"The Film Maker"

MASON DELSSON
<u>HOLLYWOOD DETECTIVE</u>

Michael P. Blattenberger

ISBN 979-8-9936871-0-0

Publisher's Cataloging-in-Publication Data

Names: Blattenberger, Michael P., author.
Title: The film maker : Mason Delsson - Hollywood detective /
Michael P. Blattenberger.
Description: Parker, CO: BookCrafters, 2025.
Identifiers: ISBN: 979-8-9936871-0-0
Subjects: LCSH Crime--Fiction. | Detectives--Fiction. | Hollywood (Los Angeles,
Calif.)--Fiction. | BISAC FICTION / Mystery & Detective / General
Classification: LCC PS3602 .L38 F55 2025 | DDC 813.6--dc23

Publishing assistance by BookCrafters, Parker, Colorado.
www.bookcrafters.net

Dedication

My continuing inspiration is my lovely bride, Catherine. She found my first manuscript after 20 years and encouraged me daily to write. Her strength and fortitude are a constant reminder of why I should keep striving to accomplish my goals by writing every day.

1

CARMEN ELIZABETH CRAIG WAS A BEAUTIFUL BRUNETTE who had developed a love of horses early in her childhood. She was a descendant of the Warner Brothers clan, who owned extensive real estate in California. She rode in rodeos as well as any equestrian competition her family could find for her to enter. She took care of the horses she rode and helped the stable master tend to the needs of the other horses her family had purchased. Her grandfather's ranch was close to where she lived in the Hollywood Hills, so she could ride her bike there if she wanted. Her mother said, "Boy, did she ever want to!!" Carmen was up early in the morning before school and fed and watered the horses, now numbering forty. Some of them were show horses, others were for racing, and the rest were just for pleasure riding around the large estate.

She rode her bike back home in the morning, showered, dressed, and readied for school. Her mother, Grace, made her a quick, warm breakfast each day. Sometimes oatmeal and pancakes, which were Carmen's favorite. Somehow, her mother made them into horses in the pan, and Carmen always told her, "Mommy, these are yummy, but it seems weird to eat the horses!" Her mother would laugh and hurry her out the door to catch the school bus.

Carmen loved school and was a very bright child. Her parents were optimistic about her. She had expressed to them early on that she wanted to study to become a veterinarian. She talked about this dream until she went to high school. There, she met boys. Being from Hollywood, all the boys were extremely cute. She was a beautiful girl with long curly hair down to her waist, and the boys began to notice. Her figure had also filled out early, so that by her freshman year, she had a voluptuous body. Her mother made her dress conservatively, but even the baggy clothes could not hide the delicious curves. She stood five feet eight inches tall. Her smile was so captivating that the family decided to provide her with a bodyguard during her college days.

One day, her girlfriend, Kathy Muller, begged her to go with her to the auditions for the school play directed by the English teacher. The play was the Broadway play written in 1961 by Neil Simon that was eventually made into a movie of the same name. It was called "Come Blow Your Horn." Kathy read for a part, and the director asked Carmen to read for the lead role of the girlfriend. Carmen was shy and unassuming and told him she was not interested in participating. She had just come to watch and support Kathy.

She was finally coaxed into reading, and it became painfully obvious that she was a "natural." She had looked at the playbook for three minutes and had memorized her lines. The director, Mr. Robert Schott, was impressed and later posted the roles on the main hallway bulletin board. The students were all in a tizzy. Kathy got a leading role, playing Sophie Baker, mother of the lead character Alan Baker. Alan Baker's role in the 1962 movie version was played by Frank Sinatra. Kathy excitedly ran to Carmen's locker to tell her she had gotten the part of Connie, Alan Baker's love interest. Carmen was reticent at first, but after her friends came and congratulated her, she began to get excited. She could not wait to tell her mom and dad. The Warners both understood Carmen's attraction to the theater, films, and later television, as their family was well-rooted in the industry. The Warners owned a large movie studio and produced many important films over the years.

After four weeks of rehearsals, the play was presented on Friday night, Saturday night, Sunday afternoon, and Sunday night. The auditorium was packed for each performance, and they got a standing ovation after each act. At the end of the final act, when each of the main cast members was introduced, Carmen got the largest round of applause. By Sunday night, she was hooked. She had never been in the spotlight before, other than winning an equestrian event, which was more for the talents of the horse she was riding. This new adulation was the audience's appreciation for Carmen's talented performance. Her parents and grandparents were over the moon. She told them she would focus on veterinary in school, and still minor in theater.

After four years of college, she graduated with a degree in veterinary. Carmen excelled academically but always found time to participate in the school's theatrical productions. She garnered quite a reputation in the community, and people loved coming to see her perform. She ended up starring in three movies and was renowned in the industry. Carmen was a large part of the success of these films. No one was surprised when she garnered awards for her performances. However, she still loved her horses, so she retired from acting and focused on opening a business.

Carmen became a famous veterinarian, even as she continued her acting pursuits. All the people throughout Southern California would bring their horses to her for treatment. She was like the "whisperer." She ran her business for five years. Then Carmen went part-time after the decision to become a mother. She decided to devote her life to motherhood.

Carmen met Dalton Craig during one of her movies, and they fell in love. He was previously married but had no children, and as he explained, his first wife really didn't love him or even act like she did. Dalton was six feet, two inches tall. He looked like Clark Gable, but his hair was colored salt and pepper. He had a neatly trimmed beard and moustache. He dressed impeccably. After four months of dating, Carmen and Dalton were married. The wedding was held on his ranch. There were over a thousand people in attendance. The celebration went on through the night, and folks still talk about it. Some say about 5000 people tell stories of being there.

Ten months after the wedding, Carmen and Dalton brought

Walker Davis Craig into the world. She was the doting mom and did everything for Wally, as she called him. She stayed home with him until he was five, and then she and Dalton tried to have a little brother or sister for Walker, but she was unable to conceive. The doctors could not figure out why. They thought the problem was Dalton. He refused to do a sperm test. After sperm test refusal, Dalton said he wanted no more children. This was crushing to Carmen. She withdrew more and more away from Dalton after this happened.

Carmen did not return to work or even have any interest in acting. She just spent time with her horses. Walker learned to ride and would occasionally ride with her, but he and Carmen did not have a strong bond when he was a teen. When he was an adult, however, they became very close. He was very driven to be like his father and be in the movie business. Walker's father, Dalton, worked long hours and became very successful. He dreamed of owning a studio, and all his efforts were aimed toward that end.

Carmen, unable to conceive again and seeing her son gravitate more towards his dad, became sullen, and her friends were worried. Kathy Muller especially spent loads of time urging her to return to acting. Carmen said, "That is Dalton's world. I want nothing to do with it."

In the land of movie stars, agents, producers, directors, and the struggle for stardom, fame, and fortune causes a city to seem like a swarm of bees trying to grab the nectar in a large flower bed. There was always a mad scramble to see who would be the next "Queen Bee." In entertainment lingo, this meant the next "NEW STARLET." This was the case in the city of Los Angeles, California, or more specifically, HOLLYWOOD.

Dalton Craig was what the media outlets called a "movie mogul." He was fifty-seven years old, six feet two inches, with a full head of gray hair, and he kept himself in terrific shape. He grew up in Gilroy, California, and left there only to go to the Los Angeles Film School located on Sunset Boulevard near Vine Street in Hollywood. Dalton became a successful producer and director when he left film school years ago. He got a great deal on a failing studio called Gemini Film Studios and owned it for twenty-five years. Lately, he had four movies in a row nominated for awards at the Oscars. Three times he won the prestigious award for Best Picture.

Dalton became more successful when bigger celebrities starred in his films. He had a profound sense of business, an excellent eye for talent, and an excellent feeling for finding a good story. Gemini Film Studios was well known for murder mysteries and suspense thrillers. One of Dalton's favorite authors was Donald James who authored four stories that intrigued Dalton. He purchased the rights to the stories and wrote the screenplay for each story in collaboration with Donald James. The movies were produced at his studios, and the two of them made millions of dollars at the Box Office. James enjoyed fame as a writer and as a screenwriter. Dalton became the "Go-to-Guy" for movie makers as Producer and Executive Director.

Dalton Craig met a lovely woman after film school named Lynda Laffarty. They had instant chemistry and began dating. Lynda was an actress when she was younger. Nowadays, she plays some of the most exotic roles, portraying women as the sexy wife or girlfriend of the lead actor in the film. She was intelligent and very much an independent woman who knew what her talents were and demanded to be taken seriously based on those acting talents. She refused to be typecast in roles that objectified women. She became very popular in Hollywood. Her relationship with Dalton became very serious, and they were married in a simple ceremony on his ranch with a few friends and family.

Their lifestyle was hectic as they both were laser-focused on their careers. This left little time to cultivate the relationship. Each had specific needs. Neither had the time, nor the inclination to satisfy the other's wants and sexual proclivities. Lynda began to seek men who paid attention to her, as Dalton did not. Dalton sought the solace of women who were subservient and revered his station in the community as an up-and-coming mogul. Lynda and Dalton drifted apart and divorced after only two years together.

She wanted nothing from Dalton, and as it was years before his success, she was not entitled to any major awards in settlement. They have agreed to remain friends for over thirty years. She even became friendly with the woman who replaced her.

To this day, either Dalton or Lynda can call the other for support, whether financial, moral, or an honest opinion. Each of them respected the other's opinion; having someone to trust was a comfort for both of them. Having help with a decision was useful, and often critical regarding one's career path in a community like Hollywood.

Dalton Craig had a routine that was familiar to all who knew him. He rose early, jogged for three to five miles through the Hollywood Hills, then returned home. He worked out in his home gym for an hour, then sat and had a cup of coffee in his outdoor kitchen while reading new scripts, then began planning his day.

Dalton had little time for serious relationships but was always attracted to beautiful women in the show business world. He dated female actors, models, and even a talent agent or two. None of these ladies interested Dalton in a significant way. He was looking for that spark that he received from the type of women that had been portrayed in so many of his movies over the years. People called him a dreamer and laughed at his naivete.

He met his second wife, Carmen Warner, in college when she played opposite him in the school's production of "Come Blow Your Horn." He played the part of Alan Baker (Frank Sinatra's role in the movie). Later, when he purchased Gemini Studios, Dalton competed with Warner Brothers Studios in this purchase bid and was shocked to see Carmen was there as their representative. Warner was represented by this lovely young woman named Carmen Warner. Both parties put in bids for the purchase but were rejected, forcing a second bid weeks later. There were sparks between Dalton and Carmen during the process, as there were during their school play together. Each remained professional through the process of purchasing Gemini Studios. Each tried to fight the personal feelings they had for each other and eventually succumbed to the heat they created.

Dalton won the bidding war for Gemini, and afterward, Carmen called to congratulate him. He asked her out to dinner, and the rest is history. They dated for a month, and he proposed. She was swept off her feet and totally in love with every facet of Dalton's character.

She accepted, and they were married. They had a son, Walker, within ten months of the union, and lived in the expansive ranch Dalton still owned. They spent twenty-five years together. Dalton became rich and more successful. Carmen's love of horses continued, and she expanded their stables so that eventually, they had success in racing, as well as in breeding horses for others here and abroad. Carmen made frequent trips to England and France to discuss horse breeding and even brought horses there for breeding. One particular trip was memorable as her trip to Dubai produced not one but six marriage proposals.

Two weeks after their twenty-fifth wedding anniversary, Dalton's wife, Carmen, was killed in a freak accident while she was riding her favorite horse, Sage, a beautiful Appaloosa breed, out on the far reaches of their ranch when the horse was spooked by something or someone. Her favorite steed, Sage, was as tame as a junkyard dog.

Long before horses were domesticated, people hunted for their meat, their hides were later used to make leather boots and coats, and their hair was used in upholstery. The hair of white horses was even used for making violin bows in the early 1800s. Carmen was aware of the horse's history but was appalled by it. Sage was one of Carmen's most requested breeders.

Since domestication, the horse has been like a household pet. Its primary role was for sport in competitive racing. The rich even rode them, using dogs for hunting foxes or other small animals. Carmen Craig had been a lover of horses for her whole life. Sage was her household pet. She owned many other horses, but Sage was like her child, her best friend, and her world.

The investigation of her death concluded that Carmen Craig was thrown off her horse into a large pile of rocks up on a hill. Since there were no witnesses, as she rode alone that day, the investigators conjectured her steed was spooked by a rattlesnake or was startled by something that made it react violently enough to throw its rider. Carmen landed on one of the large boulders that were virtually everywhere on their property. She hit her head on the rock and was killed immediately. The horse stayed by her side until she was found that afternoon by her stable master, Erikson Howard, who had gone to look for her. He found she was unrecognizable due to the total disfigurement of her face from the accident. He recovered her phone with which he called the police, then Dalton. After their initial investigation, having no witnesses, the police declared the death accidental, caused by her fall from the horse.

The funeral, which was a closed-casket affair, had been difficult for Dalton as their marriage had reached twenty-five years when Carmen died. Even though they had drifted apart emotionally, he loved her dearly. Their son, Walker, took Carmen's death extremely hard, as he blamed himself for not riding with her that day, as she had requested.

The day after her death, Walker became a recluse, was listless, stopped riding, and moved back into his father's ranch, where he eventually lost interest in most things, especially contact with the outside world. Even Dalton's first wife, Lynda Laffarty, whom Walker had become extremely close to, tried all she could to get him out of the funk he was in. Efforts in this regard were all to no avail.

All efforts from friends and family were also unsuccessful in touching his heart and bringing him back to normalcy. No one had any success in bringing him out of the funk he had fallen into. Walker just could not seem to bounce back from this tragedy. He spent much of his time in his old room, alone.

Mason Delsson was the investigator in the Carmen Craig case. He had been a Detective in the Los Angeles Police Department for fifteen years. Everyone thought Carmen's death was an "open and shut accidental death case; at least everyone on the ranch reported it as such. Mason felt there was something that seemed untoward, and he wanted to find the answers to the many questions he had. He knew it would be difficult knowing Hollywood types as he did. He saw them as a very closed group, cult-like in their operation. When it came to sharing information with outsiders, especially the police, people became very guarded. It was like pulling teeth to get any substantial information from this group.

Mason Delsson had been a police detective for so long that he had begun long ago to trust his instincts when solving these matters. He distrusted nearly everyone else involved. These instincts usually proved to be correct and surprisingly accurate.

Dalton buried his long-time wife, lover, and friend soon after the autopsy. She had died of a blunt force trauma to her skull, which was consistent with the reports from those who were called to the ranch by Erikson Howard. Erickson found her on the ranch after searching for three hours. After the funeral, a week after Carmen's death, Mason called Dalton Craig and asked for a meeting.

Dalton was a remarkably busy man, as you would imagine, always running the operation of his business very late in the afternoon in his large Hollywood studio. It was difficult to corner him for a sit-down, but Mason was persistent, and they met late on Friday night at Craig's Gemini Studios.

Mason Delsson walked into the office of Mr. Craig after getting through security, the outer secretary, and the private secretary, Dolores Madison. After sitting in front of Dolores's desk, admiring her legs for almost fifty minutes, Dolores stood after her desk phone buzzed and said, "Thank you so much for your patience. Detective Delsson, Mr. Craig will see you now."

Mason followed her into a spectacular office. It took up the entire fourth floor of the studio headquarters, and you could see the ocean. There were many sailboats out on the water, so the view was amazing. The office was glass on three sides.

Mr. Craig's desk was in the middle of the room and a step up off the floor. The desk area was twenty feet by twenty feet square, with a support pole in each corner, making the area look like a royal office for a king. There were six cushioned chairs covered in tan leather in front of the desk. The desk chair Dalton sat in was large enough for two people to sit in, and it swiveled around to be able to see the view over a large U-shaped credenza. The office was full of trees in large pots, flowers in hangers on the ceiling, as well as flower arrangements on the tables and cabinets. There were two couches in front of the solid wall behind the visitors' chairs, with four television screens. The windows had floor-to-ceiling drapes, and when closed, could darken the room, making it a viewing room.

There was a mahogany conference table to the right of Dalton's desk with twelve chairs around it. In the corner where the side glass wall met the solid wall at the head of the conference table was a fully stocked bar. It had twelve barstools in front of it in white leather over soft cushions. The furniture was expensive, as were all the other decorations, and awards lining the wall over the door. Seated at his desk, Dalton was often inspired by those awards to work harder.

Dolores Madison entered the room from the bar area and brought Mr. Craig a beverage. It looked like a cosmopolitan in a stemmed glass. Dolores asked in a very flirtatious, sexy voice, "Mr. Delsson, can I get you anything? Coffee, tea, water, cocktail?" Mason didn't know she almost added "me" at the end. Dolores was very attracted and in awe of the much younger Detective. She was normally very prim and proper, but she felt something different being around Mason Delsson. Dolores was seeing another man at the time, but he was away overseas. She felt like he was the one, and she pledged to herself that she would wait to see if this man returned to woo her like he told her he would.

Mason replied, "Maybe just water, please?" Dolores walked to the bar and brought Mason a bottle of water. She smiled at him and then walked away. He watched as she walked to the bar and back and admired her long, slender legs as well as her flawless figure. He thanked her, then she left and closed the door.

Mason made a mental note to speak with her when she was away from this environment. He knew she would be more inclined to share pertinent information, if she knew any, away from her boss and the safe confines of the studios. He also had an ulterior motive for wanting to speak with her, but he let that thought fade as he had to conduct this interview.

Dalton gulped down half his drink and began, "Well then, Detective, how can I help you today?"

Mason, taking notes, said, "I just have several questions to ask you. These are purely routine and in no specific order. We are trying to close our investigation of the circumstances surrounding Carmen's death. First, let me say how sorry I was to hear of your wife's passing."

Dalton nodded. Mason continued, "Your wife was out riding on the day she was killed. Was she a frequent rider?"

Dalton replied, "Horses were her life. She loved to ride and was a great breeder. We even had a few thoroughbreds that we raced years ago. Carmen and I met in college doing a play together. There were sparks. We met again five years later when I was trying to buy Gemini Studios. Carmen represented her family's studio, which also had an interest. We began our relationship that day."

Mason then asked, "Was she alone on that day?"

Dalton sighed, then said, "She rode all over the ranch for years and knew the grounds better than anyone. She often rode alone as she did that day."

Mason's nerves about his next question made him begin to perspire, but he forged ahead, knowing that asking such a personal question would certainly change the dynamics of the interview. He asked, "Did your wife have a large life insurance policy?"

Dalton frowned and said, "Can I ask why it is important for you to know that?" Mason knew this was coming.

He replied, "Mr. Craig, we are just trying to do our due diligence. We want to know if it was substantial and who the beneficiaries are."

Dalton looked at his watch and said, "I want to cooperate fully with the authorities. So yes, she was insured for fifty million dollars. My son and I are beneficiaries in succession."

At that moment, the intercom buzzed. Dalton said, "Yes, Dolores."

Dolores' voice replied from the intercom, "Your six o'clock appointment is here whenever you are ready."

Dalton said, "Thank you, Dolores. We'll just be a few more minutes."

Mason gathered all of his determination and asked, "Mr. Craig, what would you estimate your late wife's financial worth?"

Dalton Craig was now angered and showed his displeasure to Mason. "She was worth... everything to me and I will miss her terribly, now that she is gone." Dalton sighed and continued, "Her financial worth is a matter of public record, but it is, in my opinion, none of anybody's business. Mr. Delsson, I must excuse myself as I have another pressing appointment waiting. Have a nice day, Mr. Delsson, and thank you for all your efforts. Good day."

Mason thanked him for the time, then he rose and extended his hand to Dalton, who also rose with an angry face, shaking the offered hand. Mason walked to the door, where he was met by Dolores Madison, who escorted him to the outer offices. Mason made note of the fact that he saw no one else waiting in the private outer office.

He walked out of the studio, wondering if the interview was cut short on purpose. He was so rattled, he completely forgot to ask Dolores Madison to meet with him, privately, so that she could answer some questions about Dalton. She might be less reticent to express her true feelings about Dalton away from his estate.

The next morning, around 11:30 a.m., Mason Delsson was seated at his desk in police headquarters. He received a telephone call from the coroner's office indicating that Belinda Cheeks, Dalton Craig's housekeeper, had left the Craig residence at 9 a.m. and was found at the bottom of a ravine, not even a mile from the ranch, a short time later.

She was found by an anonymous caller just down the street from where she worked as a housekeeper for Dalton Craig. The vehicle she was driving had careened through a guardrail and overturned several times. Miss Belinda Cheek was dead at the scene. The coroner, Trudy Pine, had been called. Trudy pronounced her dead at the scene, saying she would order an autopsy to be completed as quickly as possible. An autopsy that she would perform as the coroner. This might give them some clue as to whether she was killed by the accident or had died by other means. The fact that the caller who reported the car accident had left the scene before police arrived begged the question: Was this an accidental killing?

Police were on the scene when Mason Delsson arrived. The officers responding said they were called by an anonymous caller who was not at the scene when she called police, reporting a car had gone off the road at mile marker 14 on the road to Dalton Craig's ranch. The female caller was gone by the time they arrived. The police had little to go on, but Mason noticed there were no tire marks anywhere on the pavement, which meant she didn't try to engage the brakes.

The woman was thrown from the vehicle, so all they could assume was that she was alone, unless the caller was either the driver or passenger. Hopefully, the autopsy would confirm the cause of death.

Mason got back to HQ at LAPD after 5 p.m. He saw Chief Corci's office light was still on, so he meandered over and tapped lightly on the door, "Hey, Chief. Got a minute?" Mason saw he was on the phone, so he went to get a cup of coffee for both of them.

Mason had so much to tell the chief of detectives, he would have to use his notes. They almost filled the notepad he was using.

Dick Corci was the Chief of Police Detectives in Los Angeles. It was a high-powered position with lots of visibility in front of news media coverage. He turned in his chair and held up one finger, indicating he was almost done with his call. He motioned for Mason to sit.

Corsi said goodbye to the caller and said to Mason, "There was another high-profile accidental death in Hollywood today. It was

Sarah Ostrov, the model-actress-producer. It was reported she died in a fall."

Sarah Ostrov was a very successful fashion model in her youth. She worked for all the top magazines and even did a few things for *Playboy*. She got into acting and starred in several movies: one series with Robin Zander, a producer, at Paramount Pictures. It became the forerunner to "Charley's Angels."

Sarah Ostrov was rumored to be the love interest of Dalton Craig for years after his first divorce. Mason realized he would have to speak directly to Dalton to confirm this. Mason thought to himself that these deaths seemed to be anything but accidental.

Sarah was a five-foot-seven-inch blonde having what could only be called a voluptuous figure. She lived in a very expensive home about five blocks from the home of Dalton Craig.

Sarah had three housemates. A lady and two men from the film business, but behind the cameras, not in front of them. The lady's name was Lynda Deene, who was extremely close to Sarah. She was a slender blonde who was an associate producer working for Sagittarius Films. The men in Sarah's home were Elijah Landon, a cameraman and physical trainer to the stars, who many thought was her love interest. Jim Thompson, the fourth roommate, worked part-time as a talent agent, but primarily was a stunt coordinator and part-time bodyguard to Dalton Craig. Jim and Sarah often rode together to the Craig home, so there were people who gossiped about whether both her male roommates were involved with her. It was confusing to many, as well as quite the topic of conjecture.

Miss Ostrov was found on one of the Gemini Studio's old movie sets by one of the extras in their latest production, Ellis Grant, who went to the wrong location for his shoot that day. She was outside the saloon on the lot where they shot western movies. She seemed to have fallen from the second-floor balcony. The balcony's railing was broken and dangling in the wind. This lot had been inactive for many months. He called the police first, then called Dalton Craig. All of Sarah's housemates would be interviewed by the police.

Jake Makenko came on the television reporting for KNBC

Channel 4 at 4 p.m. in Los Angeles that afternoon, "Today, we learned of another accidental death in Los Angeles County. A woman named Belinda Cheeks was found not far from the home of her employer, Dalton Craig. She has worked as his housekeeper for the past five years. Miss Cheek's vehicle went off the road and was found at the bottom of a ravine. Miss Cheeks, 35, was reported to be alone in the car, and the police on the scene indicated she was found dead when they arrived. There were no obvious tire marks on the road to indicate she tried to stop. The coroner, Trudy Pine, said she would conduct an autopsy by the next day or so. We have little else to report other than that. The police will continue their investigation. This is Jake Makenko reporting from Malibu Beach for KNBC Channel 4." His report ended.

Dalton Craig was shown Jake Makenko's news report. He and his lawyer, Sam Barfield, discussed whether or not to make a statement to the press about the series of accidents. Then they discussed if the deaths were not accidents. Maybe someone was responsible for the deaths, and maybe he should have Jim T. with him at all times. Dalton made a call to Mr. Thompson to arrange just that.

On the eleven o'clock news on Channel 4, Jake Makenko came on again to do a special report. Jake has been a long-time, familiar face on several news channels in Los Angeles, reporting the police matters. Jake said from his news desk, "We have had another accidental death reported by the Los Angeles County Sheriff's Department. Miss Sarah Ostrov, 36, was found in a backlot at the studios of Gemini Films. Actor Ellis Grant found her while looking for the place he was due to shoot a scene. Miss Ostrov was an actress, model, as well as an alleged love interest of Dalton Craig.

"The Los Angeles County coroner, Trudy Pine, estimated that Miss Ostrov had died only an hour or two before being discovered. The actor, Ellis Grant, told the authorities that he saw no one else or any vehicles around when he found the body.

"The Police's preliminary investigation revealed that Miss Sarah Ostrov had visitors that day, as reported by her housekeeper, who lived on the grounds, but saw no one enter or leave the home. She only saw the cars in the drive when she returned from the store. Guests, who were familiar with the house, went around back to the pool area to see Sarah. The housekeeper, Janelle Phillips, had not seen her or anyone else leave the house.

This is the third accidental death of someone close to Dalton Craig. His wife, an alleged lover, and his housekeeper. All of them have taken place in the past three weeks. It seems suspicious. Maybe they are connected and maybe they are not, but I wonder. We will continue to follow this case for future developments. Mason Delsson thought about the job ahead sitting in his office at Police Headquarters.

He left the office to visit Dalton Craig at his home. There was a large gate at the entrance to this palatial home with a speaker box with a call button on it. Mason rolled down his window, pushed the button, and waited for someone to answer.

Someone behind the security camera said, "Can you state your name and the purpose of your visit, please?"

Mason replied, holding up his badge to the camera, "My name is Mason Delsson. I am with the Los Angeles Police Department, and I wish to speak to Mr. Craig."

The voice said, "Please drive through and come to the front of the house." The gate slowly opened, and Mason drove down a long tree-lined road that opened into a view of the large house behind the circular drive and the large fountain with a statue of a woman holding a bowl, which sprayed water into its surrounding pool.

Mason parked in the circular drive at the front door of the home. He walked up to the front door and rang the bell. The double doors were ten feet high and almost as wide. They looked very heavy. A man dressed like a butler came and opened the door and said, "This way, please. Mr. Craig is on the veranda." Mason followed the butler. He asked him how long he had worked here for Mr. Craig.

He replied, "My name is Sam Barfield. I am Mr. Craig's attorney. I have been with him for twenty years or so."

Mason asked, "How often do you come to the residence?"

Sam Barfield replied, "Not very. I was just concerned about how Dalton was taking the news of the recent accidents."

Mr. Craig was, indeed, on the back patio sitting at a table under a huge umbrella. Mr. Craig said, "I expected to see you, Mr. Delsson. How can I be of assistance today?"

Mason said, "May I join you at the table?"

Dalton replied, "Of course, Mr. Delsson, have a seat. Can I get you a beverage? I am having a cosmopolitan on the rocks."

Mason said, "I would very much like a drink as it sounds delicious, but I am on duty.

Dalton said, "OK. Fine. Maybe just water?" Mason nodded. Dalton said to Sam, "Bring us two of these, holding up his empty cosmopolitan, and a bottle of water for Detective Delsson."

Dalton looked at Mason as if to ask, "What's up?"

Mason took the opportunity to ask as many questions as he could before the lawyer returned. Mason said, "Mr. Craig. Are you killing these people around you?" Mason held his breath. He always dreaded having to ask such a blunt question to a person who may be innocent, but he had learned that sometimes a person's response was the window to their soul.

Dalton Craig paused for a second and said with a smile on his face, "Mr. Delsson, if I were to kill anyone, it wouldn't be in my own 'backyard' or the people I care so much about."

Mason noted Dalton mentioned where the deaths happened before he mentioned those who had died.

Dalton continued, "By the way, I had nothing to do with any of the recent accidents. I know you are just doing your job, but I can't help feeling a bit violated as I have just lost my wife, and a lifelong friend as well as my trusted housekeeper who was like family to us. My attorney and I were discussing the possibility that my life may also be in danger, so I have a bodyguard assigned around the clock until we confirm these deaths were accidental or somehow planned."

Mason forged ahead, "Mr. Craig, do you ride horses?"

Dalton said quickly, "I have been known to get up on one over the years, but it is not something I relish. That was my wife's passion, and she instilled the same love of the equines in my son, Walker. He was a champion rider when he was much younger. It's the only thing I have seen him take to other than a large glass of tequila. To be honest, I have always been slightly afraid of those beasts."

Mason, being the skeptic he was, thought Mr. Craig was being less than honest with him about needing a bodyguard or even being afraid of horses. He also needed to find out how many people were employed at the house. He would interview them all. Mason asked, "How many people are around here on your property regularly?"

Dalton replied, "Well, on any given day, we have several ranch hands, a few stable people, two or three maids, and my assistant. There is also my son, from time to time, when he and his mom rode horses together. Sometimes my ex-wife, Lynda Laffarty, rode with her. When Walker was out on his own, he visited us for dinner two or three times a week, but since his mom died, he moved back home. Now, he is here every day with me."

Mason probed further, "Mr. Craig, you have lost a wife, a housekeeper, and an alleged girlfriend in a matter of days. Can you explain that? Do you know anyone who would want to hurt your wife, housekeeper, or girlfriend?"

Dalton pondered this question, "Well, Mr. Delsson, I have never considered it. My late wife was in many organizations and was adored by most of those who knew her. Judging by the turnout at her funeral, I would estimate that she had thousands of friends and admirers. She was a generous person and gave large sums of money to a lot of different causes. She received a considerable fortune when her dad passed away. She may have had a sister but as far as I know, she was an only child, the sole heir. She became mega-rich very quickly."

Mason asked, "Did she have one or two close friends?

Dalton answered, "She had many, but now that I think of it, she did have a small group of five or six other ladies she frequently saw and had over to our home at least twice a week. With my work keeping me in the studios for much of the time, she made our home welcome to those six women. They also traveled together. They became like her second family."

Mason said, "Could you give me their names? I would like to interview them as well. Speaking of that, I would also like to set up a day when your son and staff will be available to do a half-hour interview. Could we do that tomorrow?"

Dalton was writing on his desk pad when he said, "I will have my staff here and ready to speak to you at ten o'clock in the morning. Here are the names of my wife's close friends."

Mason said, "Thank you, Mr. Craig. I will see you in the morning. Thank you for your time." He got up and found his way out to his car. He was shocked at the names on the paper. The names Dalton had listed were Lynda Laffarty, Cricky Amherst, Jen Sandrew, Susie Crull, and Kathy Muller. Mason knew every one of these powerful and influential women. They were also known to everyone in Hollywood, and if something needed to be done, these ladies could surely get things accomplished.

After an hour's ride, Mason arrived back at his office at HQ. He went to the coffee machine and ran into Chief Dick Corsi. Mason said, "I just spoke to Dalton, and he seems genuinely crushed by the deaths of his wife and housekeeper. He did give me the names of her six best friends. You will be surprised at the names on the list."

Dick Corsi said, "Why don't we sit and chat in my office if you have a couple of minutes?"

Chief of Police Dick Corsi was originally from the Buffalo, New York area. He started as a Buffalo policeman and worked his way up the ladder to Chief of Detectives. He worked as the Chief of the Key West Police Department for a short time, then moved west to Los Angeles. He was tall and handsome with great people skills. He also had a knack for being able to understand the criminal mind, which made him successful as a leader. Those who knew him were impressed with his dedication to bringing criminals to justice. He was revered by the men and women he led on the force, who tried to emulate him.

The Chief's office was much larger than the cubicle Mason had. There were large windows on the wall facing west, looking out at the ocean. On a clear day, you could see Catalina Island. There were couches in front of the windows. The Chief's desk was in the center of the room with a small conference table behind it. Mason sat in one of the black leather cushioned chairs in front of the large mahogany desk. Chief Corsi began, "Help yourself to the coffee. So, who is on this notorious list?"

Mason began reading the names with a comment for each. "Lynda Laffarty. This was Dalton's first wife. Lynda was a long-time actress and was, by all accounts. an attractive woman with a great figure. Nowadays, she is generally cast in the part of the mother in her movies. She is allegedly in a torrid romance with screenwriter Shawn Harper, who is from Lake Tahoe but now lives here in Los Angeles.

"Christy Amherst. She was an actress originally from Buffalo, New York. She played the villainess in movies but was famous for the many commercials she had done over the years. She inherited the Los Alamitos Raceway from her late husband."

"Jen Sandrew. She was married to a man from Iowa who owned a chain of gyms across the country. When he died two years ago, she was left with his fortune. She sold the chain of gyms, and she now owns a boutique on Rodeo Drive called Elegant Lace."

"Susie Crull. She is an actress and was never married, but lives with Kevin Syracuse, who is a producer at Sagittarius International Pictures. She was successful in films and now owns a fancy restaurant in Malibu Beach called Armory Square West."

"The final name on the list is Kathy Muller. She is described as a buxom blonde from back east who was in pictures for years. She had won five Oscars and even had a Tony for a show on Broadway. She was very popular in Hollywood and was notorious for throwing some of the wildest parties at her home. A few years ago, she purchased a restaurant in Marina Del Rey at the Ritz-Carlton Hotel. It is called Retreat Two."

Mason said to Dick, "I am going to call each of these women in for an interview, and I am guessing one or more of them knows something about the death of Carmen Craig."

Dick Corsi sat back in his large office chair, staring out the window. He turned to Mason and said, "So you think the death of Carmen Craig was more than an accident?"

Mason replied, "I have nothing to go on but my instincts, Chief. It just feels like something is going on below the surface that stinks."

Chief Dick Corsi said, "Well, let's start with interviews of the lady friends of Carmen and review the tapes together."

Mason left to call Lynda Laffarty to schedule a meeting for the next day.

Mason finished his calls to all the ladies on the list of Carmen's friends and went home. The interviews began at 9 a.m. and lasted an hour and a half each. The last would be done by 4:30 p.m. So, Mason knew he would be tired and in need of a tequila afterwards.

Lynda Laffarty walked into Police Headquarters at 9 a.m. She was escorted into one of the interrogation rooms by a secretary who asked if she wanted a bottle of water. She sat looking around the office, waiting.

Mason walked into the room and handed a bottle of water to Miss Laffarty, saying, "Good Morning, Miss Laffarty. I am so glad you are here today. I have a bunch of questions about Carmen Craig. I want this to be rather informal so you can relax."

Lynda looked Mason up and down, assessing him. She liked what she saw but thought she would reserve final judgment until after their chat. She responded, "No problem, Detective. I will do anything I can to help find out why Carmen died."

Mason said, "What do you mean exactly, Miss Laffarty? We already know how she died. Do you have a different theory about her death?"

Lynda Laffarty pulled a tissue out of her small purse and

said, "Detective. I know Carmen was a very accomplished rider on horseback. It seems strange after all these years, that is what killed her."

Mason paused as he watched Lynda's facial expression, then asked, "What do you think happened?

Lynda said, "Well, I do not have a theory. I just miss her and want there to be conclusive evidence that this was an accident. It was so unbelievable that she would have an accident like she did. The people who were on the scene initially from the fire department said her face was so disfigured, they were not sure it was her until after DNA testing could be done. Based on her clothes, hair, body type, and especially the jewelry she was wearing that was easily identified."

Mason responded, "Well, Miss Laffarty. Did you ever ride with her? If you have a feeling that something else happened, what could it have been? Do you know of anyone who would want to perpetrate harm to Mrs. Craig?"

Lynda thought for a moment that she would have to be careful when she responded. She was starting to daydream about Mr. Delsson in some naughty scenarios, so she had to stay focused. Lynda finally got her wits about her and replied, "OK, Detective. Let me take those questions separately. You have me a bit flustered with the number of questions you asked, and this is the first time I have been interrogated by the police."

Lynda began softly in a voice that gave Mason goosebumps all over, "I have ridden with Carmen, but she was much more accomplished than I am. I do have a premonition that something must have happened to cause her death. I think there are a few people who would want to see her out of the picture, quite frankly."

Mason said, "Would you care to name any of those people?"

Lynda, with a straight face, said, "Allie Campwick, Dalton's current girlfriend and, of course, Walker Craig, her son."

Mason's eyes went very wide. He almost couldn't speak, but said, "Why do you think her son would have anything to do with his mother's death?"

Lynda said, "Dalton and I have an iron-clad pre-nuptial agreement. Her son may know about what his mother and father had in the way of an agreement, but I can't confirm it. However, I suspect they had one. Walker may have thought Carmen would have been in line for a lion's share of his father's money. Maybe he didn't want her to have any of the money he might inherit from Dalton. She and Walker lost their closeness as he got older and realized how much power his father had. It might have been put into the will that he gets nothing based on his lack of performance in anything that could be described as work. Walker seemed to lack any motivation to sustain his interest in working. He just expected his folks to take care of him.

Lynda grabbed a tissue from her purse, wiped her eyes, then continued, "As far as his girlfriend goes, and I will call her that out of respect for my ex-husband, Walker may think his father might have redone his will, so she may also be in line for Dalton's wealth. My feelings for Walker have changed of late. We were, for years, very close, but watching him as he has grown has caused a fissure between us because of his laziness, rudeness toward his mother, and frankly, his lack of respect for me. Unfortunately, his father is unaware that he is a spoiled brat. His father thinks Walker can do no wrong."

Lynda now took a drink of water that had been placed on the table in front of her. She continued, "Dalton thinks Walker is an upstanding citizen in the community. I am not sure why he thinks that, but he has said as much to me. I chose not to address it with Dalton."

Mason looked at Lynda and said, "If Dalton's son is worried about his inheritance, there might be more targets for future accidents. Maybe you should speak to Dalton about how you feel, unless you would like me to talk to him. Dalton may even be a target."

Lynda shrugged and said, "Do what you think is right. I owe no allegiance to Dalton Craig or Walker, for that matter. If that is all you have for me, I have to leave for another appointment today." She rose and walked out the door.

After Miss Laffarty left the room, Mason saw that he had fifteen minutes before his next interview. He telephoned Randy Keene, who was a private investigator and had done work for Mason in the past. When he answered his phone, Mason said, "Hello, Randy. I have a case I would like you to help with. Are you available today?"

Randy said, "As a matter of fact, I am not busy with anything right now. When should I stop by to see you?"

Mason said, "If you could get here just before noon, that would be great. Thanks. See you then." They ended the call.

There was a knock on his door, and Robin Zander, the Detective Division secretary, stuck her head in the door and said, "Mason, your next interview is here. Shall I seat her in the conference room?"

Mason said, "Yes, please, Robin. Thanks."

Mason jotted down more notes on his pad regarding questions for Cricky Amherst. He got up and walked toward the conference room down the hall.

Mason stepped into the conference room and was taken aback by the woman who sat at the table waiting for him. Christy Amherst was a beautiful brunette. She was dressed in a silk-looking red dress that came down to about three inches above her knees. She had long legs that stuck out from under the table, and her shoes looked expensive. They were red with a bamboo-wedged heel. She even smelled great. Her perfume almost took his breath away. He cleared his throat and said, "Miss Amherst. Thank you so much for taking the time to see me today."

Christy Amherst, or Cricky as she was known to her friends, had a look on her face that said to him she was giving him the once over to see if she liked what she saw. She was smiling when she said, "Detective Delsson. It is nice to meet you. How can I help you today?"

Mason asked, "What was your first thought when you heard that Carmen Craig had died?"

Christy replied, "I was initially horrified. I wondered how it happened because of her knowledge of riding, the horse, and the terrain."

Mason continued, "Do you think Carmen had any enemies?"

Christy thought a minute, then said, "You know, everyone loved her except the people you would have thought should love her."

Mason said, "That is confusing. What do you mean by that?

Christy said, "She dreamed of a family nucleus for herself that she witnessed in her own family. She worked her whole life to be the apple of her husband's eye and the love of his life. Although she had a special bond with Dalton, she was never close to her son, as much as she doted on him. She had given up everything to raise him. Everyone else she met was close to her and made her feel like family. We even spoke about it one day. She said she felt emptiness in her heart, feeling she failed to create a special bond with her only child."

Mason said, "You didn't mention any enemies."

Christy said, "I know of no one but those in her family. The kind of relationship she had with Dalton was strained because he philandered, and her son, Walker, never treated her with respect. If you ask me, they were all after her money. She comes from a rich family. She was the great-great-granddaughter of one of the Warner Brothers. She inherited a lot of money and property from her father when he died."

Mason was glad they were taping all the interviews, as he thought taking notes would have been intrusive, and he could not have kept up. He then asked Christy, "Which one of them was most likely to have perpetrated an act of violence on Carmen?"

Christy looked at him with a menacing stare and said, "Are you asking me who killed Carmen Craig?" Mason just nodded. She paused, then said, "I don't know, and I have no proof, but my money is on someone in the family wanting to get rid of her to expand their inheritance."

Mason asked boldly, "Did you kill Carmen Craig?"

She laughed and said, "Wouldn't that be ridiculous? She was my

best friend. Also, I was not in line to inherit any of her vast millions."
At that point, she rose and said, "I am done here, Mr. Delsson. Good
luck in finding her killer if that is what you think happened." She left
quickly. He had no more questions to ask, so he let her go.

Mason was sitting there, waiting for the next interview, and
his head was spinning. His cell phone rang. It was Randy. Mason
answered, "Hello, old friend. Are you close to my office?

Randy said, "I hope to be there in two minutes."

Mason said, "Run right up. I only have a few minutes. Thanks."

Two minutes later, Randy came into the office. Mason waved
him in. Randy was from a town back east and worked in that small
town in New Hampshire, posing as a house painter.

Mason said, "I don't have a lot of time, but I need you to follow
Lynda Laffarty and find out what she is up to. I think she knows
more about the death of Carmen Craig than she is telling us. See if
you can get her on tape talking to whomever she visits in the next
week or so."

Randy said, "I am on the case, Mason. I will check in daily to let
you know if I get anything."

Mason said, "Thanks." He walked Randy out. Then Mason got in
his car to drive to his appointment with Jen Sandrew.

Jen Sandrew was originally from Chicago, Illinois. She studied
kinesiology and became a Pilates instructor as well as teaching
yoga. She was discovered in one of the local gyms by a female
producer and became a star very quickly. She was a talented
performer, and audiences loved her. Jen had six films under her
belt, which were all wildly popular. She was married for a short
time but was now single, living in Beverly Hills.

She owned a small chain of four women's clothing stores. called
"Elegant Lace." There was one on Rodeo Drive, one in Lake Tahoe,
one in San Diego, and one in Palm Springs. They primarily sold
ladies' lingerie. She had received a call from Mason Delsson from
the LA Police Department requesting an interview, but due to her
schedule, he thought it might be easier if he came to her Rodeo
Drive Store.

Mason walked into the Elegant Lace and was uncomfortable. There were 12 or 15 women in the shop when he entered. They all looked him up and down. A salesgirl, Sydney, greeted him. Sydney McKeller worked for her Aunt Jennifer for four years. She asked if he was Mason Delsson. He replied, "Yes, I am Detective Delsson. Is Miss Sandrew available?"

Sydney said, "Follow me, Detective." Hearing who he was, all the women in the store began whispering to each other. They watched the gentleman be led up the six steps in the back to the loft office, where Jennifer Sandrew sat waiting at her desk.

Jennifer rose as she hung up the phone. As she came around to greet Mason, he saw that she wore a beautiful lavender lace top that clung to her alluring body like a second skin. She had a matching skirt and purple five-inch pumps that matched her ensemble. He was almost unable to say hello when she shook his hand. She said, "Hello. Mr. Delsson. Please have a seat." Mason sat in one of the two pink leather swivel padded armchairs in front of her desk. He would have to take notes this time because he was not at HQ, where he would have videotaped the interview.

Mason finally found his voice after clearing his throat and said, "Thank you for squeezing me into your busy schedule. I won't take much of your time. Let me ask, who do you think killed Carmen Craig?" Mason watched closely for her reaction to the question. He found it best to begin with shock and awe in his questioning of a potential suspect.

She flinched, looking a bit shocked, but quickly responded, "I was under the impression that she died accidentally from a fall off her horse. Do you have any reason to believe she was murdered?"

Mason wrote in his notes, then, ignoring her question, asked, "If you thought someone had caused her death, who do you think it could have been?"

Jen said, "This is very unnerving, Mr. Delsson. I was very close to Carmen and saw or spoke to her every day. The thought that someone might have actually caused her death is very upsetting."

She paused a moment, then said, "If it was anyone, it was probably her son, Walker Craig."

Mason jotted more notes and said, "Why would you think Walker would want to kill his mother? Were they ever at odds in front of you? Did you ever see him physically mistreat her?"

Jen said, "I didn't say I think Walker killed her. I am saying that I would not be surprised that she didn't die accidentally. Walker might be the only one I know who would have any possible justification. Their relationship was strained, and he expressed quite often his displeasure that his father and mother were not close. I think Walker knew of his father's secret liaisons and blamed his mother for causing discord between his parents, even though they presented themselves as deeply in love. My guess is, Walker feared his father's new love interest would cause a divorce and marry his father. Because he wanted no one else to lessen his inheritance from his father when he died, Walker was always trying to come between his father and any dalliances he had. I know Dalton has had a few health challenges of late. He knew his mother would not leave him any of the money she would inherit from Dalton, nor any money from the estate she received from her late father, because of their strained relationship and his lazy attitude toward work."

Mason asked, "Jennifer, what kind of relationship did you have with Carmen Craig?"

Jen quickly said, "What are you implying, Mr. Craig? Do you think we had more than a close friendship?"

Mason said, having watched her reaction again to the question, "I am sorry, but I wasn't insinuating anything but rather trying to find out how close your friendship was with her. Did she ever express to you that she feared for her life?"

Jen said with a sad look on her face, "Well. She always thought that because of their strained relationship, she would be a likely candidate for Walker's ire if he didn't inherit all his father's wealth. I don't have any real proof that he threatened her, but I think she feared him."

Mason said, "I have one more question. Is there anyone else you can think of who would want to see Carmen harmed or out of the picture?"

Jen Sandrew said, "I have known the principals in that family for many years, and I don't think anyone would want to see any harm come to her. She was genuinely loved by everyone."

Mason followed up with, "Do you think Dalton would have had anything to do with her accident?"

Jennifer Sandrew thought for a moment while looking deep into Mason's eyes. She finally answered, "I think, Dalton truly loved her. They had been through many challenges and were still together. So, NO. I don't think he had anything to do with it."

Mason, not letting it go, asked, "Miss Sandrew, you mentioned challenges they went through. Could you give me an example or two?"

Jennifer was not as confident when she answered this time. She shyly said, "I think Dalton had a few dalliances with younger women from his studio. The first couple of times hurt Carmen, but she learned to ignore them as long as he was discreet. Sometimes he was not as discreet as they had agreed to. So, Carmen decided that the two of them could play that game and took on several lovers of her own. Both male and female."

Mason said, "So, Dalton had a few other women that he played with during their marriage?" Jennifer just nodded to confirm. Mason said, "Can you tell me the names of the lovers that both Mr. and Mrs. Craig entertained?"

Jennifer Sandrew said, "I never knew who either of them was seeing, as I have enough trouble keeping my own life in order, but they seemed to both be okay with the arrangement."

Mason then asked, "Is there anything else you would like to add?"

She said, "No. Detective, but I am anxious to learn if you find any evidence to prove her death was not an accident."

Mason rose from the chair. He put his notebook away and extended his hand, saying, "Thanks for your time and candor, Miss Sandrew. Please keep our conversation private. If you think of anything else that would help in the case, call me." He handed her his business card, then went down the steps and walked out of the store.

Randy Keene sat across the street from the home of Lynda Laffarty. She lived down the road. It was a few miles from her ex-husband, Dalton Craig's ranch. He was waiting to see if anyone visited Lynda, as Mason had asked. He also watched to see if Lynda left the property.

It was 10:30 a.m. when a black Audi A5 entered the Laffarty property. He recognized the driver immediately. She was the lady who owned the Los Alamitos Raceway. Randy was a bit of a gambler and was lucky enough to have some influential friends who associated with Miss Christy Amherst. Twenty minutes later, the black Audi left, heading south on Laurel Canyon Boulevard toward Hollywood. Randy followed the Audi as he had many targets in his investigation's history.

Susan Crull, Sue to her friends, walked into Police HQ at 2:30 p.m. ready for her interview with Detective Delsson. She was dressed to the nines and looked like the movie star she was. Her latest film, "Eyes of the Wicked," had garnered her an Academy Award nomination, so she was in the tabloids daily. She was a thin blonde with a petite figure. She was dressed in a wild print dress that came down to five inches above her knee. Her shoes looked expensive, her legs were long, and she walked with an air of importance. Sue lived with Kevin Syracuse, who had produced her movies out of Sagittarius International Studios.

Sue was led by Diane Smythe, who was one of the Report Techs on the floor, to the small conference room Mason was using for the interviews. The cameras were turned on and rolling, then she buzzed Mason's office. He answered, and Diane said, "Your 2:30 is in the conference room. Everything you asked for is ready." He knew she meant the cameras.

Mason said, "Thanks, Di." He went directly into the conference room to start the interview, "Hello, Miss Crull. It's a pleasure to meet you. I'm a big fan of your work. Thank you for coming today.

If you are ready, we can begin unless you have questions for me." Sue shook her head no. Mason began, "Miss Crull, how close were you with Carmen Craig?"

Sue took off her stylish sunglasses and replied, "Please call me Sue. Carmen was one of my best friends. She had advised me a lot during my career, and we have spent tons of time together both in town and during our travels across the globe."

Mason continued, "Do you have any reason to believe that Carmen was murdered rather than dying accidentally?"

The shocked look on Sue Crull's face told him volumes. She was a bit choked up, then seemed to turn angry, "Do you have evidence that she was killed? If so, I can tell you those who did it!" Her face was red initially, but then she calmed down.

Mason wasted no time. He probed further, "If she didn't die from a horse-riding accident, who do you think might have wanted her dead?"

Sue said, "Maybe I am speaking out of turn, but I was really angry when she died. I have ridden horses with her for years when I am not working, and I felt it was very curious that she was on her favorite horse and fell or was thrown off. She hit the rocks face-first, they said, hit her head, and died. She broke that horse in, and she has fallen off horses since she was a kid. It is baffling."

Mason asked again, "We may have reason to believe she was murdered." Knowing he had no evidence, he forged ahead, "Who do you suppose would be the leading candidates? Is there anyone you can think of who might have wanted her out of the way?"

Sue again looked shocked, "You think there was more than one person who killed her?"

Mason clarified, "You said before you could tell me 'those who may have done it.' So, I assume you think there is more than one person who you thought had a reason or a wish to kill her."

Sue Crull realized how he had baited her, so she became more cautious, "Let us just say that a person with her kind of money, anybody who was in line to inherit it, might have reason to do something like that. I thought she mentioned a sister once, but I am not sure. I know she and her husband, Dalton Craig, had a son that she didn't see eye to eye with, and there may be more."

Mason said, "Did you ever have any quarrels with Carmen?"

Sue said, "We were practically sisters. We have never had a disparaging word since we met twenty years ago. She was the kind of person you could go to for a shoulder to cry on or to give you moral support. I don't know anyone outside of her greedy family who ever said a harsh word toward her."

Mason took a stab at getting more information, "Do you think one of her relatives would kill her for the money?"

Sue said, "I guess that is something you will have to find out, Mr. Detective. If you have nothing further for me, I need to get to another appointment."

Mason said, "I have all I need. Thanks again for coming in today. Have a nice evening. Sue, please keep our talk private for now. Thanks."

After Sue left, Mason called his lawyer friend, Denis Shinto. Denis answered his private line, "Hello."

Mason said, "Hello, Denis. Mason Delsson here. I was wondering if I could pop in to see you tomorrow morning. I have some questions about Dalton, Carmen, and Walker Craig, and maybe we could speak about the will situation."

Denis responded, "What time do you need me?"

Mason said, "I'll be in at 9 a.m. if that works."

Denis replied, "You are on the calendar, my friend. See you then."

Just as he hung up, Diane Smythe knocked lightly on the door and peaking in said, "Your last appointment is here in the conference room waiting for you. Did you need me to bring you anything?"

Mason said, "Thanks. Yes, please. A black coffee would be great." Diane left. Mason went down the short hall to the conference room. He entered and was shocked to find a beautiful woman seated before him.

Kathy Muller was the owner of Retreat Two, a restaurant in Marina del Ray inside the Ritz Carlton Hotel that featured gourmet cuisine with Italian food being the mainstay. She was very elegantly attired in a gray business suit. The jacket was tailored to fit her like a glove. She wore a pink collared blouse under the jacket, and Mason could see her dark pink bra beneath the blouse. She wore a matching skirt that came down to an inch above her knee. Her tanned legs needed no stockings, and she wore what looked like very expensive high heels in gray. It was a lovely ensemble. The sight of it was one that Mason saved in his permanent memory bank.

Mason said, "Hello, Miss Muller. I am Detective Mason Delsson. Thank you for coming today to answer a few questions. Is there anything you'd like to say before we begin?" He noticed the diamond stick pin on her lapel.

Kathy Muller said, "Yes, Detective. I noticed you gave me quite a leering once over as you came in. Do you approve of my look?"

Mason, of course, blushed a bright red. He was busted. He replied, "Well, Miss Muller, I am sorry if I offended you, but quite frankly, I have been in Los Angeles, California, for over three years now. I will never be accustomed to seeing such extraordinarily beautiful women. Please forgive me."

Kathy Muller smiled her sweetest smile and said, "I didn't want to embarrass you, Detective, but while you gave me the once over, I took a long look at you as well. I must say thank you for the compliment as well as the leer at my body. I can honestly say I have never seen a more handsome policeman. May we begin?"

Mason wanted to go in a whole different direction than he had initially planned, but his instincts took over, and his mind told him not to think with his little head. He knew this reaction from Miss Mason might be a diversion to get him off his game. As difficult as it may be, he forged ahead, "OK, Miss Muller, what was your relationship with Carmen Craig?"

Kathy took a deep breath and replied, "We were long-time lovers, Detective."

You could have blown Mason over with a soft breeze. He was

quite taken aback. Not only by the vision in his mind, but her absolute candor.

He asked, "Was this a public or private affair? By that I mean, was this people's general knowledge?"

Kathy Muller knew she had Mason in uncomfortable waters, but she replied, "Well, Detective, Carmen and I spent a lot of time together, went on vacation together, but we never announced it to anyone. Neither of us cared who knew, but we were as discreet as we could be to not embarrass members of her family or mine. We had been together for ten years before she and Dalton agreed to stay together for Walker and appearances but see other people discreetly."

Mason then asked, "Do you think her death had anything to do with your relationship with her?

Kathy's reaction was quick and venomous, "Of course, it was not. She and I were very discreet. Even our close girlfriends have no idea about our relationship. I frankly don't think it was an accident. She and I are very experienced riders, and she would never have put herself in a situation where she was in a dangerous area with her horse, Sage. I just wish that I were with her that day, but I was called away by my son, who was having an emergency and needed my help."

Mason asked, "How do you think she died?"

Kathy said, "I have no evidence to make any claims about her accidental death, but I have my suspicions."

Kathy's phone rang loudly, and it startled both of them. She looked at the phone and saw who it was and declined to answer. She said, "My apologies, Detective. I thought I had definitely shut off the ringer on my phone.

Mason continued, "Miss Muller, who do you think may have had reason to kill Carmen Craig?"

Kathy paused and looked around, "Well, Detective, I noticed you mention her by name each time you've asked a question, which means you are probably videotaping this interview. If you are, I would like a copy, and you limit the people who have access to it. I am not thrilled with you, knowing you didn't ask me first. Studying law for several years, I know it is within my rights to have knowledge of it and give my consent beforehand. Shame on you."

Kathy Muller continued, "My thinking is, if someone had anything to do with Carm's death, it would have to be Walker Craig. Walker thought that after Dalton's death, Carmen would inherit the bulk of Dalton's money. Walker wanted not only his share but also everyone else's share of the money. I have no proof. That is why I am so sad I was not able to be there with her when she passed. Not only because her death could have been prevented, but also because people should never die alone."

Mason said, "Had Carmen ever been unfaithful to you? If she had, would you have killed her for it?"

Kathy laughed, "There was no reason for her to cheat on me. We had both been cheated on in our marriages, so to alleviate this, we brought others into our bed. I, of course, tell you this in confidence, and now you will really have to give me a copy of the tape."

Mason was convinced Kathy was not his killer. He said, "I will deliver you a copy of the tape tomorrow. Thanks again for coming in today."

Kathy Muller said, "It was my pleasure, and thanks for listening. By the way, I am looking for another bed partner if you ever want to audition for the role. Here is my card. Call me anytime." With that, she got up and extended her hand to him.

Mason shook her hand and said, "I will certainly think about that in the next hour or so, and as I wrap up this case, I will let you know. I will drop the tape off at Retreat Two tomorrow, and maybe we could have dinner. If you are available at six o'clock."

After shaking hands, Kathy went to the door and said, "I will see you at six tomorrow. Good night and happy fantasies."

Mason sat looking at the camera and said, "I'll cut that part out before giving the tape to anyone."

Mason walked into the office of Shinto and Associates on Elmwood Avenue just outside the Rodeo Drive area. Denis greeted him at the reception desk and said, "Good Morning, old friend. Let's talk in my office. Can I offer you a beverage?" Mason declined and followed Denis into a very large office on the second floor.

The room was all walnut wood from the large desk in the middle of the room to the wall-to-ceiling bookcases along one side. His desk looked out at a wall of windows that framed the mountains to the east. Mason sat in the chair Denis pointed to. It was a deep brown leather, and it was a very comfortable armchair. Mason began, "Denis, how much do you know about the Craig family?"

Denis replied, "Dalton, the late Carmen, and their son, Walker?" Mason nodded affirmatively. Denis continued, I used to work for Carmen before she got married. When her father died, she found a lawyer-financial advisor who could advise her on the millions she received in inheritance. What do you specifically want to know?"

Mason said, "I think Carmen may have been killed. I have no proof at this point, but the case evidence just doesn't add up. Here we had a woman who was a lifelong horse rider and breeder of horses. She allegedly fell off her favorite steed, face-first into some rocks, and was then found unrecognizable. Carmen rode almost daily and usually with someone. The day she was found, she was alone. Do you know the financial status of Gemini Studios? Was Walker almost estranged from his mother?"

Denis replied, "That is an interesting hunch, my friend. Knowing you like I do, your bloodhound senses are usually correct. Carmen spoke often about how Waker was close to her as a very young child, but as he became a teenager, they became distant. He was lazy and spoiled by his father, which created a lot of anger among all three members of the family. It caused Carmen a lot of pain to see her only child drift apart from her. It was only in recent months when I ran into her at a restaurant that she told me she and Walker were becoming closer again and even rode almost daily."

Mason then asked, "How much was Carmen worth? Did she actually own Gemini Studios?"

Denis said, "I don't think so. Dalton Craig has done well in the film business. He is wealthy in his own right." I am not aware of how much money her father left her, but I know it had to be a significant number."

Mason asked, "Did Carmen ever mention that she was afraid for her life?"

Denis said, "No, she never spoke of that. She did say that having all the money she inherited made her uneasy and vulnerable. Especially the trend in the country toward violence."

Mason said, "Well, I won't take any more of your time. Thanks for seeing me. We'll have lunch soon. Give my regards to your wife, Irene." Mason left and went to his office.

* * *

Lynda Laffarty and Christy Amherst pulled into the parking lot at Retreat Two. They had planned to meet Susie Crull, Jen Sandrew, and Kathy at her restaurant for dinner and discuss the interviewing talents of Detective Mason Delsson.

Randy Keene had followed the ladies to the restaurant and taken two or three pictures of them going inside with his high-speed camera. He used a Canon DSLR with a Canon EF75-300 mm lens. He returned it to his briefcase and went into the restaurant and sat at the bar. A pretty, sexy barmaid, Mel Barstow, asked him, "What'll you have, sir?"

Randy said, "Just a draft beer. I am waiting for a friend."

Lynda and Christy were seated at a table in the back private area by the hostess, Suzi Cooke. The waiter, Greg Solomet, came over and took their drink order. Lynda began, "I just wanted to get here early to chat before the rest of the ladies arrived. I was taken with Mason Delsson. He looked so strong, and I could tell he would be good in the sack. He's got those bedroom eyes and soft but strong hands."

Christy laughed, "There is nothing better than listening to you size up a man and describe why you want to sleep with him. How on earth do you tell whether a man will be good in bed? Maybe you should write a manual for those of us who cannot."

Lynda said, "Well, it is simple, Miss Amherst. The look in a man's eyes will tell you all you need to know. If a man looks you up and down, what you're wearing, and how you fill it out, it will give you a hint. If he maintains eye contact with you during the initial conversation, it is a good sign, but I always watch for where his eyes are on me when I look away and look back. He doesn't have time to shift them from your boobs or your ass, depending on where he is looking. Then you know he wants more."

Christy laughed, "So, how can you tell his strength translates into a great lover?"

Lynda said, "It is the feeling of shaking a man's hand that tells me. If he looks like a bodybuilder and he crushes your hand when you shake, he will be rough and insistent on his pleasure. If he grabs your hand weakly, he is a fish. The man who grabs firmly and stares in your eyes is a passionate and caring lover."

Kathy Muller walked into her restaurant and said hello to Suzi Cooke at the front desk. She went into the kitchen and saw the chef at work. Bobby Pinkess was her head chef. His mastery of the menu was amazing, and he could make anything taste grand. His specialty sandwich was fried octopus. It sounds awful, but it melts in your mouth. Kathy yelled to him, "Hey Bob, do you have anything special for my girls tonight?"

Bob said, "I am making alligator fritters and breaded zucchini. I also have added some octopus and steak on skewers to mix the plate up." Kathy laughed and could not wait to tell them what they had eaten when their meal was done.

Kathy walked out to the bar to see Mel Barstow, her sexiest barmaid, working, and had her cosmopolitan already poured. She said, "Thank you, Mel. This is why I keep you behind the bar."

Kathy drank it down, then said, "Send another with a round of drinks for the girls at the table. She walked through the room and saw that the tables were full. She was glad her business was working so well. She attributed it to great food, great help, and great service. Her recipes were good, and the people she hired worked hard, and she compensated them well. She had worked hard all her life to make the business what she dreamt it would be.

She got to the private dining room just as Sue Crull and Jen Sandrew entered the restaurant. They came separately but walked into the private dining room together.

Greg Solomett, one of the waiters, joined them as they took their seats and had drinks for everyone, including Sue and Jen, who had just arrived. Greg said, "Would you ladies like me to bring your food now or wait for a few minutes?"

Lynda said, "We haven't even looked at the menu to choose what we want for dinner."

Greg just smiled and said, "Miss Muller has already ordered for you."

Kathy Muller said, "Greg, give us ten minutes, then bring the food.

Lynda started, "Well, who besides me thought Detective Delsson was a hunk?

Sue Crull said, "I thought he was cute, but his questions indicated they don't have an idea how Carmen died. I think he was on a big fishing expedition."

Jen Sandrew said, "I was not impressed with Mason Delsson. His questions were more about my relationship with Carmen. I mentioned her strained relationship with Walker, and he insinuated that I said Walker killed her. I put him straight on that one, saying Carmen mentioned she was threatened by her son's dependence on his father's money. He wanted all of it when Dalton passed on."

Christy laughed, "Well, let me tell you. I was quite taken with Mr. Delsson. He looked me up and down, and I was glad I was sitting down because it made my knees weak. I felt tingly all over, if you know what I mean. Then he began the interview, and his demeanor was somewhat gruff and accusatory. I had to straighten him out. Then I realized I still wanted him."

Lynda said to Kathy, "Miss Muller, it appears we all want to jump his bones. What are your feelings?"

Kathy said, "He asked right away what my relationship with Carm was. I told him frankly that we were lovers. He asked if she was ever unfaithful." All the ladies laughed at that remark. Kathy continued, "As you all know, Carmen and I have been close friends for some time and have shared our bed with others, so there was no need for us to stray."

2

GREG SOLOMET APPEARED WITH TWO HELPERS and delivered the meal. The three men bustled around these ladies like bees to a beehive. The meal was an elaborate culinary display. There was a large dish of lasagna just oozing with sauce. There was a large bowl of salad with greens, tomatoes, cheese, beans, and a plate of three dressings beside it. There was also a plate of fried meat on a stick. They looked like chicken tenders but were fried octopus, steak, and chicken. It also had three different dipping sauces to pair with it. Greg also brought two bottles of Cabernet Sauvignon and wine glasses for each of them. He said as his two helpers left, "Please enjoy, ladies. If you need anything else, please don't hesitate to ring the bell that is on the table. I will be back to check on you regularly." He left them to their feast.

The ladies were all talking at once. They were oohing and aahing over all the items before them. They each thanked Kathy for choosing the meal as they tasted everything. The wine was poured by Jen as she was closest to it.

Lynda said, "So, which one of us should have Mr. Delsson first?" They all laughed, but each of them secretly wished it would be them that the group would choose. They each felt he was attracted to them, as they recalled his lingering looks during their separate interview. Would he even want any of them?

Jen said, "He is more my age, and I am a single lady looking for a man to help me with my sleepless nights. I could probably get very used to making my daily goal to satisfy this man's pleasure for the next three or four decades. I get tingles just thinking about what it would feel like in his arms."

Christy perked up, saying, "Honey, we are all single ladies and need a man to make us sleep well at night. Mr. Delsson would not discriminate regarding the age of a woman. As Lynda told me, if a man shakes your hand firmly and stares into your eyes, he may be telling you that he is a passionate and caring lover. He wants me."

Sue Crull said, "I think we should each try our best to bed him and see which of us has the 'right stuff.' I think he'll choose any of us depending on what he is looking for. It will probably be me because I am so much more attractive than all of you!"

Lynda said, "I think this calls for a small wager between us. We should all have free rein to try to land this shark and see who is the first one to put their hooks on him. Ladies, thoughts?"

Sue Crull said, "I have an extra $200 that is just burning a hole in my Gucci wallet."

Christy responded, "Why don't we make it interesting, ladies? I will wager $500 to see if my feminine charms are the most attractive in this group of old hens."

Jen said, "I have my $500 with me now. It is not in a Gucci bag like Sue Crull here, but I am itching to spend on something extravagant.

* * *

Mason Delsson picked up the phone in his office and dialed the number of Walker Craig. The maid picked up the phone, "Craig Residence."

Mason said, "This is Detective Mason Delsson from LAPD. I would like to speak to Walker Craig if he is available."

The maid said, "Mr. Craig is currently in a meeting. Can I have your number so he can call you back?" Mason gave her his private number, and they hung up. Mason wondered how long it would be before Walker called him back. He then called Sam Barfield at his office downtown.

Sam's secretary answered the phone, "Barfield and Associates, how may I direct your call?"

Mason said, "This is Detective Delsson from LAPD. May I speak to Mr. Barfield, please?"

The secretary said, "Hold the line, please, while I check to see if Mr. Barfield is available."

Mason heard a click and waited. He anticipated being told he was in a meeting or on another call. He would just have to go to his office, he thought.

A voice brought Mason out of his reverie when he heard, "Sam Barfield here. What can I do for you, Mr. Delsson?"

Mason said, "Mr. Barfield, thank you for taking my call. I have several questions about Mr. Craig and his financial plans, as well as his will. Would you like to do this over the phone, or would you prefer if I come to your office?"

Sam Barfield said, "You are scheduled to come to the ranch and interview the staff today at ten o'clock. Why don't we talk when I see you? Your interviews may take some time, so I'll have my secretary put out some sandwiches for us."

Mason said, "Thank you. That would be appreciated. I have a lot of questions to ask you. I will see you at ten. Talk to you then, goodbye." Mason was somewhat encouraged but realistic. He wondered if Dalton's lawyer would share anything, and if he did, would it help his investigation? He also wondered how the interviews with the staff would go.

* * *

Dalton was frustrated knowing his son had no forethought about his future, other than, Daddy would pay for this or that. Dalton tried to remain calm and said, "Listen, Walker. You need to start your life. Be independent. Choose a career path. Meet a lady and settle down. If you start a family, that will be your responsibility to support it. Not your mother and me.

I have spoken to you more than once to begin preparing for your future by deciding on a career path. If you want to take over the studio and learn how to run this business, you should work in it as much as you can. So, when I leave it to you, you will not lose what I have built. If you want to go in another direction, you must begin now and prepare your legacy. I can no longer support your unmotivated existence."

Walker had gone to school but was never motivated to do anything because his father doted on him all the time. He would hang around the movie lot at Gemini Studios. He was tolerated because he was Dalton's son. He became quite a nuisance and got into loads of scrapes with other directors at age sixteen. He had a knack for upsetting the in-house productions with his obnoxious behavior. It got to the point that Dalton had to sit him down and read him the riot act.

Dalton had said, "Sit down, Walker. I need to tell you a story." Walker loved it when his dad would relate a story because most often it was about some starlet he had a tryst with or one that had done something scandalous on one of the sets at Gemini. This talk turned out to be different. Dalton went on, "You are my son, Walker, and I love you, but you have to get focused on your life. You have done nothing with your life because I have spoiled you rotten, and you get away with all kinds of mischief because I am your father. It has now affected my business. Not that it is more important than you, but if I don't have continued success, our fortune will be in danger, or it could be entirely lost."

Walker remembers hearing that speech like it was yesterday. His father had told him, if he didn't get his own life on track, he would never inherit either Gemini, his film empire, or his riches. Dalton had told him, "Go to school and make something of yourself. Find something that will drive you to make a living on your own and create a life for yourself. I won't support you until you pick an area of interest and make it on your own. My riches and business will be left to my wives."

Walker went to college and worked hard. He found investments and the stock market very interesting. As his interest grew, he realized his father had been right. He felt so much better about himself when he had a goal to attain. He became an expert in trading stocks and anything financial. He graduated from Stanford University. He went on to build a large financial firm. He did taxes, was an advisor to people on buying and trading stocks, as well as the kinds of things to invest in that would both make money and be used as a tax write-off. His father had set him up with the finances needed to open his business. Dalton even found that Walker was an excellent advisor for Gemini Studios. Walker, however, continued to sponge off his father, and mother's wealth and good fortune. This was short-lived. After his mother died, Walker seemed to fall apart. He moved back home and became reclusive.

* * *

Walker had just left Lyndsey Shaft when he fell hopelessly in love with Karena. They told everyone they were soulmates and became inseparable.

Walker met Lyndsey at his father's studios and became enamored with her. They dated, and even though Lyndsey Shaft was a few years older, they were happy. In a few years, Walker became disenchanted with Lyndsey. She was not the domestic type, and Walker wanted children. Lyndsey was not crazy about the idea. Then she became distant toward Walker. Their sex life became a drudgery for both of them. They separated after two and a half years together.

Then he met Karena Katrinka. She was a model and worked for a studio in Hollywood that was a rival of his father's, called Sagittarius International Films. They began dating, and she was welcomed into the Craig family. Walker's business was thriving. Karena had become more and more famous. Walker had to work hard to maintain his business.

Karena Katrinka was a starlet/model who had been raised in Poland. She had come to this country to seek fame and fortune. She was hired by Monika Losserio, who was an Agent for the SAG AFTRA Screen Actors Guild (American Federation of Television and Radio Artists). Monika was an old friend of Patrick Jameswick, who ran Sagittarius International Films. They got Karena loads of work doing runway modeling, then had her branch out into films. Karena met Walker Craig at one of those Hollywood parties that lasted until dawn.

Karena got pregnant about four months after she began dating Walker. Dalton asked him if he was going to marry Karena. Walker said, "What do you think, Dad?"

Dalton said, "Son, that is something you and Karena have to decide if it is important for you both. If you do, however, based upon your birthright, you would be well advised to have her sign a pre-nuptial agreement." Walker said, "I see where you are going, Dad, but I don't have any money or an estate to protect."

Walker would often travel and be gone for long periods, as he spent time in Europe cultivating business there for foreign billionaires who needed to be advised on buying and selling in America's stock market.

Walker feared he would lose Karena to someone else due to his constant absence. He was finally motivated to work and be successful, if only to independently support his lifestyle, and the one Karena had become accustomed to now. Sadly, Karena lost the baby. She and Walker drifted apart emotionally while Walker forged ahead with his career.

Karena became a regular around Dalton's house. She had even changed agents. She hired Ryan Parker, the agent, to help her slip away from Sagittarius Films and sign a contract to work for Gemini. Dalton was thrilled to hear this and promised to make her rich and happy. The first two films she made for Gemini won her an Academy Award, and they made millions of dollars. She became close to Dalton and flirted with him all the time. This caused Dalton's girlfriend, Allie Campwick, to be very upset and jealous of the time they spent together. Allie was co-owner of Elegant Lace with Jen Sandrew. She worked a lot to make her business grow, so she was absent as Dalton had time to, as she termed it, play with little Miss Karena.

Karena spent a lot of time away from Walker's house when he was away. She began to hang out at a local gym to keep fit. She hired a trainer by the name of Elijah Landon. He owned a gym where he did private training sessions. They flirted and neither of them hid their feelings for one another. The rumors flew around the social circles in Hollywood. This kind of gossip spreads like wildfire.

Dalton heard from the grapevine that his son's love interest had found herself a plaything for when Walker was out of town. His name was Ryan Harper, and he was a screenwriter working for Patrick Jameswick at Sagittarius International. Neither Harper nor Landon knew that Karena Katrinka had another lover outside of Walker. She hoped Walker wouldn't find out. It was Dalton Craig.

* * *

Monika Losserio was the agent people in Hollywood went to for actors, but her specialty was people in the music industry who were not yet in the mainstream, but very talented. Patrick J. Hart at Sagittarius International called her to say they were making an updated version of The Wiz. He called Monika and said, "Monika, I want to put together an ensemble of young talent. Can you help?"

Monika said, "I just discovered a new group back in upstate New

York called Familiari. They are a quartet with two brothers and two sisters that play all kinds of instruments, and the harmony they sing is incredible. Do you want me to send them for an audition? I think the group is currently in Las Vegas doing a few shows. I can set up an audition for next Friday at one o'clock."

Patrick said, "That works perfectly as the team is meeting here at noon. Thank you."

Monika got on the phone and called Vincent Thomas. He was the leader of the group, and she got him while on a break in rehearsal at the Bellagio in Vegas. She said, "Vinnie, this is Monika Losserio in LA. I have a client who is producing a remake of the musical, The Wiz. They would like your group to audition. I am leaving tickets for the four of you at the Las Vegas airport to fly Southwest to LAX. You are scheduled to leave this Tuesday at 1 p.m. If you need to ship your instruments, I can give you the name of a company there, and they will pick up your stuff and fly it here. I will pay for everything. How does that sound?"

Vinnie said, "Let me talk to the group, and I will call you back in ten minutes." It was eight minutes later when Monika's phone rang. "Yes. We will gladly do it," said Vinnie.

Monika laughed, "I guess you guys are ready to be stars!" They ended the call.

Vinnie said, "Carmella, Roman, and Clara, pack your bags. We are going to Hollywood. It is something we've all dreamt about, and now we have got our shot. Let's do this thing!!" They flew to Los Angeles the next day.

* * *

Lynda Laffarty sat at the table in Retreat Two after several of the ladies left. She sat across from Jennifer Sandrews. They were discussing how hard they worked, and Jen said, "Listen, my partner at Elegant Lace and I are going to Tahoe on Friday. We are looking at three new locations to open a new branch. We may stay four days, do some skiing and a bit of partying, do you want to join us?"

Lynda said, "You mean Lake Tahoe? Oh, that sounds delicious. I don't know about skiing, but my good friend Kathy Muller, who is my usual travel partner, loves to ski. We were just discussing it, so I will call her, and the four of us can go. I will call and get a reservation for two rooms at the Ritz-Carlton-Lake Tahoe."

Jen said, "Kathy can probably get us a deal. Also, my friend, Lynn Fuda, is the head chef at the Café Fiore Restaurant. It has the best Italian food. You'll all love it. I have been to Tahoe many times, and there is so much there to see and explore. We will have a great time. There are a lot of single men who are always there to choose from as well. We will have a super relaxing vacation. We will drink, sleep, eat, and chase men."

Lynda said, "That sounds like a getaway."

Jen Sandrew thought, *I must call Allie Campwick, my partner, and make sure she will have staff cover our time away in Tahoe.* Jen said to Lynda, "This trip will get us away from the buzz of Hollywood, and we'll be able to get some peace." Jen called Allie, "Allie, we are going to Lake Tahoe for the weekend. Can we get the staff to cover the store for us?"

Allie was excited, "Yeah, girl. That sounds like a plan. I will get the staff to rally around for us and clear our calendars. You can give me the trip's particulars when I see you tonight for dinner. I have been wanting to get away with you on a vacation out of town."

Kathy Muller drove to her home with Christy Amherst in the car. She said, "Christy, why don't you come to my place for dinner this evening? I will have the help put together a nice spread, and we can plan a getaway for you and me."

Christy said, "I would not mind getting out of town for a short exodus, but I was just talking to Christopher Erickson. His fashion show, presenting his spring line, is next weekend in New York City. I have an invitation. Why don't we attend? We can stay at Trump Tower. Donald has extended an open invitation, so I can call and confirm the availability. They are in the 700 block of Fifth Avenue at 56th Street. The show is at Vuitton in the next block up Fifth."

Kathy Muller pulled into her house's driveway and said, "I am going to pack a bag for Tahoe. You and I will have a separate vacation for just the two of us."

Christy got into her car and drove home after confirming her reservations on the plane for NYC and at Trump Tower. She thought it would be more fun in Tahoe, but she had plans for New York City that were pressing. She could relax anytime.

* * *

Mason Delsson sat at his desk in the LAPD building. He was watching the tapes of his interviews with Carmen Craig's friends. He suddenly noticed something in Kathy's interview. When she spoke of inheritance, he noticed something on her face. She seemed in a peaceful, happy mood, like she was getting some money.

Mason knew he had more work to do. There were more people to interview. He wanted to speak with the staff at Dalton Craig's home. He especially wanted to speak with Walker Craig and ask where he was on the day his mom fell off her horse.

Mason called Dalton Craig's residence. Sam Barfield again answered the phone. Mason said, "Is this Sam Barfield?"

Sam asked. "Who may I say is calling?"

Mason replied, "Sam, this is Detective Delsson of LAPD."

Sam said, "I am Sam Barfield, and I was just leaving the house to go to my office. How can I help you?"

Mason said, "I would like to come to the ranch tomorrow and complete my interview with Mr. Craig and also speak to each one of his staff. I think it would be easier than having them subpoenaed to come downtown to do an interview."

Sam said, "I will speak to Mr. Craig and see if he is available tomorrow. Even if he is away, you could certainly stop by the ranch and speak to everyone here. What time would you be coming?"

Mason said, "I can be there by 9 a.m. if that is not too early."

Sam said, "That will be fine. If Dalton can be available, I will make sure he is here." They ended the call.

Mason wondered to himself if Dalton would even be there.

Mason then called Randy Keene, his private investigator. When Randy answered, Mason said, "Randy. Mason here. What do you have for me?"

Randy said, "I have a report I am dropping off at HQ today."

Mason said, "Great. I have another assignment for you. I need you to set up a stakeout at Dalton Craig's home after I see you. I want to see if he leaves the ranch tomorrow."

* * *

Jen Sandrews, Kathy Muller, Lynda Laffarty, Sue Crull, Cricky Amherst, and Allie Campwick boarded an early flight on Friday morning for Lake Tahoe. The plane was owned by Dalton Craig. It was a Hawker Beechcraft 4000. Lynda had asked her ex-husband to approve the use of it for the trip with a few of her girlfriends. Dalton, always having a sweet spot in his heart for his ex-wife, immediately said yes to her request and called to make sure the plane and pilots were ready.

The plane took off at 9:30 a.m. from LAX. They touched down in an hour and twenty-five minutes. Tahoe had one runway, and it was a bit rough landing, but they arrived safely. There was a white limousine waiting for their arrival, and their driver, Tony Strong, took their bags and made them comfortable in the limo. Dalton had ordered the bar to be stocked, and Tony would chauffeur them during their stay.

The limousine took the ladies on a fifteen-minute drive to the Hilton Vacation Club at South Lake Tahoe. The views were so scenic that everyone commented on them. Their driver also offered some insight into the place's history.

They had two rooms on the fourth floor overlooking the Lake. In one room were Lynda, Cricky, and Kathy. Allie, Jennifer, and Sue took the adjoining room. The views were spectacular. Kathy said to her roommate Lynda Laffarty, "I don't know about you, but I am starving. I had nothing but black coffee for breakfast."

Lynda replied, "I love the room. You did a great job getting the reservations. I found a place not far from here, called Boat House on the Pier, that looks like they have a great dinner reputation. I'll call the girls next door."

Kathy Muller called Tony and asked if he would mind taking them to dinner. He asked, "When would you like to go?"

Kathy said, "We can be in the lobby in fifteen minutes. Does that work?"

He said, "I'll be waiting." She let the other ladies know.

Exactly, on time, the six ladies assembled in the lobby, and there stood Tony Strong with the door open to the limousine. Tony

Strong was a former physical therapist working in his home state of Colorado in the Denver area. He worked with several agencies serving the disabled population, as well as in conjunction with several orthopedic doctors. The money was fine, but the salary that Dalton Craig paid him for his various duties far exceeded the six figures he earned back in Colorado.

He met Dalton during a tour of the Gemini Studios and noticed that Dalton's gait was slightly akimbo. Tony asked Dalton about it and told Dalton, he was a physical therapist and would gladly help him work out those kinks. He said to Dalton, "If I can't improve your walking and relieve your back pain in three visits, you don't have to pay me. If you want to retain me, I will only charge you $125 per hour session."

Tony has been with Dalton ever since. Tony smiled as the four ladies climbed into the spacious gray limousine. He was dressed in a dark gray uniform with a gray pilot cap as well. The ladies were all chatting at once, so he asked Kathy, "Are your plans to go to the Boat House on the Pier?"

Kathy said, "Yes, sir, Tony. That is exactly where we are going. By the way, do we have to tip you extra if one or two of us consume too much libation and need a special assist to the hotel room?"

All the ladies laughed as they intended to unwind a bit on this trip. Tony waited until the laughter subsided, then said, "Ladies, I do not accept tips. Mr. Craig has taken care of all the financial needs."

The ladies looked seriously at each other, paused, then laughed loudly for the next five minutes. Kathy said to Jennifer Sandrews, "Well, Miss Jen. It looks like we are in good hands this evening." That began the conversations in earnest again on their way to Boat House.

The ladies were summarily impressed when Tony pulled the limo up to the front door. The place was right on the lake, and you could see sailboats on the water, for as far as you could see.

The ladies walked into the Boat House and found it to be a very swanky place. They were seated by the hostess, who turned out to be the owner, Catie Gaynor. She said to them, "Your waiter will be Jake Stone. He will attend to your every need."

Jake Stone was right behind her when she left. He introduced himself to the ladies, "Hi, I am Jake, I will be your waiter tonight. Here are the menus. Can I start you off with something from the bar?"

Lynda ordered a scotch on the rocks, Jennifer asked for a Cabernet Sauvignon, Allie said, "Give me your best margarita."

Kathy said, "I am drinking red wine as well, so bring us a bottle of the Cab for us to share."

Jake said, "I will bring these and take your food order upon my return." With that, Jake left the table, thinking he would love to have a romantic encounter with any of these ladies.

Lynda said, "OK, Ladies, which of you would like the waiter?" Everyone laughed.

Kathy replied, "He is a bit young for me. I don't want to have to teach anyone pleasure at this point."

Allie said, "I find him yummy. I would like to trip the light fantastic with him a time or two."

Jen said, "I guess we know who will get Mr. Stone." Just as she said this, Jake reappeared with their cocktails.

Kathy said, "Give us another few minutes for food."

* * *

Mason Delsson sat in his favorite coffee shop at the table by the window. He did his best thinking there. He was going over the report he had received from Randy Keene. Randy relayed to him in the report that the two ladies he was tailing were planning a trip. It turned out Lynda would go to Lake Tahoe with four other ladies, and Christy was headed for New York City for a fashion show of some kind. Mason sat there watching the customers come into the coffee shop and take their coffee to go. A few sat at tables. He saw a blonde come in who looked familiar. He hoped she would stay and sit at a table. He really would like to meet her.

He was in luck. She grabbed her coffee when they called out her name, "Deyna."

It was an unusual spelling, and the way he knew it was by seeing her name on her cup as she walked past him and sat at the next table.

Deyna Doll was a fashion designer and owned a shop near the coffee shop. She had a sketch pad with her that she opened upon sitting down and began doodling. She was working on designing a bikini bathing suit for the spring line. Mason looked for an opportunity to begin a conversation. He said to her, "Deyna, that is a lovely name for a lovely lady. By chance, are you sketching me?"

Deyna never raised her head to look at him. She whispered, "Busy. Sorry."

Mason was not the type to allow her not to respond by at least looking up at him and speaking to him. He said in a soft voice, "I know you are busy, but I just need a few minutes of your time. Let me know when you are ready to talk."

Deyna Doll just sipped her coffee as she drew on the sketch pad. She never looked up at him. Mason sat there for over ten minutes reading the report from Randy Keene. He had finished his coffee and was just about to get up to leave. He envisioned saying, "Nice talking to you, Deyna. I hope we meet again." It was a snide remark, but he was not used to women just ignoring him. He thought it was arrogant of her not to even acknowledge his presence for more than two words of dismissal.

He was gathering his papers, ready to stand up, when she looked up and spoke to him, "I am sorry, Mr. Delsson. I was right in the middle of a creation and didn't want to lose my focus. What do you think?" She turned her sketch pad around so he could see what she had drawn.

Mason just whistled, then said, "Wow! That was worth the wait. I would like to see you wearing that. Maybe in a dark purple with white trim for the ties. If I knew there was a chance you would wear that for me, I would definitely take you out to dinner at one of the finest restaurants we have here in Los Angeles."

Deyna assessed him more closely. He had a good eye, it seemed, for fashion, and he was quite good-looking. She had not had a date in weeks while preparing for this show. Her assistant, Dalia Davenport, who had been with her for years, said, "Deyna, you need to find a man. You are too tense and becoming bitchy. I mean, very bitchy. I can recommend someone if you'd like." Deyna had declined, not knowing Dalia's taste, but now looking at Mason, she thought she would make a real effort to give this a whirl. He was dreamy.

Deyna said, "That is a very good suggestion, Mr. Delsson. Thank you. I will include that color in the samples."

Mason then realized she had called him by name. He had no name on his cup as he was a regular. He wanted to finish the conversation, but she was gone, waving back to him over her head.

* * *

Dalton Craig had finished his latest project with a new writer, Fitore Fantazee. She had spoken to him at a cocktail party months ago, and when she met him said, "I have a script I'd like you to read."

Dalton took one look at her and knew he would read it, just so he could see her again. Fitore was from Puerto Rico and had been here for years as an actress. She was five-foot-eight with jet black hair that she wore down to her shoulders. She had the most beautiful green eyes he had ever seen. When they spoke, he did not notice anything but her beauty until she thanked him and walked away. He was mesmerized but the sway in her luscious hips. It was her legs in those five-inch heels that grabbed his attention. She stopped at the bar, turned around, and found Dalton still staring at her. She smiled and waited for her drink. Dalton noticed her chest was even more voluptuous than the view from the rear. He was helplessly star-struck and knew without a doubt he would read her script and call her again. He hoped the script was good so they could work together.

Gemini Studios was in luck. Fitore Fantazee was as talented a writer as she was a beautiful woman. The story was about a starlet who was a killer. She sought rich men, found a way to get them interested, which was never difficult, then she would slide her way into their hearts, planning to then inherit or steal their money. The story was entitled, "Captivating Temptress."

During the making of the movie, Dalton was so smitten with Fitore that he invited her to take a weekend trip with him to Lake Tahoe to celebrate the completion of the film. He said, "Fitore, I have enjoyed working with you to get this film in the can and ready for distribution. How about you and I go to Lake Tahoe for the weekend?" Fitore accepted his invitation after giving him several reasons that it was a bad idea to mix business and pleasure. Dalton was persistent, and she acquiesced. The next day, he sent a car for her. It brought her to the private plane section of LAX. They boarded and were off to Lake Tahoe to stay at The Hilton Vacation Club in South Lake Tahoe.

Dalton had the steward on his jet bring them champagne that had been chilling all morning. It was just past noon as Dalton asked, "Are you hungry? I can have the steward bring us some snacks or a sandwich. If not, we can go to lunch at one of the best restaurants in Lake Tahoe."

Fitore said, "Let's wait until we get settled in the hotel. I am better able to focus on eating when I am on the ground. Flying is only for drinking."

Dalton laughed, "I understand completely. It took me a lot of air miles before I could be comfortable eating anything substantial. After we settle in at the hotel, I know a great place for lunch right on the Lake. It's called The Boathouse on the Pier. I think you'll enjoy the food and the ambiance."

* * *

Jake Stone returned to the ladies' table to take their orders for food. He brought another cocktail for each of them, which they greatly appreciated. Jake said, "What can we start you with this evening? As he took their orders, he looked longingly at the young brunette called Allie.

She looked to be a few years younger than him, but she had a beautiful smile and a great body. He had noticed her when she was walking into the restaurant. Kathy ordered the Chilean Sea Bass. Jen asked for the Caprese Chicken Linguini. Lynda and Allie both ordered the Carne Asada Steak. Lynda then ordered another round of drinks for the table and Jake made a note.

Jake took Allie's order last and watched as she smiled brightly at him while she blushed a lovely shade of red. Dinner was divine. They adjourned to the bar and had four more drinks. All were drunk on the way back to the hotel.

The next morning, the ladies slept in as the hangovers were something many didn't experience often. By noon, they were ready for lunch but chose another restaurant. Kathy said, "We might have been quite loud and raucous last night, so I think we should find somewhere else for lunch.

* * *

That morning, Tony Strong had two calls for the limousine to go to lunch, so he called his buddy, Kirt Leoz, to grab another car to take the ladies to lunch. He would drive Dalton and his guest to the Boathouse.

Tony Strong held the door open for Dalton and Fitore. She was quite a fine-looking lady, but Tony maintained his professionalism by not leering. She was very chatty with Dalton when they rode to the restaurant. Dalton was quiet and listened well. He wanted things to go well as he was quite smitten with this beautiful lady. She was not only stunning but also very adept at writing stories and screenplays.

They entered the restaurant and sat at a small table for two on the outside deck. It was unseasonably warm, and Fitore shed her jacket to sit in the sun. She looked out onto the lake and was quiet. The waiter, Jake Stone, recognized Mr. Craig and knew he had better be on his best behavior. Jake said, "Good afternoon, Mr. Craig. It is great to see you. What can I get you both?"

Dalton did not recognize Jake, but Dalton was cordial. His motto was a fan was a fan. He said, "Let us have a bottle of Dom and menus."

Jake said, "Yes. Sir." He left the menus for them and hurried to chill the champagne.

After five minutes or so, Jake returned to Dalton's table with champagne and two glasses. He asked Dalton, "Did you want me to open the champagne now, sir?"

Dalton said, "Yes, and we are ready to order."

Dalton and Fitore both ordered the Chilean Sea Bass for lunch and a bottle of King Maui Sauvignon Blanc. Jake left quickly and returned with their wine in minutes. When saw them come into the parking lot, recognizing his limousine, chilled the wine Dalton liked.

Dalton said, "Jake, this bottle is already chilled. Thank you."

Jake said, "I saw you come in and made sure I had the wines you like available."

Dalton said, "Maybe you had better chill another bottle. Fitore seems to like this one."

Jake smiled, "I already have two more chilling, just in case. I'll be back with your food in a minute."

The Sea Bass arrived, and it was delicious. They had one more bottle of King Maui as they chatted out on the deck at the Boathouse. Dalton was very taken with Fitore. She was very sexy and seemed to be into him as well. He asked her, "What would you like to do today?"

Fitore said, "I think it would be nice if we went up on the mountain and drank the afternoon away."

Dalton replied, "You are going to spoil me, young lady. I will have our driver take us to this sexy mountain retreat. We can ski if you'd like or just sit in the chalet and drink."

Tony Strong received a text from Dalton that said he wanted to go to the Ritz-Carlton in Truckee for some skiing.

Tony texted back, No worries, Mr. Craig. I can have you there in twenty minutes."

Dalton looked at Fitore and said, "We are on our way to the ski resort as soon as I pay our tab." Fitore was elated. She had always wanted to ski in Lake Tahoe, but never seemed to have the time or anyone to go with her.

She said to Dalton, "Oh, no. I don't have any of my ski outfits or my skis!"

Dalton laughed, "I'll have our driver stop in town to shop. Is that okay with you?"

* * *

Lynda Laffarty awoke with a severe hangover. It had been a while since she had that much to drink. She looked to the other bed in the room and saw it was empty. Kathy must have gone down to the coffee shop, she thought. Lynda grabbed her phone and texted Kathy, Where are you K? Coffee shop?"

As Lynda walked into the shower, her phone buzzed. It was Kathy calling. Lynda answered, "Hello, Miss Partyer. How did you sleep last night?"

Lynda said, "I am just getting into the shower, I don't know for sure yet. I had a lot to drink last night. What did we end up doing?

Kathy answered, "Well, Miss Lady. You flirted with every guy at the bar last night but never hooked up because you were so inebriated. We came back here to the room, you threw off your clothes, were stark naked, you jumped into bed, and were all over me. I made you stay on your side of the bed, and five minutes later, you were sound asleep."

Lynda tested the water, and it was ready. She almost stepped under the rain shower spray with her phone. She said, "Oh my goodness, I am so sorry. Please forgive me. Listen, my shower is ready, so I will meet you in the coffee shop in twenty minutes."

Lynda ended the call and stepped into the shower. She thought to herself that it had been a long time since she had been romantic with anyone, so she had to be careful. She needed to be sober when she expressed her sexuality. Especially to someone whom she had never been with before like Kathy.

Lynda finished her shower, dressed, took the elevator to the lobby, and walked into the café. She went to the counter, ordered a coffee, and went to the table to join Kathy.

* * *

Dalton and Fitore skied for over an hour and decided to head into the lodge. Fitore said, "I am a little cold because I don't have my favorite ski jacket. Thank you again for buying all of these wonderful clothes that must have cost a fortune. I must admit that I feel sexy in them, but I am ready for a hot toddy."

Dalton said, "Let's head to the lodge. I have to agree, the clothes look incredibly sexy to me. I was thinking of something other than the lodge to warm you up, but we'll start with a few drinks to get your blood temperature up.

They stowed their skis and headed into the bar area. They sat at the end of the bar and ordered. The bartender's name was Blake Koleman. He asked, "What'll it be, folks?" Miss Fitore ordered a hot-toddy, and Dalton ordered an Apple Cider Margarita.

Blake asked, "What bourbon would you like, miss?"

Fitore replied, "Do you have any Yamazaki Single Malt?"

Blake said, "Yes, I do, Miss Fantazee. Great choice. The tequila for you, sir?

Dalton said, "A Patron Reposado. if possible."

Blake said, "Coming right up, folks."

After their second drink each, Fitore said, "I am toasty warm right now. Are you hungry?"

Dalton smiled, "I am for you, sweet thing! I could probably force myself to put on the feedbag as well. Let's get a table." Dalton paid the tab and left a $100 tip for Blake.

Dalton and Fitore Fantazee approached the hostess, who was a tall redhead named Faye. Faye asked, "Would you like your usual table, Mr. Craig?"

Dalton grinned and said, "Yes, please, Faye. That would be great. How nice to see you." Shaking her hand, he placed a fifty-dollar bill in her palm.

Faye said, "This isn't necessary, Mr. Craig, but thank you very much." Dalton just smiled and held the chair for Fitore when they reached the table.

During their dinner, Dalton got to know all about Fitore and asked her many questions about her youth, her family, and her dreams. Fitore was born in Puerto Rico but came to this country as a small child. She was only four years old, but even then, her parents were teaching her what English they knew. This would serve her well the next year when she began school in Miami. She was active in school and very popular because of her beauty. She was in the drama club, cheered for the sports teams, and even took ballet lessons.

Fitore wanted to go to Juilliard to study voice and ballet, but her parents wanted her to be the first in their family to go to college. They thought it would serve her well when her interest in the silliness of singing and dancing faded, and she had to support herself. Little did they know that her talent was so special and her drive to be successful in the entertainment field was so strong. Fitore would not only impress the folks at Juilliard, but also the scouts from Hollywood. She was given a full scholarship to the school and became an amazing talent with their guidance. With Fitore's constant hard work, she graduated from Juilliard as the valedictorian. She got an agent and landed a show on Broadway. Her next goal was to get into Hollywood movies.

* * *

Monika Losserio was waiting with her limousine driver in the luggage area at LAX. It was only minutes before she saw the group of them riding down the escalator that led to the baggage area. Monika stood at carousel number six as she saw their flight number from Vegas appear on the lighted display. She recognized Vinnie Thomas immediately as she had heard him play at a Solomet concert in New York a while back. Monika greeted them, shaking Vinnie's hand, "Welcome to Los Angeles. You all look fabulous. I have my driver, Jimmy, here to help with your baggage."

Vinnie said, "I hope you don't mind, but we all brought instruments just in case." Then he introduced the rest of Familiari, "Monika. This is Carmella Rae. This is Roman Marks, and of course, Clara Lynn." They all exchanged pleasantries, and when they saw their bags arrive, they went to the carousel and pointed to or grabbed them with Jimmy, the driver. Jimmy had rented a large flatbed cart to load all their bags for transport. He knew most of the security team, and they were all familiar with him, so he was double-parked right outside the baggage claim.

Their bags were loaded into the trunk. They were on their way to the Hollywood Historic Hotel on Melrose. They had separate rooms, two of which were adjoined. The ladies took one set of adjoining rooms, and the gentlemen took the other. They were across the hall from each other. Monika asked them out for dinner as they would audition the next afternoon. The limousine picked them up at 7 p.m. and took them to Spartina's on Melrose, where Monika greeted them in the lobby. They sat down and decided on pizza.

The dinner chat by the group centered around the audition, what roles each would play, and when they could rehearse. Monika had made plans for them to visit the Paramount Theatre first thing, have a light lunch, and return for their audition. The audition went very well.

The director, Mary Beth Lancaster, was very excited to find young people so talented. She cast Vincent in the role of the Tin Man; Carmella fit well in the role of Dorothy because of her energy; Clara was versatile, so she won the role of Glenda, the Wicked Witch; and finally, Roman made an outstanding Lion. The group went into rehearsals in two days, so they had to make plans back home to be gone for a while.

The group enjoyed their sojourn into the Hollywood scene. After rave reviews, Familiari ended their run at the Paramount and returned to the East Coast.

* * *

Mason Delsson sat in his home office this morning. It was very early, and he was on his second cup of coffee, and when he looked at the clock, it was 4:45 a.m. He was going through the interviews he had done with Dalton Craig and his staff at the ranch. He paid particular interest to the four friends of his second wife.

When he looked at his notes from Dalton's interview, he noted that he also wanted to check out Sam Barfield, Dalton's attorney, to see if he had a police record of any kind. Mason logged into the Police computer system and typed in a search for Samuel Barfield. He was shocked to see what came up on the computer screen. It said that Samuel Barfield was arrested in 2015 for allegedly causing the death of his pregnant girlfriend, Chrissie Christmas. It went to trial, and Barfield was acquitted because the DNA evidence found at the scene of her accidental fall showed the prints were not Barfield's. Chrissie had fallen off her balcony while Sam Barfield was out of town for three days, presenting at a law conference in Chicago, Illinois.

Mason made a note to check the personal will and testaments of both Carmen and Dalton Craig. He felt instinctively that this did not seem like any accident but rather a planned murder. Mason made notes about Dalton as well. He found that even though Dalton Craig was rich and famous, as well as a self-professed "Don Juan." Mason didn't see him as someone who would perpetrate crimes against those he loved. Sam Barfield was another story.

Next, Mason looked at his interview with Lynda Laffarty. She seemed to be pointing a finger at several people other than herself. He would check to see if she was in the will of either Dalton or

Carmen, which would give her a possible motive to bring harm to those listed to inherit Dalton or Carmen Craig's wealth.

When Mason looked at the Christy Amherst interview, he was gob-smacked, his mouth agape, and his mind also reeling. As Mason asked her about her relationship with Carmen, he was asking the question with his head down. When he saw the tape, he noticed her flinch and how uncomfortable she looked. Was it her reflecting on something she had done, or was she thinking she had been accused of having something more than a close personal friendship with Carmen? Mason wondered if they had more between them. He wondered if they were lovers. He should have asked Christy about her relationship with men, if she had any. That would have given him a better sense of where her head was. He began jotting down questions he had for each of these ladies when he had a chance to follow up with them.

He had not taped his interview with Jen Sandrew as he had to go to her store, Elegant Lace, to talk to her. He did take some notes, but they were not enough for him to assess whether Jen had anything but a friendship with Carmen. She was surprised to hear the police were investigating her death as a homicide, wanting to help in any way she could.

The next interview he had was with Susan Crull. She used Sue when she introduced herself, but Mason felt it did not suit her. She was more formal and decided he would call her Susan. He watched the videotape of that interview and saw no indication of guilt when they discussed a potential homicide. He wrote a note to ask each of them where they were on the day Carmen Craig died. He felt like kicking himself for being distracted from his game by these beautiful women. *How could he not have asked that question,* he thought to himself.

The last interview he had on tape was with Kathy Muller. He remembered being shocked that she openly admitted she and Carmen were lovers. Was there any reason for them to have a lovers' spat? Did one of them cheat on the other, with Carmen ending up dead?

Mason decided that he would talk to Walker Craig. He wanted to ask him about his relationship with his mother, Carmen, and what Walker would do if he were to inherit his father's estate with all the vast property and movie rights.

Mason wondered who would receive the ownership of the Gemini studio and all that property. He decided to make calls to the ladies and ask where they were on the day Carmen died.

Mason's first call was to Lynda Laffarty. She got a voice message that said, "Hi, you have reached Lynda. Sorry, I will be out of town for a week or so. Leave a message and I will call you back when I return. You have a great day."

He was next called Cricky Amherst. Again, he got a voice machine. This message said, "Hello, Cricky Amherst here. I am in New York City for the week at Fashion Week. Talk to you when I return. Leave a message." She never changed the outgoing message from NYC to Lake Tahoe after deciding to join her friends in Lake Tahoe.

Mason was getting frustrated. He was mad at himself for leaving so many strings untied in the investigation. He should also have told those interviewed not to leave the city unless they called him first. Now he would have to wait.

Mason decided to try to reach Jennifer Sandrew. He screamed in frustration when he heard the voice machine pick up. Her message was, "Hi, you have reached Jen Sandrew. I am on vacation with my partner, Allie. Leave a message as the manager in the store, Sydney McKeller, is checking the machine twice a day, so she will help if she can. See you soon, and thanks for calling."

Mason wondered why all of the people he had interviewed were out of town. Mason picked up his phone again and called Walker Craig. He answered, saying, "Hello, this is Walker. How can I help you?"

Mason said to Walker, "This is Mason Delsson from LAPD. I would like to speak with you about the recent deaths. Can you come to my office?"

Walker replied, "I am going into town this afternoon. I can stop by the station around 2:30 p.m., if that works?"

Mason said, "That would be great. Thank you so much. I will see you then."

Mason thought to himself that he should probably try to get in touch with Sue Crull. She is the only one of Carmen's close friends whom he had initially interviewed but needed to see again.

Mason dialed the number of Bello Da Ball Boutique in Hollywood. A man answered, "Hello, this is Bello Da Ball. How can I direct your call?"

Mason replied, "Let me speak to Susie Crull, please. This is Detective Delsson from LAPD."

The man said, "Miss Crull is not available, Detective. She is currently out of town at fashion week in New York. Can I take a message for her?"

Mason tried to remain calm, but the man could hear that his voice was filled with emotion. Mason said, "To whom am I speaking, please?"

The man replied, "This is Kevin Syracuse, and I am looking after the shop while the owners are traveling. What is your message?"

Mason asked, "When do you expect her to return from New York?" Kevin Syracuse answered, "She is due back on Tuesday as long as the airlines cooperate."

Mason said, "Please ask Miss Crull to contact me at her earliest convenience, as I have some follow-up questions for her to complete our investigation. She has our number. Thank you, Mr. Syracuse. Have a nice day." With that, he hung up.

* * *

Back in Lake Tahoe, the ladies wanted to take advantage of the summer-like weather that had appeared in Tahoe during their visit. They called Madison Tours to ask about booking a sailboat tour of the lake. Kathy was the initiator, so she made the call.

"Madison Tours," said the man who answered, "This is Del. How can we help you today?"

Kathy Muller asked, "Yes, do you have any sailboat tour availability today? I have a group of four ladies who need an adventure, get some sun, and spend time relaxing."

Del said, "I have two boats available today. What time would you like to sail?

Kathy said. "We are close, so would an hour be too soon?"

Del Madison was used to customers calling at the last minute, expecting to find a boat available. It just so happened that the fleet was almost all in dry dock for the upcoming winter, but he had two schooners that were still in the water. At this time of year, customers were few and far between, so he would give them a good rate. Del said to Kathy, "Well, you are in luck. I was just getting ready to take a party of six men out for a ride in ninety minutes. The cost is..."

Kathy interrupted him, "The cost is no issue. We will be there at 1 p.m. sharp. My name is Kathy Muller for the party of four ladies. Thanks so much. Goodbye."

* * *

Mason Delsson sat in his office reviewing his notes on the interviews he had done on the case of Carmen Craig's death. He knew he had missed something, but he couldn't put his finger on it. At twenty minutes after two o'clock, Walker Craig walked into Police Headquarters in L.A. He said to the desk Sergeant, "I am here to see Detective Delsson."

The Sergeant at the desk said to an intern sitting farther down the desk, "Kip, can you escort Mr. Craig to conference room two?"

Kip Stanton walked Mr. Craig into the conference room and asked, "Can I get you coffee or a bottle of water?"

Walker replied, "I would love a bottle of water, please."

"Comin' right up!" said Kip.

Mason walked into the conference room and handed Walker his

water. Walker said, "Thanks. Did you knock over Kip on your way in here?" He laughed.

Mason did not. Mason remained professional and sat down, pointing for Walker to sit across from him. Mason began, "Thank you, Mr. Craig, for coming in today. I am investigating your mother's death and would like to ask you some questions."

Walker said, "OK. I am ready."

Mason, remembering his earlier faux pas, said, "Where were you the day your mother died?"

Walker began to cry. Large tears began to fall down his cheeks, and he grabbed a tissue from the table and dabbed at his eyes, trying to regain his composure. He immediately apologized to Mason. "Sorry, Mr. Delsson. I thought I had cried enough tears since her passing that I could talk about her again."

Mason made a note on his pad and waited. Walker seemed to take a deep breath and then said, "Well, to answer your question, I was away from the ranch that day. My mom had asked me if I wanted to ride, but I wanted to see this woman I knew, audition for a part in one of my father's movies. I have been seeing her for a few weeks, and I thought she would be perfect in the film. She landed the part in the film that day without needing a callback, so we went for an early dinner, and we returned to her place for the evening. Regrettably, when I returned to the ranch the next morning, I was told my mom was missing. Shortly after that, we were notified that her body had been found after accidentally being thrown from her horse, where she must have struck her head on the rock below her, and died instantly."

Mason said, "Please accept my condolences. I must ask, what was the name of the girl you went to watch in the audition?"

Walker thought for a moment, then replied, "I know this is routine, but she really would rather not be linked to me just yet, as she wants to make it in this town without my or my father's influence. I will cooperate, but I want assurances that her name will be kept out of the case reports."

Mason said, "I understand her concern, but I need her name.

If after questioning, there seems to be no connection to your mother's death, we will ensure her name is not made public."

Walker said, "Her name is Keisha Kane. As I said, we have only been on one date. I don't know all that much about her."

Mason asked, "Can I get her contact information?"

Walker was again reticent to provide any personal information but did say, "I have not seen her, nor do I have a way to contact her, but she works with an agent, Monica Lasserio. That is all I know."

Mason had dealings with Monica in the past, so he knew she would be cooperative. Walker was getting impatient with Mason, so Mason asked him, "Mr. Craig, you seem to be getting anxious or exasperated with my line of questioning. Is something wrong?"

Walker Craig seemed to sigh with a deep breath and respond, "Mr. Delsson, I have a few pressing appointments and a business to run, so if you have no further questions, I will excuse myself."

Mason knew he was annoying Walker, so he pressed on to see if he could get to the bottom of what was bothering him. Mason then took out his phone and called Monica Lasserio, "Yes, Monica. This is Mason Delsson. I am here with Walker Craig, and he has given me the name of an actress you represent, by the name of Keisha Kane. Can you tell me when the last audition she was sent to?"

Walker began to fidget, listening to only one side of the phone call. He wondered what Monica was saying.

Mason said, "Thank you, Monica. I will call her now." Mason watched Walker carefully as he dialed his home number. Mason's machine answered, and he made like he was talking to Keisha Kane, "Hello Keisha. This is Mason Delsson of the L.A. Police Department. Monica Lasserio gave me your number as your name came up in our investigation of Walker Craig. He said he was at your audition the day his mother had the accident. Can you verify that Walker was there?"

Mason waited as long as he could, watching Walker fidget. Mason said into the phone, "Thank you very much, Keisha. We will follow up with you in the next couple of days to get a written statement from you. You enjoy the rest of your day."

Mason looked at Walker and said, "I have no further questions for you. We are through here today. Thank you for your time."

As Walker walked out, he thought to himself, *he had had much better interviews with the police. He wondered if Mason Delsson thought he was hiding something about his mother's death.* Walker was glad he had left the ranch but sad he had not ridden with his mother the day she died. The mystery of her death would haunt him every day.

* * *

After Walter Craig left headquarters, Mason called Keisha. Picking up on the first ring, she said, "Hello, this is Keisha."

Mason said, "Miss Kane, this is Mason Delsson, a Detective with the Los Angeles Police Department. I got your number from Monica Lasserio. I have some questions for you in completing our investigation of the death of Carmen Craig. Would you be available to stop at police headquarters today or tomorrow?"

Keisha thought for a minute, then responded, "Detective Delsson, is it? I have just had an injury recently as one of my horses stepped on my foot and some bones were broken. If you could come to my residence to speak with me, I would be more than happy to help in any way I can. Why don't I text you my address, and you can text me back when you will be here?"

Mason said, "Sorry to hear about your injury. I appreciate you making time for us to speak with you. Is this afternoon at 4 p.m. a convenient time?"

Keisha said, "That works perfectly. I will see you then. Goodbye."

Mason's phone buzzed with a text from Keisha. Her address was 527 N. Beverly Drive, Beverly Hills, corner of Carmelita Street. He dated a lady who lived nearby, so he was familiar with the neighborhood. It was on his way home, so it was convenient. At the next stoplight, he texted back: Thx, CU Then.

* * *

As Mason sat at his desk, wondering how all the people he had interviewed were doing. Many of them had gone out of town. He would look to fill his work calendar with tracking them down first thing next week.

Mason opened his computer and googled the name Keisha Kane. When the woman's picture appeared on the screen, Mason was startled. The woman on his screen was a striking redhead. He read the short biography under the photo. It read: *Keisha Kane from San Diego, California, is a veteran actress and has been one of the most successful stars of the pornographic genre in the last five years. She was under contract with Catalina Films for the past three years. Now, she is looking to freelance in the industry, as well as attempting to move into legitimate movies.*

The article went on to give her agent's name and contact information. There were a few pictures included in the article. None of the photos were of Keisha nude. Mason decided to have his questions ready for his interview later. He thought there may be some nude pictures of her on the internet sites, but he was not familiar with searching for porn. Maybe later, he thought.

Mason telephoned Keisha Kane. When she answered, he said, "Miss Kane, this is Detective Delsson from LAPD calling. I am just finishing up at my office and am heading to your place. Do you need anything from the store that I can pick up and save you a trip?"

She replied, "How very thoughtful. If you happen to pass a liquor store, could you possibly pick up a bottle of tequila for me? I just ran out. Pick something you like, just in case I can twist your arm to have a cocktail with me."

Mason said, "I can pull into the liquor store on Melrose on the way. See you in a few." They ended the call, and as Mason walked to his car, he wondered why she was out of breath and why she was planning to offer him a cocktail when he arrived. This should be quite interesting, he thought to himself as he pulled into traffic.

* * *

Thirty minutes later, Mason pulled into Keisha's home. It was a corner lot that had a U-drive in front of what looked like a fortress, hidden behind a retaining wall that covered the front and side exposure to the street. He walked up to the front door carrying a bottle of Fortaleza Reposado and a small bag of limes. Mason rang the bell, and a voice said, "Hi, Detective. I will hit the buzzer, and you can come in. I am in the first room on the left upstairs at the top of the staircase."

Mason opened the door and entered the home. It took his breath away. The staircase she mentioned was this enormous two-sided grand entrance into the home.

He walked up the stairs and looked at some of the art hanging on the staircase walls. He recognized a few of them. They were Andy Warhol's iconic Marilyn Monroe, the Campbell's Soup can, and a self-portrait of him surrounded by multi-colored flowers.

Mason knocked at the first door on the left, even though the door was open, Keisha said loudly, "Come on, Detective. I see you brought me some Tequila. Thanks so much. Come have a seat across from me."

The room he had entered looked like the library. Its walls were lined with shelves of books. There was a large-screen TV over the fireplace. There were three large couches, each with a recliner next to it. A large oak desk was on the far wall with two cloth chairs in front and a high-back rolling office chair behind it. Mason had not noticed. but looking out the window, he could see the ocean in the distance.

Keisha said, "If you open the Tequila, I will mix us a couple of drinks." Mason quickly divested the bottle of its wrapping and handed it to her. He noticed she was dressed in a long, silk pink gown with lace trim. Her long legs were exposed, and he noticed a walking boot in pink as well.

As Keisha leaned forward to pour the drinks, her gown opened, and he was presented with quite the expanse of cleavage. She was busy putting ice in the glasses and pouring the Tequila, Triple Sec, and Gardonne. Mason asked, "What is that you're pouring?"

Keisha replied, "Oh. Gardonne is an orange cognac liqueur similar to Grand Marnier. I do not use regular mix but the limeade drink, which is lower in calories and makes the drink smoother. You can give me your opinion." Keisha began shaking the silver shaker, squeezing a lime in each glass, and pouring the mixture. She handed a glass to Mason, who rose to take it from her and sat back on the couch across from her. They each tasted the concoction, and it gave Mason a chance to assess the lady of the house.

Keisha was a beautiful woman. Mason guessed Keisha to be in her early 40s. She had green eyes that sparkled, which enhanced her brilliant smile. The gown was flowing, but with her seated, it hugged her form like another skin. Mason could see that she had a very voluptuous figure.

Before he began to feel more awkward than he already was, Mason began the discussion, "Thank you, Keisha, for allowing me the time to speak to you. I recall you were out of breath when we last spoke on the phone. Is everything all right?"

Keisha laughed, "As I mentioned on the phone, I have a few broken bones in my foot, so it takes me a while to get around. If I am too far away from the phone, I try not to miss the call, so I hobble off to it as quickly as I can. Without crutches, I get out of breath quickly. I thought I was in decent shape for an old lady, but my huffing and puffing has made me realize I need to get back into some cardio as soon as I can. Now, what can I help with?"

Mason thought to himself that from where he was, she looked pretty damn in shape for however old she was. Mason took out his pad a began going through the questions he had written down beforehand. This would give him a chance to see her reaction when queried.

Mason said, "How well did you know Carmen Craig?"

Keisha replied, "Not as well as some, but we were friendly. She and I had been on many auditions for movie roles over the years, in our younger days. We talked at parties often, and I even dated her son, Walker, a time or two. When she and I spoke of him, she seemed relieved that he was dating. He was quite a shy person in his early life."

Mason continued, "Are we alone in the house? She nodded, "Yes, we are. I live alone. I have a maid come in daily for a few hours to help with cleaning and meal prep. She has been with me for years."

Mason asked, "Are you married or seeing someone?" Keisha had a strange look on her face. He made a note of it.

She replied, "That is an unusual question, Detective. Are you interested in seeing me socially?"

Mason was now more flustered than upon arrival. He gathered himself and replied, "Not at the moment, I was trying to elicit whether you were romantically involved. If I were to have a beautiful lady such as yourself in a relationship, I would certainly ensure she had someone here to take care of her just in case she needed something that she could not do for herself."

Keisha almost seemed to blush when she said, "That is very sweet of you, Detective. To answer your question, I have never been married and am not currently romantically involved."

Mason said, "And you have a maid that works part-time?"

Keisha said, "I am getting around better now, and I confess to being an independent type-A personality and a bit of a stubborn mule."

Mason looked Keisha straight in the eye and said, "Did you have anything to do with the death of Carmen Craig?"

There was a long pause, and Keisha glared right back at Mason. It started to get uncomfortable for both of them when Keisha broke the ice by saying, "Detective Delsson, I know you are only doing your job and looking for a reaction, by asking these direct and unsettling questions, however, I had nothing to do with her death. I know of no one who had anything to do with her death, and I know of no one for sure who had anything against her or something to gain from her death. Why do you ask? I had heard she fell off her horse and landed on a rock or something."

Mason knew he was dealing with a very savvy lady. Keisha

never flinched when he asked the last question, but he would forge ahead in search of clues.

Keisha drank down her tequila and began to fill the mixer with ice. She poured some more elixir into it and began to shake it. She leaned over and refilled her drink and topped off Mason's half-empty glass. She raised both the glasses, handing his back to him full again, and said, "Detective, here is to the late Carmen Craig. May you uncover the mystery of her death, if there is one."

They drank in silence for a moment. Keisha was giving the police detective the once-over, more closely now. She liked what she saw. She guessed that he was as old as her, but noticed his salt and pepper hair was meticulously in place. He was slender, yet she could see he was fit. He had a slight of two or three days' growth of beard, and his suit was clean and quite stylish. His shoes sparkled.

Keisha decided to take the offensive, "Detective, can I ask you a question?" Mason nodded. Keisha queried, "Are you married?"

Mason was shocked by this and simply said, "No. Why?"

Keisha continued, "Do you currently have someone romantically in your life?"

Mason laughed, "Are we seriously doing this?"

Keisha said, "Well, if you can ask, so can I. Mr. Delsson, I find you very attractive, and as we are both unattached at the moment, I suggest we see if you are as attracted to me as I am to you. We can go from there."

Mason laughed again, saying, "Miss Kane, I make it a rule not to get involved with the people I include in any of my investigations. This is very flattering, but I think it would not be wise to go down this road."

Keisha was not giving up and said, "So are you saying that you do not find me attractive?" At this point, Keisha stood, dropped her robe, and stood glaring at Mason straight into his baby-blue eyes. She wore a very skimpy negligee in lavender that came to just below the Vee between her legs. Mason could see that her panties were a similar lavender and quite translucent. He could feel the beads of perspiration forming on his brow.

He said, "Keisha Kane, you are one of the most beautiful creatures I have had the privilege to lay my eyes on in all my forty-four years. So, yes! I find you extremely attractive, and if you feel half the electricity that I am currently experiencing, no pun intended. I think I must make an addendum to my rule about the women I encounter in my investigations."

Keisha stepped around the coffee table between them and held out her hand. Mason rose, taking her hand. Keisha put her arms around his shoulders and waited. Mason leaned in, and their lips met. They both felt the electricity, and each moaned onto the other's lips as their kisses became more heated.

Keisha dropped her arms and stepped back. She looked into Mason's eyes and said, "Detective, do you have any other questions? If not, I am going to escort you to my bedroom and make mad passionate love with you."

Mason said, "Keisha, that is, by far, the sexiest invitation I have heard in the last thirty years. Yes, I have one more question. On your last audition, was Walker Craig there to observe you?"

Keisha said, "No. Now follow me and bring the drinks." Off they went to the bedroom laughing.

* * *

Walker Craig waited until he got home. He picked up the phone and used the speed dial to call someone. The phone rang three times before it was answered. The voice said, "Hello, I am not available. Leave a message at the beep."

Walker replied after the beep, "I just met with an LAPD Detective, and he wanted to know if I had an alibi for the day my mother died. I said to him that I was at your audition. If he contacts you, let him know I was there." Walker hung up the phone.

Keisha thought *I better call him back and let him know.* She dialed the phone and got a busy signal. She sent Walker a text: W- you hung up before I could get to the phone. I wanted to tell you that he came to see me, and I told him no when he asked if you were at that audition. Call me back.

* * *

Del Madison had just finished fueling his fifty-foot schooner that was tied up on the large dock. He looked up and saw the six ladies appear on the walkway to the dock. The tall blonde said, "Are you Del?"

Kathy Muller looked at this man and thought he looked very familiar. She said, "The lady in the office sent us down here to take a cruise around the lake."

Del Madison noticed that all the ladies were very attractive and knew it would be as pleasurable for him as it would be for the ladies to sail today. The weather looked good now, but there was a prediction for a late-day storm, so he didn't want to be out long on the water. He said, "Good afternoon, ladies. Welcome to Madison Tours. The guys will help you onto the vessel and escort you up to the front. Once we are underway, you can walk about, but make sure you use the railings. After we leave the dock, you can sun on the lounges and there are no restrictions on clothing coverage. I will be making a few announcements and descriptions of the different sights, but if it gets too annoying and you would rather just relax, please let me know. We also have a bar with drinks available once the crew gets us underway. If you don't have any questions, we can shove off."

Kathy Muller, Jennifer Sandrew, Allie Campwick, Sue Crull, Cricky Amherst, and Lynda Laffarty sat watching the crew prepare the vessel for departure, and all were quiet. As Captain Del barked orders to the crew, he paused and asked, "Would you ladies like something to drink? I'll send one of the crew to take your orders in a minute."

It was two-fifteen when they set sail. They were gone about a half hour when they came to an island about one hundred yards from shore. Del picked up the microphone that led to all the speakers on board. He said, "Ladies, off to your right is the famous Island of Witches. It is not too big and has an excellent beach which is as pristine as the morning snow of Colorado. If you want to go skinny dipping or just lay out and tan in the altogether, we have a small dingy that will take you there."

There was buzzing among the ladies and four of them wanted to go. Lynda, Cricky, Allie, and Sue. Kathy and Jennifer decided to stay aboard. They told the others they would stay and chat. Twenty minutes later, the dingy was lowered and four ladies and two crew members left the schooner for the island. Del said to the ladies, "Stick with the crew and you'll be fine."

They took several blankets, a picnic basket with cheese and wine, as well as tanning oil. The dingy reached the beach and one of the crew members walked the boat in close enough so the ladies could disembark. The dingy was anchored and the crew set up several large blankets for the ladies. One of the crew stayed with a large rifle and the other stayed on the dingy which was now moored not far offshore.

Sue lay on a blanket while the others disrobed and walked into the water naked. Sue thought to herself that even at her age, she was a bit shy and not as adventurous as Allie, Lynda, and Cricky. The three ladies in the water were in great shape and drew constant attention from the two crew members.

After about two hours, the wind picked up on the beach and the sand began to spray the ladies. The sun went into the clouds, and they decided to return to the schooner, as the sky began to look ominous. The ladies began to dress and put the blankets around them as the temperature had also dipped.

Kathy and Jennifer were on the deck bar having drinks and chatting about men, mostly. The change in weather caught them by surprise as well. They were ushered into the cabin to wait for the dingy to return.

* * *

It was a very, choppy, dingy ride back to the large boat. The ladies were very nervous and quiet as they approached the large boat Where Del and the other crew were waiting to help them back on the ship. The crew quickly raised the dingy in its original place at the starboard stern. Once they were all accounted for, the anchor on the large ship was raised, and Del Madison headed straight back to port. The sky was almost pitch black, and the thunder and wind made for a scary return to land.

Forty minutes later the schooner pulled into its slip at the pier. Four more crew appeared to secure the schooner and help escort the six ladies returning to dry land.

Del's wife, Dolores, was relieved when the ship was secured as she knew after years on the lake how brutal these storms could be, to say nothing of the danger for all on board the large sailing vessel.

* * *

Kathy Muller called for a driver to pick them up and return them to the hotel. He arrived in five minutes. Everyone was grateful. It was quiet on the ride to the hotel when Cricky said, "Hey, Guys. What are we doing for dinner? I am starved."

Allie Campwick shouted from the back of the limo, "How about Harrah's? They have a great American menu and the casino is beautiful. They open at 5:00 p.m."

Jennifer Sandrew shouted, "I vote for that. My stomach is growling." There was a group consensus, so Lynda called and made reservations for 7 p.m. They were happy and eager to go back to their rooms and get ready.

Meanwhile, the skies opened up and the rain began. It seemed like a monsoon as you could barely see out the windows. When all six met in the lobby, the bell captain had four bellhops with large umbrellas at the ready to take the ladies to the limousine. The limo stopped under the front door's canopy. They were able to exit into Harrah's without getting dampened by the deluge.

They were seated at a large table toward the back of the dining room of Friday's Station. Their waiter was named Jason. He was a tall, good-looking young man who looked to be mid-twenties. He had blonde hair and blue eyes, and his tanned skin made him look like a surfer.

Kathy ordered a white wine, Sue followed suit. Cricky ordered a Margarita, Jennifer ordered a Jack Daniels and Coke, Allie ordered a vodka on the rocks with a lemon twist, Lynda and Sue ordered a Cabernet Sauvignon. Jason handed them dinner menus and said, "Ladies, thank you. I will return to take your dinner orders."

Lynda took a liking to the young waiter saying, "I wouldn't kick him out of my bed." The ladies laughed.

Allie said, "Really? Look at all the surprise looks on our faces."

The laughter got even louder just as Jason reappeared with the drinks. He jokingly said, "You ladies were probably talking about me, weren't you?"

Now the laughter at the table got the attention of everyone in the restaurant. Seeing the looks on the ladies' faces, Jason blushed but kept his professional demeanor. He set each of their drinks down in the correct order which was especially noticed by Lynda. She said, "I am ready to take your orders dinner. Ladies?"

All of them had perused the menu and were ready. Allie ordered first, "I will have a salad with oil and vinegar on the side and a bowl of lobster bisque soup for my entre. Jennifer followed with, "I would like another Jack Daniels, and I'll have the filet mignon, medium, with a vegetable. Cricky went next, ordering, "I want the chef salad with Thousand Island dressing and the Chilean Sea Bass."

Jason asked, "Would you like a side with the bass?"

Sue replied, "Yes, maybe I'll try the asparagus."

Kathy went next saying, "I'll have another white wine. I want the prime rib, medium with a baked potato." Jason was standing to the left of Lynda. He looked down at her and was impressed with her abundant cleavage.

He was about to ask but Lynda began her order, "If you could fit on a plate, I would order you to go and take you to my room." Some of the ladies gasped but most giggled.

Jason said, "I think that can be arranged Miss; however, did you want something to eat with the ladies?"

Again, the laughter brought everyone's eyes in the room to their table. It was now Lynda who blushed and said, 'Well, I should probably save my appetite for later, but I guess I will have the lobster bisque to start then a rib eye, medium, with garlic potatoes for the entre. Bring me another Cabernet when you bring the food, please."

Jason said, "Thank you ladies. I will put a rush on these meals so I can prepare for my pressing engagement I have right after dinner." Jason walked toward the kitchen listening to the roar of laughter at the ladies' table.

* * *

Dalton Craig and Fitore Fantazee left the ski lodge and decided to go to dinner. She said, "Do you have a favorite restaurant here in Tahoe?"

Dalton replied, "Well, as a matter of fact, I have already made reservations at the Friday Station in Harrah's. I thought we would have dinner, then test our luck in the casino."

Fitore said, "Did you leave enough time for me to ravage you, shower, and dress before we leave the hotel?"

Dalton laughed, "You are a mind reader too? You bet I did."

He called their limo driver who said, "I am here at the door of the lodge, sir." Dalton knew it was not Kirt but someone Kirk had hired to assist him. He took Fitore by the hand and walked her to the front door.

She said, "Dalton, I have been very impressed, not only by your elegance, but the care everyone takes in service to you. I hope I can emulate the loyalty and passion I have seen expressed toward you since we arrived."

Dalton said, "Fitore, my dear, you are so beautiful and classy. You add to any elegance I may have. I can't wait to return to our suite. I will give you a chance to unwind, but I would love the opportunity to worship every ounce of your being."

The limo arrived and the driver held the door as they entered. He said, "Mr. Craig, my name is Winston, and I will be your driver this evening. If you have made reservations for dinner, I will be available upon your exit from the hotel."

Winston drove them back to the hotel and as they strolled toward the elevators, the clerk at the front desk called to Dalton, "Mr. Craig, I have several messages for you if you have time, Sir."

Dalton said to Fitore, "One second, Doll. Let me grab those messages, they might be important." He walked ten steps over to the clerk who handed him three message slips. Dalton looked at the first slip of paper. It was from his son, Walker, it read: Dad-police were here again today asking questions about Mom's death. They were asking for an alibi. Call me. Walker-

Dalton wondered why Walker would feel this information was important enough to leave at his hotel in Tahoe rather than call him on his cellphone. He walked toward Fitore as he read the second. It read: D- I heard you're in Tahoe with a lady friend. Maybe we could meet for a drink. L-

Dalton wrapped his arm around Fitore's waist and escorted her toward the elevator. She said, "Is everything all right?"

Dalton laughed, "It is now that I have you this close to me." They stepped into the elevator and pushed the button for the fourth floor. Dalton looked at the third message. It read: Mr. Craig-Tried to leave a message. Mailbox full. I am worried. Dolores.

Dalton put the messages into his pants pocket as he and Fitore exited the elevator. He got to the room, and she began to undress quickly. Dalton did as well. He marveled at her body, and she was impressed by his. They fell on the bed together.

* * *

After a delicious meal at Harrah's Friday Station Restaurant, the ladies decided to head to the bar. Everyone did shots of Tequila. In no time at all, they were surrounded by men. Most of them had paired up with a much younger man. Lynda did not see anyone who might tickle her fancy, so she just ordered another shot of Tequila for everyone. She said to Cricky, "I am going to the ladies' room."

When she almost reached the restroom, the men's room door opened. Jason, their waiter, walked out. He almost bumped into Lynda, and she let out a slight yelp as he grabbed her by the shoulders. He said, "Sorry. I was just coming to see if you ladies had stopped at the bar. Here you are trying to tackle me at the restrooms."

They both laughed and she replied, "Stay right here. I am bored at the bar, but I have to tinkle. Will you have a drink with me?"

Jason said, "I'll be right here."

Jason Carney had moved to Lake Tahoe from back East. He had gone to school in the small town of Tonawanda, New York which is not far from Niagara Falls. He ran a small clothing exchange after high school and did some modeling. He decided to move west to California. Some friends he made there urged him to work in Tahoe as they were always looking for waiters and the clientele were generous tippers.

Lynda came out of the ladies' room and there stood Jason. She put her arm around his waist and led him to the bar saying, "Come on young man, let's get drunk."

All of her friends were gone. She thought they were in the restroom but after twenty minutes or so, she figured either they had hooked up with the guys they were talking to or gone to another bar. Jason leaned in toward her and whispered, "Lynda, I want you to know you are the sexiest woman I have seen since I came to Lake Tahoe. I knew the minute I began serving you and your friends that I wanted to be with you. Then you began flirting with me. I didn't know if you were serious or just trying to impress your friends. The only thing I knew for certain was that I wanted to get to know you. I was on my way to the bar to look for you when I almost knocked you down near the restrooms."

Lynda felt a tingle run through her body. He was that close to her ear and that was big erogenous zone for her. Plus, his words made her realize that he was into her, as much as she was into him. She replied, "I would like to leave after this drink, but I have a roommate which doesn't work for me. Do you have a place we can go where we could have a little privacy so I could tear your clothes off?"

Jason laughed warmly, smiling a very broad smile, "I have a place here at the hotel. It's not fancy but we'll be alone. I'll take you there whenever you're ready."

Lynda took her drink and downed it in one gulp. She said, "Let's go." They got up and walked toward the elevators.

Jason said, "I am a little nervous bringing a lady to my room. You're my first and you are quite the knockout."

Lynda said, "Flattery will get everywhere my new, young friend. No need to be nervous at all. We'll go as slow as you need to with this. I don't have any plans for tomorrow."

As Lynda and Jason came around the corner, they found the elevators thirty feet away. The doors opened and Lynda watched as Dalton with a beautiful woman, exited out of the door and walked toward the dining room. They never saw her and Jason as they were approaching from the other direction.

The elevator smelled like the couple who just left. Lynda recognized Dalton's cologne, Earl Grey by Jo Malone. Jason stood behind her and brought her back to the present by kissing her neck. The next thing she knew, the elevator doors opened on the sixth floor. They walked a short way before he opened the door for her to room 609.

The room was elegant. The fireplace was burning, which gave the room a glow and brought the temperature to a comfortable level. It had a small sitting area with a small cocktail bar. There was a couch and loveseat with a matching rocker in front of a large TV hanging on the wall. There was another door which she assumed was the bedroom and bath. She said, "This looks cozy." She walked to the floor-to-ceiling window that overlooked the lake. In the distance, she could see the mountain and skiers transversing down the slopes under the bright lights.

Lynda said, "Wow, Jason. That is some view you have here." As she turned around, Jason said, "Yeah, and the view out the window is nice, too."

Lynda laughed and said, "Aren't you sweet? Come here." Jason walked to her, and they embraced. They kissed gently at first but soon the heat began to build quickly.

After a minute or two, Lynda pulled free of his embrace and said, "Can you show me the bedroom? I would like to get more comfortable."

They walked hand in hand through the second door. This did indeed lead to the bedroom and en suite bath. The bedroom had a large king-size bed, and the curtains were open, with the same view of the mountain skiers.

Lynda said, "Give me a minute to freshen up." She walked into the bathroom and closed the door.

Jason went out to the small bar and grabbed two glasses and a bottle of Tequila. He checked the phone and saw he had a message which he would answer later. When he walked back into the bedroom, Lynda was lying on the bed with the covers turned down.

Lynda wore a skimpy, pale blue negligee with a pair of matching panties. Her blonde hair was cascading on the pillows she had propped up. She said, "You look very overdressed Mr. Carney. Won't you join me? Set the Tequila down, we won't be needing that just yet."

Jason nervously giggled, "If this is your idea of going slow, I am in big trouble when you decide to speed up." As the warm glow from the mountain slopes softly lit the room, Lynda watched Jason undress. She marveled at his patience and his exquisite body. He looked like a swimmer but much fitter. She began to feel that tingle again, this time throughout her body. Jason was in his boxers and joined Lynda in bed. They kissed and the sparks began to fly as they quickly got naked. They were alone in the world and exhilarating passion filled that world.

They had fallen asleep. Jason awoke first. He gazed down at the beautiful sight next to him on the bed. He could not believe he had been lucky enough to have a lady this classy in his bed.

Lynda opened her eyes and saw Jason staring down at her. She smiled with contentment and said, "Let's get dressed and go someplace for breakfast." They dressed and were gone in ten minutes.

3

DINNER WITH DALTON WAS AS ELEGANT as Fitore thought it would be. He was friendly to the staff, both men and women who seemed to gravitate to him anticipating his every wish. They were waiting for the check and decided they would go to the bar for a quick nightcap. The bar was circular with a mahogany top that looked almost fake as the shine from the Polyurethane finish reflected objects around it but provided excellent protection. Sitting at the bar, you could see behind it, the slopes out of these tall eight-foot windows on the rear of the room. As night falls each night, the lights from the ski resort illuminate the patio just outside the bar and put a romantic glow over the bar area, creating a romantic mood in the restaurant's views.

Dalton asked Fitore if she wanted champagne and she replied, "No thanks. If it is okay with you, I would like a Jack Daniels and coke."

Dalton laughed, "Now you're showing me the kind of girl I love." He called the barmaid over. She had Aubrey on her name tag. Dalton said, "Aubrey, this lovely lady beside me would like a Jack and Coke. I will have a double shot of Patron."

Aubrey replied, "Coming right up, Mr. Craig." She scurried away quickly.

Fitore smiled and said, "Dalton, does everyone at this hotel know you? If I didn't know better, I would guess you are the owner."

Dalton smiled broadly back at Fitore and said, "Well, if you don't know the owner of the hotel's name, you certainly may put your employment at risk."

Fitore was surprised, "Oh my word, Mr. Craig. I had no idea that you were my host for the trip. I found it odd that the room we are in had clothes in the closets, three bedrooms, and two jacuzzi tubs as well as a fully stocked bar. I am surprised your name is not on the marquee outside."

Dalton was enjoying this very much and told Fitore, "Sometimes it is better to stay under the radar rather than blow your horn everywhere you go."

* * *

The ladies from Hollywood had returned to one of their suites and were chatting. Jennifer Sandrew came out of her bedroom having changed into a much sexier outfit. She wore a bright red dress that ended three inches above her knees. Her five-inch pumps matched the dress perfectly. The neckline plunged in a vee almost to her naval. It was obvious she wore no bra. Christy said with a whistle, "Wow, someone is going out to hunt big game tonight!"

Jennifer replied, "I saw an old business associate of mine going into the bar as we came back up here; so, I thought I would go down and crash his party and have a nightcap."

Christy laughed and said, "Shall we expect you to return before breakfast then?"

Jennifer said, "Well, you never know about these things. I wouldn't worry. If I am not back by morning, I promise to meet you in the restaurant for lunch at noon." All the ladies laughed, because they were just talking about retiring for the night. Jennifer threw a small mink jacket over her arm and waved goodbye over her shoulder to the ladies as she walked into the hallway and down to the elevators.

Fitore said to Dalton after their third drink, "Mr. Craig, I am feeling a bit tipsy and would like to freshen up with a shower. It may sober me up somewhat. Why don't you have another drink and give me a half hour before you come upstairs."

Dalton kissed her on the cheek and said, "I will be counting the minutes. I have a few calls to make so hopefully the time will go faster."

Fitore left and walked to the elevators. Dalton tried to get Aubrey's attention, but she was serving a new couple at the bar. He looked out the windows at the skiers and pulled out his messages to return some calls. He felt the barstool next to him move as someone sat down. A voice said, "Is anyone sitting here, sir?"

Dalton swiveled his stool around to engage the sexy voice he had heard. His mouth flew open, and he was speechless for a minute. There, next to him sat his ex-wife's friend, Jennifer Sandrew. Dalton said, "Well, what a nice surprise. Don't you look ravaging this evening? What brings you to Tahoe this time of year?"

Jennifer said, "Are you going to buy me a drink, Mr. Craig?"

Dalton laughed, "Isn't it just like you to answer a question with a question? Yes. I will buy you a drink. Jack and Coke?"

Jennifer replied, "Yes. It is sweet of you to still remember my choice of drink. How are you, Dalton? I mean besides the beautiful lady who was on your arm earlier."

Dalton replied, "I am great. I just looked at my messages a minute ago. I checked my phone, and it was turned off. Probably my subconscious mind telling me to relax and enjoy my week. I got three messages at the front desk but yours was not one of them. I was pleasantly surprised to see you. I won't ask how you've been because I can see quite plainly that you are fabulous. You look beautiful in the dress. Of course, you always were a stunner! I think I may have told you that more than once. The lady I am with is a writer/producer for the studio and we seemed to have a lot in common, so I invited her here. I have a few things going on here, so I brought her along. Who are you here with?"

Jennifer took a sip of the Jack and Coke the bartender had just delivered, then said, "Well, I am not with a man but then you can probably guess the names of those I am with."

Dalton thought for a moment and said, "OK, you are probably with at least three or four other ladies in one or two suites. Most likely it's Lynda, Christy, Kathy, and Sue."

Jennifer laughed, "Almost right. I am also with Allie Campwick who works with me at Elegant Lace. I didn't tell the girls who I was coming down to see. They were all getting ready for bed and I said, 'I saw a friend and wanted a nightcap anyway.' So, I took a chance. Where is the lovely lady you're with?"

Dalton said, "She went up to the room to freshen up. I told her I would be up soon as I wanted to return calls to the folks that left messages." That seems boring now that you're here. Do you want to go someplace quiet?"

Jennifer Sandrew and Dalton had dated for a few months after he left Lynda, his ex-wife. Dalton had come into her store looking for some lingerie for a "friend." Which, of course, meant a lady he was now seeing. When she pressed him on it, Dalton said it was a gift for his secretary. She had said it was a very personal and sexy gift for a secretary. He told Jennifer that he and his secretary were close, and dated in the past, but were no longer an item and it was her birthday, and he knew she loved lingerie. Jennifer asked him at the time if he wanted her to model something for him in her office. Dalton, of course, said he would love that. They picked a few choices and went to her office. She locked the door and told Allie not to disturb them. She remembered how she had stripped completely in front of Dalton and tried to model the lingerie, but Dalton had other ideas. He attacked her and they had mad, passionate sex. Jennifer thought back and realized it was to this day, the best sex she ever had. Now she wondered if it would happen again.

Dalton and Jennifer walked out of the bar together arm and arm. Two hours later, Dalton walked into his hotel suite to find Fitore naked and asleep on the large, king-size bed. Dalton walked into the other bedroom's ensuite and quickly showered. He dressed in a hotel robe. He went to the bar in the living room. He had a double shot of Tequila, picked up his phone, and returned the call from Walker.

It was late but Dalton knew it must be important enough for Walker to leave a message. Walker picked up the call on the first ring, "Dad, where the heck were you. I have been trying to call but either your voicemail is full, or your phone has been off."

* * *

Dalton said, "Sorry, Walker. I must have shut off my phone, so as not to get messages from the front desk. What's up?"

Walker sat in his living room. He had been drinking but not enough to affect his faculties. He replied, "I spoke to Mason Delsson from LAPD today and he wanted to know if I had an alibi for where I was on the day my mother died. I told him I was watching an audition for a friend of mine, Keisha Kane. I wasn't there that day and Delsson is more than likely going to follow up with her. What should I do?"

Dalton poured himself another drink. He took a long sip and said, "Well, do you want me to come back to town and fix this?"

Walker breathed a sigh of relief and said, "I hate to bother you but that would be amazing."

Dalton said, "I'll fly out first thing this morning and call you then." Dalton hung up his phone and went into the bedroom to lie down. Fitore never stirred. He slept.

Dalton awoke at five o'clock that morning. Fitore was still asleep. He rose, got dressed, and left her a note. It read: *"Fitore, please accept my apologies. I flew back to LA this morning for an emergency. I left you asleep. You can call the driver and have him fly you back or you can stay, relax, and enjoy the room. You can charge to the room whatever you need, and I should return the first thing tomorrow. If you decide to return to L.A., my driver will let me know. Regards, D."*

* * *

Fitore awoke feeling refreshed, but it was as if she was drugged. She couldn't remember if Dalton had returned to the room the night before, but his side of the king-size bed had been slept in, but he didn't answer when she called his name. She wondered where he could be.

Fitore went into the shower, and the hot shower seemed to rejuvenate her. She needed coffee desperately. She walked naked into the kitchen and saw the note from Dalton. She thought to herself, *I wonder what the emergency was back home. He said he would return so I should just enjoy the solitude until he returns.*

She was going to make coffee but decided to order breakfast and coffee from the hotel room service. She ordered two hardboiled eggs, rye toast, and a pot of coffee. She put a rush on it and used Dalton's name. They said they would be up quickly.

Fitore went to the bath and grabbed a white robe to put on. She walked back into the kitchen to get her phone and there was a knock at the door. She wondered who it was as she had just ordered breakfast five minutes ago. She looked out the peephole and to her surprise, there stood a waitress from the restaurant with her breakfast. She opened the door, and there stood a lovely lady with a white blouse and a short black shirt. Her name tag said: Robin Rapple.

Robin said, "Breakfast for you and Mr. Craig, Ma'am. Where would you like me to set this down?"

Fitore said, "Thank you so much. Robin, please place it on the patio. It is so nice outside this morning. We'll have it out there on the balcony."

Robin walked to the sliding glass door and opened it. She placed the tray down and said, "Would you like the umbrella opened, Miss Fantazee?"

Fitore said, "Robin, do we know each other?"

Robin said, "I am a big fan of your work, Miss Fitore. I was bartending last night at the service bar for the waitresses when you and Mr. Craig came into the bar. I want to someday be in movies like you. If you have any advice on the best way to get in, please let me know. I would be most appreciative. Knowing that you are with Mr. Craig, gives me hope that you have the influence I sorely need."

Fitore looked more closely at Robin and saw that she was, in fact, a beautiful girl. She had long black hair that was so shiny it looked like a plastic wig. Robin stood five feet, eight inches in her flat shoes. Fitore guessed her figure to be 36D-24-36. She also had the bluest eyes she had ever seen. It had been a long time since a woman had caught her eye.

Robin must have been right out of college when she encountered her first experience with a lady. That woman was a bit older than she, but it was an amazing time, as she remembered it. Fitore said, "If you could open the umbrella, that would be appreciated. If you have a few minutes, I could speak with you now. Have a seat."

Robin pulled the chair out next to Fitore and sat down. Fitore began, "You are a very beautiful lady, Miss Robin. You would look good on the big screen. Have you ever done any acting?"

Robin looked closer at this beautiful lady and got chills down her spine. She hadn't felt attracted to a woman in some time, but there was something about this lady. Maybe it was her accent that made her voice ooze with sexuality. Robin replied, "Yes, Miss Fantazee, I did a few plays in college, and the past three years I have been fortunate enough to do some summer stock right here in Tahoe."

Fitore said, "That's great. Please call me Fitore. I think you and I are going to be good friends. I have just completed another screenplay, so I am looking for someone new to play the ingenue." Fitore's robe was draped open as she reached across the table for the coffee pot.

Robin thought to herself that this may be my chance. She asked, "Do you think I would be able to audition for a role?"

Fitore responded, "I was going to ask if I might take some photos of you. I would run them by my team when I return to L.A."

Robin said, "I would love to pose for you. When would you be available?"

Fitore said, "Let me get my phone. I will take some preliminary shots of you right now if you have some time?" She got up from the table, not bothering to refasten her robe. She knew she looked good and hoped her guest would think the same. She hadn't often been this attracted to a female, but Robin was so beautiful and luscious, she would make an exception.

Robin looked at Fitore's nude body and felt herself get a tingly feeling all over. She began to breathe a bit heavier, and her palms were sweaty. She said to Fitore, watching her come back to the table with her robe still open, "I have no make-up on, and I am dressed in my uniform."

Fitore stood over her getting her phone ready, then said, "That's even better if we see you in a natural environment. The light is quite good out here, so just stand near the railing."

Robin stood, straightening her skirt, and walked to the railing. Fitore began taking pictures before Robin was even ready. Fitore said, "That's great. Enough of you in uniform, would you be comfortable doing a few risqué shots for me?"

Robin was ambivalent about nudity, but she decided, at that moment to go for it. She asked, "Do you want me to disrobe right here?"

Fitore was excited, now as well. She said, "Well, the light is just right and there is no one around. Let's do some in your lingerie, then maybe a few nude shots. There are a few bedroom scenes and some nude scenes as well, but they'll be tasteful and elegant." Robin took off her blouse first, then her skirt. She had on a lacy green lingerie set that was very sexy and revealing. She slipped off her shoes and again posed by the railing.

Fitore was taking pictures the whole time, then said, "Let's go inside now. I am losing the light. I'll get us a drink before we continue in the bedroom?"

Robin said, "Okay."

* * *

Dalton Craig was dropped off at his home at 10:30 a.m. He immediately went to look for Walker. His lawyer, Sam Barfield, was just coming in from the pool area with a towel wrapped around him. He was startled when he saw Dalton. Sam asked, "When the hell did you get here? Where is Fitore? Did you drop her off at her place first?"

Dalton laughed, "Lots of questions for a man swimming naked in my pool. Have you seen Walker around?"

Sam said, "He was leaving very early and when I asked where he was going, all he said was, "I have an appointment.""

Dalton walked toward his office and Sam followed. Sam said, "Oh, by the way, you never answered even one of my questions. How are you?"

Dalton said, "Hey, Sam. Put some pants on unless you have a few fillies outside by the pool. If so, go tend to them. I'll call when I need you."

Sam left the office and continued on his quest for some orange juice and champagne, as he was requested by the ladies to make some Mimosas. He had three ladies waiting on the pool deck for him. One was a redhead, and the other two were blondes. The redhead was Avery Summer. She was a tall dancer with a perfect figure. She was originally from Tulsa, Oklahoma. Blondes were Celia Shaw and Scarlett Redding. Celia danced in the same club and did some acting work in some small films. Scarlett was a dancer in a club that was in downtown L.A., and she came from Las Vegas.

Sam retrieved two bottles of Cristal champagne and a bottle of orange juice. He walked back out to the pool, and Avery was sunning topless on a chaise lounge while Celia and Scarlett were in the shallow end of the pool. These two were in a lover's embrace and kissing each other passionately. Avery heard Sam and went to help him. She said, "Ooh. Bubbly! I could use this as a remedy for my hangover."

Celia and Scarlett heard the conversation at the umbrella table on the other side of the pool. They sauntered over, arm and arm, and Sam watched as they seemed to glide effortlessly up the steps at the near end of the pool. Scarlett said, "Sam, we didn't mean to start without you, but we got a little heated when you didn't come back right away."

Sam said, "No worries, Ladies. I enjoyed the show. Dalton is back, and he doesn't look happy. He was asking about Walker. Did anyone hear where Walker was going this morning?" The ladies all shrugged their shoulders.

Scarlett said, "He didn't say anything to us, but he seemed preoccupied. He usually would at least ask for a lap dance or make a lewd remark. Today, we got nothing from him."

Celia added, "It may have something to do with the cop that was here yesterday."

Sam finished pouring mimosas. He said, "Last one in has to shower alone tonight.

* * *

Cricky Amherst woke after an early night with the ladies. They all crashed around 1:00 a.m. She made a pot of coffee and jumped into the shower. Minutes later, Lynda Laffarty appeared in the bath and said, "Room for another?" She walked naked into the large walk-in shower, which could easily fit 6 or 8 folks.

Cricky said, "Good Morning, Sweet Cheeks. Sleep well?"

Lynda said, "I slept like a dead woman! How much did we have to drink last night?"

Cricky replied, "Some of us had more than others. You were the winner. You started ordering shots of Tequila. After one, we all signaled the bartender to only serve you. The rest of us had our limit at that point. I think we shut you off after four shots."

They showered, each admiring the other's naked form. Each of them had seen the other naked once or twice, but being up close and personal was a little different. They finished and wrapped themselves in the hotel-provided white fluffy robes. Lynda followed Cricky into the kitchen, where they found Kathy, Allie, and Sue sitting at the coffee bar.

Kathy said, "Cricky, you must have made the coffee. We made a second pot knowing that Miss Lynda would need several cups to open her eyes after what she drank last night. By the way, does anyone have an idea about what we had for dinner?"

The ladies laughed as none of them could remember. Allie asked, "Did anyone hear from Jennifer yet this morning?"

Lynda said, "She was dressed to kill and looked to be on the prowl, so I am guessing she landed her prey and is at this moment waking him with the oldest reward in the books."

All of the ladies laughed except Allie. Allie was worried about her boss as she seldom caroused at night. Kathy piped up and said, "Allie, I wouldn't worry too much just yet. Jen has been known to sow her wild oats when she is on vacation or sees a man she would like to snuggle with. We'll give it until noon. If we don't hear from her by then, we'll send out the militia!"

Kathy said, "I guess it is my turn for the shower. Allie got up and followed her. They both undressed and got into the shower. Kathy said, "This is a nice surprise. I have been admiring your body since we got here."

Allie said, "I wanted to see you as well. I was worried about Jennifer, but then the thought of joining you in the shower erased any of that worry from my mind.

The two women embraced and began to soap each other's bodies. They kissed, and it got progressively more erotic. Kathy said, "Shall we go to your room?" Allie could only moan when Kathy let her hand trail over Allie's chest.

Allie said, "We had better go quickly before I attack you right here in the shower.

Kathy and Allie went by Lynda's room and saw Lynda and Cricky in a naked embrace. Seems like their sexual needs were also being met this morning.

* * *

Mason Delsson sat in the chair in his home office. He was awakened this morning with a call from Keisha Kane. She said, "Good morning, Mr. Delsson. I trust you slept well when you arrived home last evening."

Mason replied, "I slept like I ran a marathon. The best marathon a man could dream about. I wanted to stay last evening, but you more than exceeded my expectations of how you would feel in a romantic embrace. I knew if I stayed, I would have to cancel all the interviews I had scheduled today. I tried to wake you before I left, but I think the Tequila had made your brain a bit foggy at that point. Thank you, by the way, for letting me enjoy your sweet amorous sexuality. I left you a note, but I had so much to tell you, I thought it was best to wait until we met again, so that I could tell you my feelings in person, Keisha."

Keisha said, "I have several appointments today, would you like to buy me dinner tonight? I found a new restaurant that I have wanted to try out. I was waiting for the right person to ask. I hope you are available this evening."

Mason saw the home office phone was lighting up, indicating I had an incoming call. He decided to let the machine answer it. He said to Keisha, "That is a flattering offer. I was going to ask you out as well, so, yes, I would love to take you to dinner. Does 6:30 sound reasonable?"

Keisha replied, "That sounds perfect. I have a couple of surprises I would like to share. The place is dressy casual, so how you were dressed yesterday would be great. I, on the other hand, feel it best to wear something a bit less revealing. I will see you at six thirty. Have a productive day." She hung up, and Mason held the phone in his hand, thinking about their night together the previous evening. It had been the best sexual liaison he had experienced in the last twenty-five years. He remembered the call he had received on his home office phone.

The light was blinking, so the caller had left a message. He clicked play and listened. The message was from Tony Strong. Mason heard, "Mr. Delsson. This is Tony Strong. Randy Keene asked me to call and let you know that Jennifer Sandrew is missing in Lake Tahoe. Randy is still talking with Lynda Laffarty, who initially talked to me about Jennifer. She told me Jennifer went out alone two nights ago and has not returned. Lynda called me to ask if I had taken her anywhere. I had not seen her at all. So, I called Randy, and he suggested I call you. Lynda asked if we could keep this information from the authorities until they were sure she had or had not hooked up with someone. They tried calling her phone, but Lynda reported that it was either shut off, or the battery needed to be charged.."

Mason said, "Thanks, Tony. I will call Randy, and we'll strategize a plan. If you see him, let him know I am working from my end." They ended the call. Mason wondered if he should go to Tahoe, but he knew he had other fish to fry in L.A. His phone rang, and it was Randy. Mason said, "Hello. What's up?"

Randy said, "Have you spoken to Tony?"

Mason said, "Yes."

Randy continued, "No sign of the woman. I searched the morgue and have no leads."

Mason said, "I thought the group was heading home today and was hoping to talk to all or some of them again today. Did any of the restaurant or hotel staff see or know anything?"

Randy replied, "One of the bartenders at the hotel thought he remembered a lady in a blue dress who took a seat at the bar next to the gentleman who ordered her a drink. When he returned with the refill, they were gone."

* * *

Fitore Fantazee went to the bar and made Robin and herself a drink. She walked back into the bedroom, and Robin had her back to the door and was removing her lingerie. She turned as Fitore entered. Robin walked to Fitore and grabbed her drink. She asked Fitore, "Where do you want me? Or should I ask, Do you want me?"

Fitore took a long gulp of her drink, set it down, and placed her hand around the back of Robin's neck. She drew her in for a long, heated kiss. Both were out of breath when they parted. Robin Ripple set her drink down and led Fitore to bed. Fitore was naked quickly. They crawled into bed and were entangled in a lover's embrace with hands everywhere and mouths covering a great deal of each other's skin.

Robin drew back and said, "I'll take that as a yes. Girl, you are so beautiful, and your passion is electric. I am going to savor this moment."

After a torrid hour and a half of lovemaking, Fitore and Robin stood in the shower, soaping each other's bodies and kissing almost nonstop. Fitore said, "I think you will be perfect for a role in my next movie. Can you come to L.A. to do test for my team? You can stay with me if you like. If not, I can reserve a room for you at my favorite hotel."

Robin now rinsed them both and said, "I have a bunch of vacation coming, so I can come to L.A. when you need me."

Fitore said, "Oh, I need you. I am still tingling. Can you come to L.A. this week?"

Robin said, "Just let me know when and I will grab a flight." Fitore said, "Well, I am staying with a gentleman here, but he had to fly back to L.A. When he returns, I will ask him when we are going back, and maybe you can fly with us. You can stay with me, and you'll have no expenses except maybe when we go shopping."

Robin purred in Fitore's ear, "That sounds dreamy. I will let the hotel know I may be leaving for a short while. Just let me know. I should get ready to go back downstairs. Thank you for a beautiful visit. Can't wait to see you again."

Fitore said, "Give me your contact info before you leave, and I will keep you posted as to what our plans are. By the way, could I interest you in joining me and my gentleman friend when he returns? I know he would love to ravage you as well as watch us together."

Robin said as she dressed and readied to leave, "I will go pack a bag and be ready the minute you call. I will be tingling all day with anticipation for all that you mentioned. Goodbye for now."

Robin left, and Fitore was sitting again at the minibar in the room. Her phone rang. She said, "Hello. This is Fitore."

The voice was a welcome relief; it was Dalton, "Hello, my Sweet.

How are you? I am so sorry for leaving, but you looked so angelic sleeping when I left."

Fitore replied, "I was a little concerned. Are you alright?"

Dalton said, "Yes. I am dealing with an emergency my son has at home, and I am a little worried. He called me yesterday, and my phone was off. I was focused on this beautiful woman I was with, so I didn't want to be interrupted."

Fitore laughed, "I was focused as well. I had an interesting day. I think I may have found a new leading lady for my next film. I will fill you in on all that when I see you. Do you know when or if you'll be returning, or do you want me to check out and return to L.A?"

Dalton said, "I have not been able to locate my son, and I am waiting for the police right now. I am planning to return today after dealing with him, but he is nowhere to be found. I will leave it up to you. If you want to return to L.A., I will send my plane back for you. If you want to relax there for a day or two, I will get back as soon as I can."

Fitore said, "I am quite comfortable here, and I needed this relaxation. I will stay and wait for you. If you need me, I will return, but I will enjoy these marvelous accommodations."

Dalton said, "That will be perfect, my dear. I am hoping to see you soon. Take care and charge whatever you want or need to the room. I have notified the hotel that you have carte blanche."

Fitore said, "That is sweet. I will make myself busy. I have some work I can do here. I hope all is well and you can return quickly to my arms."

Dalton asked, "Are you charging everything to the room? I don't want you to be shy about what you charge."

Fitore said, "Dalton, you have been very generous. If I eat at the hotel or want something to drink while at the pool, I will charge it to the room. If I go elsewhere, I will use my own money. I am not shy about spending yours or my money."

Dalton was pleased, "Thank you, Fitore. I will do my best to return soon. Take care."

* * *

Mason Delsson was back at the Craig estate. He rang the bell, and a ravishing blonde answered the door. "Yes. May I help you?" Mason showed his badge, and the girl said, "Right this way, officer." She turned and walked to the staircase. She was wearing or almost wearing a bright yellow bikini. She had long legs and was about five feet nine inches. Mason almost tripped while watching her rear end ascend the staircase to Dalton's office.

Mason thought to himself, *I have been here three times now, and all of the people here were gorgeous.*

They reached the office, and she opened the door, leaned in and said, "The police are here, Mr. Craig."

Dalton said, "Just a minute. I am just ending a phone call." He picked up the phone on his desk and said to no one, "Thanks, goodbye."

As Dalton waved her in, she stood back and let Mason pass. He had to rub across her body to enter the room. He scolded himself and refocused. He said to Dalton, "I got here as quickly as I could. Have you heard from your son?"

Dalton said, "Yes, thank goodness. I just got off the phone with him. He is in Las Vegas waiting for me to see him there. We were unable to connect as my phone was off while I was in Tahoe. To be honest with you, he was rattled after he spoke to you. He was severely affected by the loss of his mother, and he gets depressed when he talks about her passing. I was able to calm him down. I will go to Las Vegas on my way back to Lake Tahoe to be with him. Thank you for responding so quickly, and I am sorry for the false alarm.

Mason said, "That is perfectly okay, Mr. Craig. I was in the neighborhood, so I was close." He walked back out the door and left.

* * *

Lynda, Christy, Allie, Sue, and Kathy were sitting in the hotel room in Lake Tahoe. Lynda said, "Well, it has been two days and there has been no word from Jennifer. What do you guys think we ought to do?"

Allie said, "I am worried that something bad has happened to Jennifer. She has never been the type to do anything this impulsive. I don't know what to do. I should go back to the store, but I don't want to go without finding her."

Christy said, "I know what you mean, Allie. I also need to get back to L.A., but my feeling is that Jennifer is a big girl, and if she is in trouble, she will reach out to one of us. We have filed a missing person's report and should let the authorities handle the situation. It would be silly to think we could find her ourselves. My gut tells me she may be cuddling up with an old friend. I vote for us to leave and let the police handle the matter."

Kathy, being the clearest thinker, said, "I think we should return to L.A. Let the LAPD know what's happened. I will call Mason Delsson, as he just interviewed each of us regarding Carmen's death. He might have the resources to look for her. What do you ladies want to do?" The ladies agreed and decided to have Lynda call Dalton to see if his plane was available. If the plane was not available, they would fly a commercial flight back to L.A.

* * *

Back in L.A., Walker Craig went to visit his old flame, Deyna Doll. She was a background singer for a group called Two Way Street. They had dated years ago and ran into each other three days ago after Walker had been interviewed by Mason Delsson from the Los Angeles Police Department. Deyna had been trying to get back together with Walker for years. They had an explosive sexual relationship that both of them thought of often. In Deyna's case, it was more often than she could handle.

Deyna lived in Beverly Hills. She had a music studio in her home. It was a perfect place where her band could practice without worrying about neighbors. The guys were just leaving a rehearsal when Walker drove into the driveway. He knew almost all of the guys, so he honked his horn as he parked next to Deyna's Escalade. They all waved as they got into their cars and drove off the property.

Deyna was expecting him, and she buzzed him into the private residence. Walker was familiar with the place, so he went in and went straight to the bar. He poured himself a Scotch and ice. He also poured some Tequila for Deyna. She walked in from the downstairs studio just as he finished mixing her drink. Deyna said, "Well, you are a sight for sore eyes. Thank you for the cocktail. I need it badly." She took a large gulp and felt the burn down her throat to her belly. She continued, "Aah! That hits the spot. We are working on a few new tunes. Some of the old Earth, Wind, and Fire songs. The music comes quickly to everyone, but the vocal harmonies are always difficult to arrange. Today was a good session, but a long one.

Deyna came over to Walker, and they hugged. They looked into each other's eyes for what seemed like a long time, but it was only few seconds, then they kissed. It was electric, just like it had been when they dated. Neither could remember why they broke apart, but their reuniting last week was so random that each knew they wanted to be with the other.

Walker was the first to break from the kiss and said, "It feels like no time has passed when we kiss. You are such an amazing lady. I guess I was out of my mind when we parted."

Deyna said, "I thought you had another woman, but you didn't for so long. I knew then that you didn't leave for another woman. I guess it was all the family stuff and work that got you into a funk. It was lovely talking to you the day we ran into each other. You seemed calmer, more together, and mature. You are even more attractive to me now than you were back then. Frankly, I could not wait until we were in each other's arms again. I can tell from one kiss that the electricity between us has not waned one iota."

Walker hugged Deyna, and they kissed again. The moans that

each of them heard from the other increased the erotic energy that flowed between them. Deyna said, "Walker, I seriously do need a shower. Pour me another drink and I'll be back before you notice I left." Walker watched as she headed to her bedroom. He watched her hips sway, and it gave him a tingle down his spine. He could not wait to see that beautiful naked form again and pleasure it.

Deyna jumped into the shower, soaped her body, and washed her hair. She would dry her hair with a towel and then wrap it around herself before she returned to the bar. She rinsed, toweled off, and walked back to the bar.

Walker had just finished mixing another drink. Deyna said, "I am ready."

Walker looked up and almost dropped the drinks. "Oh my! What a vision. I love it when you're fresh out of the shower. You look amazing." He handed her the drink which she took and gulped down half of it. She placed the glass back on the bar and put her arms around Walker.

She said, "Would you like to see how I redecorated the bedrooms?"

Walker said, "Yes, I would. Lead the way."

Deyna laughed, "I think you remember the way to the sleeping area." She entered her room and flipped on the lights that were set at a soft glow. Deyna walked to the bed, turned around, and dropped the towel. Walker was awestruck. His mouth was agape, and he thought she had asked him a question, but his brain was not processing anything but visual input. The blood was rushing to another part of his body.

Deyna almost yelled at this point to get his attention, "Walker. Can you hear me? You seem to have gone into a trance. What do you think of the changes in the bedroom?"

Walker blinked and heard her this time. He stuttered but finally responded, "Holy Moly, Miss Deyna. You have certainly resculpted your delicious body. I wholeheartedly approve. Wow. Is there a 'touching' portion of this show? Do you have any oxygen handy?"

Deyna laughed but was pleased he noticed and was impressed.

She answered, "My dear, Walker, you may approach the queen and take any liberty you so desire."

Walker took two steps forward and fell to his knees. He began to worship her body like he did long ago. They both filled the room with erotic sounds and moans. Deyna finally pulled him to his feet and pushed him onto the bed. She began to disrobe him quickly. He frantically tried to help. Deyna was finally able to get him naked and jumped onto the bed, atop him. It was then that the electricity began to spark. They changed positions at least four times, the timers had turned on the lights around the outside of the home, and the room began to brighten. Deyna and Walker lay next to each other after two hours of adult wrestling. They had trouble controlling their breathing, and each was covered with a thin film of perspiration.

It was Walker who caught his breath and voice first, "Double D. That was the best sex ever. Not only with you but also for me with anyone. You are amazing. We are amazing together. Do you want a steady guy in your life? I will do all I can to be that man and give you as much joy as I just experienced."

Deyna smiled, rolling over to caress his chest, "Walt, you have gotten better and still the best man I have ever met, who knows how to satisfy a woman. Oh, by the way, why were you asking for oxygen?"

Walker laughed as he hugged her closer to him, "I just ran out of air when I was worshiping you, and I was going to pass out from lack of oxygen."

They both laughed. They rested. After thirty minutes of silence. Walker began, "Deyna, the reason I called was to see you again, of course, but also to pick your brain about a personal matter."

"I think I know what you are going to ask but go ahead. I will tell you if it is what I thought."

Walker took the next half hour to explain in detail the conversation he had with Mason Delsson from the L.A. Police. "There was just something about the look on his face when he was asking the questions about my mom's death. You know how guilty

I felt about not being with her that day. He made me feel like it was me who killed my mother."

Deyna's mothering gene kicked in, and she hugged Walker as she lay next to him in her bed, "Walker, you didn't kill your mother. It was an accident." She kissed his forehead, and he tightened his grip around her shoulder.

"Deyna, you always could calm me down. I feel so safe in your arms. I think I am going to do a separate investigation and see if I can find anything the cops haven't found."

Deyna said, "I know a good private detective if you want one. His name is Josh Polland. I can give him your number, or I can set up a meeting for you two to have a meeting."

"That sounds like a plan. Let me know when you set it up. The least I can do is talk to him and see what he thinks about the case and whether he will take on the case."

* * *

Dalton had just spoken to Randy Keene, who told Dalton that Jennifer Sandrew was reported as missing in Lake Tahoe. Dalton got a chill running down his back. He wondered if anyone had seen him with Jennifer at the bar in Tahoe. He wondered if they had found her yet.

Dalton called Fitore in Tahoe. She answered the phone in their hotel room on the first ring, "Hello."

Dalton said, "What a tingle I get just hearing your voice."

Fitore was very happy to hear his voice, "Hello, my love. I have missed you so much. Are you returning here?"

"I am on the plane as we speak. I should be back in your arms in twenty minutes."

Fitore screeched with glee, "Oh, Dalton, that is such great news. I shall be ready. Do you want something to eat upon your return?"

Dalton said, "If you are up for it, I would like to take you to a restaurant I haven't visited in a long time called Café Fiore. It is about ten minutes north of where you are. I have called for reservations for one hour from now. Can you be ready?"

"I am nude right now, but I will be ready when you get here. Mr. Craig."

"Okay, my dear. See you soon." He ended the call thinking about her being nude.

Fitore jumped from the couch in the hotel room and went to the shower. She spent ten minutes primping, and when she came back into the bar area, her hair was combed in an upsweep, she donned black thigh-high nylons, a short black mini dress with five-inch black heels. She had a white chinchilla winter coat ready to slip on when Dalton arrived.

* * *

Dalton's plane landed ten minutes after his call to Fitore. Kirt Leoz was standing on the tarmac waiting with the long black limo. Dalton exited the plane and was walking into the lobby of the hotel ten minutes later. He walked off the elevator down the hall to his suite and swiped his door key. It opened, and he walked into the room. There stood this vision in black that took his breath away. He went to her open arms, and they embraced. Their kiss was passionate, and they were both out of breath when it ended.

Dalton said, "Miss Fitore, you look incredible, but you already knew that. Let me change my suit and we'll leave for the restaurant. It's Italian cuisine and I hope you like it. An old friend of mine is the owner, and she is a great cook. Her name is Lynn Fuda. She is originally from back east but now lives in Tahoe full-time.

Fitore watched as he changed his suit. She got excited looking at his naked body. He was a beautiful specimen of a man. Even at his age, he looked like he could make love all night long. She knew he could because she had experienced it many times.

Dalton then held out his hands to the side and said, "Well, do I clean up well enough to accompany a queen to dinner?"

108

Fitore laughed and said, "You are a Greek god whose wish is my command. Let's go to dinner, I am starving."

Dalton said as they walked to the elevator, "You have been eating while I was gone, haven't you?"

Fitore replied, "Yes, but not necessarily food. I will explain when we are at our dining table." The limo drove to the restaurant.

Kirt held the door for Fitore and Dalton as they entered the restaurant. Dennis Bellowso, the maitre d' welcomed them to the restaurant. He said, "Welcome to Café Fiore, Mr. Craig. Wonderful to see you, sir. I have your regular table ready for you. Please follow me."

Dalton and Fitore walked behind Dennis, who had their menus in hand. They stopped at a small table near the window in a darkened part of the room. Dennis held the chair for Fitore, then put down the menus. He said, "Mr. Craig, can we make you something special tonight?"

"Have Ms. Fuda come out if she has a minute."

"Very good, sir. Richard will be your waiter this evening. He is one of our veterans."

Dennis Bellowso left the table and within a minute, Richard Bruce appeared and said, "Good Evening, folks. My name is Richard, and I will be your server this evening. May I start you with a cocktail before you order?"

Dalton looked at Fitore, who nodded and said, "Do you feel like champagne tonight or shall we drink Tequila? Richard, we'll have a couple of your famous margaritas, please. When you bring them, we'll have looked at the menu, and then we will order."

"Very good, sir." He walked toward the bar.

Dalton said to Fitore, "What are you in the mood to eat tonight?"

Fitore laughed and said, "You mean besides you?"

Dalton's phone rang. It was Sam Barfield, his lawyer. He said, "It is my lawyer, Doll. I should take this. Excuse me."

Sam said, "Dalton, I just wanted to give you a heads up. They found the body of Jennifer Sandrew this morning in Lake Tahoe. Her body was floating on the other side of the Lake from where you are. I just heard from Randy Keene, who is in Tahoe. Should I have him call you, or what do you want to do?"

Dalton said, "That is so sad to hear. I did not know she was in Tahoe with the girls. I am having dinner at the moment, so if you could take care of the particulars, I would be grateful."

Sam said, "The Tahoe Police should have notified them by now, but I'll check. They wanted to fly back to LA today, but in view of the situation, I will help them rearrange their plans if they wish. Have a nice evening, Mr. Craig."

* * *

Dalton hung up. He looked at Fitore and said, "What have you decided for dinner?" Just as he spoke, Lynn Fuda walked up to the table and greeted him with a Hello.

Lynn Fuda was originally from Syracuse, New York. She was married a couple of times and had five children in total. When her last husband passed, she inherited several properties, which turned out to be worth lots of money. She moved between Florida and Spain for a while. Then Lynn decided to open an Italian restaurant. Her son, Michael, said that she should go somewhere where there was money, influencers, and a place where there was a lack of good Italian restaurants. He suggested Lake Tahoe. Lynn had purchased the small restaurant that used to be a seafood place. She named it Café Fiore. It had become the go-to place on the Lake.

Lynn said, "It is so nice to see you, Mr. Craig."

"Oh, please call me Dalton."

Lynn replied, "Is there anything special you would like to eat tonight, Dalton?"

Dalton looked to Fitore, who said, "How is the seafood here?"

Lynn replied, "I have some nice fresh swordfish, and I just received some sea bass from San Diego this morning."

Dalton said, "I would love the sea bass. How about you, Fitore? What are you in the mood for?"

Fitore said, "I would like to try the swordfish."

Dalton said, "My apologies to you ladies. Lynn, this is Fitore Fantazee. Fitore, this is Lynn Fuda, the owner of this great restaurant and she is an old friend of our family."

Fitore said, "It is so nice to meet you, Miss Fuda. Dalton has been raving about the food here since we left for the café."

Lynn said, "Nice to meet you as well, Miss Fantazee. Haven't I seen you in movies?"

Fitore was impressed with this woman. Lynn was beautiful in her own right. Lynn's hair was long, brown down to her shoulders. She was dressed in an apron, but her clothes beneath it were exquisite, and she was blessed with a great shape. The fact that she recognized her made Fitore feel comfortable with her.

Dalton said, "I will have some of your famous lasagna as well."

Lynn said, "I will let your server know, and I will begin to cook the food. It was great to meet you, Fitore."

Lynn left for the kitchen. She told Richard on her way that Dalton had ordered, and he just needed to get their side choices and keep their drinks full.

* * *

Lynda Laffarty's phone rang as she walked back to her room at the hotel. She did not recognize the number but said, "Hello."

The voice said, "Ms. Laffarty, this is Sheriff Antonio de LaPaz in Lake Tahoe. I regret to inform you that the body of Jennifer Sandrew was found. Her body washed up on the west side of the lake. It looks like she had a large hematoma on her head, but we'll have to wait for the coroner's report to determine whether she fell and hit her head or if she drowned and was struck in the head in the water. Do you know her next of kin?"

Lynda cried and tried to keep her wits about her as she listened to the sheriff. She said, "Thank you for the call, Sheriff. Will you let me know when the coroner releases the body so we can arrange to get it back to L.A.? I think she had a sister. I will ask her business partner, Allie Campwick, if she knows how to contact the sister." They ended the call, and Lynda wept.

It was a few minutes before Lynda could collect herself and call Allie Campwick. Allie answered the phone on the first ring, "Hello, Lynda. Did you hear anything?"

Lynda braced herself and said, "I am afraid Jennifer is gone."

Allie screamed into the phone in disbelief. She said, "How? Where did they find her? Did someone have something to do with her death?"

Lynda said, "Come to my room and we'll do this together"

Allie said, "That is very nice, Lynda, but I have a million things to do and arrangements to make. Please let me know who your contact was in Tahoe so I can speak with them directly."

Lynda said, "I think it would be best if you come to my room and make the arrangements. I'll get the rest of the girls here immediately, so we can all be on the same page." Allie agreed.

Lynda hung up the phone and texted the other girls to come to her room as soon as possible.

Within 10 minutes, all the ladies had assembled back in Lynda's room to support each other.

Cricky said, "Lynda, do you know what happened to her? Where was she found? Was she with anyone? I remember thinking that when she left the hotel room, she was alone and vulnerable. My worst fears have now been realized. Are the Tahoe Police doing the investigation?"

Lynda tried to calm Cricky down some, but she knew her personality, and that calming would take time. Lynda replied, "I don't have any details, but as soon as I do, I will contact you. The Tahoe Sheriff Antonio de Lapaz may be calling us all to ask a few questions. Don't be surprised if it is sooner rather than later."

* * *

Mason Delsson answered his office phone. It was Antonio de

Lapaz, the Sheriff in Lake Tahoe. Antonio said, "Hello, my friend. How are things in Tinsel Town?"

Mason replied, "Same as always, Antonio. Hectic. How about you?"

Antonio de Lapaz said, "Just wanted to give you a courtesy call about Jennifer Sandrew. She was here in Tahoe for a few days with some friends. As these women returned to their room Wednesday night, Jennifer left them after midnight to meet someone. She didn't say who she was going to see. I've been running down leads since we got a call first thing Thursday morning. She was spotted on the beach on the west side of the lake, either left there, or more likely floated up and landed there. It is improbable that she fell in on the east side where her hotel was and floated to the other side of the Lake in eight or so hours. It, however, is not impossible. If we come up with anything, I will call you."

Mason said, "Thanks for the call. Antonio. Talk to you soon." As soon as he hung up the phone, Mason called Randy Keene. "Randy, they found Jennifer..."

Randy interrupted Mason, "Yes, I know. She was found dead in Tahoe. She was with Kathy Muller, Cricky Amherst, Susan Crull, Lynda Laffarty, and Allie Campwick, her business partner. These five other women were still in their hotel suite when Jennifer left to go out. I have already checked around the hotel and found only one waiter who remembers seeing Jennifer come into the bar and sit next to a grey-haired gentleman. They didn't stay long because when he came back to the bar to get the next round of drinks for his tables, he noticed the bar was empty and Jelly Morton, the bartender, was alone, washing glasses. Do you want me to come back to L.A. or stay here to see what I can see?"

Mason replied, "Hang out there and work with Sheriff de Lapaz."

Mason tried to call Lynda Laffarty to set up a meeting, but he got her answering machine. He left a message for her to call him. He decided to visit Elegant Lace, the store owned by Jennifer Sandrew and Allie Campwick. He left the office and drove to Rodeo Drive.

* * *

Lynda Laffarty and Kathy Muller were talking in the kitchenette of Lynda's room. Kathy asked, "Do you know what exactly happened?"

Before she got into too many questions, Lynda stopped her by saying, "She was found by two fishermen when she floated up onto the beach on the other side of the lake Thursday morning. That's all the information I have. The Sheriff from Tahoe may call to ask more questions, so expect it, if not, a visit from Detective Delsson here in L.A. Put your thinking cap on, like we all are at this point. See if you can replay in your mind what happened on your trip. The Sheriff was looking for anything Jen did or said that could be a clue. Thanks. Gotta go, Goodbye."

As soon as they hung up, Lynda began running through her mind each day's events since they arrived in Lake Tahoe. She was curious about how abruptly Jennifer went out that night after complaining of being tired during their activities. She was looking for any sign.

Lynda said, "I think one of us should go with Allie to get Jennifer's body. Maybe I will call Dalton and let him know what happened to our friend. I will ask to borrow his airplane."

Sue said, "That is a great idea. Allie will surely appreciate the company. Let me know if there is anything I can do. "

Lynda sat on her couch for a minute to collect her thoughts, and her cell phone rang again. She jumped this time as her mind was elsewhere in deep thought.

It was Dalton. "Lynda, I just heard about Jennifer. I am so sorry for your loss. Is there anything I can do?"

Lynda almost laughed. She replied, "You must be a mind reader. I was just about to call you. I was wondering what I would say to you. Do you think we could borrow your airplane? I want to offer it to Allie to fly to Tahoe to bring Jennifer's body back here to L.A."

Dalton said, "That is the same thing I was thinking. I know you all must be mortified that she died on the trip you all took together. What do you think happened?"

Lynda said, "Well, after a night of drinking on the water, we decided to go back to the hotel and get some sleep. We were planning a shopping trip early the next day. Jennifer decided to get dressed again and go out. We let her go alone. She never made it back." Lynda was now in tears.

Dalton said, "I wish I could be there to comfort you. I am sure it was no fault of any of you ladies."

"Dalton, thanks for being there for us. We don't even have a clue."

Dalton replied, "It is the least I can do. I spoke with a friend of mine who is in Tahoe. He did some investigating when he heard about it from one of his police buddies and found a hotel worker who said he saw her that night. He told my friend she met an older gentleman there, but when he returned from taking a drink order at one of the tables he was serving, the bar was empty. I want you to know that I was that gentleman. I had just sent the lady I was with back to our room and finished another drink when Jennifer walked in and sat down. She said she saw me earlier when we came off the elevator going to dinner. Jen decided to come down to the restaurant to see if I was still there. She said that when she saw me, she knew she still had feelings for me and asked if I was interested in rekindling the relationship that we had way back in the day."

Lynda said, "Oh my goodness, Dalton. What did you tell her? You may have been the last one to see her alive."

"I told her that I was flattered. I told her she was a beautiful, desirable woman that I found very attractive, but I didn't think I could see her again. First, she is friends with a lot of folks in the business. She is close to you. Secondly, and most importantly, she and I had drifted apart, wanting to see other people. I didn't want that for either of us again. She said she understood and left."

Lynda asked, "Did you follow her to make sure she was not upset?"

Dalton replied, "No. She was cordial when she left, and I went back up to my room. I got an emergency call from Walker, and I left my lady friend a note of apology and flew back to L.A. for the day. I didn't get back until later the next night."

Lynda wondered if he was telling the truth or maybe hiding something. She asked him, "Did you speak to the authorities?"

"I tried to call Mason Delsson, but he wasn't in his office, so I left a message. I am sure he will call back today."

Lynda said, "Thanks for telling me this, Dalton, and I appreciate the use of the plane. I won't take any more of your time."

* * *

Dalton said goodbye and hung up. Just as he did, Fitore walked naked out of the shower, walked to the bar, and fixed them both a cocktail. She delivered his drink to him as he sat on the patio. Dalton said, "I don't want you to catch your death out here, even though the view is gorgeous. Why don't you and I stretch out on the bed and talk?"

Fitore put one hand on her hip, spun herself around on one foot, so he could get a view of her from the back. and swayed her hips, invitingly walking back toward the bedroom. Dalton was quick to follow.

Dalton dropped his robe as he entered the bedroom and joined Fitore on the bed. The passion was evident for both of them. Thirty minutes into their tryst, Fitore noticed a thin film of perspiration on her own body and steam coming off of Dalton. They were well practiced and knew what each other liked. They were physical, loud, and signaled their ecstasy with simultaneous moans. Dalton was now on his back, and Fitore was also trying to catch her breath. She looked over toward him and said, "There are no words for me to express the pleasure you give me."

Dalton took a long sigh and replied, "Chica, you ring all my bells as well. You are an incredible lover. I am lucky to be with you here in this lovely setting. By the way, I was wondering when you would like to leave here; would you like to return to L.A. tomorrow?"

Fitore said, "That sounds like a plan to me. Let's go out for a nice dinner tonight and maybe leave first thing in the morning. I have one more sexy lingerie set for you for tonight.'

Dalton agreed. They ate dinner in the hotel restaurant and returned to their room. They showered, made love, and fell asleep in each other's arms.

4

THE LADIES RETURNED from the Tahoe excursion and were all back at work, except, sadly, Jennifer Sandrew. Lynda Laffarty and Allie Campwick flew this morning on Dalton's plane back to Lake Tahoe mortuary to retrieve Jennifer's body. Dalton told Lynda he was checking out this morning, and he would have his driver stop at the mortuary. He would have Jennifer's casket taken to the airport and loaded into the plane's cargo hold. Dalton and Fitore would meet the plane as it refueled, and they would return with Lynda and Allie to Los Angeles.

As Dalton walked through the Lake Tahoe airport, he walked by a woman who caught his eye. He didn't want to disrespect Fitore, so he was very discreet. She was somewhere around 5 feet 8 inches tall with dark, red hair to her shoulders and a body that looked as if she had been in the gym regularly. He lost her in the crowd, but he made a mental note in his head to search for the woman he saw in the airport's corridor sometime soon. She reminded him of his late wife, except for the color of her hair, and maybe her youthful appearance. This woman was classy and beautiful. He was distracted having Fitore at his side, but he silently racked his brain trying to place where he knew that woman.

Lynda and Allie waited in Dalton's plane when they arrived at Lake Tahoe. It wasn't more than ten minutes until the plane was refueled that the door opened, and Dalton and this breathtaking woman entered the fuselage. They were to sit up front. Dalton walked them halfway back down the aisle to say hello. He said,

"Ladies, I am so sorry for your loss. The driver confirmed that the casket had been loaded. Allie, do you have a funeral director in place?"

Dalton then said, "Ladies, may I introduce Miss Fitore Fantazee. She is an actress as well as a producer/ screenwriter. We may work on our next project together. Fitore, this is Lynda Laffarty, an ex-wife and old friend. This is Allie Campwick, who was a business partner with the lady who died."

Allie said, "Yes, I already gave the funeral home address to the driver. Thank you again, Dalton, for the use of the plane and all you've done."

Dalton said, "No worries at all. Glad I could help. I have two drivers meeting us at LAX, one for you two, and the other for me and my friend." Lynda's eyebrows rose upon hearing this, and Dalton did not fail to notice.

The ladies exchanged pleasantries, and Lynda was warm but took a very discerning look at the tall blonde. She wondered how long Dalton would dally with this lady. She asked herself if she still had feelings of jealousy. It had been too long since she and Dalton parted.

It was a short flight back to LA. Allie was on the phone planning for a one-day wake and funeral for her partner, Jennifer Sandrew. Lynda closed her eyes and thought about Carmen Craig. Lynda had never thought of Carmen dying any other way but simply falling off a spooked horse and hitting her head on a large rock. Now Jennifer was gone. Lynda had an uneasy feeling about all the deaths she had seen in her circle in a short amount of time. She wondered if she was on the killer's list. Trying to calm herself, she wondered if Dalton was the perpetrator of these accidental deaths.

* * *

The plane landed and taxied to a private hangar, where Dalton's plane was stored. Just as Dalton had indicated, two limousines were waiting for them as they deplaned. Dalton sat Fitore in one, then went to make sure the drivers and pilots waited for the casket to be loaded by the folks from the morgue. Lynda and Allie both thanked Dalton for bringing them back. It was expedient and saved them a lot of money and time.

Dalton watched them drive off, then returned to his limo, where Fitore sat waiting patiently. He said, "Would you like me to drop you off at your home, your office, or would you join me for a swim and a few drinks at my humble abode?"

Fitore laughed. She had thought about this during the whole flight back to L.A. She replied, "Dalton, thank you for a lovely time in Tahoe. I looked at my phone on the way back and realized my schedule shows several important meetings for me to attend, as well as an uncountable number of emails to return. So, if you could drop me off at my residence, I would appreciate it greatly. I am hoping to get a rain check for the swim and drinks invitation."

Dalton said to Kirt, the driver, "Take Miss Fantazee to her home first, please." Kirt Leoz waved through the glass window and drove back to Beverly Hills.

* * *

Mason Delsson walked into Elegant Lace in Beverly Hills. He asked the clerk if Allie Campwick was available. The clerk, Sydney McKeller, asked, "Who may I say is calling?"

Mason flashed his badge and said, "Detective Delsson, L.A.P.D."

Sydney said, "Just a minute, Detective. I will see if she is available. You might want to look around and shop for your favorite lady." Chuckling, she walked toward the back office.

Mason walked toward a rack of negligees. He thought of Keisha Kane and wondered if he should bring her a gift. Maybe just to look in on her to make sure that she was okay. He smiled and quickly picked out two outfits. One of the bra and panty sets was black. The other was purple. Mason brought them to the cashier as Allie Campwick walked to him from the back office.

Allie said, "Welcome back, Detective Delsson. How may I help you today?"

Mason blushed as he saw Allie look down at the counter to see his purchases. He said to Allie, "Can you spare a few moments to answer a question or two?"

Allie said, "Sure, come up to the office when you're done with your transaction." She turned and walked back upstairs. Mason watched every step she took and marveled at how fit she was. Beverly Hills was indeed filled with countless beautiful women. He would never get tired of "girl watching" as they used to call it when he was younger.

* * *

Lynda returned home, retrieved her mail, and went into her office. She began sifting through the envelopes, and she spotted one that had a familiar return address on it. It was from Sagittarius International Pictures, Inc., Patrick J. Hart. CEO, Hollywood, California. She opened it first. It read:

Dear Lynda,

I hope this note finds you well. I was unsuccessful in my phone calls to you, so I dropped you this note. I have just returned from a long stint in Lisboa, Portugal. I wrapped up the film last week and finally got home.

I wanted to set up a meeting with you for two reasons. First, I have a movie idea that I would like to pitch to you to star in and direct. It is a real, different murder mystery. It was written by an old friend of yours.

Secondly, I selfishly wanted to see you again as I not only missed your company but also your beautiful personality. I have thought of you often since our last time together.

My schedule is open for you if you're interested in having dinner with me. We can dine here, out by the pool, or visit one of our favorite eateries. Your choice.

Please contact me when you return from your trip.
Warmest Regards, Patrick

Lynda spent the next few minutes remembering the times she and Patrick shared. He was a very passionate man. So classy and very attentive for someone who possessed such power and influence.

Lynda picked up the phone at her office desk and dialed Patrick's number. He answered after three rings. "Hello, this is Patrick."

Lynda replied, "Well, Mr. Hart. How wonderful to hear from you. I am sorry I missed your calls, but I took a short trip to Lake Tahoe with friends and wanted to focus on them. How are you, and how did your filming go in Portugal?

Patrick Hart was elated by Lynda's call. "Lynda, it is great to hear your voice. I was very involved in the shooting and editing of the film. My team and I just finished the edits and music adaptations. We will release it around Valentine's Day. As I said in my note, I would love to have dinner with you. Are you available?"

Lynda said, "I am very available for such a handsome and talented movie mogul. Let's get together on Friday at your place. If you still have the same chef, it will be a treat. Shall I pack a bag? I would love to go into hiding for a bit."

Patrick was very happy now. "That sounds like a great plan. Stay as long as you can stand me. Cat is still my chef, and I will let her know to prepare a special meal of your favorites. She will be happy to see you, but not nearly as happy as I. Shall I send a limo for you around 4 p.m. on Friday?"

Lynda replied, "Oh, that would be super. Thanks. I will talk to you on Friday. She decided to drive over to Elegant Lace and pick up a few new things to wear for Patrick. She jumped into her Mercedes-Benz CLE 300 and drove to Rodeo Drive. She was lucky to find a parking spot right in front of Elegant Lace.

She entered, and Sydney greeted her with a warm, "Hello, Miss Lynda. How are you? Can I help you pick something special today, or would you like to browse?"

Lynda said, "Hi, Syd. I have a few things in mind, so I could use some help. Thanks," Sydney took her right to the section of their slinkiest lingerie. It is exactly the kind of thing Lynda was looking for. "Oh, this is perfect. Let me browse for a few minutes. I will call if I need you." Sydney gave her a thumbs-up and walked back to the register to cash out another customer.

* * *

Mason sat in the same chair he used when he last spoke with Jennifer. This time, he was with Allie. He began, "First, let me express my deepest condolences for your loss. I know you must have been very close."

Allie said, "Thank you. It has been difficult, but strangely, we were prepared for the potential of one of us leaving. We just didn't plan for this. I think I will be fine, and I have already had a couple of offers to join as partners."

Mason said, "That must be comforting to know. Are they friends that you trust?"

Allie thought of whether to tell him and then said, "You know, it is funny you mention it. I was just thinking about the very issue when you arrived here to see me. The two friends, who were on our recent trip, made offers. Lynda Laffarty and Christy Amherst were generous in their offers. I have known both forever, but I have a few concerns about both, but that is a matter I must work out by myself."

Mason said, "How well did you know Carmen Craig?"

Allie replied, "She and I were riding partners, and she gave me a loan to start this business. We saw each other at least once a week for cocktails or dinner. She was a great lady. I miss her every day. We became close when I was asked to help with breeding horses."

Mason then asked, "Do you know how much money she had?" Allie laughed, "Well, I have heard some numbers, but we never spoke of it. I know she made a recent change in her will. She did not express to me what the changes were, but I could certainly guess."

Mason asked, "Do you know who is in her will to receive her money?"

Allie said, "Well, I don't know the particulars, but she indicated there were a few people in her family and people close to her husband whom she wanted to make sure would never see any of her inheritance.

Mason said, "What do you think happened to your partner, Jennifer, up in Lake Tahoe?"

Allie said, "You know, I have known her for years, since right after school, and she was always very tight-lipped about her personal life with men or women. I don't know for sure which she preferred. When she left the hotel that night, she was dressed as if she were on the prowl for a man, but that is a guess based on how she was dressed. She had changed into her LBD (Little Black Dress) and high red heels. Her hair was down to her shoulders, as opposed to her always wearing it either up or in a ponytail. I don't have the slightest clue what fate befell her that evening."

Mason said, "One more question, Miss Campwick. Did you have an intimate relationship with Jennifer Sandrew?"

The shocked look on Allie's face told Mason he had hit a nerve. Now he was waiting for her answer. Allie got her composure and said, "First of all, I can't believe you just asked me that question. Secondly, even if I did, her going out alone that night in Tahoe would not have been a reason for me to kill her. And finally, Jen and I were good friends and partners in a thriving business."

Mason said, "Thank you for your time, Miss Campwick. I will leave now, but I want you to know you really could have answered with a simple yes or no. Good day."

Mason got up, grabbed his bag of lingerie, and walked out. He looked at Sydney McKeller's face as he was leaving. He guessed that Allie was probably gesturing toward him in some way that made her laugh. He just smiled and got into his car.

* * *

Randy Keene and his team were now asked to keep close tabs on Kathy Muller, Christy Amherst, and Sue Crull. Mason had already directed Randy to follow Lynda Laffarty. Randy reported to Mason when he returned to his office. Kathy Muller and Sue Crull were observed at lunch in Beverly Hills. They were overheard talking about Dalton Craig and his new girlfriend, as well as the last will revision of Carmen Craig. Mason asked, "Did you get any more detail than that?"

Randy said, "Well, they were discussing who they thought was listed in her will because they were conjecturing that neither Dalton nor Walker Craig was, but it was a guess."

Mason just whistled, "Anything else?"

Randy said, "I spotted Lynda returning from a shopping trip today, and two minutes after she returned home, Christy Amherst drove up her driveway and entered without knocking or ringing the bell."

Mason said, "Okay. Great work. You and I should meet early tomorrow to strategize and compare notes."

Randy said, "We can meet at the donut shop at 7 a.m. if you wish."

Mason said, "Perfect. I was just going to suggest that. You know cops and donuts!" They both laughed and ended the call. Mason's phone rang. It was Lynda Laffarty. He let the call go to voicemail, and he would listen to it later at the office.

* * *

Sydney McKeller went to Allie's office and asked her if everything was okay. Allie said, "Oh, I guess. That Detective just asked me some very personal questions that upset me. I will be fine. I see he bought some lingerie."

Sydney said, "Yeah, I know. He has good taste. It is nice to see a gentleman comfortable enough to make a purchase such as this with as much confidence as he did. If you don't mind me asking, what did he ask you that upset you? Maybe we should report it to his superiors."

Allie Campwick said, "He asked me whether I had an intimate relationship with Jennifer." Sydney walked to her, and they hugged for a long while until the front door's bell rang, signaling someone entering.

* * *

After the visit to Elegant Lace, Mason stopped at the liquor store and picked up a bottle of Tequila. He got back into his car and called Keisha Kane. She answered quickly this time, "Hello, Mr. Delsson. How long are you working today?"

Mason replied, "I have finished working today, Miss Kane, and wondered if you were available for a short visit."

Keisha Kane was now excited, "Why, Mr. Delsson, whatever do you want from me this evening?"

Mason said, "I have a bottle of your favorite Tequila, and I purchased you a gift. I would like to toast to your beauty and give you the gift." Keisha said, "I will leave the garage door open, drive in, and close it after you. I will be waiting in our favorite place with ice and limes at the ready. Hurry!"

When Mason returned to Keisha Kane's home, he drove into the open garage and parked next to her Mercedes. He grabbed the wrapped package from Elegant Lace, the bottle of Casos Amigos Tequila, and closed the garage door as he entered the house. He got a bit disoriented as he had come in the front door the last time he visited the Kane home. He walked through the kitchen and saw the grand staircase to the second floor. He walked silently up the staircase to the third room on the left. He heard the clinking of ice in glasses and knew she was there. He walked in and saw her. He thought that he would never get used to having his breath taken away just by the sight of her. Keisha looked up and smiled, "Hello, Stranger. It is so nice to see you again. I see you come bearing gifts."

Mason said, "I have a little something for you to thank you for your stunning hospitality and ravishing beauty."

Keisha blushed and said, "Open the bottle, my love, so we can toast to our new friendship." Mason undid the stopper of the Casos Amigos bottle and poured liberal amounts into each of the glasses Keisha had prepared on the coffee table.

Mason lifted both glasses, handing one to her, and lifted his glass in a toast.

Mason said, "To Keisha, the most beautiful and beguiling lady I have ever known."

Keisha slinked their glasses again and said, "To Mason Delsson. May our friendship be long-lasting and our lovemaking always passionate." They clinked glasses and each took a swallow.

* * *

Dalton Craig sat by the pool at his enormous home and sipped on his vodka and soda. He watched Sam Barfield come out of the house onto the patio carrying another large bottle of Grey Goose vodka and a pitcher of ice. Right behind him in a wild print bathing suit was James Thompson, his bodyguard and confidant. James went straight to the diving board, did a precision jackknife, and slipped into the water almost without a ripple. Dalton watched as James finally appeared at the other end of the pool, having swam its length all the way underwater. The water dripped off his body like water off a swan. He exited the pool without a ladder and came to the table. He said, "Sometimes you just need to cool off on hot days like these. May I join you gentlemen in some libation?"

Sam laughed, "As big as you are, who would deny you anything you might request? I am glad I am not a woman you might pursue!" All of them laughed.

Dalton poured each of them a healthy amount of vodka on ice with some twisted lime wedges. He handed each a glass and said, "Here is to the good life. May we live forever."

They clinked glasses and both said, "Here. Here." Then drank.

Sam started by asking, "How was your trip with Fitore to Tahoe?"

Dalton said, "It was magnificent until one of the ladies vacationing with Lynda and her friends went missing, then was found dead floating in the Lake."

Sam looked surprised, asking, "Did you know her?"

Dalton said, "Yes, as a matter of fact, I used to date her years ago. Fitore and I had dinner at the hotel, and she left to prepare for us being intimate together, and I stayed in the bar having one more drink. Jennifer Sandrew appeared next to me at the bar minutes later.

Sam interjected, "No kidding!"

Dalton continued, "Jennifer said to me, 'Well, hello, Mr. Craig. Is this seat taken?' I was a bit surprised to see her, but I bought her a drink. I told her I was with someone, and she explained her feelings for me and asked if we could get together again. I cordially declined after telling her how flattering it was for her to ask. She gulped down her drink and left, saying she was sorry to have bothered me, but she understood.

"I then received a call from my son. Walker, who seemed quite frantic after being interrogated by the police again. He felt like they were trying to accuse him of murdering his mother. I went back to the room. I left a note for Fitore as she was sleeping soundly from the liquor she had consumed.

"I jumped on my plane and returned here to L.A., where Walker and I talked most of the night until he had calmed down, and I felt he was stable. We had a plan in place to ensure you would be supporting him at the next encounter with the police.

"I returned to Tahoe the next morning, and Fitore was sunning naked on the patio of the room. We had a nice reunion. We went to dinner, and I heard that Jennifer Sandrew had been found washed up on the shore across the Lake. I consoled the ladies with Jennifer on the trip. I offered to bring her back on the plane to L.A. as we were returning the following day."

Sam said, "Wow, I should go write that down. It was a firsthand account of your steps during the visit to Tahoe and how you assisted in the return of the body to L.A. Are you feeling okay about all that?"

Dalton said, "I am saddened by her death and wonder what happened to the lady after she left me that night. I hope the police find out."

* * *

Keisha Kane opened the gift Mason Delsson had brought her. She was surprised and pleased that he had purchased some very expensive lingerie. It was from Elegant Lace, her favorite store. She said, "I must thank you properly for this very expensive gift, Mr. Delsson. I think I can do that best in my bedroom. Why don't you pour us another drink and meet me there?"

Mason said, "I like the way your mind works, Miss Kane. You should plan on me gifting you quite often in the future."

As she walked toward the bedroom, she said over her shoulder, "The gifts are only icing on the cake. I just want to thank you for keeping me company."

She was gone, and Mason made the drinks. He thought to himself that he had a lot of questions to ask the ladies who had vacationed in Lake Tahoe, as well as Dalton Craig, who just happened to be there, when one of his ex-girlfriends was found dead. Then he was distracted by the vision he saw as he entered Keisha's bedroom. Keisha wore the purple lingerie he had just purchased. It fit superbly, and she looked like a million dollars. He just whistled and said, "Wow. Keisha. That is the way all women should look when they are entertaining a gentleman. It is a perfect fit, and you look amazing."

Keisha said, "Thank you, kind sir. You have too many clothes on for this viewing and the official thank you that is about to be bestowed on you. Please disrobe, Mr. Delsson." Keisha climbed up onto the bed, and Mason handed her the drink he just made. He then stripped as quickly as he could. Once completely naked, he crawled up between her legs and began to lick and kiss his way from her ankles to her mouth.

He lingered as they kissed, then she broke away and said softly, "Please make love to me, Mason." For the next hour or so, Keisha thanked him for the gifts, and he provided the warmth and affection she desired. Once they reached their crescendo, they both lay in each other's arms, and they slept.

When Mason awoke, he dressed and drove back to his office. He told Keisha the case he was working on had just gotten a new twist. He sat at his desk and tried to jot down some questions for each of the ladies who went on the ill-fated trip to Lake Tahoe. At this point, he counted four deaths that may or may not be attributed to Mr. Dalton Craig. He had a hunch that the motive may be his late wife's last will revision.

* * *

Mason wondered if he could find out when the reading of the will would take place, if it had not happened already. He also wanted to know who the new lady in Dalton's life was. He worked into the wee hours of the night to complete all the tasks he had outlined for himself. He slept on the often-used, comfortable couch in his office. He would get a fresh start in the morning.

Mason awoke in the middle of the night. He looked at the clock on his desk in the office, and it said: 5:10 a.m. He was awakened by a nightmare. He remembered it, so he got up and grabbed a pad from the top of his desk. He wrote down the dream before it left his mind.

Carmen Craig was in the dream, and she was talking to the four other ladies whom he was investigating. Mason saw Belinda Cheeks, a female housekeeper in the Dalton Craig house. There was Karina Katrinka, a female actress/ director who worked for Dalton and died in a mysterious accident on a movie set at Dalton's Studios. Sara Ostrov, a famed movie star and producer at Dalton's Studios. The last woman was Jennifer Sandrew, a female who owned a lingerie shop but dated Dalton Craig off and on for many years. Carmen was talking to all of them, and she said in the dream: *We must get our revenge!* Mason woke with a start.

Mason looked at the list and realized, these five women all had been in some kind of relationship with Dalton, and now, they were all dead. He put on a pot of coffee to start his day.

* * *

Lynda Laffarty had received a call from Richard Bruce in Tahoe. The message he left said, "Lynda, I am on my way to LA as we speak. I will be in town for a week as I have two or three auditions. I will be at the Beverly Hilton. Maybe we can get together for dinner some evening. You have my number. Give me a call."

Lynda was glad she had stopped at Elegant Lace and purchased five new lingerie sets. She would call Richard later and invite him to her house. Then she thought twice and decided to take him to her favorite restaurant. She didn't know him well enough to bring him to the house. She did, however, find him delicious.

Lynda called Richard at 2 p.m. He answered on the second ring. "Hello, may I help you?" he said, not recognizing the number.

Lynda said, "Hello, Mr. Bruce. Yes, you can help me, all you want. This is Lynda Laffarty. How are you today?"

Richard Bruce was now a happy man. He said, "I am extremely better than I was five minutes ago. Thank you for getting back to me. I was wondering if you had any plans this evening for dinner?"

Lynda said, "As a matter of fact, I do." Richard was crestfallen. Lynda continued, "I am having a dinner meeting with a business associate. Can we meet on Saturday at 6:00 p.m.? Take an Uber to Spago on N. Canon Drive in Beverly Hills. I have reservations for 6:00 p.m. I hope that works for you. After dinner, we can have drinks at your hotel if you are interested in that."

Richard said, "All of that sounds perfect. I will be at the bar waiting. Thanks."

* * *

Mason reviewed his notes and thought his dream about these five ladies was a little unusual, if not unnerving. He would try to get in touch with Dalton Craig again. He called, and Sam Barfield, his lawyer, answered. Mason said, "Sam, this is Mason Delsson. LAPD. I would like another ten minutes with Dalton."

Sam said, "We are working at home today. Stop by anytime."

Mason said, "Thank you. I will be there in thirty minutes." He wanted to ask Dalton about the girl who died in Tahoe, and also when the will of his late wife would be read. If they were not forthcoming with the information, he realized that Sam Barfield's assistant, Jan Ridilla, who had gone to school with Mason, would know. Maybe he could get the information from her.

Mason then called Kathy Muller. She owned Retreat Two restaurant in L.A. He would try to see her today as well. He called the restaurant on the off chance it would be open this early. Kathy answered the phone on the first ring, "Hello, Retreat Two, This is Kathy, how may I help you?"

Mason said, "Hello, Ms. Muller. This is Mason Delsson, LAPD, I was wondering if you would be available this afternoon. I have a few questions I would like to ask you."

Kathy Muller replied, "You are in luck, Mr. Delsson. I am here at the restaurant, and I have already helped prepare things for lunch, so I am available. What time would you like to stop in?"

Mason said, "How about 1:30 p.m.?"

Kathy said, "Perfect. I'll see you then." They ended the call. Kathy reflected on her last interview with Mason and knew he would probably ask about Jennifer's death as well. She would help as much as she could.

Mason walked into Retreat Two. He was greeted by the hostess. She said, "Would you like a table for lunch?"

Mason said, "No, thank you. I am here to see Kathy Muller."

The hostess said, "I was expecting you. Please follow me, Sir."

Mason watched this tall blonde lead him to the back office, and it reminded him of watching the girls in the Miss America Pageant walk down the runway. She knocked on the first door next to the kitchen and heard Kathy Muller say, "Come in."

Mason was surprised when Kathy stood up behind the desk. She had on a Chef's jacket, and she appeared exactly how one would think a chef would dress. Kathy said, "Hello, Detective. Please have a seat."

Mason sat in one of the two chocolate brown leather-stuffed chairs in front of her desk. Looking around, he saw no windows in the office. There was, however, a flat-screen TV on the adjacent wall with a film running of people walking down the Boardwalk at what looked like Venice Beach. Mason began, "Miss Muller, please accept my deepest sympathies for the loss of your friend Jennifer Sandrew. It must have been quite a shock to be on vacation for relaxation and have this happen."

Kathy said, "Thank you, Detective. It was quite a shock. Please call me Kathy; Miss Muller makes me feel like an old school marm." She laughed as she sat back down in her expansive desk chair.

Mason then began his questioning that he had strategized in the past week, "Kathy, I have been thinking about all the deaths we have seen in the past few months. We have had five females die. They all have some connection to Dalton Craig. What do you make of that?"

Kathy replied, "I am not sure I understand what you're asking, Detective."

Mason rephrased his question, "Kathy, do you think Dalton Craig has had anything to do with the five women's deaths in his small social circle?"

Kathy said, "Well, Detective, I was just thinking about that exact thing when we flew back to L.A. from Lake Tahoe. He lost his wife, Carmen. His housekeeper, Belinda, was killed in a car accident not far from his residence. Sara Ostrov, whom he dated and worked with, was found dead from an apparent fall off a balcony on a back production lot of his studios at Gemini. Then Karina Katrinka was found dead in a theater on another back lot of Gemini Studios.

Finally, Jennifer Sandrew, whom Dalton dated, was found floating in the water on the west side of Lake Tahoe. I think there is a connection. They all may have been pressuring Dalton to either take care of them, give them money or security, or put them in his will. Maybe he wanted to rekindle their relationship and had turned him down."

Mason was impressed that Kathy had put together the same scenario that had woken him up the other night from his nightmarish dream. He said, "I have put that same deduction together. What do you think could be the main motivation for the killings?"

Kathy said, "Oh. So now you are calling these deaths murders?"

Mason replied, "I guess until I can prove otherwise, I am referring to them as such. How much do you know about Carmen Craig's love life outside her marriage to Dalton?"

Kathy laughed, "That is the last question I expected to hear from you today. Wow! You folks don't pull any punches, do you?"

Mason replied, "I am a professional. I have been trained to ask hard questions. I am blunt, so those being interrogated can't think of a good lie. I have found that people with something to hide tend to hem and haw when asked a point-blank question."

Kathy said, "Now I am being interrogated?"

Mason replied with a straight face, "This is an example of what I am talking about. I have asked you four questions, but you have provided no answers. but replied with four questions. This is how those people stall for time to figure out an acceptable scenario to provide as an answer instead of the truth.

Kathy laughed, "I find it interesting talking to you. You are the first man I have met in a long time who can get into an exchange with me and present a challenge."

Mason said, "Oh, so you think this is a checker game to provide you with a challenge, so you can tell this to your cronies when they are looking for drinking stories? Well, let me explain to you, Miss Muller, I am a police Detective. I could very well have subpoenaed you to come downtown to my office to answer these questions under the scrutiny of a polygraph. So, meeting you on your turf, so your day is not disrupted, I expect you to answer my questions with the information I am requesting rather than trying to outwit me. If you continue, you will find yourself on the murder suspect list and potentially in a holding cell at LAPD Headquarters.

Kathy said, "Well, Detective, you don't have to get your shorts all twisted in a bunch. Although your statement sounds a bit like harassment, I will answer your questions to the best of my ability, and I apologize if you have felt violated."

Mason said, "That discourse may make for some interesting repartee for your ladies' parties; however, Miss Muller, my question still is, what do you know about the men in Carmen's life during her marriage to Dalton?"

Kathy got a serious look on her face and said, "I remember Carmen became disenchanted with Dalton's infidelity after five or ten years. She was tired of watching him have trysts with this or that ingenue. Carmen decided that her loneliness was no longer going to restrict her sexual satisfaction. She dated Patrick J. Hart, who runs Sagittarius International Pictures. They were just good friends, I think, but she adored him. She then went out with William Truman, who was a New York lawyer who came out to Los Angeles to become one of the best-known lawyers/agents to the stars."

Mason then asked, "Do you know who was named in Carmen's will?

Kathy said, "No, we never spoke about her money and who she would leave it to. Sorry, I could not be more helpful. "

Mason said, "That is all I have at this time, Miss Muller, so I will say goodbye." He rose and left to return to his office. On his way there, he called his old friend, Janet Ridilla. She worked as an aide to Sam Barfield. Sam was Dalton's lawyer, so he may have worked with Carmen also.

* * *

Janet answered the phone, "Office of Samuel Barfield, how may I help you?"

Mason said, "Hello, my friend, this is Mason Delsson. How have you been? I miss seeing you out and about."

Janet was always happy to hear from Mason. He always made her laugh. She replied, "So nice to hear from you again. I am well. I keep myself busy, and I, too, miss getting together with old friends. What can I do for you?"

Mason asked, "Did Sam work as Carmen Craig's attorney?" Mason said, "Do you know when Carmen's will is to be read and who the beneficiaries at Sagittarius are?"

Janet said, "That is privileged information, my friend, but because I trust you need it for a case you are working on, I will have to go get the file. I will put you on hold for a minute while I retrieve the information. I'll be back."

Janet returned to the call and said, "Mason. This is private information, so keep it under your hat if anyone asks how you got this. Carmen Craig and I were friends. She spoke to me about the beneficiaries of her estate. She felt that Dalton already had enough money, and her son, Walker, would inherit his father's money, so Carmen decided to donate a large part of her estate to Horse Breeding Associations across the country. I think, if my memory serves me, she named a dozen people to receive some money from her estate. The list of names is Jen Sandrew, Sara Ostrov, Christie Amherst, Belinda Cheeks, Lynda Laffarty, Kathy Muller, Christopher Ericsson, several cousins, and me. There are twenty-one different designations."

Mason wrote down the names and asked, "Janet, how much is each of you going to receive?"

Janet said, "I know it was a significant amount. but I have no exact figures. We'll find out next Thursday at the reading of the will."

Mason asked, "Where is the will being read? Who is reading the will?" Mason was very excited to get this clue and find out the amount each of these individuals was to receive. He knew this information could provide some clues for determining the perpetrator of these killings.

Janet replied, "Carmen's financial advisor and friend, Erick Schrank, is reading the will on Thursday at 10 a.m. at the Beverly Wilshire Hotel on Wilshire and El Camino Drive. Did you need an invitation?"

Mason replied, "No, I think I will just go with you, Miss Ridilla." They made plans, then hung up.

Mason returned to his office and looked at the names from the list Janet had given him. There were six women he knew. The one man whose name he was given was Erickson Howard, the Craig Estate Stable Master. The fourteen people were a mystery until the day the will was read. Mason thought that the day of the reading would be an interesting experience. Hopefully, it would shed some light on those who might have killed for money.

* * *

Fitore Fantazee walked into her house after picking up the mail from the front hall and dropped everything at the kitchen table. She picked up the phone and immediately dialed up her new friend, Robin Ripple. Robin was working at the restaurant but was on a break. She looked at the phone and didn't recognize the number, so she let it go to voice mail. Robin went back to work.

Fitore left a message for Robin Ripple, the lovely girl she had been served by in her request for room service in Lake Tahoe. The message she left was formal and to the point. - Robin, this is Fitore. I am sorry I haven't called since we met for the photo shoot, but I was whisked back to L.A. by the gentleman I was staying with in Tahoe. I have decided to set up an audition for Monday afternoon. I have left a paid round-trip ticket for you at the United Airlines ticket counter at the airport in Lake Tahoe. If you can get away for the audition, pick up the ticket and fly to LAX. Text me at the number I gave you and let me know what flight you will be on. I will send a car to pick you up and bring you to my home. I thought it would be easier for you and fun for us to continue our getting to know one another phase of our relationship. If you have any questions or can't come for some reason, please call me and let me know. We can adjust those plans to meet your needs. Regards, FF.

Robin was ecstatic when she read the text from Fitore. She didn't want to sound overanxious, so she had to wait thirty minutes before texting her back a message that read: Fitore, thank you so much for the kind invitation. I have some time off coming, and the season is slowing down so it's perfect timing. I will take my two-week vacation, fly out Friday, and be in LA by 1:15 p.m. If that works for you, just text OK. It is so gracious of you to invite me into your home. I'll wait to receive my tickets and follow your directions on where to go. I can't wait. This is so exciting. I can't thank you enough. Warmest Regards, Robin-

Fitore had just stepped out of the shower and noticed the text. She was nude when she read it and felt a warm tingling in her core as she thought about her new friend and soon-to-be housemate. She was excited to introduce Robin to her team as well as her new lover, Dalton Craig. Fitore texted back: There are fresh sheets on the bed. A car will be there at 1:00 to pick you up at the airport. Bring a swimsuit or two, a cocktail dress, and some sweats. That's all you'll need. C U, F.

Robin was packed and ready as she walked into the Manager's office at the hotel and asked for her two-week vacation. The Manager was just about to ask her if she needed some time off, so she granted the wish and gave her two weeks' pay to hold her over and guarantee she would return.

Fitore Fantazee picked up her phone and sent a text to Dalton Craig. Dalton, I have a new ingenue arriving on Friday afternoon. I would like to entertain her for a while, then take her to dinner. Can you meet us at Andy's at 6 p.m.? It's on Santa Monica Boulevard. Anderson Paak owns it. He and Bruno Mars are generally there at night if they are in town. It will be fun. Thanks, Fitore.

Dalton Craig was just about to call Fitore Fantazee when he got her text. He called and left a message. I will meet you at Andy's at 6 p.m. Thanks.

Dalton reflected on how many women he had been with since his first wife, Lynda, and he had split up. He considered himself to be a very lucky man. The women were all beautiful, sexy, and he enjoyed their company. He wished that he had been more loving toward his second wife, Carmen. He realized, in that moment, that she was the one he was really trying to replace in his life. He began to cry, thinking about the opportunity he had missed with her.

5

ERICK SCHRANCK WAS A FINANCIAL ADVISOR to many of the stars. He handled billions of dollars for his clients, managing their investment portfolios. Carmen Craig was one of those clients. Erick had an office in L.A. on Wilshire Boulevard, but there were too many people to count in the Beverly Wilshire Hotel conference room that Thursday morning. He was prepared to read the final will of Carmen E. Craig. Erick's secretary, Denise DeLeo, counted heads as all the attendees finally took their seats. She handed Erick a note that said: 20 of 21 here.

Dalton Craig sat at the opposite end of the conference table from Erick. Also at the table were Walker Craig, Carmen's son, Kathy Muller, Christie Amherst, Allie Campwick, Lynda Laffarty, Christopher Ericsson, and Denise at Erick's side, taking notes. There were additional relatives of those present and Mason Delsson, who sat in the very last row.

Erick Schranck began to speak, and the chatter ceased immediately. He began, "Welcome all to the Reading of Carmen Craig's Will. This was changed and finalized a month before her passing. I have papers to sign for those who are named within this document. Please do not leave before signing, or you will forfeit your inheritance. These were the wishes of Carmen Craig. Carmen Craig's total assets at the time of her death were two trillion dollars.

There were discernible gasps from those attending the reading. People were looking at one another and wondering. Their thoughts went wild. Each had a strained look on their face. They refocused and were brought back to the present by Erick Schranck, who continued to speak.

Erick said, "Carmen writes."

"If you are hearing this, you have heard of my passing, and my will is being read. Please know that I loved you all and will miss you dearly. These are the final assignments of my net worth. My lawyer has reviewed this document, and my financial advisor will read it now:

For my Horses' maintenance and Stable upkeep, I leave $200,000,000.

To the ASPCA, I leave $100,000,000.

To my Stable Master, Erickson Howard & Staff, I leave $4,000,000.

To Ian Cheeks, son of my late Housekeeper, I leave $5,000,000.

To Owen Cheeks, Belinda's youngest son, I leave... $5,000,000.

To Lynda Deene, partner of Sara Ostrov, I leave $10,000,000.

To Dolores & Del Madison, I leave $35,000,000.

To my Sister/Brother's children, Mark C. I leave $25,000,000;

Jim M. I leave $25,000,000; & Sarah E. I leave $25,000,000.

To my favorite Charities: Hospitals. I leave $20,000,000.

Cancer Research, I leave $20,000,000.

Brain Injury Research, I leave $20,000,000.

To my friend, Kathy Muller, I leave $10,000,000.

To my friend, Christy Amherst, I leave $10,000,000.

To my friend, Alexandra Campwick, I leave $10,000,000.

To my friend, Lynda Laffarty, I leave $10,000,000.

To my nephew, Christopher Ericsson, I leave $20,000,000.

To my stepson, Eric Slay, I leave $20,000,000.

To my Fiduciary, Erick Schranck, I leave $15,000,000.

To Erick Schranck's Assistant, Denise DeLeo, I leave $5,000,000.

To lawyer, Sam Barfield, for will contests, I leave $2,988,000.

To Sam Barfield's Assistant, Janet Ridilla, I leave $3,000,000.

To my son, Walker Craig, to repay money spent on me, I leave $10,000.

To Dalton Craig, I leave $100 for each marital infidelity $12,000.

Subtotal $600,000,000.

The final assignment of the estate's remaining assets will be put in trust for THE CEW of America $1,999,400,000,000 .

This is the end of my reading of the will. Any questions or formal protests can be made to the financial advisor's office within 15 days in writing. Thank you all, and for those of you named, please see my assistant, Denise, before you leave. If you leave before signing these papers before the advisor walks out, you will forfeit any monies assigned, and they will be returned to the trust. If anyone wants to contest the will, please let Denise know, and she will give you the forms that you must sign. Just so you know, the trust will pay any inheritance tax on the money that was just awarded. If you have any questions, please have your tax accountant call my office."

Erick Schranck folded his paperwork and stood up. He said, "Ladies and Gentlemen, thank you all for attending this reading. Enjoy the rest of your day.

The crowd of folks began rising from their chairs and speaking softly to one another. Many began a line in front of Denise DeLeo's end of the table to sign the forms that were required. Everyone seemed to be in a state of shock, not only because of the amount of money they were about to receive, but also the money that was left in a foundation trust for who knows what purpose. Many questions were asked about what the CEW was. Erick responded that he was not at liberty to divulge that information.

Dalton Craig and his son, Walker, immediately walked out of the conference room. The chatter within the room was deafening. Erick had to tell everyone that they needed to keep their voices to a minimum until they had left the room.

Sam Barfield knew that Dalton would be hopping mad, but Sam decided to stay to sign his papers. He would go directly to Dalton's home afterward and devise a plan to file papers to contest the will. He asked for them from Denise, then he left.

Lynda returned to her home after listening to the reading of Carmen's Will. Lynda was disheartened that she received the same money as her friend but understood no one left their husband's ex-wife any money. In this case, Carmen had.

When Lynda walked in the door, she put down her purse and keys and clicked on the answering machine to listen to the messages. She had one message. It was Richard reminding her that she was to meet him at Spago for dinner. Lynda stepped into the shower, dried herself, performed her magic getting ready, and was in an Uber, forty-five minutes before six o'clock.

Lynda walked into the bar area at Spago and found a seat in the middle of the bar. A handsome bartender was working behind the long, oak bar as she sat on the stool. She thought she remembered him, but as he got closer to her, she could read his nametag. It read: Ryan M. Now she remembered him. He had served her before, but she thought it was in Lake Tahoe.

Ryan walked over to Lynda and said, "Well, hello, Miss Lynda. Fancy seeing you here. Can I mix you a drink?"

Lynda said, "Hi, Ryan. I'll have my usual."

Ryan answered back quickly, "Super. One dry martini on the rocks, and pass the vermouth over the glass quickly. Coming right up."

Lynda was impressed. She must have made an impression on young Ryan. She would keep that in the back of her head. He was certainly attractive and just her type.

Ryan came back with the drink and said, "This one's on me, Miss Lynda. Just holler when you need another."

Lynda was going to say something very seductive, but her thoughts were interrupted by a voice in her ear. The male voice said, "You look absolutely delicious. May I sit in this chair?" Lynda turned and saw Richard Bruce. He was a magnificent-looking man. He had dark curly black hair, was a shade under six feet tall, was built like a linebacker for the Rams, and had the most beautiful blue eyes. He smiled at her, and Lynda melted into her barstool. She could barely speak when he sat in the seat next to her.

Richard began, "It is so fabulous to see you again. You never fail to impress, not only with your attire, but also with how well you fill out whatever you wear. It is like Christmas to my eyes. How have you been?"

Lynda was flattered but leery of getting too far ahead of things. She said, "I am starving. Why don't we sit at our table and order, then we can chat?

Richard said, "Can we get you another cocktail?" as he motioned for the bartender.

Ryan was in front of them in a flash. "Yes, sir. What can I get you?"

Richard said, "She'll have another, and I'll have a Jack and ginger with just a little ice."

* * *

Sam Barfield drove to the Craig Estate and parked in front. He walked back to the pool area, and there sat Dalton and Walker at an umbrella table, close to the water. Dalton said to Sam, "What the hell is CEW?"

Sam knew it would be the first question to be answered so he had done some research on the drive to Dalton's after the will reading. He said, "I guess it is that either a sister or cousin to Carmen, will be the trustee for the money she left. I can't believe that Carmen would cut off both of you from her estate."

Dalton said, "I am not surprised with all the philandering I have done over the years, but to leave her son without an inheritance is shocking."

Walker looked up from his cell phone and said, "I just googled CEW and there is no such person or organization listed. Maybe I should call Grandma Warner and ask her if she knows."

Sam said, "Dalton, did you want me to contest the will on your behalf?"

Dalton was as furious as Sam could remember. Dalton responded, "That is the least you should be thinking about. I want to know how my late wife had over a trillion dollars. She rarely picked up a check at any restaurant we dined at. I want a full accounting of my bank accounts to make sure she was not siphoning off money from them."

Walker said, "I just spoke to Grandma Warner. She invited me to her house for dinner. I will attend and report back my findings."

* * *

Kathy Muller, Allie Campwick, and Christy Amherst were walking out of the Beverly Wilshire Hotel together. Kathy said, "What in the hell is CEW?"

Christy said, "Whatever it is, they are worth a boatload of money. It is of no consequence to me, however, as I just inherited $10 million."

Kathy replied, "I hear you, girl. I just can't help wondering if we have all been duped. I will call Lynda and see what her take is on the matter."

Christy said, "What do you mean duped?"

Kathy said, "Far be it from me to look a gift horse in the mouth. I was jotting down the numbers that Erick read off and I got six hundred million dollars in assignments before we got to the one

Trillion, 999 Billion, 400 Million dollars assigned to CEW. You would have thought that over the past fifteen years or so, we would have heard of this CEW organization before now. Also, why did she not leave her husband, Dalton, or her son, Walker, any of her wealth?"

As Kathy Muller unlocked her car and got in, she said to Allie and Christy, "I will call Sue and invite her and you both to dinner at my house tonight around 7 p.m. I will throw a couple of steaks on the grill and make a nice salad. I have been dying to have you guys taste the wine I bought the last time I was in Sonoma."

Christy said, "You're worried about two trillion dollars? You have more to think about than anyone else. Besides, you have ten million dollars to spend or at least decide what to do with it. I know I am thinking exactly that."

As they got into their separate vehicles, Allie Campwick said, "Can you imagine that Carmen was worth TWO TRILLION DOLLARS? I am very appreciative of the money she left us all, but you could have blown me over with a feather when he announced what she was worth at the time of her death."

* * *

Mason stayed at the reading until Janet Ridilla had signed her papers to receive her inheritance. They walked quietly to his car. When he held the door for her, she slid into the front seat and buckled her seatbelt. Mason got in by the driver's door, buckled up, and started the car. He looked over at Janet, who seemed to still be shocked. He said, "How does it feel to be a millionaire?"

Janet was still flabbergasted, "I don't know if it has sunk in yet. It is starting to feel good, though. What did you think of the announcements that were made?"

Mason said, "Did you know about this CEW trust? They seemed to be the big winners today. Much to the obvious disgruntlement of her husband and son. Would Sam know anything about this trust business?"

Janet replied, "I will ask, but judging from the look on his face when the last assignment was announced, his jaw was down to his chest, and his eyes looked like he had just done two lines of cocaine!"

They both laughed, and Janet said, "Keep your eye on the road, Mr. Delsson. I want a chance to spend some of my inheritance."

Mason stopped laughing and asked, "Janet, why do you think she left you that much money?"

Janet answered, "Well, now that I have had a few minutes to reflect, I have done many menial jobs for Ms. Craig over the years. I wish I knew more about this mysterious CEW. I mean, inheriting that kind of money must be astounding."

Mason's car had reached Janet's home. He stopped and let her out. She parted by saying, "Thanks for the ride, Mason. I owe you lunch at your convenience. Enjoy the rest of your day."

Mason wondered what his new flame, Keisha Kane, was up to. He phoned her and she picked up after only two rings, saying, "Well, Howdy, stranger. How have you been?"

Mason said, "Busy. I noticed you answered after two rings. I am on my way past your place and wondered if you'd go out to dinner with me this evening. You can wear your dressy clothes with some exotic frilly things underneath them."

Keisha replied, "I am hungry for food as well as you. I can be ready in ten minutes as I just got out of the shower. How fancy do you want me?"

Mason said, "You are always fancy. Whatever you wear gets my blood boiling, so be comfortable."

Keisha said, "Okay. I'll be ready."

Mason replied, "I will be there in ten minutes. I will pull around to the back door." He hung up the phone.

He reflected on what Janet had said. She told Mason she wished she knew more about the CEW organization that received almost two trillion dollars. He had a hunch and would wait to research it when he returned to his office tomorrow.

He pulled up to Keisha Kane's back entrance and tooted the horn twice. He barely finished when she bolted out the door. He noticed that she had no cast on her leg. She smiled as she approached the side door. She got in, and her perfume followed, filling his nostrils with his new favorite aroma. She leaned over to him and kissed him long and hard on the lips. She said, "Hello, Handsome. Thanks for the invite. I am so happy to be seeing you again. Where are you taking me…for dinner?"

Mason replied, "My favorite Italian restaurant, Vitello's. It's in Studio City off Ventura Boulevard."

Keisha said, "I have heard of it, but I've never been. I love trying new places. What is their signature dish?"

Mason said, "I don't know if they have one, but my favorite is the ravioli."

They drove from Keisha Kane's on Beverly Drive in Beverly Hills to Vitello's in Studio City. The drive took just under thirty minutes.

They used valet parking and walked into the restaurant. They were greeted by Christy Christia, the Hostess. She seated them by the window at the side of the dining room. Mason and Keisha sat on the same side of the booth. They could look out the window at the beautiful sunset over the Pacific Ocean. Their waiter approached with a towel over his arm. Keisha thought it was fancy. He said, "Good Evening. My name is Ryan, and I will be your waiter this evening. May I start you out with a cocktail?"

Ryan was the son of Kathy Muller, who owned Vitello's, as well as Retreat Two in Marina Del Ray. He was destined to become the Manager/owner of Vitello's. His mother wanted him to learn each facet of the operation by doing that job, so he could relate to the needs of his staff concerning hiring and management.

Mason pointed to Keisha, who asked Mason, "Should we drink Tequila tonight?"

Mason said to the waiter, "Bring us a small bottle of Casamigos, two glasses, and some limes."

When Ryan returned minutes later, he set down the bottle, two glasses, a large saltshaker, and a plate full of wedge-cut limes. Ryan asked, "Shall I open the bottle and pour, sir?" Mason nodded. Ryan poured each one of them a shot. They did their first shot without salt or lime.

Keisha said, "I would like to order my food, the IN-Vogue Salad and the Shrimp Scampi."

Mason followed with his order, "I will have the Strawberry Arugula with goat cheese with the vinaigrette dressing. For my entree, I'll have House Ravioli with butternut squash sauce and pesto." Ryan said without writing anything down, "Very good. I will bring the salads out in a few minutes."

As Ryan left, Mason poured the second shot of Tequila for him and Keisha. Salt and lime were used this time. Keisha leaned over to whisper into Mason's ear, "I hope the dinner doesn't take long, I have another set of lingerie that I would like to get your opinion on. Oh, and by the way, I am not wearing any underwear. Maybe that will motivate you to finish the meal quickly." They laughed and drank.

After dinner, Mason and Keisha were both drunk. They had left but one shot in the bottle of Casamigos. Mason paid their check, and they walked outside where an Uber was waiting for them. Mason left his car rather than drive Keisha home. They stumbled into the rear entrance of Keisha's home, and both began undressing the other. Keisha stopped him and said, "I think I would like a nightcap. You get the drinks, and I'll change into something more comfortable." She walked to the bedroom, and Mason went to the bar.

He poured two shots of Tequila without spilling a drop. He was pleased with himself. Now the challenge he faced was to walk to the bedroom without spilling any Tequila. He walked slowly. He was glad he did because as he walked into the bedroom, Keisha was already sitting at the end of the bed, waiting. She had on a flowing lavender, floor-length silk robe. Mason could see she had on a bra and panties set underneath. Both were skimpy, and both were dark purple.

Mason said, "I am glad I was prepared. I almost dropped the drinks. You look amazing. You are sexy when you wear stuff like that, but you're even sexier when you are naked."

"I'll drink to that." Keisha stood, dropped her robe and took her drink from Mason, clinked his glass, and downed the shot. She handed him back her empty glass and unsnapped her bra, what little there was of it. She quickly stepped out of her thong and crawled onto the bed. She said, "I am ready. Get your clothes off, NOW!!!"

Mason was awakened by the sun shining through Keisha's bedroom window. He looked to his left, and he let his eyes roam over her nude body. He knew she was not that young and had no enhancements, but he was amazed by her firm, supple body. He got lost in the view as he heard her whisper, "Good morning, are you drooling over this body or are you still drunk from last night?"

Mason laughed and said, "Lady, sue me, but I will look at that body, dressed or undressed, for as long as my eyes still work. You are wonderful to look at and even nicer to play with. Each time I wake up, after a night of loving you, I just have to pinch myself to see whether or not I am dreaming. It is a very special feeling to see you like this in the morning, knowing our lovemaking is so perfect."

Keisha whispered again, "Do you have time for another session? I need a quick shower, then I want to jump your bones again."

Mason said, "As a matter of fact, I have nothing pressing until much later this afternoon. Let me wash your back." They showered and returned to the bedroom, after grabbing a quick cup of coffee. Mason kissed her all over, then she returned the favor. They made love for what seemed like hours but was much shorter, and after their very loud crescendo, they rested.

Keisha said, "It is afternoon, did you want me to make you some lunch?"

Mason laughed, "Boy, how the time flies when you are in my arms. I have to shave and dress. I have an appointment in an hour, but thanks anyway. I will take a rain check."

Mason shaved, dressed, and kissed Keisha, who was naked in her bed. He said, "If you get lonely, call me. I will just be trying to find a murderer." She kissed him back, said goodbye, then fell back to sleep.

* * *

Dalton Craig sat at his desk planning his next movie. He wanted to make it in Paris. He thought about his secretary, Jodi Panicee, wanting a vacation. He would send her to Paris to find a location like the one they had discussed for his next film. Dalton called her into the office. He said, "Jodi, I need you to go to Paris and find the locations for the next movie. You can take a friend with you. Spend the time vacationing on the company's dime. I will have my plane fly you there, and you can pick a hotel. I recommend the Ritz in Paris. Get the Executive suite. It is 4000 francs per night, but well worth it. The Ritz is a three-block walk to the Seine, and a six-block walk to the Eiffel Tower. You can take the corporate card with you to charge dinners and such."

Jodi was thrilled, "Thank you so much, Dalton. I will find a few great locations and get lots of pictures. Of course, as usual, I will make all the arrangements with the local officials to get permits, etc. I will be gone for eight days. Thank you for this assignment. It will be a pleasure to do the research for this film." She left Dalton's office and called her friend, Greg Solomet, hoping he was available.

Greg Solomet was living in California. He was tired of the everyday grind of his 9 a.m. to 5 p.m. office gig, so he decided to try his hand at acting. He felt like he could pull the wool over anyone's eyes and get from them what he needed. He had met Jodi Panicee in the Retreat Two Bar about three months ago. They had talked about going to France together. He was looking to buy a piece of property. She was just looking to experience the romance of the City of Light, as well as get a little work done for Dalton Craig.

Greg answered his phone without recognizing the number. "Hello, Solomet. I hope you are well. I would like you to join me on a trip to Paris. How soon can you pack a bag?"

Greg remembered her voice instantly, "Hello, Jodi. I am well. Tell me the details of your proposed trip."

Jodi said, "I will pick you up in a limo on Friday at 10 a.m. We will fly in my boss's jet to Paris. I have booked us a room at the Paris Ritz Hotel in the Executive Suite for eight nights. I have to work on setting up locations for the company's next film, but it will be an all-expense-paid vacation for us. Interested?"

Greg laughed, "Well, Ms. Panicee. I would love to accompany you to Paris. I am looking to purchase some property there, and coincidentally, I spoke with my realtor there yesterday. This works out beautifully. I can see the properties he has found for me, I can see Paris again, and I can have the pleasure of your company for eight glorious nights. My bag is packed, and I await the limo on Friday."

Jodi was elated. "That is fantastic. I will see you Friday morning at 10." She hung up the phone and began packing her bag with her most daring lingerie, eighteen of her fanciest dresses, and of course, a few toys to heighten the sex. She thought about the last time she and Greg had been together. She shivered. He was the consummate lover and was seemingly head over heels for Jodi. How exciting this would be.

* * *

Deyna Doll was a sparkplug of Ecuadorian birth. She had met Walker Craig when they were taking classes together at the University of California, Los Angeles - Berkeley. She was working on her master's degree in business administration. Walker was seemingly just spending his father's money. They dated a few times, and it became obvious that there was incredible chemistry between them. She was the manager of the Los Alamitos Racetrack. She worked for Christy Amherst. They handled a ton of cash at the track, so she hired a security firm to make sure it was handled with care.

Walker sent the security company his father, Dalton, used at the Gemini studios over to the Racetrack,. This turned out to be a fantastic marriage for both of them. Walker made some money on the referral, and Deyna covered the security for Christy Amherst.

Walker Craig was sitting around the pool at his father's house. He had two gins and tonics today, so he couldn't drive. He wanted to see Deyna Doll today. He called the driver, James, and told him he was going to the racetrack today.

James Thompson knew that the only track that interested Walker was the Los Alamitos Racetrack. He would be able to visit his friend, Tonya Mountain, who worked supervising all the betting ticket windows at the racetrack. James brought the limo around to the front of the Craig Estate, waiting for Walker. He came out dressed like he was going to the Kentucky Derby.

James Thompson drove Walker in the limousine to the Los Alamitos Racetrack. He dropped Walker at the door and said, "I will park the limo and be in shortly. I want to visit my friend, Tonya. I will be at the betting windows, then I will come find you." Walker barely acknowledged James and walked into the door of the racetrack. James parked the limo in the VIP lot as usual. and went in through the same door.

James saw Tonya working at a betting window. He knew that meant she was filling in for someone. He waved, and she waved back. He went to find Walker. It was a quick search as Walker had found Deyna Doll working at the last betting window, closest to the track seating doors. That meant they were very short-staffed today. James heard the bell sound for what looked like the fifth race. That meant betting stopped, and the windows automatically closed. The patrons then all left the windows to go outside to watch the race.

All of a sudden, chaos ensued. Seven or eight men burst into the betting window areas through the back entrance. They brandished long guns and wore masks. They were all dressed in dark blue coveralls, which were the uniforms of all the horse paddock staff at the racetrack. One tall man was the leader and yelled at the tellers, "Open your money drawers, then get on the floor. Anyone hitting the alarm will be shot." The robbers then began to work in pairs, loading money into their bags and making sure the tellers were lying face down.

Deyna Doll had opened her drawer, lay on the ground and reached out to hit the alarm. As Walker stood on the other side of Deyna's window, he saw one of the men dressed in black aim at Deyna. Walker screamed, "NO, NO, NO!" The man in black shot at Deyna, then shot at Walker. He must have emptied the clip as he reloaded, as the leader yelled for all of them to move out. James crawled on his hands and knees to get to Walker. He didn't know how many were injured, but his main concern was Walker.

The robbers must have finished their mission at the window. As they left through the back door, they dropped two teargas canisters behind the tellers. James heard a lady scream, "They are gone. Somebody hit the alarm, I can't see mine." James continued to treat Walker's wounds. He had been hit in the left shoulder. James removed his shirt and tried to stop the bleeding.

Walker said, "Deyna, are you okay?" Deyna did not reply.

James said to Walker, "Can you walk? We need to get out of here. We can deal with Deyna later."

Walker blacked out. He had lost some blood and went into shock. James saw that he had been hit more than once. Racetrack security came rushing into the betting area from the viewing stands. They used walkie-talkies to radio for help from the paramedic units scattered around the racetrack. The paramedics arrived within minutes and began CPR and treatment.

The police arrived within minutes after that, as the scene got very loud, as there was a lot of yelling from the tellers as well as the police. The area was cleared of tear gas, as all the doors were open. You could hear multiple sirens of approaching emergency and police vehicles.

James watched as paramedics, with stretchers, arrived in the area. They attended Walker as well as some others behind the windows. James called Dalton on his cell phone. When Dalton answered, James said, "I am at the track with Walker. The place was robbed, and he got shot. Paramedics are here and will take him to the hospital. I will go with him and call when I know where we are going."

Dalton said, "Oh, my Lord. Call me when you hear. Is it bad?"

James said, "Too early to tell. I will call when I know anything." They ended the call.

The paramedics asked James, "Are you with him? Is that your shirt?" James nodded. The paramedic said, "Did you know you were hit?"

James was shocked. "No. The adrenaline must have kicked in." James was given treatment quickly for two superficial wounds on his head.

The paramedics had Walker on a stretcher and said to James, "Can you walk? You can come with us to the hospital in the ambulance. I have a shirt that may fit you if you want."

James said, "How is my friend?" The paramedic lifted his side of the stretcher and said, "His vitals are stable, but he has lost a lot of blood. We'll know better when we get him over to Los Alamitos Medical Center on Cherry and Katella. It is only a few blocks from here."

As they walked out to the ambulance, James saw another stretcher come out and noticed it was Deyna Doll. The woman that Walker was talking to when they were shot. James couldn't tell what her condition was, but he figured her going to the hospital meant she was still alive.

In the ambulance, James called Dalton, who picked up his phone immediately. He yelled to James, "What's happening?"

James replied, "We are in an ambulance and just pulling into the hospital at the Medical Center in Los Alamitos. Walker is still unconscious but is receiving oxygen, and his wounds will be examined first. Are you coming to the Medical Center?"

Dalton said, "We are on our way. I will have Sam drive me. How are you?"

As James was taken into a treatment room at the Medical Center, he said to Dalton, "I didn't even know I was shot until the paramedics got to the Racetrack. I am fine so far. I will update you when you get here. Talk to you soon."

The ER doctor came in immediately. Dr. Gracia asked, "How are you feeling?" James responded, "I am fine. I didn't even know I was shot."

The doctor laughed, "You wouldn't believe how many times I have heard that. It looks like you have two wounds. One on the side of your head, but above the left ear. The second is right in the part of your hair. They are both superficial and can be closed with just a few stitches. We will have you out of here in no time."

The nurse, Diane Deal, entered the treatment room with the supplies the doctor needed. She said to James, "You look very familiar. Have we met before?"

James replied, "Yes, I think you went out with my friend Walker Craig."

Diane turned red. She immediately was embarrassed, remembering how that encounter ended. Suffice it to say, it ended poorly. She said, "Oh, now I remember. Thanks."

James asked the doctor, "How is my friend, Walker Craig? I rode with him in the ambulance."

The doctor said, "That is confidential information, and I am not at liberty to discuss his status with you. Are you family? FYI, I don't know the status of all the cases that come in. I only know those that I am working on."

James looked at Diane but said nothing. His eyes seemed to ask her to check on Walker. She knowingly nodded and left the treatment room. She knew Walker would not want to see her, especially if he was here being treated, but she vowed to find out.

Dalton sat in the waiting room, full of worry and waiting to hear how his son's condition was progressing. Dalton thought of Walker's mother, Carmen, and wondered what she would have done. Sam Barfield was there, but he couldn't confide in him about his personal feelings. He was afraid he might lose Walker. Sam tried to engage Dalton in conversation, but Dalton was very quiet and unresponsive. Sam worried about whether Dalton could take another death in his immediate family.

James Thompson entered the waiting room and saw Dalton. Dalton stood and gasped in horror as he saw the bandages wrapped around James' head. Dalton said, "Oh, my goodness, James. You were shot as well?"

James replied, "Just a couple of scratches. I'll be fine. Do you think I should stay with Walker? Maybe we should send some security, and I will stay with you. Thoughts?"

Dalton responded immediately, "You should go home and relax. Take some time to recover for a few days. I will call and get security for both of us, just in case. I will have Sam drive you home, and I will stay with Walker."

James said, "Thanks, Dalton. I will call as soon as I can return. We can leave whenever you are ready, Sam." They left Dalton at the hospital amid his thoughts. James and Dalton had few words during their trip to James' house.

When they arrived, Sam asked, "Would you rather stay at my house? I could order a nurse to come in, and the staff will take care of your needs."

James said, "I'll be fine here on my own, but thanks. See you in a day or two."

* * *

Jodi Panicee awoke on Friday in a mood that could only be described as elated. She had finalized her packing and was dressing for her trip. She had her red bra and panties on with a pair of thigh-high nylons that were tinted red. She had done her make-up, and her dress was laid out. She sat at the kitchen table, drinking a cup of coffee. She texted Greg Solomet, who was traveling with her today. Are you ready? The limo will pick me up in twenty minutes and drive to your place to get you. We should be at the private area of the airport in plenty of time to go through customs and be ready for take-off.

Greg Solomet had just closed his suitcase and sat down to finish his cup of Earl Grey tea. He heard his phone buzz. It was a text from Jodi. He was excited not only to see her again but also to travel free to France on her boss's dime.

Jodi and Greg both had an agenda they would share in detail when they arrived. Greg was there to look for property to buy for his retirement/vacation home. He would also help Jodi look for appropriate locations for her company to film their next feature film. He grabbed his phone and texted her back: Packed and ready. Waiting for you, Doll. Can't wait to see you and spend a great time together.

Jodi, seeing limo had arrived, put on her dress and sent Greg a text. The limousine is here. See you in twenty minutes.

Jodi and Greg Solomet arrived at the airport and went through immigration. They were escorted to the plane by the pilots and made themselves comfortable.

* * *

The doctor walked to the waiting room and asked for Dalton Craig. He nervously stood and greeted Dr. Chris Garcia. Dr. Garcia said, "Mr. Craig. Your son, Walker, is now out of the woods. It was touch and go for a bit, but he responded to treatment quite well. He lost a lot of blood, and his body went into shock. His heart went into Atrial Fibrillation, but the heart specialist was here today so we did an Elective Cardioversion. His heart has responded and is back into normal rhythms. He was wounded three times. Two in the arm and once in his chest which caused the most loss of blood and put him into A-Fib. That bullet went close to his heart but missed it. It went clear through his body and caused no other major damage. We will keep him for four or five days just to make sure there are no more complications. Do you have any questions?"

"When can I see him?"

"He is very groggy at the moment. If you go in and he is awake, only stay for five minutes. Tomorrow, he will be more conversant."

"Thank you so much for all you've done, Dr. Garcia. I just want to see him for five minutes and I will let him rest. There will be a security team here soon to keep an eye on him. I hope that is okay with the hospital."

Dr. Garcia said, "That will be fine. Are you expecting any trouble?"

Dalton replied, "I hope not. It is always better to be prepared in the oft chance someone wants to finish the job while he is most vulnerable."

A nurse whose name badge said Diane said, "Come with me, Mr. Craig. I will take you to him. He is in the post-op unit right now, but we will move him to a regular room in the next few hours. He will be in room 501, later tonight." Diane Deal, Walker's nurse, led Dalton back to the recovery area on the first floor. In the third cubicle down, lay Walker. He had tubes coming out of him and he looked pale.

Dalton gasped when he saw Walker in this condition. He had not been an athletic child and did not play sports. As far as Dalton could remember, Walker had never been in the hospital. This was one hell of a way to begin. Dalton saw Walker's eyes were closed so he just put a hand on his arm. Walker opened his eyes and half smiled at his father. Dalton said, "Nice to see you made it through. The doctor said you did great and should make a full recovery. They have put you on plenty of medication to keep you comfortable. I will let you get some sleep. Call if you need anything. I will give the nurses my phone number so they can call. I will see you first thing tomorrow."

Dalton leaned down and kissed Walker on his forehead. Walker gave a weak smile, then closed his eyes. Dalton could not remember the last time he showed any affection to Walker. His instinct to do so had him a bit shaken. He gave Diane his telephone number and left to wait for Sam to come back to get him.

Sam walked into the waiting room ten minutes later and asked Dalton if he wanted security for Walker. Dalton said, "They are already here. Thanks for asking. Let's go home."

All the way home he thought how lucky he was that he didn't lose his son. He vowed at that moment to do whatever it took to rekindle their friendship and loving relationship.

* * *

Mason Delsson drove to his office directly from Keisha Kane's home. He got a cold bottle of water out of his small refrigerator and winced in pain when he took a long swig. He felt a twinge in his bottom right jaw. He knew the familiar sign of a cavity. He made a note to call a new dentist he was referred to by his neighbor, Catie Gaynor. He found the card in his desktop file, Lone Tree Family Dentistry. Amber Parkridge, the office manager, scheduled Mason for an appointment to see Dr. Freeman on Friday afternoon.

Mason's assistant brought Lynda Laffarty in for her appointment, and she sat in the chair opposite his desk. She was dressed in a flowery print summer dress. It was five inches above her knees and provided a wonderful view of her very shapely legs. The neckline was a deep vee and her cleavage was evident. She had on beige platform open-toed sandals which highlighted her hot pink polished nails that also matched her fingernails. She even wore pink sunglasses.

She said, "Detective Delsson, thank you for seeing me today. I wanted your help in finding the person who killed my friend, Jennifer Sandrew."

Mason said, "I have just begun my investigation so what can you tell me about your trip to Lake Tahoe."

Lynda seemed to tense up, then she began to speak, "It began with Jennifer saying she wanted to go on a vacation to Tahoe. Jen, Christy Amherst, Allie Campwick, Kathy Muller, and I were the designated group. We flew on Dalton Craig's private plane, which he offered to us when he heard we were going. We got a suite for the five of us at the Hilton Hotel Vacation Club. We were having the best time. Everyone in the group took a day to do individual excursions. We met back at the hotel and went to Lynn Fuda's Pianeta for dinner. We had a great time and shared small bits of our day. We ate and drank and decided to crash. On the way up to the room, I saw Dalton Craig come off the elevator with this stunning woman and head to the dining room in the hotel. I thought I was the only one who noticed, but after five minutes in the room, Jennifer came out of her room, dressed to the nines. She said she was going on the prowl, which is our code word for finding a man. We all laughed because Jennifer was the most unlikely to dip her fishing pole into the lake, so to speak. When she didn't return the next morning, we assumed that she had landed the fish she was looking for."

Mason said, "Let me stop you there. Did you see Jennifer with Dalton?"

Lynda replied, "No, I did not. I did, however, ask the bartender when I got down to the bar again if he had seen anyone other than the stunning brunette with Dalton."

He answered, "I saw a woman sit next to Dalton at the bar when Fitore left. She ordered a drink and walked away with it after speaking to Dalton for a few minutes. When he paid the bar tab. I saw him exit the restaurant and go out of the hotel. I know this because I had cashed out and was on my way to meet up with my girlfriend."

Mason then asked, "Why would you bring up the name of your ex-husband when talking about the death of your friend, Jennifer Sandrew?"

Lynda answered, "Well, Dalton dated Jennifer for a while after he and I broke up. That's how I first met Jennifer. I went into her store, Elegant Lace, looking for something new for this man I had just met. She recognized me and started a conversation. She asked my permission to date him. I found that quite hilarious. I told her about his philandering, and she just laughed. She said, 'I know all about his ability to stray. I watched them from afar when he dated Sarah Ostrov who was a close friend of mine.'"

"I gave Jennifer my blessing. They only dated for a few months then he broke it off. She never talked about it, and I never asked her about it. When I saw Dalton at the same hotel where we stayed, and Jennifer ran out to go on the prowl, I wondered if he had met her. The bartender, Jason, confirmed it and thought he remembered that they didn't leave together but had a drink together. Then, she turned up dead the next day."

Mason asked, "Dalton seems to be in the center of all the recent deaths we have been tracking. Do you think that Dalton killed Jennifer?"

Lynda replied, "I am just reporting the things I observed while in Lake Tahoe, Detective."

Mason said, using an old technique, "So you do think Dalton had something to do with Jennifer's death."

Lynda was onto his game, "Are you trying to entrap me, Detective Delsson?"

Mason replied quickly, "No, not at all, Miss Lynda, I am just trying to let you help me solve the murder of your friend. Do you have anything else to report?"

Lynda was done playing games with this gumshoe, so she said in her sweetest tone, "Detective Delsson, I think I have relayed all the information I have to you." Mason watched as Lynda got up and walked away. He again focused on her body and admired her curves as well as her classy sensuality.

* * *

Greg Solomet got off the plane first when he and Jodi landed in Paris, France. He led the way to the luggage carousel to await the delivery of their bags. Once they arrived on the belt, Greg put them on a flatbed cart through customs and walked toward the limo area. He hailed the limo with his sign placard that read: Solomen/Panicee. The limo pulled up quickly, and the driver jumped out of the vehicle with the trunk open. He confirmed they were headed to the Ritz Hotel and loaded their bags. They were on the way. Jodi was impressed that Greg had been able to negotiate customs so quickly and procure the limo to take them to the hotel.

When the limo dropped them at the Ritz, the doorman retrieved their bags and put them on a cart. The desk clerk signed them in and rang the bell for the bellboy, who appeared within seconds. The desk clerk said, "Please take these folks to room 609. Thank you. Folks, enjoy your stay."

Jodi raved about the room. "I will have to thank Dalton for the wonderful accommodations. I think we can work with this setup. What is your plan for tomorrow?"

"I spoke with my realtor yesterday and she said that she had five properties to see tomorrow. Do you want to go with me, or do you have appointments of your own?"

Jodi said, "I have maybe ten locations to see. I don't have to do them all in one day and think I will start with the first five. The realtor is coming in a limousine at 9 a.m. He said it may take three hours or so today."

Greg said, "Why don't we meet for lunch here at the hotel tomorrow around 1 p.m.?"

Jodi replied, "That works. What about dinner tonight? Do you just want to go downstairs and get dinner?"

Greg said, "Let's shower first, then we can go. I will call down and reserve a table while you jump in the shower."

Jodi asked laughing, "Do you want to join me so we can save water?"

Greg said, "You start the water, and I bet I beat you into the shower!"

Greg and Jodi showered together. They started to become amorous, but Jodi said, "I need a glass of wine and maybe something to eat before we get swept away in the erotic delights tonight."

Greg was toweling off and watched Jodi exit the shower. He said, "I have a table ready downstairs. How soon can you be ready?"

Jodi said, "My hair is done, and I will put on a dress and drive you crazy at dinner knowing I have nothing on underneath."

They both laughed. It took them only minutes to dress. Greg grabbed his room key and off they went.

They were seated and ordered a drink. The waiter, Francois, returned with the drinks, and they looked at the menu. Jodi ordered organic spaghetti with prawns. Greg ordered the Turbot, pan-fried, potato purée, Grenobloise condiment, and Beurre Blanc sauce. Their waiter brought French bread that they nibbled on until the food arrived.

Dinner was served within fifteen minutes. They shared each other's dishes, and both were impressed with their orders. They ordered a bottle of French wine and sat at the table until they finished the wine.

At dinner the next night, Jodi asked Greg, "Did you find a property you like here for your new home? I am curious to know what the going price is for a home here in Paris."

Greg said, "I found three, but I am going to let the realtor hassle with the owners on the price and get the best deal. Any of the three would be perfect. All of them are stand-alone homes with private backyards, although small, each has a pool and cabana. They are all three bedrooms and are accessible to transit and markets. We will see how good the realtor is at her job."

Jodi replied, "That is great. All the locations sound fabulous. I had a great day as well. I was able to secure five different locations right in the center of Paris for Dalton's movie. I also found four properties in the countryside. I sent him pictures of each, and he was over the moon with all of them."

Greg asked, "Do you know what the movie is about and who wrote it?"

Jodi replied, "I am not sure, but I think it is a who-done-it and Dalton wrote the screenplay. He has only done one or two since taking over the studio, but I feel like this could be quite the blockbuster."

Greg asked, "What do you want to do tomorrow? It is supposed to be an excellent weather day, warm and dry."

Jodi said, "I would love to ride on one of those boats that float down the Seine River."

Greg said, "I was just looking through the paper this morning, and I found this notice for a cruise dinner. It is called; Paris-Capitaine Fracasse, three-course Seine River Dinner Cruise. I will make reservations for tonight."

Jodi screeched with joy. She jumped into Greg's arms and kissed his face a hundred times. She said, "I am so happy right now I have always wanted to do that."

Greg made the reservations and that night they lived Jodi's dream. She said to Greg when they returned to the hotel, "Mr. Solomet, This evening has made me quite amorous. I am going to change and freshen up. I hope you will join me in having a nightcap. I have some erotic goals for this evening for you and me."

Greg went to the mini bar, poured two drinks for them, then carried the drinks and the wine bottle to the bedroom. There he found Jodi in a yellow lingerie that looked like it was painted on her.

* * *

Lynda went home after the interview with Mason Delsson. She was stressed out over the line of questioning and couldn't help but wonder if she was a suspect in Carmen's death. What would she have gained? She was already in Carmen's will. Lynda had no clue she would inherit that kind of money from her long-time friend as well as the wife of her ex-husband. The fact that she was left so much money and Carmen left nothing to her son and husband was troubling to Lynda. The whole business of talking to the police was very uncomfortable for her.

Lynda got into the shower and readied for her dinner date with Richard Bruce. He was an actor, and living here in L.A., but had lived abroad for a few years. They lost contact until he called the other day. She was excited to see him and wondered what his status was. Single, divorced, married? She would see soon enough. She dressed and decided against wearing panties. She wore thigh-high nylons and a demi-cup bra supporting her large breasts.

When she was ready, called for an Uber and within minutes it arrived. She said to the driver, "Take me to Spago's but I don't want to get there until eight minutes after six p.m." The driver knew they would be there ten minutes too soon, so he took the long way. It was a scenic drive through Malibu, and they arrived exactly at 6:08 p.m., on the dot. Lynda handed him thirty dollars in cash and said, "Here is something for you for being so efficient. If this dinner doesn't work out, I may call you again for a ride home.

The driver, Devin Willis, handed Lynda his business card. It read: Call Willis for a Cruising Experience. He said, "Call me on that number if you need me tonight or any time you need a lift."

Lynda slid his card into her purse and smiled, saying, "I will keep that in mind. Thank you. Maybe I will see you later." She walked into the restaurant and went to the bar where Richard said he would be waiting.

Richard rose from his barstool when she appeared. His breath was immediately taken away. She was more beautiful than he remembered. She wore a short black dress with sexy ankle-high black high-heeled boots. Her brunette hair was cut short in a bob and Richard began to perspire remembering what her body looked like under that dress. She could only be described as zoftig and her legs showed she was either a runner or walker. Richard thought she was the sexiest woman he had ever seen.

Lynda walked up to him, and he was conscious of his arousal. She noticed the arousal she had inspired. She grabbed Richard on his shoulders and locked eyes with Richard, their lips locked. It was the kind of kiss that old lovers exchanged. They parted and both were out of breath. Richard said, "I remembered you were beautiful, but you still took my breath away. Let me order drinks for us, then we can sit down for dinner.

Richard called over the bartender and said, "When you get a chance." Holding up his empty glass.

The bartender came immediately and asked, "The same for you; how about your lady?"

Richard replied, "The same for me and the lady will have a glass of cabernet." Richard turned to Lynda and said, "I don't think I have seen you look better. How have you been? Are you hungry? What have you been up to since I saw you last?"

Lynda replied, "I am fantastic. I was so looking forward to seeing you again. You didn't disappoint me. I was in Vegas not too long ago with my girlfriends from Syracuse. We had an amazing time, and I drank too much wine. Richard, you look amazing as well. You have been working out. I can't wait to take your clothes off and see how you've progressed. Let's order dinner so we can leave and go to your place to do some naked wrestling."

Richard motioned for the waiter, and he was there before Richard put his arm down. Blake, the waiter, said, "Are you ready to order folks?"

Richard pointed to Lynda who said, "I would love to try the Austrian White Shrimp Pizza."

Richard said, "Thanks sounds great. We will have that, Blake, and two more drinks, please."

Blake hurried away to place the order. This gave Richard and Lynda time to catch up. Richard said, "I heard an old friend of yours died in an accident in Lake Tahoe?"

Lynda took a breath and said, "There are so many people who were once in my life that have met their demise. I am a bit frightened by the possibility that these 'accidental deaths' are not so accidental."

Richard looked concerned, "Do you think something untoward has happened to those people who died?"

Lynda said, "Richard, Let's not speak of these things tonight. I want to know everything you have been up to since we last saw each other."

Richard said, "Do you know how long it has been since I held you in my arms?"

This statement brought about some silence as Lynda thought back and tried to remember the last time she had seen Richard. Lynda said, "I think it was Cinco de Mayo, three years ago when we met in New Orleans. There was a bar on Bourbon Street that made Hurricane cocktails."

Richard replied, "It was Pat O'Brien's on Bourbon Street. We had a great time and went back to the hotel around 4 a.m. We made love like it was the end of the world and didn't wake up until 3 p.m. the next day."

They laughed and remembered the days of passion they had shared. Blake Coleman, the waiter, brought another round of drinks along with the pizza they ordered. They were both starving and finished the pizza quickly.

Richard said, "Hey, Miss Lynda. The pizza is gone. We finished our drinks, so does that mean we are done here and should return to my house for some wrestling?"

Lynda replied, "Mr. Bruce, are you trying to take advantage of an old friend who has had too much to drink?"

Richard answered, "Why, yes, Miss Lynda. I think it is time for me to take you back to my expensive bachelor pad and have my way with you."

Lynda remarked, "Pay the tab, and I will call an Uber. It looks like I might get lucky tonight."

Devin Willis pulled up his Uber in front of Spago. Richard and Lynda entered the vehicle, and Lynda gave him Richard's address. She said, "Richard, Thank you for a lovely evening but I think something we had tonight, didn't agree with my tummy. I will drop you off first because you are closer. I will call you tomorrow when I am feeling better. I am so sorry to have to cut our date so short. Will you forgive me?"

Richard looked dumbfounded and replied, "I am so sorry I made you sick. I hope you feel better. Please call me tomorrow and let me know if you are feeling better. Please know that I understand. I think."

Richard had a premonition while he sat at his kitchen table. He decided to drive by Lynda's home and got into his car, even though he had had too much to drink. It was a distance, but he was curious to see if she was sick, went home, or maybe had another engagement.

It took about thirty minutes for Richard to get to Lynda's house. There was no sign of the Uber nor were there lights on in the house. There were no signs of life. Did she even go home? He wanted to stay and satisfy his curiosity, but he was angry at that point, so he drove home.

Richard got home about midnight. He had a message on his answering machine. It was from Lynda Laffarty who said, "Richard. It is Lynda. I wanted to call and apologize again for cutting our date short. I was violently ill after getting home and am going straight to bed. Please let me make this up to you when I am fully recovered. Goodnight, my love." Lynda's voice made him excited. He decided to jump in the shower and go to bed.

6

MASON DELSSON SAT IN HIS OFFICE and pulled out a yellow legal pad. He was going to try to do this systematically. He wanted to find the person or persons responsible for the deaths of all the recent accidental deaths. He began by making a list of those who died and thought detective work is a pretty gruesome occupation. I should retire and become a podcaster and find a topic to discuss daily.

The list of the deceased:

Carmen Craig. The wife of Dalton Craig. mother of one son, Walker Craig. She was rich by inheritance but acted in movies and became a veterinarian after she retired. No enemies are known at this point.

Belinda Cheeks. She worked as the housekeeper for the Craig family for fifteen years. She had an ex-husband who lived in Colorado. She was educated but preferred to work for the Craigs. No known enemies.

Sarah Ostrov. A movie actress and director for Gemini films. Dated Dalton Craig for a time. Janelle Phillips, Sarah's housekeeper, was the last one to see her alive.

Karena Katrinka. A model from Poland. She lived at the Craig estate for a time and dated Walker Craig. They parted amicably years ago, according to those who knew her.

Jennifer Sandrew. A Hollywood socialite. She was a former model and film star who retired to open a business on Rodeo Drive called Elegant Lace. Her partner, Allie Campwick, was rumored to be her lover once. The business was very successful, and the ladies got along well in their partnership.

Mason sat at his desk reviewing the list when the telephone rang. It was the Chief of Detectives, Rich Corsi. The Chief said, "Mason. Chief here. I don't know if you saw on the wire this morning that Lynda Laffarty was found dead this morning by her pool man, who comes every other day to work on the pool. She was found naked on her pool deck in the back of her home.

Mason gasped when he heard the news. He had just spoken to the woman the day before. He asked the Chief, "Are there any witnesses? Was she shot, stabbed, or did she fall?"

Chief Corsi said, "I don't have the forensic report, but she wasn't shot or stabbed. The coroner, Trudy Pine, indicated there was a bruise on the head, but that could have been from her fall. Trudy said she would know more after the autopsy."

Mason said, "Thanks, Chief. I will follow up with Trudy first thing tomorrow." They ended their call. Mason sat and added Lynda Laffarty to his list of the deceased.

<u>Lynda Laffarty</u>. Former wife of Dalton Craig, an actress, a member of Carmen's closest friends' group, and recently awarded $10 million from the estate of Carmen Craig.

Mason knew who was behind the deaths. He would have to find the proof and links to the evidence left by the murderer. Mason knew his instincts had been right. These deaths had not been accidental.

Mason quickly went down the list of people he wanted to speak to about Carmen's death. Cricky Amherst, Sue Crull, Dolores Madison, Allie Campwick, Walker Craig, and Keisha Kane. He would start with Cricky Amherst who had been on the trip to Lake Tahoe with Lynda Laffarty and their friends. He messaged Robin Zander, the secretary for Detectives, and gave her the list of appointments for the rest of the people on the list to come to his office.

Mason's first call was to Dolores Madison. She had worked for Dalton Craig for the past fifteen years as his private secretary. If anybody had an opinion of Dalton, it would be Dolores. Dolores answered the phone, "Hello, Dalton Craig's office, how may I help you?"

Mason said, "Miss Madison, this is Mason Delsson of LAPD. When I saw you last, you were rushing me out of Dalton's office, and I forgot to arrange an interview with you. I would like to interview you at my office, so you are away from your office and are more comfortable talking about the Craig family. How late are you working today?"

Dolores Madison said, "I am leaving at noon today as I have some errands to run for Mr. Craig, and I will be downtown and could stop in around 2 p.m. if that works for you?"

Mason replied, "That would be perfect. Thank you so much, Miss Madison. I will see you then." They hung up their call.

Mason then dialed the number of Los Alamitos Racetrack, which was owned by Cricky Amherst. A young woman answered, "Los Alamitos Raceway. How can I direct your call?"

Mason said, "I would like to speak with Miss Amherst, please. This is Mason Delsson for LAPD calling." The operator put him on hold, and the next voice he heard was Cricky Amherst.

"Hello, Detective. How can I help you today?"

Mason replied, "Are you going to be in the city sometime soon? I would like to speak to you about the recent events here in town."

Cricky said, "I am going shopping right after lunch, so I will be available around three-thirty. Would you like me to stop by your office?"

Mason said, "That would be amazing, Miss Amherst. Thank you so much. I will expect you then. Goodbye."

Mason then buzzed Robin Zander, "Robin. I have scheduled interviews with Dolores Madison and Christy Amherst for today. Did you have any luck contacting the others?"

Robin replied, "Thanks. I was just about to call Miss Amherst. I have scheduled all of the others for tomorrow. You have Susan Crull at 8 a.m., Allie Campwick at 9:30 a.m., Then, Walker Craig at 11, and your final interview is with Keisha Kane at noon. She said she would pick you up for lunch if that is all right."

Mason said, "Robin. Those are perfect. Thank you so much. Talk to you later."

Mason was in his office again when Robin called him on the intercom, "Detective Delsson, there is a Miss Dolores Madison here to see you.

Mason replied, "Please send her in, Robin. Thanks."

Dolores Madison walked in looking like she was ready to tee off at a local golf course. Mason said, "What is your handicap, Dolores?"

Dolores laughed, "Golf!" They both laughed.

Mason said, "Well, I have finally met someone I can play golf with. Does your husband play?"

Dolores replied, "Yes, he does, but if it takes longer than an hour and a half, he gets antsy and walks off the course. We taught our children to play when we were younger, and during that time, I don't think either of them ever heard the ball hit the bottom of the cup on the green from within four feet. Del always said, 'That's good. Let's move on.'"

Mason said, "That sounds like my ex-wife when I was doing a chore. I would get eighty percent of it done, and she would call it good. Then she would finish it herself."

They both eyed each other up for a minute or so when Mason continued, "Ms. Madison, I wanted to ask you a few questions away from the Craig Estate. This way, you can feel free to say whatever is on your mind, freely. My first question is, Do you think Dalton Craig killed his wife?"

Dolores never flinched, "Well, Mr. Delsson, I have been around the Craigs for years, and one, I think they were in love. Two, Mr. Craig was in the office all day on the day Carmen died. Three, each of them agreed to an open marriage, and there was never any open animosity between them. Finally, they were both independently wealthy, and neither needed money from the other."

Mason jotted down some notes and asked, "Did you ever hear them quarrel in anger?"

Dolores laughed, "Detective, they were together for twenty-five years. I think I heard them quarrel twice. Once, to make Walker more responsible for his chores around the estate, and on another occasion, they had words over the casting of a movie that they co-produced. Other than that, it was the best relationship, other than my own, that I could honestly say, both partners were hopelessly in love."

Mason jotted notes again and asked, "Dolores, are you in love with Dalton Craig?"

Dolores almost fell out of her chair she laughed so hard. She composed herself and said, "You have yet to meet my husband. Had that happened, you would never have asked that question. I loved my husband since he rode his bike past my house when I was sixteen years old. I loved him then, and I love him today many times over. He is my rock, my lover, and my best friend."

Mason laughed along with her as he again made some notes. He said, "Dolores, who do you think was responsible for Carmen's death?"

Dolores thought a moment and replied, "I am not convinced that she is dead. No one saw her body except when Erikson Howard, the stable manager, found her. He was not as upset as you would have expected one to be when their long-time boss was found with her head smashed against the rocks while out for a ride on her favorite steed. I have no proof, but it is just my theory."

Mason said, "So, if that was not Carmen, riding Carmen's horse in Carmen's clothes, who might that have been?"

Dolores laughed, "You, Mr. Delsson, are the Detective here. You figure it out. I may be way off base, but sometimes you just get a feeling, a premonition, a hunch, as you cops say."

Mason said, "Last question, have you ever seen or heard Carmen had an enemy or someone she just didn't get along with?"

Dolores said, "I didn't have a lot of contact with Carmen as I worked for Dalton. We didn't have many social interactions. Men loved her as she was so beautiful and rich. Women loved her because she was a ladies' lady. By that I mean, she was always one of the girls. Sensitive, kind and always there to help someone in need. So, I can't say I ever saw her in a situation where there were angry words exchanged. Only a few times with Dalton and a handful of times with her son, Walker. Their relationship was strained over the years."

Mason said, "Thank you again, Dolores. It was a pleasure speaking with you. Have a great rest of your day."

Dolores Madison walked out of the conference room and Mason read over his notes. He now realized that he had more questions than when she walked in to see him.

Cricky Amherst walked into Police Headquarters thirty minutes later. They sat in the same conference room where he and Dolores Madison met. Mason welcomed her as she was seated. He noted she was dressed much more fashionably than when he last saw her. He said, "Thank you for coming in today. I have a few questions, and it shouldn't take too long."

Cricky said, "No worries, Detective. I was on my way into the city to do some shopping and have lunch with some friends."

Mason began, "You had an incident last week. You were robbed, and a few people were shot. Can you give me an update?"

Cricky said, "Sure. The people who robbed us got away with $450,000. That is a sizeable sum, but much of it is insured. We think we know who the culprits are. One of the tellers, Deyna Doll, thought she recognized the voice of the leader of the crew that robbed us, so we have some good leads. Regarding the people who were injured, I am happy to report that all are either home recovering or out of danger in the hospital. The two most serious victims were Deyna Doll and Walker Craig. Miss Doll was shot four times and went into shock. The doctors put her in a protective coma so her body could begin to heal. She is no longer in a coma, and the surgeries were successful. Her doctors indicate she should have a total recovery. Walker Craig was shot three times. He lost a lot of blood and had two surgeries, which saved his arm and repaired his shoulder. He is scheduled to be discharged tomorrow, so he can recover at home. Jim Thompson, Walker's bodyguard, was shot twice in the head. The wounds were superficial, and he lost some blood. He was treated and released. He did, however, remain in the hospital guarding Walker Craig. There were four of my employees who were also injured, but all were treated and released. Though we lost some money, we were lucky not to lose any of those who were shot."

Mason said, "Thank you for the update. That is much more information than I received from the hospital. Now, I know you and Carmen Craig are close friends. Did she ever share with you any feuds she had with anyone?"

Cricky said, "No. Never. She got along with everyone. Why do you ask?"

Mason replied, "What would you say if I told you that Carmen Craig may not be dead?"

Cricky felt her face go numb. She began to cry, "Why would you say that? They buried her. Have you heard from her? Are you trying to trick me?"

Mason said, "Calm down, Miss Amherst. It is just a theory. I had to ask you a shocking question to get your reaction. I know you are an accomplished actress, but no one can portray that kind of emotion at the drop of a hat. Keep this conversation to yourself, please. I have some other people to talk with, and I want to get their natural reactions as well."

Cricky said, "Can you tell me why you think Carmen is still alive?"

Mason Delsson thought a minute, "I don't usually divulge my investigation information, but I think I can trust you to not share this. The only person to see Carmen was her stablemaster. Carmen left nothing for her family. Most of her wealth was left to a trust fund. Things just don't add up."

Cricky said, "Well, that was a pretty foul thing to do to someone who loved her as much as I did. Shame on you. I will keep this a secret, but if she is alive, do you think she would contact anyone?"

Mason said, "Probably not. If it is true, then she wanted to drop out of the world and start a new life. I haven't uncovered any evidence of that being true. I just talked to someone who has the same hunch, so I thought I would check it out."

Mason and Cricky exchanged pleasantries, and Cricky left to meet her friends. She was upset at first, then calm as she sat in her car driving to Rodeo Drive, mulling over what had just happened.

* * *

Coroner Trudy Pine called Mason at 5 p.m. just as he was leaving for the night. She said, "Mason, I spoke with Chief Corsi, and he said you are going to lead the investigation on the Lynda Laffarty case. I am having my assistant drop off the report to both of you in the morning. I wanted to give you a heads-up before you saw it."

Mason replied, "Trudy, thanks for the call. What did you find?"

Trudy replied, "It looks like she was hit with a blunt weapon, in the back of the head and fell forward. There were abrasions on her face that would indicate she fell forward. If she had just fallen forward, there would have been a large hematoma on her forehead, but there was not. She was found face up floating in the Lake. My report indicates she was struck from behind, fell forward, received the abrasions from the fall forward. There were no signs of a struggle. My conclusion is, she was murdered. We are checking hematology for signs of drugs."

Mason said, "Thank you for the clarification. It sounds like we have a mass murderer in our midst. That makes six deaths seemingly all accidental, but more than likely planned and executed to look accidental. I will await the report and call if I have questions. Thanks again. Good night."

Mason thought of going to Keisha's place and spending the night, but he thought better of it as he was going to interview her about the murders tomorrow, so he stayed home. He made himself a drink, took a shower, and went to bed. He woke up early and glanced at his alarm clock; the time was 6:15 a.m. Wow, he still had half a drink on his nightstand from last night, which meant he had fallen asleep around seven o'clock. He slept for almost twelve hours. He made a mental note to slow down a bit. Out of habit, he showered, dressed, and drove to work.

Susan Crull was seated in the waiting area when he went to get coffee. Mason said, "Good Morning, Miss Crull. You are a bit early, but I can see you if you're ready."

Sue stood and walked up to Mason and shook his hand, "Good morning, Detective Delsson. Yes, I am ready and hope I can be of some help."

Mason escorted her into the conference room. They sat on opposite sides of the table. Mason began, "Can I get you a water or coffee?" Sue shook her head no.

Mason asked, "Are you aware of all the deaths of your friends and others connected to Carmen Craig and her husband, Dalton?"

Sue Crull was not nervous at all and spoke in a very confident manner, "I have been grieving and confused about all my friends. I have some questions for you when you are ready."

Mason said, "Be sure to remind me before you leave. My first question is if Carmen Craig was murdered, who might have been the person you would think is most likely to have done it?"

Sue replied looking shocked and surprised, "Are you saying her death was not an accident?"

Mason shook his head no and said, "I said if it wasn't an accident, who would you suppose would have a motivation?"

Susan Crull was now off her confident game. She thought for a minute, "I am just trying to wrap my head around the idea that her death was not an accident. Sorry. Carmen Craig was the most popular person that I have ever met. To my knowledge, she never had any enemies, nor have I ever witnessed her having an exchange of an angry word with anyone." She paused and thought for a minute, so Mason waited. Sue continued, "Now that you ask, there were some people who were very envious of her. Her looks, her money, her husband, and her talent for breeding and training horses. I cannot think of anyone who would go to the extreme level of envy that one would kill her."

Mason jotted notes, even though he was recording the interview, "What kind of relationship did you have with Carmen Craig?"

Sue replied quickly, again very confident, "Carmen and I were friends for years. She was the type of lady you could trust with your deepest secrets and your troubles, or someone to comfort you if you needed it. She was the ringleader of our group of six or seven ladies who met regularly and traveled together. She brought us together individually into the group and we all became friends because of her. I miss her dearly."

Mason was poker-faced when he dropped the next bomb. He said, "Miss Crull, what if I told you that Carmen Craig did not die in a fall from her horse?"

Sue gasped aloud and held her hand over her mouth, "Oh, my goodness. Are you saying she is alive?"

Mason waited, watching her reaction, "I have spoken to some folks who are not convinced she died in the accident that was reported. Does that sound like something that Carmen might have done?"

Sue was still in disbelief, "Are you saying that she faked her death?"

Mason said, "Miss Crull, I am conducting this investigation of all these seemingly connected deaths. There are some reasons why people have put forth these theories, and as the investigator, it is my job to look at every possibility. We have no one who witnessed any of the deaths, so anything could have happened. The deaths could be a part of a bigger picture. These questions are to be kept in confidence and shared with no one. I am saying, I don't think she died accidentally. Did your fiancée, Mr. Syracuse, know Mrs. Craig?"

Susie Crull gathered herself and said, "Kevin and I have seen them socially for dinner once or twice and at parties with friends, but he wasn't close with either Dalton or Carmen. He was with a different studio, so they were actually in competition at times for movie rights, scripts, and actors, as well as professional industry people."

Mason knew this was not something he wanted to delve into more deeply, so he said, "I have no more questions for you. What did you want to ask me?"

Sue said, "I wondered if you knew who robbed the Los Alamitos Raceway? My business partner, Deyna Doll, was shot and almost killed in that incident. She and I run a clothing store on Rodeo Drive called Bella Da Ball. I wanted to know if they had found the robbers who shot her, because I wanted to know if Deyna was still in danger. I also wondered if I was in danger. Deyna and I spoke briefly in the hospital, and she said something like all the deaths were in some way connected to Dalton Craig. I wasn't that close to the situation, but Deyna has been kicking around L.A. for a couple of decades. She and her husband, Dennis, traveled in those circles."

Mason replied, "So, you are asking if I know who the robbers were, and are you and Deyna in danger? At this point, all I can say is that I don't know. When I spoke to Cricky Amherst, she said Deyna had recognized the voice of one of the robbers. I don't know whether anyone has asked her yet."

Susan Crull and Mason agreed that neither had any more questions for the other. Mason said, "Miss Crull, thanks so much for coming in today. If I hear anything positive about Carmen, I will call you. Goodbye."

Mason looked at his watch and saw it was 9:05 a.m. Allie Campwick was in the waiting area when he went to his secretary, Robin Zander, and handed her his notes. He checked the video room and put in a new tape. Robin brought Allie Campwick into the conference room.

Mason walked back into the conference room at 9:15 a.m. and said, "Good morning, again Miss Campwick. Thank you for coming in for questioning. I will begin so we can get you back to your job as quickly as possible. Let me start by asking what your relationship was with Carmen Craig."

Allie seemed a bit nervous, so Mason made a note. Allie answered, "Well, that is an interesting story. After Dalton Craig divorced his first wife, Lynda Laffarty, I was introduced to him at my fashion store by my partner, Jennifer Sandrew. Dalton was in buying some lingerie for "a friend." He and I seemed to hit it off, so every time he needed lingerie, he would ask for me. I hadn't seen him in months when he came into the store one day and asked me to lunch. I asked him why he was not around for a while. He told me he had divorced his wife and was tired of the running around/chasing women scene. I told him I would go to lunch, but I was hesitant to get involved with such an alleged womanizer. He said it was just lunch. Long story short, I fell for him after a few dates, and we dated for a few months, had a falling out, and we parted. A month or so later, I met Carmen Warner. She was a friend of Jennifer's and began coming in quite often to buy new lingerie. She and I became friends. When I told her I had dated this guy for a while who was a movie producer, she said she was also. When we found out we were both talking about Dalton Craig, we laughed and laughed. She said we should be friends because she was friends with his ex-wife, Lynda, and another girl as well. I later realized Carmen was talking about my partner, Jennifer Sandrew. Carmen invited me into the group as many of us were dating or married to Dalton. He remained friends with all of us and thought it was funny we had all become friends." Allie took a breath and laughed, "Did I answer your question, Detective?"

Mason lied and said, "I wish I had this on tape, so I wouldn't have to decipher these notes. I found the answer fascinating and that is certainly helpful in piecing together some things I was hoping to solve. Let me ask, who do you think murdered Carmen Craig?"

Allie was shocked and looked horrified at the question. She said, "Really? You think she was murdered?"

Mason replied, "It is not important what I think, I am asking what you think."

Allie said, "If that is true, that is more horrible than her dying accidentally. I never saw her exchange harsh words with anyone. I always wondered though how she could be so close to so many of the people Dalton had been with. I know now that she had loads of money, but I have no clue who might want to kill her because I assumed all her friends were as rich as she was. That is until I attended the reading of her will. The fact that she left so much money to those in our friend's group, including me, is still shocking."

Mason had all the information he wanted but he continued, "Allie, we spoke briefly after Jennifer was found dead, do you have any idea who would have wanted her dead?"

Allie teared up and grabbed a tissue out of the box on the conference table. She finally said, "I still have not come to grips with her being gone. She and I were not close personally, as you might expect. I found her friendly, a great businesswoman, but there was always a distance between us when it came to personal things. That was fine with me. She has a sister who inherited Jennifer's half of the business. She wanted to sell her half as it brought so many memories back for her. When I received the inheritance, I gave her a very generous offer. Sorry I am being so gabby. To answer your question, I have no clue who would have wanted to kill her."

Mason didn't share with Allie, his revelation about who he thought was responsible for the deaths of all these women. He wanted to ask another question, "What was your relationship with any of the following: Lynda Laffarty, Sarah Ostrov, Belinda Cheeks, Karina Katrinka?"

Allie replied, "The only name I recognize is Lynda Laffarty because she was part of the group. She was in our group and seemed to be the leader after Carmen died. I was very good friends with her. So, I am still grieving over my three friends."

Mason thanked her and escorted her out to reception. He looked at his watch and noted that his next interview was in five minutes. He used the restroom. He then saw Robin Zander escorting Walker Craig into the conference room. Mason had to brace himself for the next hour or so.

He ran into Sam Barfield on the way to the conference room. Sam said, "I am going to sit in on the interview if you don't mind. Walker was a bit shaken after his last interrogation with the police. I wanted him to feel supported."

Mason said, "No worries, Sam. I promise not to use any Nazi tactics."

Mason sat across from Walker Craig and Sam Barfield. He offered them water or coffee, and they declined. Mason began. "Walker, I was sorry to hear of your mother's passing. Please accept my condolences. Were you and your mother close?"

Walker looked at Sam. Sam nodded. Walker replied, "Yes. We were very close."

Mason asked, "I learned that your mother was quite the equestrian. Did you horseback ride with her often?"

Walker again looked at Sam for a nod of approval. Walker replied, "Yes, we rode together often. I was supposed to ride with her..." Sam cleared his throat, and Walker stopped.

Mason looked at Sam and said, "Counselor, if you interrupt my questioning again, I will have you removed from the room. Do I make myself clear?" He got no response from Sam. Mason continued, "Walker, I heard you were upset the last time you were questioned. Can you tell me why?"

Walker again looked at Sam and Sam blinked his eyes twice. Walker began to answer but this time Mason stopped him, "Hold on one minute, gentlemen. I am uncomfortable with your lawyer telling you which questions are okay to answer. You have not been charged with a crime so you should have no hesitation in answering these questions. I thought you might be interested in aiding us in the investigation of your mother's death. If you have any information that you want to share, I will gladly listen. If you don't want to talk with me without your lawyer, we can certainly put out a bench warrant for you as a potential hostile witness in a murder case. I get the sense that you may have something to hide. If you don't, I suggest you comply and answer these questions. Your call."

Walker looked at Sam saying, "I will answer the questions. I have nothing to hide. If you want to stay, sit back over my shoulder so you can't give me any help on what questions to answer."

After Sam got up and walked to the chair near the back of the room behind Walker, Mason said, "Okay. How often did you ride horses with your mom?"

Walker replied, "When I turned fifteen years of age, I stopped because I was focused on what Daddy wanted. When I started college, Mom and I rode about every other day. She and I got much closer."

Mason said, "There have been six women found dead that either were married to, dated, or worked for your dad. How does that make you feel?

Walker began to nervously fidget, but answered, "I am not a private detective. I was saddened when I learned of each of their deaths, but I do not know anything about the circumstances, nor do I think my father is responsible for any of them if that is what you're implying. Dalton Craig has a reputation as a ladies' man and will always be that. I can't think of a reason for him to cause the death of anyone, much less the people he loved and cared about."

Mason made a note in his book. He was filming the interview, but he knew it would make Walker curious. He was just writing down the next question. Then he asked Walker, "Did you have anything to do with these deaths?"

Walker jumped to his feet and began yelling, "Are you accusing me of causing someone's death? I loved all those women, too. Not like my father did, but I was fond of each of them as they were influential in my life. I don't think I want to answer any more questions, Detective Delsson. Am I free to go?"

Mason said, in a firm voice, "No. Sit down. I am not finished questioning you. If you jump up and start raging again like a madman, I will think it is because you are guilty, and we'll discuss how we will deal with that if it becomes the case."

Walker sat and became very quiet. Mason continued, "How long were you and Deyna Doll dating?"

Walker glared at Mason and said, "We dated for a month before she met her current husband, Dennis."

Mason knew he was almost finished with him, but asked, "Did you know she dated your father?"

The look on Walker's face did not hide that he didn't know, but kept his voice controlled saying, "Yeah. No big deal. I think she mentioned it, but my dad was always seen with a pretty dame on his arm."

Mason had one more question, "How did you feel when you heard Lynda Laffarty was found dead?"

The knuckles on Walker's hands were white as he clenched his fists. He answered, "Detective Delsson, I have already told you how I felt about all the ladies who are gone. Are you trying to further torture me by dragging this questioning out?"

Mason said, "Thank you, Mr. Craig. You are now free to go. You have given me all the information I was seeking. Have a good day. Goodbye."

Walker briskly walked out the door followed by his attorney, Sam Barfield. Walker was talking under his breath, and it was obvious he was upset, but Sam looked at him putting his index finger on his lips and Walker stopped talking as they exited out into the parking lot.

Mason stopped at Chief Corsi's office, who waved him in. Mason said to Dick, "Well, the interviews are going great. I just saw Walker Craig lose his composure, big time. When I asked him whether he had anything to do with the six deaths, he screamed and yelled and wanted to leave but I made him sit down. He started the session having his lawyer giving him signals on whether to answer the questions until I threatened to subpoena him under a bench warrant. That seemed to get his attention. My hunch tells me that either he or his father, Dalton, is responsible for all these women dying. I just have to go over the deaths one by one to see if we can get any evidence to support that. I have four more people I am questioning, then I will sit with you and run it all by you and get your take on which way to go."

Dick Corsi said, "It sounds like you have things going in the right direction. Keep following your nose as they say. Keep me posted."

Mason said, "Thanks, Chief. Talk to you later." Mason went back to his office. It was almost noon, and he knew that Keisha Kane was coming in. He would ask her some questions and then take her to lunch. He would have to concentrate when she was here because her mere presence shook him to his core.

Robin buzzed Mason to let him know that Keisha had arrived. He said, "Can you send her to the conference room?" Robin said, "We are on our way."

Mason walked into the conference room to see Keisha Kane seated where he usually sat. He said, "Do you mind sitting on this side, my notes are here, and I have my back to the window so I can see if someone comes in."

Keisha laughed, "Are you saying you would rather me sit on the side where the camera is pointing?"

They both laughed. Mason said, "Well. To be perfectly honest, yes. We will be filming so I don't have to take notes. Are you okay with that?"

Keisha said, "Can I review the tape, I would like to see what I look like on the police camera?" They both laughed as she changed seats.

Mason, getting serious, began, "Keisha did you know any of these six women who were killed accidentally? Carmen Craig, Sarah Ostrov, Karena Katrinka, Belinda Cheeks, Jennifer Sandrew, or Lynda Laffarty?

Keisha said, "I knew all of them. Do you want me to describe my relationship with each of them?"

Mason said, "Yes, please."

Keisha began, "Carmen and I were lovers. After she found out her husband, Dalton, was seeing other women, she came to me and confided in me. One thing led to another, and we made love which relieved her stress. She and I were an item for two or three years off and on. She was not a lesbian but like all women, needed to be loved more frequently with someone she trusted.

"Sarah Ostrov was a beautiful lady who worked for *Playboy* and *Penthouse* in different capacities. We met on one of those photo shoots. We became friends. I was the other woman when she was seeing Dalton. It didn't last long because Dalton found out and put a stop to it.

"Karena Katrinka was a very shy lady and was in love with this man who treated her poorly. She took all she could, he had cheated, and they divorced. I was just a support mechanism for her.

"Belinda Cheeks was Dalton's housekeeper, so I knew her only briefly. She was a great person who had more talent than being a housekeeper but never took advantage of it.

"Jennifer Sandrew was a beautiful woman who liked guys and gals. She was a business wizard, but her relationship with Dalton did a number on her. I think she loved him, but he had moved on, which broke her heart.

"Lynda Laffarty was a good friend. She divorced Dalton and somehow became friends with all the women who were in his life, including Carmen Craig. They became a group and often did dinners and trips three or four times a year. Lynda was a very sexual person and had many lovers after she divorced Dalton. Is there anything else you want to know?"

Mason made a few notes but asked, "Do you think any of them were at odds with Dalton to the point he would kill them?"

Keisha replied, "Yes. All of them!"

Mason looked up from taking notes, looked Keisha in the eye, and asked, "Did you have a relationship with Dalton?"

Keisha laughed and said, "Why don't you ask Dalton."

Mason said, "That is funny. Can I take a raincheck on lunch? I have an emergency dentist appointment."

Keisha laughed and said, "No worries. Call me so we can get together again soon."

* * *

Mason went to his dentist's appointment on Friday afternoon. He was greeted by a hygienist, Carla Parker, who quickly took X-rays. She then cleaned his teeth. The doctor, Kelly Freeman, came in afterward, looked at the X-rays, and asked, "Do you want to do the cavity today or wait?"

Mason laughed, "Your girl has got my mouth pretty numb now, so you might as well do it now if you can."

Dr. Kelly said, "I will give you a shot to numb the area, and we should have you out of here in twenty minutes." She administered the shot, it numbed the area, and she came back to see him. Dr. Kelly drilled out the cavity, filled it, and did a fluoride treatment for him.

Dr. Kelly walked him out to the front desk. Kristen Valdosta, the insurance coordinator, confirmed his insurance while Amber Parkridge scheduled another appointment for him. As he stood at the desk, another hygienist, Ashley Quattro, brought another woman to the desk who was finished. The woman was a very attractive redhead. Mason thought he recognized her but couldn't place her. He was on his way out, and as he opened the door to leave, he heard both Ashley and Kristen from the desk say, "Thanks, Elizabeth. See you next time."

Mason thought that if he wasn't already somewhat involved with Keisha, he would try to get the lady's name from the dentist's office. He drove to Police Headquarters and went directly to his office. He called Erick Schrank to set up an interview. Erick agreed to meet at LAPD headquarters Saturday morning, at 10 a.m.

* * *

Mason then went to Dalton Craig's estate, and Sam Barfield again answered the door. Mason asked Sam, "Hello, Sam. I am here to see Erickson Howard."

Sam let him in, picked up a phone, and dialed the four digits for the Stable Master's office. Sam said into the phone, "I need Mr. Howard to come to the main house. There is a Detective Delsson here to talk to him." He hung up and said to Mason, "You can use the dining room to speak to him. Go in and have a seat." He pointed to the next room.

It looked like a dining room where there was a long twelve-foot dining table with armchairs at either end, and five chairs on either side. It looked to Mason to be a walnut carved set, beautiful and expensive. He waited for fifteen minutes, but no Erickson Howard appeared.

Mason called out to Sam, "Hey Sam. When do you expect Mr. Howard will arrive?"

Sam walked in and said, "He said he would be right over. I will go out to the barn area and check on him if you want."

Mason said, "I would appreciate that. Thanks." Sam left, walking out the back door. Mason decided to follow him at a distance. Sam walked briskly, so Mason did have some difficulty keeping up without being noticed. Sam walked into the stables, and Mason waited.

Sam could be heard calling out for Erickson Howard. He called three times and waited. Sam asked one of the stable boys where Mr. Howard was. The stable boy said, "Mr. Howard took his favorite steed out early this morning and has not returned yet. He didn't tell anyone where he was going. He just said, "I'll be back."

Sam turned to return to the house. He saw Mason standing halfway there and stopped to tell him, "He apparently was out riding since early this morning. He may be checking fences or water troughs around the property. I don't know when he'll return. When he does get back, I will tell him that he needs to set up an appointment with you ASAP."

Sam and Mason walked together back to the main house. Mason said, "Thanks for looking for him. I will await his call when he returns. Goodbye."

Sam said, "Goodbye, Mr. Delsson. I'll talk to you soon."

***

Mason wanted to talk to Deyna Doll. She told the police she thought she recognized the voice of one of the people who robbed the Racetrack. Mason stopped by the hospital. It was on his way to the office. He flashed his badge to the receptionist and asked what room he could find her. The receptionist, Chris Lebek, said, "Miss Doll is in room 405."

Mason took the elevator, noting he never liked the smell of hospitals for some reason. He exited to the fourth floor and went to the head nurse's desk. He asked for Deyna Doll. The nurse on the desk was Diane Deal. Mason noticed she had an elegant face, and from what he could see under the uniform, her body was elegant as well. He focused on her face, "Which way to Room 405?"

Diane Deal said, "You're here to see Deyna Doll?" Mason nodded.

Diane said, "I'm sorry, you missed her. She is down in physical therapy, so I couldn't speculate on a time she would return to her room."

Mason said, "Thank you. May I inquire about her status?"

Diane said, "No, you may not. We are not obliged to give out that information that is governed by HIPAA regulation."

Mason grumbled under his breath but remained professional, "What time do visiting hours run to?"

Diane Deal smiled and said, "Visiting hours are from 2 to 8 p.m. Patients need their rest, so we allow time in the morning for therapy, testing, and doctor visits. We cut them off at 8 p.m., so the patient can have some private time after their dinner."

Mason felt better so as he left, he told Diane, "Thanks for the information."

***

Mason left the hospital and decided to visit Erick Schrank, Carmen's financial advisor and the man who read her will the other day. Mason arrived at 2 p.m. and Denise DeLeo greeted him, "Good afternoon, Detective Delsson. What can I help you with today?"

Mason said, "I am here to talk to Erick if he is available."

Denise said, "He is on the phone right now. I will check to see if it is a long call." She got up from her desk and went into Erick's office.

Mason thought to himself that he was running into a lot of very sexy women lately. Denise had a beautiful face and was, as anyone could see, a very classy lady.

She returned as Mason was daydreaming, "He will be out in a minute to see you, please have a seat. Can I get you a water or something?"

Mason held up his hand while sitting down and said, "I'm good."

Erick came out into the outer office and said, "Detective Delsson, nice to see you. Please, come back to my office, and we can talk."

Mason followed him back to the rear office. Mason said, "Sorry to show up unannounced, but I was in the area and thought I would save you a trip to Headquarters."

Erick closed the door and motioned for Mason to sit in a chair opposite him at his work area desk. Mason began, "Mr. Schrank, I need your help. I have reason to believe that the person responsible for Carmen Craig's death is also responsible for five other deaths. In your discussions with Mrs. Craig, did she ever indicate to you that she feared for her life for some reason?"

Erick took a deep breath as he leaned back in his large, padded, leather chair. He said, "Detective Delsson, I have had many discussions with Mrs. Craig. All of which are confidential. We mostly spoke about what she intended to do with her significant wealth. If there was anything that she mentioned to me in these talks that was untoward, I would have called you upon hearing of her untimely death."

Mason said, "OK. Can you tell me what CEW is? They received the majority of the money she left in her will. Who has access to the money received? And where was the money designated?"

Erick took another deep breath. "Detective, under the terms of the contract that I signed to manage Mrs. Craig's finances, I cannot disclose what CEW is, even if I knew. Mrs. Craig set that trust up before she and I began working together. All I have is the name and destination of the account. I get semi-annual reports for our tax reporting, but other than that, I am afraid I can't be of any help."

Denise DeLeo knocked at Erick's office door, entered, and said, "I am sorry to interrupt, but you have two phone calls on hold, and your next appointment is waiting." She closed the door and left.

Mason looked at Erick's phone, and there were, indeed, two lines blinking. He said to Mr. Schrank, "I guess that is all I have, Erick. Thanks for letting me drop in. I will leave so you can get back to work. Have a nice day."

Erick said, "Thanks for understanding. Good day."

Mason let himself out of the office. He noticed that a woman was waiting as Denise had indicated, so he felt better that he wasn't bum rushed out of the office. The woman was dressed well. She wore a large, wide-brimmed black hat. Her black dress was elegant, and her five-inch heels completed the ensemble nicely. She also wore very large black sunglasses that almost hid her face completely. She reminded him of a movie star. Mason said to Denise, "Thanks, Ms. DeLeo, for squeezing me into Erick's schedule. Have a great rest of your day." He left the office.

* * *

Greg Solomet walked into the bedroom of their hotel room with two drinks. He found Jodi in a skimpy yellow negligee that made him stop and stare. Jodi cleared her throat to get Greg's attention. She said, "I take it from the look on your face, Mr. Solomet, that you approve of my choice of sleepwear."

Greg handed her the drink he made for her and said, "A toast to the negligee makers all over the world, and to the beautiful women who wear them. You look mouth-wateringly delicious. Cheers." They clinked glasses and drank.

Greg grabbed both drinks and set them on the nightstand. He took Jodi in his arms, and they kissed. Their hands were all over one another. Their breathing became quicker and louder. Jodi broke the kiss, grabbed Greg's hand, and led him to the king-size bed. They quickly lay naked in an embrace, became amorous, and their love dance began. Jodi was loud during these trysts. Greg loved the sounds and chatter that Jodi voiced to describe the action while Greg attempted to match her ferociousness. They were both completely spent and fell asleep.

* * *

Mason walked into the hospital once again. He rode the elevator to the fourth-floor reception desk and asked if Deyna Doll was in her room.

The nurse, Diane Deal, said, "You are in luck today, Detective. She just returned from therapy fifteen minutes ago. Her room is 405-B."

The nurse pointed down which hallway Mason should take. He arrived at the room, knocked, and waited for a reply. He heard, "Come in if you don't have any pills or needles."

Mason walked in and saw Deyna dressed and looking like she was ready to leave the hospital. He asked, "Miss Doll remember me? I am Detective Mason Delsson from LAPD. Are you leaving the hospital today?"

Deyna replied, "Unfortunately, no. The doctors tell me I should stay a few more days. I agreed if they took all the tubes out of me and let me dress in street clothes. I can walk around the floor for some exercise, but not outside yet. Please have a seat."

Just as Mason sat on the long couch built into the wall adjacent to her hospital bed, a man walked in dressed in a business suit. Mason assumed it was the doctor, but the man walked over to Deyna, leaned down, and kissed her passionately. He said, "How are you feeling today, Chica?"

Deyna said, "Better, honey. This is Detective Delsson from the LAPD Detective Mason, this is my husband, Dennis Bellowso."

The men shook hands. Mason said, "Deyna, I have but a few questions. If you are not feeling up to it for any reason, please let me know. I will try to be brief. I heard from my source at the racetrack that on the day of the robbery, you indicated you thought you recognized the voice of one of the robbers. Is that true?

Deyna did not hesitate, "Yes, Detective. The voice I recognized sounded like Kevin Syracuse, but I may be mistaken. He runs Sagittarius Pictures. He lives with my friend, Susie Crull. We have had dinner with them many times. He has a distinct accent from New York."

Mason said, "Deyna, it seems unlikely that a man who runs one of the largest film studios in Southern California would stoop to the level of robbing a racetrack. If he were caught, it would jeopardize all of his hard work over many years."

Deyna replied, "Well, Detective, if you delve into his financial stability and recent failures of the movies he has produced out of his studio, you might find a probable rationale for the venture. All that man talks about at parties and gatherings is how much he hates Dalton Craig. He blames Dalton for stealing all his good employees, the cameramen, grips, producers, and writers. Gemini Studios, which Dalton owns, can afford to pay these professionals much more money because, as he says, Dalton's rich wife. Kevin's Sagittarius Studios has not had a hit movie since they produced the Snow Villain series."

Mason jotted down some notes and said, "Deyna, how much money did they end up getting during the robbery?"

Deyna said, "I have spoken to Christy Amherst over the past several days as she calls to check on me daily. The Raceway's accountants estimate that the haul was in the neighborhood of $450 thousand. We have a safeguard against robbery, so we deposit regularly. Because it was a weekend when they hit us, we had over three days in receipts on hand ready to be picked up by our bank courier, Brink's Security."

Mason said, "How big is the grudge that Kevin Syracuse has against Dalton Craig?"

Dennis, Deyna's husband, answered, "I have heard him say that he wanted to destroy everything that Dalton Craig cherishes."

Mason asked, "Deyna, who at the racetrack knows what the money pick-up schedule is?"

Deyna replied, "Just Cricky Amherst and me. Why?"

Mason said, "The robbery could have been random. In my experience over the years, no crime happens randomly. Do you think it could have been someone inside the racetrack that tipped them off about when you would have the most money on hand?"

Deyna replied laughing, "You know. I thought about whether Cricky had tipped them off so she could collect the insurance money. Then she told me that Carmen Craig had left her $6 million in her will. So, any shortfall that Ms. Amherst would have had would have been cleared up by that money. I trust her, but I don't know her that well. She may be the one. I will have to watch her spending in the next few months."

Making a note, Mason asked, "Deyna, there are six women who've died who were connected to Dalton Craig in some way. Do you think he could be responsible? All of which, by the way, were seemingly accidental."

Deyna quickly said, "I don't know him, but if Kevin Syracuse could rob a racetrack of $450 thousand, I suppose Dalton may be capable of doing anything because of the power and influence he wields."

Mason stood and said, "That's all I have, Miss Doll. Thank you for your candidness and your time. I hope you recover quickly. Have a nice day. Nice to meet you, Dennis." Mason left the hospital.

* * *

Mason was on his way to see Keisha when his cell phone buzzed, "Hello, this is Mason."

It was Randy Keene. Randy said, "Hey, Mason. I just want to let you know that I am back in 90210. Not much happening in Tahoe so I got back this morning. I met my wife, Michelle, for lunch downtown and saw something interesting that I thought I would share."

Mason said, "I can always count on you to brighten my day, Randy. What have you got?"

Randy continued, "Michelle and I were at The Rooftop on Wilshire when she asked me, 'Isn't that Kevin Syracuse from Sagittarius Studios?' I looked over and he was seated at a table no more than twenty feet with two other people. He was sitting with Erickson Howard, Dalton Carig's stable master, and Diane Deal, Walker Craig's nurse when he was taken to the hospital after being shot. I was thinking Walker might have known he was being targeted so he was lucky his dad provided security for him in the hospital in the event it was more than a random shooting."

Mason said, "That is very interesting. Stop by my office this afternoon if you're free. I have an idea."

Randy said, "I will be there by three o'clock. Talk soon."

Mason got back to his office and sketched out a plan of surveillance on Kevin Syracuse and Erickson Howard. Mason wanted to question Mr. Howard about finding Carmen Craig dead.

Mason called Keisha Kane, who blew him off for lunch the other day to see if she was upset with him and if she was available to have dinner with him. Mason got her answering machine. He left a message: "Hi Keisha, I wanted to know if you and I are still okay. I wanted to take you to dinner soon. Tonight, if possible. Give me a call if you are interested in seeing me. This is Mason. Miss you. Goodbye."

* * *

Jodi Panicee was dressing for dinner. It would be their last night in Paris, France. Greg was taking her to a very fancy restaurant. It was a great vacation for them and very productive. Greg had purchased a house in the center of Paris within walking distance of the Eiffel Tower. They had dinner at Milagro on Bouquet Street. They wanted to walk back to their hotel, but it started to rain so they hailed a cab, went back to the hotel, and had a nightcap at the bar. They retired early to prepare for a long day of travel to the U.S.

Jodi was pleased, not only with the vacation time with Greg, but also the fact she found and arranged for the use of twelve different locations for Dalton Craig's Gemini Studios' next movie. She knew Dalton would be pleased.

They flew to Munich, Germany where they had a short layover, then took a Lufthansa Airliner directly to LAX. They arrived in Los Angeles at 9:00 a.m. It had been a long day, and they were picked up at the airport by a limousine that Dalton had scheduled for them. Dalton wanted to hear all about the locations Jodi had secured so he invited them both to stay at his home to recover from the trip. Jodi and Greg were both able to sleep on the plane, so they were somewhat refreshed when they arrived at the Craig Estate.

Sam Barfield welcomed them back and showed them to their room. He said, "You folks can freshen up or rest for a bit. Dalton had the chef prepare a lavish lunch for us."

Jodi thanked him and said, "I think we may swim before lunch, unless you have an objection to that."

Sam replied, "Oh, by all means. It is a beautiful day, and the pool is heated to a comfortable temperature. Dalton doesn't like swimming in cold water. I have some errands to run so I will see you at lunch."

Sam left and Jodi and Greg unpacked. They changed into their swimsuits to prepare to go down to the pool. Greg wore board shorts, and Jodi had on the tiniest bikini. Greg had never remembered seeing one smaller. Greg said, "Wow. I think you look magnificent in the iridescent green suit. I hope I don't drown looking at you in that while we're swimming."

Jodi laughed and grabbed her bag with their towels, donned her coverup, and they went down to the pool. A servant brought over two large Bloody Mary drinks when they chose a table. He said, "Compliments of Mr. Craig."

They walked into the pool together after each took a sip of their drink. The water was a perfect temperature, and Greg swam laps while Jodi slipped into the jacuzzi. They got out of the water just in time to be welcomed officially by Dalton Craig.

Dalton said, "Welcome back you guys. How was your trip?" I hear it was productive. Can we freshen your cocktails?" He sat at his usual table, and his Bloody Mary was waiting for him.

Jodi and Greg grabbed their drinks and went over to Dalton's table. Jodi began, "I don't know if you two have met. Dalton, this is Greg Solomet. Greg, this is Dalton Craig." The men shook hands, and everyone sat.

Dalton said, "I have invited a bunch of folks here tomorrow night for cocktails and finger foods. They are all scheduled to work on our next movie, *Drugs Do Kill.* Jodi, I will need you to fill them in on the locations you've secured. Are you prepared?"

Jodi laughed, "Yes, Sir, Mr. Craig. I have a slide presentation on my computer so we can show it on the pull-down screen at the outside bar. Would you like to review it prior?"

Dalton said, "I am so lucky to have you working here. I knew you would be on top of this. Nice work. Everyone is coming at 7:30 p.m. We can eat a light dinner at five inside if you like. I will wait to see the slide show tomorrow."

Jodi and Greg Solomet decided to go out for dinner after they had lunch and rested. They dined at Retreat Two. Jodi ran into some friends, and Greg went to the bar for another drink. He physically ran into Kevin Syracuse. They both laughed, as they had been roommates in college and hadn't seen each other in years. They drank together and Kevin told him of his plan to destroy Dalton Craig.

Greg told him he was staying at the Craig Estate with Jodi Panicee. Kevin proposed to Greg that he could make $250,000. Greg said, "I am all in." They set up a plan for Dalton to have an accident in his pool. Both of them were excited about the plan. Greg more so about the money he could make. Greg said nothing to Jodi.

* * *

As house guests gathered, the chef's assistant wheeled out to the pool area, the food that was prepared. He had fresh drinks for everyone, and their place settings were laid on the table. Juan, their server, uncovered a plate of chicken salad sandwiches, salmon rollups, assorted pickles and olives, sliced fruits, and several different kinds of bread.

They were joined by Sam, and everyone selected the buffet offerings. Juan said, "If you don't see something you'd like just ring the buzzer next to Mr. Craig's chair."

Dalton had a polite conversation with Greg about what business he was in and how he enjoyed Paris. Greg replied, "I first want to thank you for the trip, the accommodations in Paris, and the hospitality here. They were all much appreciated. I am working for an international investment company that has relationships here in the United States as well as in Europe. I will spend half the year here at home and the other abroad. Without letting anything out of the bag, I wanted to say that Jodi did a spectacular job lining up all the potential locations in Paris. I was able to find a wonderful house not far from the Eiffel Tower. It overlooks the Seine River and was more affordable than I had anticipated. You are always welcome to use it when you're abroad or visiting Paris."

Dalton said, "That is very gracious of you. Thank you. I was just talking to my date for this evening, and she was telling me how much she wants to visit Paris. You know, all women have this romantic dream, so I might just take you up on the offer." Juan appeared and began to clear away the dishes and asked if he could bring more drinks.

At six o'clock, Fitore Fantazee took an Uber to the Craig Estate. She was going to spend a few days with him before he began his next project so she figured they would be in bed much of the time. Dalton rose from the table, surprised that Fitore was there as she walked out onto the back patio.

Dalton said, "What a nice surprise. We are just finishing a light dinner. Would you like me to have the chef fix you a hot plate?"

Fitore said, "No, thank you. I had a big lunch."

Dalton turned her toward the table and said, "You know Sam. This is Jodi Panicee, my assistant, and her friend, Greg Solomet." They all exchanged pleasantries, and Fitore sat at the table. Dalton turned to offer Fitore a drink, but he was beaten to the punch.

Juan appeared quickly and asked, "Hello, Miss Fantazee, can I get you something from the bar?"

Fitore said, "Vodka on the rocks."

The folks at the table were chatting about nothing in particular when Jodi said, "I am going to relax upstairs, then change for company. Greg, will you accompany me?"

Greg said, "I would love nothing better. Dalton, thank you for lunch. I will see you later. Nice to meet everyone."

Sam Barfield noticed Jodi and Greg walking out of the pool area. He saw that Dalton Craig was scowling, his face turned red. Sam asked him, "What don't you like about that situation?"

Dalton said, "I know Jodi took him to Paris, but I also know that she expressed interest in my son, Walker. When I spoke to Jodi about it, she was filled with excitement. She said that she has had a crush on Walker since she began working for me here."

Sam said, "So, what concerns you? Walker getting hurt or Jodi breaking Walker's heart?"

Fitore rose and said, "I am going to shower."

Dalton said, "Okay, right behind you."

To Sam, he said, "Either would anger me."

Sam said, "Do you have a thing for Jodi?"

Dalton said to Sam, "NO! Don't try to read my mind. I am going to shower and change as well. I will see you at seven."

Dalton rose and took a quick dip in the pool and swam four lengths. He crawled up the ladder, grabbed a towel off one of the lounges, dried his muscular body. then left.

Juan began clearing the table to set up for the evening's festivities and asked Sam if he wanted more to drink. Sam said, "No, thanks, Juan. I think I may need to be alert have my wits about me tonight, just in case the crowd gets a bit unruly. I can step in and be the voice of reason. I am going upstairs to change as well. See you later."

Juan finished setting up the tables around the far side of the pool, where Mr. Craig wanted the podium set up in front of a large TV screen that could be rolled down for viewing. He made sure the bar was stocked with plenty of liquor, and the champagne was on ice. Juan then jumped into the pool to relax for a few minutes before the evening's festivities.

The waiter and waitresses from the catering company arrived. There were decorations, posters and lights to be hung. The setup crew got to work on that first. Then the hibachis were set up next to the bar. The food and silverware would soon adorn these tables. There was even a disc jockey setting up to play music before and after the meeting.

7

AT 7 O'CLOCK SHARP, the majority of Dalton's guests began to arrive. Most stood at the bar, got their drink, and began chatting with the people they knew. By 7:15 p.m., Dalton appeared on the patio with his date. He said, "Guys, this is my friend, Fitore Fantazee." Then he walked toward the bar.

Dalton looked handsome as always, as if he were starring in the movie they were about to make. Fitore had donned a sexy little black dress with black six-inch pumps. She wore a beautiful pair of dangling diamond earrings to complete the outfit. Her long red hair made her stand out like a beautiful stop sign, just more voluptuous.

Fitore was on Dalton's arm and was introduced to all the folks who had gathered. Many were familiar with her work, and everyone was impressed by her beauty. Dalton brought her to the end of the bar and sat her down. He whispered in her ear, "I don't think you have anything under that glorious black dress, and I am anxious to get you out of it later tonight." Fitore moaned in his ear, then ordered a drink.

By eight o'clock, everyone had consumed a few drinks and eaten from the tables of finger food that Juan had been carrying out from the kitchen. Dalton called everyone's attention. He said, "Ladies and Gentlemen. Thank you all for gathering tonight. I am very excited to get our new project off the ground. I am also excited to work with each of you and tap into your legendary talents so we can put another great story on film. As we wanted to use three different locations, I will now introduce my assistant, Jodi Panicee, who will give us a presentation on the locales and timelines. Jodi."

There was polite applause as most knew Jodi and were anxious to see what she had to offer. Jodi walked to the middle of the bar and addressed the group. All eyes were on her as she stood at the podium next to the large white screen in front of the bar. Jodi grabbed the microphone and began, "Good evening, everyone. So nice to see all these familiar faces. I am grateful for the opportunity to show you what we have as locations for our film. We will begin at our Gemini studios one week from tomorrow."

Now, folks were paying close attention. Jodi continued, "Monday morning, we will begin our table reads beginning at 8 a.m. Each of you will receive a schedule of where and when you are needed on set. By Wednesday, we will have made script changes, if any, and will begin filming at noon. We will complete the week and the week after here in Los Angeles. On the 15th, most of you will fly to Lake Tahoe. Reservations at the hotel have already been made. We will be there for four weeks at various locations. We will then take a group of you to the Paris, France location. We have booked our group at the Ritz Hotel. We should complete filming in two weeks, but we may be there another week to do stills and rewrites if needed. I have a brief slide show to give you an idea of where the filming will take place."

Jodi turned around to the massive white screen that the bartender had already rolled down for her. Jodi turned on the projector connected to her computer. She began with the hotel at Lake Tahoe. "We will stay at the Hilton Vacation Club on Sky Run. Each of you has a room, and meals eaten there will be charged to your room. The other locations in Tahoe will be the Lakefront Fishing Emporium run by Del Madison, as well as several restaurants along the lake, specifically Café Fiore, Harrah's, and Retreat West. Here are some random shots from the middle of town. Lots of shopping and small shops. Now our smaller group will fly to Paris for two or possibly three weeks. Here are slides of the Hotel, the in-town locations, as well as our locations in the

French countryside. This concludes the presentation. Does anyone have any questions? Did I miss anything?"

No one asked a question, so Dalton clapped in applause. He said, "Nicely done, as expected, Jodi. Thank you. Those all looked so inviting. I can't wait to begin shooting this film. We have all the finalized scripts for each of you in this film. Jodi will hand them out as you leave this evening. Once again, thanks to Jodi for a great presentation."

The applause died down as folks began milling around and getting drinks. Dalton walked over to Jodi, and they embraced. He said, "Great job, Doll. Can't wait to see you on the beach in France."

Jodi replied, "You mean one of the nude beaches?"

Dalton said with a smile, "So kill me because I have fantasies."

They both laughed, but Jodi knew it was something she wanted. She longed to be with Dalton for a long time. She wondered.

The next morning, Dalton packed and left for Lake Tahoe. Fitore was disappointed she only had one night with him, but he assured her he would bring her to Paris after the crew left Tahoe. Fitore was happy and left for home.

* * *

Mason Delsson knew he had a dental appointment today, so he rose early. He knew Susan would be ready and waiting. He got out of his car at 9 a.m. Amber and Kristin greeted him melodiously. He sat for maybe thirty seconds when Susan appeared from the back area and beckoned him to follow her. She looked beautiful as always, and he thought how everyone in the office of women was a real beauty. He reminded himself to ask Kristin about the "Elizabeth" that he saw on his last visit a week or so ago. Susan began the cleaning process, and his thoughts were on her instructions. Forty minutes later, she was finished and praised him for the improvement in his tooth care.

Dr. Kelly came in and checked the work Susan had finished, and asked Mason if he had any issues.

Mason said, "No, Dr. Freeman, Susan has taken me under her wing, and I think all is well."

Dr. Freeman walked him out to the reception area, saying, "Kristin, make an appointment in four months for Mr. Delsson to see Susan. Have a great day, Detective."

Mason replied, "Thank you, Dr. Freeman. Nice to see you."

As Mason got to the door, he was almost knocked over by a woman who entered quickly without seeing him. He caught her in his arms and steadied her. The woman began to apologize immediately, "I am so sorry. I am late. I wanted to get in to see Dr. Freeman, and now I am apologizing to you as well as her. Are you okay?"

Mason looked at this beauty and said, "I saw you the last time you were here. I will forgive you if you have a drink with me later." Mason handed her his card.

She said, "That is very sweet, but I am leaving the country for a while, and I am seeing some as well. Thank you, though." She hurried off as Ashley, her hygienist, was waiting for her.

Mason walked to his car and realized it was the same woman he wanted to find out about, and she was involved. That was no surprise. He drove to his office, wondering where he had seen her before. He grabbed for his revolver and realized he had left it on the kitchen table at home because he didn't want to leave it in the car at the Dentist's office. He swung by the house to retrieve it. He noticed his new neighbor, Catie Gaynor, out in her front yard planting some flowers. She waved and said, "Hi, Mason. Hey, can I ask a favor of you?"

Mason walked over to where she was kneeling in the front flower bed, "Getting a jump on the yard work before the heat hits? What do you need, Miss Catie?"

Catie stood, and Mason stepped back. He gave her as discreet a once-over as he could. She had on a tank top and a pair of short shorts. She replied, "My friend, Ryan, is coming to the house erect a gazebo this weekend. Would you be willing to help if I offered to make lasagna for you both?"

Mason said, "Sure. How early did you want to start on Saturday?"

Catie replied, "Would 9 a.m. be okay? I can have coffee and bagels ready if you want."

Mason said, "I will be here bright and early then. Have a good day, Catie." He went back into his house and grabbed his revolver. He drove off, going back to his office.

* * *

Randy Keene was waiting for Mason in Mason's office, "Hi, Detective Delsson, nice hours you have coming at 10 a.m."

Mason laughed, "I was out of my house at 7:30 as I had a dentist appointment. Not that it's any of your concern, young man. Do you have any new information?"

Randy opened his notebook and began, "I have been following Mr. Kevin Syracuse for the last three days. He has met some very interesting people. As far as I can tell, they had nothing to do with the film industry. If I had to make a guess, they looked like old-time mobsters. I am having my associates run down their names from the pictures I have taken. I saw a group of them drive off in a car with Nevada license plates. I am checking with my contacts in Vegas. Syracuse and Diane Deal seem to be very chummy. She has had him over to her place four of the last five nights. We overheard them at a restaurant in Beverly Hills the other day, talking about Carmen Craig. We didn't get much detail, but we have our ears on so to speak. I will let you know as soon as we hear from my guys in Vegas who these guys are. We will continue our surveillance of Mr. Syracuse."

* * *

Dalton had packed a suitcase for his trip to Lake Tahoe. He wanted a few days to set things up before the film crew arrived. Fitore left earlier that morning as they enjoyed a leisurely morning around the pool. Dalton closed his suitcase and called his butler to take it downstairs.

An Uber would take him to LAX to fly to Tahoe. He would stay again at Hilton's Vacation Club Resort. He was a frequent visitor, so he was given the same suite each time he visited. He called Jodi and asked her to come downstairs so he could give her final instructions. Jodi Panicee appeared looking ready for a day at the pool. Dalton said, "Jodi, I wanted to remind you to stay as long as you want here at the ranch. Greg seems like a nice guy, so please enjoy your time together. The place is yours. You can join me next week in Lake Tahoe, as I will not need you there before then."

Jodi asked, "Can I give you a ride to the airport?"

Dalton laughed, looking at her skimpy bikini, and said, "With you dressed like that, we might not make it on time for my flight. Thanks, but I have an Uber coming to take me. I will call you if I need anything before you arrive, but I think we are all set to begin. I will set up meetings with the crew and work on my schedule for shooting the scenes in Tahoe. I may even have time to finalize some of the things we need to schedule when we go to Paris. I will be busy. That is why I am going alone." They were saying their goodbyes as Dalton's Uber arrived.

Dalton arrived late Saturday morning and went straight to his room. He made several calls to his crew to set up meetings when they arrived in five days. He spent the rest of the morning visiting the locations and making his notes regarding dressing room availability, as well as camera locations and lighting needs. Dalton had a late lunch. Afterward, he sat on the veranda and had a few drinks. He again reviewed the actor's lines from the script. He looked at his notes for the thirty scenes he would shoot at this location. He wanted to give the actors their stage directions for each scene. He had dinner in the hotel restaurant, then retired.

Jodi and Greg drank all day and didn't eat. Jodi crawled into bed and slept.

Greg Solomet was found floating almost at the bottom of the pool. Greg was dead.

* * *

Mason Delsson was dressed in shorts and sneakers with a tank top. He walked next door at 9 a.m., where he was greeted at the door by Catie Gaynor. She was dressed in short shorts and a black workout bra. She looked radiant as if she had been up for hours. She invited him in, and her friend Ryan Parker was already there, having coffee at the kitchen table. She introduced them, and she offered Mason coffee.

He said, "No Thanks. I had two cups this morning while going over my emails and notes from last week. I am ready to go whenever you are." They all rose from the table and went out the sliding door that led to the deck. Ryan had unpacked many of the pieces of the gazebo already, so they began quickly. Ryan and Mason worked well together. Mason found out in their chats that Ryan was an agent in the film industry but primarily worked for an insurance company in town as an IT Manager.

Catie added, "Ryan is a virtual genius when it comes to computer programs, and he is my primary source when I get stumped by something or have any kind of technical issue." The guys worked through the afternoon and were finished by 2 p.m. Catie served lasagna for them.

* * *

Randy Keene was in Mason Delsson's office when he arrived. Mason sat, and Randy began, "I could not wait to see you and wanted to be here in person to tell you what we found out. We went up on the telephone pole on the Sagittarius Studios lot. We tapped into Kevin Syracuse's office phone. I didn't go through police channels as we wanted it to be secretive. We heard him talking to the guys from Vegas. We have identified them as Julius Greco and Freddie Caputi. Both are ex-cons with a long arrest record for each of them. I checked with my sources in Las Vegas and confirmed they are with the Labella Crime Family. We have them on tape setting up another hit, but they used code names for the targets, which are a man and a woman. It looks like Diane Deal is the person they are using for the woman. The man is a secondary target for some reason."

Mason said, "I think I know who they are targeting. I had suspected that the person I was thinking of, Kevin Syracuse, was the mastermind behind the killings. Syracuse wanted to keep out of the dirt, so he hired others to do his killing. Randy, if you could please, keep your whole team on him. I am going to visit Mr. Syracuse once I piece together the evidence that we have that points to Kevin's guilt."

Randy said, "We are on it, Boss. I'll have my team check in every hour with any new developments."

Mason went to the funeral of Lynda Laffarty. There were a few hundred people in attendance, along with the pastor and a few close friends. He felt sad because she had so much family and so many friends in her life; it was a shame to see the sparse showing.

After the funeral, Mason drove to Sagittarius Studios. He was let in the gate and directed to the office of Kevin Syracuse. He got to the building marked office and parked the car. He walked into the office, and there stood Antonia Myers. She said, "Hello, Detective Delsson. How are you today? How can we help you?"

Mason said, "I am looking to speak with Mr. Syracuse if he is available."

Antonia said, "Oh, I am so sorry. He is out scouting locations this morning. Can I have him call you, or would you like to set up an appointment to see him? What is your visit regarding?"

Mason thought for a moment and didn't want to reveal his hand. He said, "We have had some deaths of folks connected to the film industry, and I was hoping he could shed some light on the circumstances of some of the people who died. If you could set up a meeting for me, I would appreciate it."

Antonia said, "Give me your contact information, and I will call you."

* * *

Mason and Ryan Parker chatted through lunch. They had a lot in common. Both loved football, and even though they cheered for different teams, each could appreciate the talent the other's favorite team had accumulated. Mason invited him to his home to watch football on opening day. They made a date for Opening Day.

Catie walked Ryan out the front door and thanked him for his expertise and hard work. Ryan expressed his thanks for lunch, "It is always delicious when you make lasagna, and yours is the best. Call me anytime if you need something."

Mason sat at the kitchen peninsula, waiting for Catie's return. When she came back in, Mason started to say something, but she cut him off, saying, "Mason, thank you again for helping erect the gazebo. I will enjoy sitting out back, out of the sun. Speaking of setting out back, I am going to grill some steaks on the grill later. Would you like to join me?"

Mason was flattered, "Yes, shall I bring a bottle or two of red wine?" Catie said, "That sounds great. Why don't we say around seven?"

Mason replied, "If I am not here by 7:05 p.m., call the police because I am dead next door."

They both laughed, and Catie said, "Be careful what you wish for, Mr. Delsson. See you later, then."

Mason went home to shower. He checked his email and found two messages from Randy Keene. The most recent said: *Call me when you get this.* The first one he sent said: *I have heard the plan that Kevin Syracuse and Diane Deal have concocted. Call me!!*

Mason jumped into the shower. He stepped out of the shower, drying himself as he went to the phone on his desk. He dialed Randy Keene, who answered on the first ring. Mason said, "Were you waiting by the phone for me to call?"

Randy said, "As a matter of fact, yes, I was. I was sitting in a bar on Melrose today and saw Kevin Syracuse walk in and sit down with Diane Deal, who had her back to me initially. I put my long-distance microphone on the table and began recording as I listened through my earbuds. I was shocked when they began the conversation immediately and Diane said to Kevin, 'Who do you want me to kill today?' I almost fell off my chair. I continued to listen. Kevin replied, 'I think it is time for Miss Christine Amherst to meet her maker.' Diane then said, 'I have been tailing her for a week, just in case. She works at the racetrack thirty minutes past closing. She is the last one there, so it should go smoothly. She won't make it to the bank deposit tonight. I will call you afterward and confirm the kill.' Kevin said, 'I will have your money ready for you when the job is done.'"

Mason said, "I will be there tonight. I will meet you a block away. I will have LAPD blues ready on the next block. We will identify Diane Deal's location. Then we will surround her. Once we see any sign of Cricky exiting the building, we will apprehend Diane Deal immediately."

Randy said, "The track closes at 11 p.m., so I will see you at 10:15 p.m. at West Cerritos and Walker Street. I only wish Kevin Syracuse were there so I could lock this guy in jail immediately, instead of waiting until later to arrest him at his home and play the tape for him. I cannot wait for that interrogation. See you later." They ended their call.

Mason dressed and went next door with two bottles of her favorite wine. He picked up four bottles of Governor's Bay Sauvignon Blanc to try and impress her. Catie answered the door in an outfit that can only be described as fetching or maybe sexy as all get out. She wore a pink camisole with a pink bra beneath it. She wore pink shorts that looked like they were painted on. Her hair was in a ponytail, and she wore beige, woven mules with a sensible three-inch heel. Catie hugged Mason and stepped back so he could enter. Mason thought she looked like a sexy, 18-year-old, but in layman's terms, she looked "HOT." Mason held out the bottle of wine, and Catie said, "Thank you so much. How did you know which wine was my favorite?"

Mason gathered himself and said, "The same way you knew what my favorite outfit on a lady was. By the way, you look delicious."

Catie blushed and said, "Thank you, Mason. Now you've made me blush."

Mason said, "I hope I didn't make you uncomfortable. I have been thinking about how beautiful you are for some time now, and I have to let you know the effect you have on me. While I am at it, I can only stay for a few hours tonight as I have a sting operation that will take place later. I would like to do this again at my place so I can cook for you. Just name the day and time, and I will fix you my famous spaghetti and meatballs."

Catie replied, "That is quite the undertaking, Mr. Delsson, cooking an Italian dish for someone who has Italian heritage."

Mason said, "I am confident you will enjoy the meal, so is that a yes to my invitation?"

Catie said laughing, "Let's see how tonight goes. I sense that we will have another meeting, but I will let you know, for sure, later." They both laughed. Mason opened and poured the wine. Catie served a sumptuous repast. Their conversation was interesting, and each flirted openly.

Mason looked at his watch and saw it was ten o'clock and time for him to leave. He stood and said, "Catie, this has been one of the most enjoyable nights I have had in a long time. I hope you will join me soon for a reciprocating meal. Thoughts?"

Catie stood as well and walked to the door. He followed. As she turned around, they kissed. It wasn't friendly. It was more like one of them brought electricity to the kiss, and sparks flew. Each thought the other had given the jolt.

Catie said, "I am free tomorrow night if you're available. That kiss was the clincher."

Mason said, "Tomorrow at 7 p.m., barring any earthquakes or firestorms. I will have dinner ready, and the wine poured. Thank you again for a lovely evening. Sleep well." They kissed again and it was hard for each of them to separate.

Catie said, "I will wear something sexier tomorrow."

Mason replied, "If that is the case, I will have my nitroglycerin ready. Just in case of a heart attack. Good night, lovely Catie." He was gone.

* * *

Mason drove toward the Los Alamitos Racetrack. He arrived at 10:10 p.m. He saw Randy's gray Cadillac Eldorado and went past it a block. He began to turn around when he saw, none other than Kevin Syracuse, sitting in an old GMC SUV. Mason went a block further and turned his car around to park behind Kevin and shut off his headlights.

Mason phoned Randy. Randy answered, "Yes, sir. Are you here?"

Mason said, "I am two blocks away from you. I am sitting watching Kevin Syracuse from half a block away from your location. Is Diane Deal here yet?"

Randy said, "Yes, she is right outside the office building that Cricky Amherst is in right now. I called Cricky and let her know she was a target. I advised her to send a female security guard out to her car and drive it away from the track. If Diane or Kevin makes a move toward the car or the office, we will intervene immediately."

They waited.

At 11 p.m. sharp, a security guard who was an off-duty LAPD officer, disguised as Cricky, left the Racetrack office. She walked to Cricky Amherst's car, which was parked in her usual spot. Halfway to the car, Diane Deal put her car in gear and raced toward the woman. Lyla Baroni heard the car approach and rolled her body into an evasive move behind another car. Diane Deal slowed down to get a picture with her phone camera.

Diane Deal lost control of the wheel of her car, which crashed into another vehicle parked in the racetrack parking lot. LAPD had three cars at the scene for backup. They moved in just after Diane's car stopped.

Randy and Mason were on either side of Kevin Syracuse's vehicle. Kevin sat there in horror, watching what had just transpired. He waited to see if Diane was okay. It became obvious she was fine as she exited her car independently. Kevin put his car in gear and made a U-turn. Randy was now following Kevin, and Mason pulled his car out in front of Mr. Syracuse's vehicle with the siren and lights on. Kevin came to a stop just two feet from Mason's passenger door.

Mason was out of his vehicle and yelled at Kevin Syracuse to exit the vehicle with his hands up. Kevin was compliant and assumed the position with his hands up on the roof of his vehicle. Randy Keene exited his vehicle and was there to advise Mr. Syracuse of his Miranda rights. He handcuffed Kevin Syracuse; walked him to his police vehicle, placing him in the back seat. Mason walked up to him and said, "Mr. Syracuse, we have been following you for several weeks now. You have been overheard talking to Miss Deal about the people you wanted to eliminate. We have you on tape several times ordering people killed. We will impound your vehicle, and you will be able to contact your lawyer when we reach police headquarters."

Kevin Syracuse just laughed. He put his head down, not wanting the press to take his picture. Mason sent Lyla to headquarters with Diane in custody, after she was examined by the medical team, and was given the thumbs up. Meaning she was OK.

Mason knew it would be a long night as he had many questions for Mr. Syracuse. He would have to wait until his lawyer arrived before he could begin his interrogation.

Randy waited for the wreckers to pick up both Diane Deal's and Kevin Syracuse's vehicles. He would then drive back to headquarters to assist Mason with the interrogation of Mr. Syracuse.

Mason sat at his desk in police headquarters. He wrote down questions for Kevin Syracuse. He was mostly interested in whether or not he had perpetrated the killing of all these women and what motivated him to do it if he had. He had suspected others, but the evidence pointed to Kevin Syracuse. He developed a list of questions for Kevin's initial interrogation. He looked them over and thought he was ready.

The list of questions read:

Why did you target Carmen Craig? Was it your jealousy of her relationship with Dalton Craig, who was your mortal enemy? What happened to Belinda Cheeks? Was she your former housekeeper, and Dalton stole her from you? Was it you who had the vehicle she was driving altered so the brakes wouldn't work when she drove to the market to do her shopping errands for Craig's estate? Or maybe you altered the brakes with someone else in mind?

He would ask Kevin about his involvement with Karina Katrinka, Lynda Laffarty, and Jennifer Sandrew, and why he was targeting Cricky Amherst, as well as his relationship with Diane Deal.

* * *

Dalton Craig arrived in Lake Tahoe and stayed at the same hotel he was preparing for the filming of his next film. After he checked in, he had Tony Strong, his limo driver, ferry him around to all the locations that Jodi Panicee had secured for the film.

He returned to the hotel at 4 p.m. and showered, preparing for dinner. He checked his emails and then dressed for dinner. He went down to the hotel bar and asked the maitre d' to pick out a table for him to dine.

Dalton ordered a Grey Goose vodka and soda with a twist of lime. A lady sat down next to him at the bar and he didn't want to seem like a lecher, but he found her attractive. He turned in his barstool and took a look at this woman. She was a beautiful redhead who was tall, thin, and curvaceous, as well as well-dressed. She looked vaguely familiar to Dalton, and he began to wonder what the easiest way would be to start a conversation without telegraphing that he couldn't remember who she was. He thought to himself, *just be honest and tell her she looks familiar. He turned toward her.*

Dalton began to speak, but the redhead cut him off by saying, "Dalton, you are here all alone. It seems unusual to see you like this."

Dalton was intrigued. He said, "Do I know you? You look so familiar."

The woman said, "I am surprised that a womanizer like you would not be able to recognize his wife."

Dalton's jaw dropped. He couldn't speak. He cleared his throat and said, "Carmen?"

The redhead said, "Hello, my love. I have seen how you wept over my casket and mourned my death. It lasted for about a long weekend. How sad."

Dalton began to stutter, "How... Why... What the hell is going on?"

Carmen Craig laughed at her husband as she watched him squirm. She let him be amazed for a minute or two, then said, "If you had been paying any attention to me or the things that were happening to me, you would have known why I went undercover. There was a plot to kill everything you loved, starting with me. Because you were so ruthless and uncaring about anyone else, except you, you missed hearing me tell you three or four times."

Dalton's jaw was still slackened, but Carmen continued, "You stepped on people in the film industry almost daily and would stop at nothing to get what you wanted. Whether you sought a new starlet, an old starlet, a script, a producer, a director, or any number of film industry crew, you stepped over whomever you needed to gain your objective. When I heard of the plot to kill me, I told you one evening, and you had your head buried in a resume of one of the starlets you sought. I think her name is Fitore Fantazee. I went to bed angry and watched as you packed a bag to leave to search out locations for a new movie."

Dalton's mouth was agape. He thought he was in a dream. He reached out and touched Carmen. He pulled his hand back like he had touched fire. He was still amazed to see her, and looking so different, he did not even recognize her. Dalton said, "My Goodness, Carmen. I am so happy you're alive. I am truly sorry for being such a disappointment in our marriage. I loved you so much at the beginning of our time together. You and I drifted apart, and

I will take full responsibility for that." He paused for a minute to study her face. "You had some work done. Your hair is much different, and your face has changed. You still have maintained your beautiful figure. In fact. It has been improved. So, I ignored your comments about someone wanting to kill you and all that I loved and adored. What then happened, out on the back trail, where Mr. Howard found you? We recognized your clothes and hair, as well as your horse watching over you. Who was the lady we buried?"

Carmen laughed, "After I heard someone was trying to kill me, I was mindful of those around me. When I was out riding, I came upon a woman who looked similar to me, but she had a gun pointed at me. When her horse was spooked by a rattlesnake, she was thrown off onto the rocks behind her. I had to think fast, so I changed out of my clothes into hers. I took her gun and her horse, leaving Sage there with her. I knew all of you would assume it was me by the clothing and Sage, my trusty horse, beside my body. I even forfeited the watch the stable folks gave me. I rode back to a friend's house and asked her to harbor me."

Dalton had tears in his eyes when he said, "I can't believe you're alive! I have so many questions about where you've been and how you are doing. What about the will and the money disbursement?"

Carmen laughed again, "I was at my funeral, dressed in black with a veil over my face. That was surreal. I also attended the reading of my will. I was in an office next door to the reading with a video feed of the proceedings."

Dalton was beside himself with amazement. He asked, "What did it feel like? Why did you do what you did with all of your money? Why didn't you confide in me?"

Carmen replied, "It was interesting to watch everyone at my funeral. I could tell the people who were saddened by my passing and those who were not. Sadly, I put you and Walker in that last category. I had decided I would not leave you or him, any part of my wealth and there and then, I was happy with my decision. I spoke to a second party who worked with Erick Schrank to execute my wishes. I developed a trust account, which only I can access. If anything happens to me, I have left instructions on how it is to be distributed. I dispersed about $600 Million to those who were loyal to me. It was so much fun seeing the people who didn't expect to receive any money get their apportioned share. It was even more fun to watch the people who received nothing, as they began to squirm and sweat, like you and Walker, for example."

Dalton still could not believe his eyes and ears as he stood listening to his "late" wife, Carmen Craig. He said, "Is that some kind of fraud? Faking your death and then watching as your money is dispersed or not dispersed. I thought we had a closeness, and that you could trust me enough to let me know what was happening, and you were in danger."

Carmen Craig got angry at his obvious inability to listen, "Dammit, Dalton! I told you twice that someone wanted to kill me before the attempt on my life. You didn't even bat an eyelash or look up from your work. As far as trusting you, I at first thought you were the person behind the threats to kill me because you had no reactions to my pleas. You have always said how jealous you were that I had inherited so much money, and you had to struggle your whole life to get where you were. I trusted you to respect our marriage vows, and where did that get me? You ran around with other women soon after Walker was born. He was all I had. You were never intimate with me again. Now I hope you understand why I don't trust you."

Dalton resigned himself to the current truth and said, "So what are your plans?"

Carmen said, in a much softer tone, "I plan to live my life away from you. You have brought me nothing but heartache and pain. I was so lonely for years that I may never be able to fully trust anyone again. Half of my friends are gone because of you. There is no reason for me to stay here."

Dalton was saddened, even though he knew what she was telling him was completely true. He said, "Why is it my fault your friends are gone? Didn't you just say that you thought I was the mastermind behind the killings?"

Carmen said, "I knew who wanted me dead. It wasn't me they wanted, but they wanted to punish you. I don't know if you'll ever understand."

Dalton replied, "Oh, I understand just fine. You are blaming me for your friends losing their lives."

Carmen angry again, "See. I cannot believe what lack of focus you have. How did you become the film magnet that you have without listening? Or is it just me you don't hear?

Trying to change the subject, he said, "Who was the woman we buried in your grave? Did you kill her, then change clothes with her? By the way, what are you doing in Lake Tahoe? Have you been here all this time?"

Carmen said, "Well, you will have to wait for the answer about the woman's identity, as I am on my way to speak to the police. I came to Tahoe specifically to talk to you. I was at the airport and saw you traveling alone. I decided this would be a good time to see you. I will talk to you again if your movie is ever completed in Paris. Tell no one about seeing me. No one would believe you anyway. Have a nice evening."

Dalton sat at the bar and watched his "dead" wife walk out of the hotel bar. He had so many questions to ask her, but she was gone before it dawned on him to chase after her. He would check with the reservations desk up front and see if she was staying here at the hotel.

He finished his drink and made his way to the front desk to check on Carmen. He found she was not registered at this hotel. Dalton had some work to prepare for tomorrow, so he went back to his suite and poured himself one more cocktail. He sat at the work desk adjacent to the bar when he thought he heard something coming from the bedroom. He got a tingling feeling all over his body. Had Carmen come back to kill him? Could she have lied about the killer being in police custody? Was his life in danger? He went to the bar to retrieve his revolver that he kept stashed there, just in case of trouble. He called out, "Is someone in the bedroom?" He held his breath as he heard another noise. He called out once more, "Is someone here? Is it maid service?"

Fear gripped him as he waited. As he was about to call out again, someone appeared in the hallway. There stood Fitore Fantazee, dressed in nothing but a skimpy negligee that barely covered her backside and was wide open so her beautiful breasts were on display. Dalton laughed out loud.

Fitore was confused as to why this man found it funny that she had arrived to surprise him in nothing but a tiny see-through wisp of cloth. Her delicious body was completely on display.

Dalton said, "Oh my word, Fitore. I am so sorry. I laughed, but it was out of relief. I thought someone was here to kill me. Come here, beautiful, and I will explain my night so far. Can I pour you a drink?"

Fitore walked to the bar and made a drink for herself. A stiff Tequila with a lime wedge. It was the same drink Dalton was having, so she made two. Fitore walked to the desk where Dalton sat. He rose and extended his arms, "You are a sight for sore eyes. Thank you so much for the wonderful surprise. You have no idea how much I wished you were here. Like in a dream, you appeared. Though you scared me half to death, I am so glad to see you."

They embraced and kissed passionately. He said, "Let's talk before I lose my concentration. Wow, you do look sensational."

Fitore replied, after taking a long drink of her Tequila, "That was quite the welcome. What is happening? I saw you had your revolver drawn when I came into the living area."

Dalton led her to the couch, and they sat. He began, "I was at the bar earlier, and a redheaded woman approached me. She looked familiar, but I could not come up with where I had seen her. Then I realized I had seen her at the airport. I started to tell her she looked familiar when she stopped me and said she was surprised that I didn't recognize my wife." Dalton paused for effect.

Fitore said, "Carmen or Lynda?"

Dalton said, "It was Carmen. It is a long story, but she told me that someone was planning to kill all the people I was close to in my life, and they were going to start with her. I am not sure of the details, but the woman trying to kill her fell off her horse and died a horrible death. Carmen changed clothes with her and took her horse, leaving her horse with the woman. She said I killed all those women. My housekeeper, Belinda; an old flame, Karina Katrinka; my first wife, Lynda Laffarty; an old girlfriend, Sarah Ostrov, whom I dated before Carmen. Then she said I killed Jennifer Sandrew, a shop owner I dated. Carmen would have made six. My son, Walker, was almost killed at the Los Alamitos Raceway and who else was on the list, I am not sure."

Fitore said, "Do the police have a killer in custody for all these killings? Am I in danger?"

Dalton replied, "You know. Carmen never told me, so I am not sure. I am tired of this. Let's go to bed so I can welcome you properly. I will provide both you and me with personal bodyguards, first thing tomorrow morning."

Dalton and Fitore went to bed and began their favorite dance. They romanced each other well into the night. Then, they slept.

* * *

Denis Schinta arrived at the Los Angeles Police Department. He wanted to speak to his client, Kevin Syracuse. He met with Kevin for thirty minutes before they came into the room and requested that both of them go to the main conference room for interrogation.

As they walked into the room, Mason Delsson, Randy Keene, and Lyla Baroni, a female officer there to take written notes, were just sitting down at the conference table. As Denis Schinta sat down, Kevin Syracuse was brought into the room. His handcuffs were removed, and the guard stood at the door. Denis Schinta was whispering to Kevin as they sat together. Mason Delsson began the questioning.

Mason asked Kevin, "Do you know why you were detained?"

Kevin shook his head no and said, "I don't have any idea why I was detained."

Mason said, "We have you on tape and video making plans with Diane Deal to have many people killed. You killed Carmen Craig as she rejected your advances before she married Dalton Craig. Belinda Cheeks, Dalton's housekeeper, was unlucky enough to take the family vehicle to the market that was rigged for Dalton to drive off a cliff. Her death must have frustrated you and your team. All of the women we found dead had a link to Dalton Craig. If anyone had a grudge against Dalton, their deaths would have certainly put suspicion on him. Sarah Ostrov was just an actress you wanted for your film, and to lie in your bed. She refused your advances and signed with Dalton, who quickly began dating Miss Ostrov. She was in love with Dalton, and he was in love with her, so you had her killed. Karina Katrinka was a beautiful young actress who you wanted for your films. She went out with you for a while but ended up signing with Dalton as he offered her a larger contract. So, you had her killed."

Kevin was shaking his head no. He started to say something, but Mason stopped him, "I am not finished, Mr. Syracuse. You hated Lynda Laffarty because she married Dalton while you were dating her. You thought she went with the man with the most money, and you couldn't stand that fact, so you plotted to kill her, and you did exactly that. Jennifer Sandrew is a sad tale. You set her up in business, but she dated you only for the money you could provide her in business. Your relationship was short-lived because she left you for Dalton Craig. This angered you terribly, so you followed her to Lake Tahoe. You killed her, then dumped her body in the lake. You will see all the evidence in discovery at court, but my guess is, you will serve the rest of your life in prison for these six murders you planned and carried out. Do you or your lawyer have any questions?"

Kevin Syracuse said nothing further; however, his lawyer, Denis Schinta, asked when they could see the discovery evidence.

Mason replied, "I will send all the evidence we have when Kevin is arraigned, and official charges have been filed. Are there any more questions at this point? If not, I will give you two gentlemen a few minutes to chat. I will send a Deputy to return Mr. Syracuse to his holding cell until Monday. You realize there will be no bail at this point due to the seriousness of the charges pending."

Mason's phone rang when he entered his office. It was Randy Keene. He said, "Mason. They just pulled Greg Solomet out of Dalton Craig's swimming pool. He and Dalton's assistant, Jodi Panicee, were there alone last night. It seems both were drinking heavily. She went to bed, and he fell asleep in a lounge chair. The staff found him in the pool with his throat cut. There was plenty of blood, and the poor guy probably never knew what hit him."

Mason asked, "Is Coroner Trudy Pine there?

Randy said, "She got here about five minutes ago. She pronounced him dead and said she would do an autopsy to determine his official cause of death. Jodi Panicee is being questioned by police now.

Mason said, "I am on my way. Where is Dalton Craig?"

Randy replied, "He went to Lake Tahoe very early this morning to prepare to film his new movie."

Mason said, "I will see you in a few minutes."

As he drove to the Craig Estate, Mason wondered about Greg Solomon's murder. He was the first male connected to Dalton Craig, who had been killed. When Mason arrived at the Craig residence there were plenty of police cars, and the media had set up locations in front of the residence. Several reporters, including Donald James, tried to get Mason to make a statement. Mason replied, "I am not the lead on this case, so I can't help you."

Mason's superior officer, Dick Corsi, was on the scene. He would deal with the press when he had sufficient information to report to them. Dick Corsi called Mason over to where the body was about to be wrapped in a body bag and put on a gurney, for transport to the morgue.

Trudy Pine said to Mason, "Detective, it seems the people you are investigating are all killing each other. I am very busy with all these autopsies. Can you make them stop for a while?"

Mason laughed and said, "If I could, I would. Do we have a murder weapon?"

Trudy replied, "Not yet. Your guys are combing the premises."

Dick Corsi interrupted and added, "I spoke to Jodi Panicee a few minutes ago. She claims she and the deceased were drinking heavily and were alone in the house after the staff cleaned up and went home. She said she fell asleep in her room but left Mr. Solomet down here at the pool, asleep in a lounge chair."

The paramedics closed the body bag and rolled Mr. Solomet out to their ambulance for transport to the morgue.

Trudy Pine said to Mason and Dick, "I will do the autopsy as soon as I get back to the office and have the report to you before the evening is through."

It was a sad scene for all the staff at the Craig Estate, especially the maid who discovered the body when she came on duty at 7 a.m.

Mason asked Dick Corsi, "Has Dalton been notified yet? Has the immediate family been notified? I think he has a daughter, whom he was very close to.

* * *

Ryan Swanson walked into Mason Delsson's office and introduced himself, "Detective Delsson, my name is Ryan Swanson. I'm private investigator and have been following Kevin Syracuse for a year and a half. I learned he was plotting to kill people close to Dalton Craig when I overheard him talking to Diane Deal at a restaurant a year ago. I decided to determine if he was talking about a movie plot or a real scenario. It turns out he was seriously trying to frame Dalton Craig so he could take over Hollywood's premium movie productions."

Mason asked, "Why haven't you come to us before now? You

could have assisted us in putting Mr. Syracuse behind bars well before he committed so many murders."

Ryan replied, "I didn't know how far Kevin would go or if the things I heard were true. My firm spent a lot of time checking his movements for the past three weeks, and the movements of all his associates. In particular, we followed Diane Deal. She seems to have been the primary assassin in all the murders. We may have lost a life or two, but now you have an open and shut case against him."

Mason said, "Okay, Mr. Swanson. Let's see the evidence you have accumulated."

Ryan opened his briefcase and handed Mason twelve videotape cassettes. He said, "Look over these tapes and let me know if you think we've done a good job."

Mason put the first tape in the machine and pressed play. He saw Kevin Syracuse in a restaurant with Deyna Doll and Diane Deal. You could see the camera zoom in, and the sound became clearer. There on the screen, they heard Kevin Syracuse talking to the two ladies about Dalton Craig. Kevin said, "I hate that man. He has stolen more women from me than I care to count. He has paid way too much money to the best cameramen in the town to make his movies. They all used to work for me. I don't think we'll ever get close enough to Dalton without his bodyguard, Jim Thompson, around, so we'll shoot for the people he loves and eliminate them."

Diane Deal said, "I would like to be designated to kill his wife. I have a friend who has auditioned for Dalton several times, and all he wanted to do was have a sexual relationship with her. She is a former Navy SEAL. This woman has been frustrated with Dalton and his whole organization trying to secure a role in one of his movies for years. She told me that the pay is twice what we can afford here at Aries Pictures, so she wants a chance to be the one to hurt him the most."

Kevin asked who the person was, and Diane said, "I will keep her in anonymity, so I will be the only one who knows her identity."

They ended their discussions, so the tape ended as they walked out of the coffee shop.

* * *

Deyna Doll arrived home. She was totally recovered from her minor injuries but was still upset at the doctor for making her stay for an extra day. The first person she called was Walker Craig. She wanted to make sure he wasn't injured at the racetrack robbery. Sam Barfield answered the phone at the Craig house, "Hello, Craig residence. How can I help you?"

Deyna recognized the voice and replied, "Sam, it's Deyna Doll. I am calling to speak to Walker. Is he available?"

Sam Barfield replied, "Deyna, how are you feeling? Are you still in the hospital?"

Deyna was a bit impatient but calmly said, "I'm fine and I am home now. Is Walker there?"

Sam said, "I just checked on him five minutes ago, and he is still sleeping. Do you want me to have him call you later?"

Deyna asked, "Did he get hurt at the racetrack robbery that day?"

Sam replied, "Well, he was shot by the same gunman who shot you. He has had some damage but is recovering nicely, thank the Lord. They kept Walker for a few days even though he adamantly argued that he was fine and needed to leave. He will be happy you called. I will tell him as soon as he awakens. Is the number you're calling from where he can reach you?"

Deyna replied, "Yes. It is my cell phone. Nice talking to you, Sam. Thanks." They ended the call, and Deyna lay down in her bed for the first time in what seemed like forever. Then she slept.

* * *

Mason spoke to Dick Corsi, his Chief of Detectives. Mason said, "With all the videotape evidence we have, the Kevin Syracuse case looks to be open and shut. Let's meet tonight and review what we have for evidence and what needs to be sent to the defense. We can strategize how best to put this guy in prison for a long time.

* * *

California's State Attorney, Camryn Thomason, and her team were ready to proceed with jury selection. Camryn told Mason that although he thought it was an open and shut case, Denis Schinta, for the defense, was a crafty litigator who should be respected and feared. The jury selection went smoothly. It took two days to complete. The judge asked for opening arguments.

Mason Delsson watched from the gallery as the defense and prosecution made their cases for the jury. Many witnesses were called for both the prosecution and the defense. It was a very contentious proceeding where the Judge, Bonnie O'Hara, often had to rule on objections from both sides. There were many side bars with the attorneys, to clarify their strategy or rule on their ill-formed procedure. After two weeks of testimony, Judge O'Hara gave the jury their instructions and had them sequestered each night so they could deliberate on a decision.

The most important turn of events for the defense was that the prosecution witnesses could not prove beyond a shadow of a doubt that Kevin Syracuse was, in fact, the mastermind behind all the killings of people who were in the galaxy of Dalton Craig. Kevin took the witness stand. His movie manuscript was placed in evidence. He described how Dalton Craig was killing all those around him. Kevin then provided alibis for each allegation. He stated, "The only thing I am guilty off is hating Dalton Craig."

The verdict was read, and Kevin Syracuse was found not guilty.

Mason Delsson was confused by the trial's outcome. Maybe he missed something major in his investigation. He sat in his favorite neighborhood bar and pondered the situation. In his mind, he reviewed the interviews and the tapes that Ryan Swanson provided. Mason wondered why prosecutors did not use any of the testimonies of Randy Keene or Ryan Swanson. Mason went home and crawled into bed. He would start fresh in the morning. He had been burning the candle at both ends. He worked on the case all day, and after a late shift, would work on a relationship with Keisha Kane. She was now being challenged by Catie Gaynor for his attention.

* * *

Deyna Doll was back at work at the racetrack. She scrutinized her fellow employees, trying to figure out who may have tipped off the robbers the racetrack would have a substantially higher deposit on hand during the weekend of the robbery. She was interviewing candidates for a security agent to provide more protection for the crew behind the betting window cages. Wendy, Deyna's assistant at the track, brought the first candidate to Deyna's office. Deyna looked up and was mesmerized by the gentleman before her. He was tall and thin with a beautiful smile. She offered him a seat and asked, "I am Deyna Doll, one of the owners. Your name is?"

The man said, "My name is Dennis Bellosow. Thank you for the opportunity to speak with you today."

Deyna reminded herself to concentrate on the interview before she blurted out something way too inappropriate. She asked, "Mr. Bellosow, your resume says you are ex-military and have a permit for concealed carry of a weapon. How many times have you used that weapon?"

Dennis Bellosow was staring at Deyna and almost missed what she said. He replied, "Miss Doll. I have fired a weapon many times while on active duty. I previously worked as a private investigator and during that employment, I fired my weapon five times when chasing perpetrators who had fired at me."

Deyna said, "Your resume does not indicate any personal information. Why is that?"

Dennis laughed, "I usually keep that private. What do you want to know?"

Deyna thought a moment and said, "Have you ever been married? Are you married now? Do you have any children? Are you seeing anyone romantically right now?"

Dennis laughed again. His laughter sent chills down Deyna's spine straight to her core. She began to perspire. Dennis replied, "Yes. No. Yes. No."

Deyna now was the one laughing, "That is very adorable, Mr. Bellosow. I hope you are more serious about security." She would not lose the upper hand here.

Dennis broadly smiled, "It is nice to see where your sense of humor is and isn't. Taking your questions in order: Yes. I have been married. My wife was killed in a plane crash after being married for three years. No. Currently, I am not in a romantic relationship. Yes, I do have a daughter, Bella, who is now fourteen. I date casually when I can, being a single father with two jobs. I prefer women who can laugh at themselves, are independent, good with children, and are open to sexual exploration. Finally, you will never find anyone more serious about the security of those I protect than I."

Deyna said, "You have read the job description. Do you have any questions for me?"

Dennis replied, "Just two questions for you. First, I would like to inquire whether you are open to suggestions on strategies for the protection of your staff that can be improved. Secondly, can I interest you in having dinner with me tonight?"

Deyna smiled and said, "Mr. Bellowso, I am looking to hire someone who will suggest how best to protect our staff; so yes. Finally, if you are hired for the position, do you think it is appropriate for me to date our Chief of Security?"

Dennis said, "If it means I will lose the job to be able to date you, then I withdraw my application. However, if I had my druthers, I would like to do both."

Deyna thought long and hard on this one. She said, "I think we should give it a try. If it becomes a problem, I guess I could hire a different security chief! You will be my personal bodyguard, and those you hire additionally will look after our staff."

He and Deyna had dinner that evening. Dennis Bellowso began employment on the next day.

* * *

Mason Delson awoke refreshed the next morning. He lay in bed, wishing he had gone to visit Keisha Kane and vowed to call her soon. He put his foot on the floor, and before he had a chance to stand and go to the shower, his cellphone rang. It was 7 a.m. He wondered who would be calling this early. He picked up and said, "Hello. This is Mason Delsson."

The female voice on the call was unfamiliar. She said, "Forgive me for calling at this hour, but I couldn't wait to talk to you. This is Camryn Thomason from the State Attorney's Office. Do you have a few minutes?"

Mason now knew who she was. The prosecutor in the failed Kevin Syracuse case. He replied, "I have not had my morning coffee yet, but this sounds important, so I will listen and put on some coffee."

Camryn said, "Mason, I went over the trial testimonies and evidence yesterday. I was frustrated and labored until long after midnight. Then, the clouds cleared, and the angels sang. The light went off, and I had my first epiphany. I could not believe how blind I was listening to the obvious and not looking at the 'what ifs.' I asked myself, what if the people testifying were telling the truth? With that premise, I restructured my strategy. The defense alleged that the conversations that were taped were all from Kevin Syracuse's house or studio. If that is true, and they were all telling the truth, someone else was the killer. I tried to look for people who had motives to kill all the people in Dalton Craig's circle. Then I knew."

Mason was excited and trying to contain himself said, "Camryn, how soon can you meet me in my office. I know it is Saturday, but I think I now know where we went wrong. I am jumping in the shower and can be at my office in twenty-five minutes."

Camryn Thomason was just as excited as Mason. She answered, "I have showered already, so I am going to jump in my car and will probably beat you to the office. See you in a few minutes."

The wheels began to spin in Mason's head as he showered. He got out of the shower and looked in the mirror, and his reflection smiled back at him. He couldn't believe he had been so myopic. He dressed, put his coffee in a travel mug, and nearly sprinted to his car. He walked into his office nineteen minutes after his call with Camryn. He saw her exit the elevator as he walked into his office. He waited and waved her in.

Mason sat at his desk, and Camryn took a seat in the comfortable chair opposite him in front of the desk. They realized they were smiling broadly at one another. They started talking at the same time. They laughed at each other's excitement, and Mason pointed to Camryn, saying, "Please, begin, Madam State Attorney, I am bursting inside waiting to hear the name of the perpetrator."

Camryn took a breath and began, "First, I will ask you, who you thought was the person who would gain the most from all these deaths? What do you think was the motive for the killings? Do you think these deaths were accidents or executed by someone? Do you think there is more than one person guilty of causing these deaths?"

Mason's mind was spinning. He had so many unanswered questions.

Camryn continued, "These were the questions I asked myself. Mason, it took some long hours into the night before it dawned on me what the answers were. We were initially looking at the wrong person, who claimed innocence."

Mason interrupted, "I have been thinking since I hung up the call from you earlier. Do you want to hear my answers to the questions? I thought, if your theory is correct and Kevin Syracuse is not the mastermind, who could it be, and did they have a strong motive to kill all these people? I, too, was reviewing my notes of the interviews and the investigation in general."

Camryn said, "Okay, I'll start with the first question. Who would gain the most from these deaths?"

Mason replied, "It could be Dalton Craig. He could have killed his wife or had her killed to inherit her money. That is a pretty strong motive, if true. I don't think any of the deaths were accidental, and I think there was more than one person responsible for them."

Camryn said, "I agree that Dalton Craig is the most likely person. However, what if Carmen is still alive? What if Carmen knew he was going to kill her, and she thwarted the person who tried?"

Mason said, "Then who was the person they found on the ranch and buried as Carmen Craig? They even read her will. What about the others?"

Camryn said, "Okay. Let's move on. We'll come back to Carmen. Let's look at Belinda Cheeks. She was the housekeeper. Maybe whoever wanted to kill Carmen or Dalton rigged the car. Belinda Cheeks was the unlucky driver who took the car to go shopping that day. She wasn't paid much as her schooling was paid for by Dalton. So, maybe they had a tryst, and she had to be eliminated."

Mason interjected, "How sad for her, if that was the case. How about Sarah Ostrov, the actress, and Karina Katrinka? They were women who dated Dalton. Why did they die?"

Camryn replied, "I looked at both of their records. Both were very poor. Beautiful but poor. Each wanted to be the next Mrs. Dalton Craig. My conjecture from what I found is each of them had Dalton doing some strange or illegal stuff. They used it to blackmail him for either marriage or loads of this mogul's money. Both of these women had worked but were not working when they passed. If they were desperate and nagging Dalton, he could have killed them or ordered their deaths."

Mason said, "Madam State Attorney, you know, we will need proof. What about the shop owner of Elegant Lace, Jen Sandrew? What about Lynda Laffarty? How do these women fit into the strategy for putting Dalton behind bars?"

Camryn laughed, "I looked at both these women. Jennifer had dated Dalton after his marriage to Lynda broke up. She either was given money or borrowed money from Dalton to purchase the boutique, Elegant Lace. She was way behind on invoices for purchases of clothing. She had quite a large gambling debt, and she had a reputation for being, at times, a fall-down drunk. She paid damages at three different restaurants while she was on one of her notorious binge drinking episodes. I have an eyewitness who saw Jennifer at the hotel bar with Dalton. They only had one drink. She left first, and five minutes later, Dalton paid his bill and walked out of the hotel. That was the last time Jennifer was seen alive.

"As for his ex-wife, Lynda Laffarty, I think she knew too much. Who do we know that's in a good relationship with an ex-spouse? She may have known Dalton planned to kill Carmen. She may have been a witness to either Sarah Ostrov, or Karina Katrinka's murder. If she was trying to blackmail Dalton because of what she knew, he might have decided to also eliminate her."

Mason was jotting down notes. He raised his head and asked Camryn, "How do you see Greg Solomet fitting into this whole drama?"

Camryn said, "Greg Solomet was almost broke when he began dating Jodi Panicee, Dalton's secretary. He was seen by one of the stable workers in a wrestling match at the pool with Jodi after everyone else had gone to bed. She was able to resist his advances because he was drunker than her. She ran to Dalton's room to tell him what had happened, but a maid appeared as Jody looked for Dalton. The said Dalton had already left for the flight to Tahoe. Solomet was still asleep where she left him passed out on a lounge chair by the pool.

"Jodi had gone to bed, but the next morning, Greg was found floating in a bloody pool with his throat slit. After his death, we searched Solomet's apartment in Beverly Hills and found correspondence on his computer with Dalton Craig. Solomet was also in possession of information about Dalton and his unscrupulous use of power to get actors to do things for less than their contracts indicated. He was stealing from himself so he could pay off the loans he was in default for on Gemini Studios, or maybe to pay off his debt from a large gambling loss."

Mason said, "It looks like all roads lead to Dalton Craig. Now, all we have to do is prove that he was either a single killer or had an accomplice."

Camryn said, "I have given this some thought. I reviewed the notes you shared. If my scenario holds any water, we must find a witness or an accomplice who will turn state's evidence."

Mason said, "That will be a herculean task, but I am up to the challenge."

Camryn left and returned to her office after laying out a strategy with Mason on how they would convict Dalton. She would use private investigators to uncover the information she knew was out there to be found.

Mason called Randy Keene to come to the office. They both grabbed a cup of coffee and went into the conference room. Mason took about thirty minutes to explain to Randy what he had heard from Camryn Thomason.

Randy said, "Wow. If this is all true, my hunch about old Dalton Craig was correct. I have spoken to a lot of people in the industry, and they all think Dalton has been whacking all these people. One of them said that Kevin Syracuse showed them the initial draft of a movie ready to go into production that tells the story of Dalton Craig. The lady told me things alleged in the movie were closer to the truth than anyone knew. People thought Kevin Syracuse was trying to punish Dalton with the movie, but all he was doing was telling the truth."

Mason was elated. "Well, we will subpoena those informants to testify. I would like to talk to Diane Deal and get her on tape. I think she is working with Dalton, as we found her at the scene, trying to kill the woman she thought was Cricky Amherst. I am sure she will likely throw Dalton under the bus. Especially, if it means the charges against her are reduced."

Randy Keene said, "I will be here for you when you need me. I have another appointment today. So, if you'll excuse me." Randy walked out the door.

A woman knocked on Mason's office door and said, "May I come in?"

Mason looked up and saw the beautiful, redheaded woman whom he had run into at Dr. Freeman's dental office. Mason stood and said, "How may I help you, Miss?"

The woman laughed, "Detective Delsson, do you have a few minutes to talk? My name is Carmen Craig."

You could have blown Mason over with a feather. He was quite taken aback. He answered, "Are you the late, Carmen Craig? Heir to the Warner Studios fortune?"

The redhead replied, "Yes, Detective. You and I have bumped into one another a couple of times at Kelly Freeman's place. May I speak with you?"

Mason Delsson offered her his most comfortable chair at his desk. He said, "Can I get you something to drink? Coffee or water?"

Carmen said, "Water would be great, thanks. I thought it was time we met, as you have been searching for my killer."

Mason laughed, "You look spectacular for being dead for six months. What is your secret?"

It was Carmen who now laughed. She replied, "Mason, if I may call you that, I would like to get the police on the right track, as you have been woefully inadequate during the investigation of my death. Please, don't take any offense. I will start from the beginning. You may want to record or video this for future court proceedings. My husband, Dalton Craig, and I were in a terrible rut after twenty years of marriage. Dalton decided he needed more spice in his life, if you know what I mean. He began to stray from the marriage to become quite the man of infidelity. I was at my favorite restaurant, Retreat Two, having dinner one evening, when I heard Kevin Syracuse talk about eliminating me. I was hyper-vigilant when that person hired to kill me showed up on a horse. She was no match for me as an equestrian. She chased me and my favorite steed, Sage, but was unfortunately not a very experienced rider, and her horse got spooked by a rattler out on the far reaches of my ranch. I should say Dalton's estate. I thought I would survive longer if whoever wanted me to be dead thought I was dead.

"I changed clothes with her as she was disfigured by her fall onto the rocks. I even gave her two pieces of jewelry that would help identify her as me. I left Sage, my trusty steed, with her and took her horse. My stablemaster, Erickson Howard, was my savior. He brought me a change of clothes and my purse. I then changed clothes and had Erickson drive me off the estate. He dropped me off at the airport, and I flew to Santa Fe, New Mexico. I stayed with a friend, Christopher Erikson, while I got things straightened out. I changed my name to Elizabeth Warner and dropped the Carmen. Then I called Erick Schrank, my financial advisor, and commissioned him to rewrite my will and set up the CEW trust.

"There were only three people who knew I was still alive. My stable master, Erickson, my financial advisor, Erick, and his assistant, Denise. Oh, I forgot, the ladies at my dental office knew, as I was forced to get a cavity filled. That is where I first saw you. I called them and asked about who you were because of the funny look you gave me. You almost recognized me, but you were thrown by them calling me Elizabeth. I got the idea from my late mother, who loved the name Elizabeth. She called me that until she died."

Carmen paused a moment while she cleared her head of the emotional remembrance of her mom and their special bond.

Mason said, "So you overheard Kevin Syracuse talking about killing you? What did you do then?"

Carmen said, "I have some old friends at the studio he owns. I had my stable master, Erickson Howard, call them and inquire about Kevin's hatred of Dalton as well as his plot to kill me. My friend at Aries Pictures told Erickson, after a hearty laugh, that Kevin was planning a film about Dalton Craig's life. He was going to release as many embarrassing facts about Dalton as he could conjure up. He wanted the public who supported his movies to know what a selfish, egomaniac Dalton had become. I had overheard him discussing the movie and thought he was serious about killing me. This made me somewhat prepared for the actual attempt on my life, which I found was initiated by my loving husband. He wanted to inherit my money to pay off his debts. The debts were caused by his overzealous payment to actresses he was trying to bed, as well as the millions in gambling debt he had incurred gambling in Vegas and Tahoe."

Mason had turned on the video camera to tape the interview with Carmen. He was jotting down follow-up questions to ask regarding Carmen's story. Carmen paused, so Mason asked, "Why do you think Dalton tried to kill you?"

Carmen continued. "I found a note he left in his office. I never went in there as that was always Dalton's private domain. I was looking for a gun to protect myself with from Kevin Syracuse when I stumbled upon a note to Madonna Hakeem. She was a former Navy SEAL. She later became a mercenary working in the United States. The note said: *C will be riding on Tuesday morning around 9 a.m. She usually wears a white cowboy hat and will not be armed. Please make it painless. D.*"

Mason said, "I wonder if we can secretly get access to the office, and we may be able to find the note. It's too bad you don't have a copy of it. That would be the kind of evidence we need to establish motive."

Carmen said, "Oh, I have a copy of it. I wanted to be able to divorce him with evidence. When I found out Kevin Syracuse was making a movie about Dalton and his goal of being the top movie executive of all time, he added to the movie that Dalton was going to kill me for my money. That's why I took him out of the will."

Mason said, "That is great that you kept a copy. It will help convict him for sure. Since you brought up the will, may I ask why your son, Walker, was not a major recipient of your fortune?"

Carmen said, "It's a long story, but he has stolen enough from me."

Mason said, "Does anyone else know you are alive?"

Carmen replied, "Just two or three people. Oh yeah, I just spoke to Dalton yesterday when I ran into him in Lake Tahoe. I had flown to Tahoe after I was attacked, where I was able to rent a house from a girl named Robin Ripple. She was headed to L.A. for fame and fortune. Dalton was shocked to see me and so befuddled that he never moved after I walked away from him. I immediately walked out of the hotel and flew back to L.A."

Mason said, "We better move fast. Is he still in Lake Tahoe? Mason buzzed Dick Corsi to have him come into Mason's office.

Carmen said, "I think he is still there. He is doing a movie there for the next few weeks, but who knows what he'll do now that I am alive."

Dick Corsi walked into Mason's office. Mason introduced them. "Chief, this is Carmen Craig. Carmen, this is Chief Dick Corsi, head of the Detective Bureau. Chief, I will fill you in on all the details, but she has evidence that Dalton Craig tried to kill her. She has a note he wrote to the assassin."

Dick Corsi said, "Ms. Craig, would you like police protection? Where are you staying currently?"

Carmen said, "I was thinking of leaving the country or at least California. I have been staying with my financial advisor's assistant. Denise was nice enough to put me up, as I was not even telling any of my friends that I was still kicking and breathing. Do you think I should have police protection? I will leave that up to you."

Mason said, "Chief, Dalton is shooting a movie in Lake Tahoe, but I think we should put her in protective custody. I plan to call Sheriff Antonio de Lapaz in Lake Tahoe. I will get a warrant and have Dalton returned to Los Angeles."

Chief Corsi agreed, and they put things in motion. Carmen called Denise DeLeo and told her she was extending her vacation. She looked at Mason and said, "I guess I am paranoid now that he knows I am alive. The less people who know where I am at this point, the better I will be."

Mason said, "I know a perfect place to set you up. My next-door neighbor is on vacation and gave me a key. I will clear it with her. I will cook dinner for you, or you can visit if you get bored. I almost want to fly to Lake Tahoe and arrest him myself. I wish I could see the look on his face when he is cuffed."

Mason called Sheriff Antonio de Lapaz, "Antonio, I need you to arrest a Mr. Dalton Craig. He is staying at the Hilton Vacation Club there in Tahoe. I can send a helicopter there to transport him if you would like."

Sheriff de Lapaz replied, "No need. You are in luck. I am going to L.A. to pick up an escaped prisoner that your guys apprehended in L.A. You can call them and let them know I will be there as soon as I put the bracelets on Mr. Dalton Craig."

Mason said, "Thanks, Antonio, I owe you one. See you when you get here. Give me a call when you're close."

Dick Corsi said, "Do you want me to have one of the female officers drive her over to your neighbor's place?"

Mason said, "Yes, I just got a text back from her saying she was happy to help." Then to Carmen he asked, "Did you want to pick up some things from your friend's? It may be a few weeks. My neighbor said that you should make yourself at home."

Carmen said, "Thank you, Detective Delsson. You have eased my mind more than you know. I appreciate the help."

With that, she was introduced to Lyla Baroni, the female officer. Mason gave Carmen the key to Catie's house. Carmen thanked him and they left in an unmarked car.

Carmen realized she felt uncomfortable in her new surroundings. Lyla said, "Carmen, I bet you are feeling uncomfortable in the unfamiliar environment."

Carmen breathed a sigh of relief, "Is it that obvious? I am in a strange home with a strange person in a dangerous situation. You're damn right, I am uncomfortable. The police are going to need me to testify in the case against my husband if they want any chance of convicting him. If that were not the case, I would be on my plane flying to Aruba. I guess we should make the best of this."

Lyla said, "If it makes you feel any better, I don't normally do this kind of duty, but you seem like a very nice person, and I think we will get along fine. Let's see if we have anything in the refrigerator we can make for dinner."

Lyla took inventory while Carmen checked the bar. Lyla said, "We are in luck. Catie must have just gone on vacation because there is plenty of food in here to cook. I can make us a salad, and there are chicken breasts ready to cook. I think I saw a grill in the back. I'll go check it out."

Carmen said, "I found a bottle of wine. Can I pour you a Sauvignon Blanc?" Lyla said, "It sounds good, but I am on duty, so I will pass on the alcohol, but thanks. I lit the grill, and it will be ready by the time we put the salad together."

Carmen had a glass of wine which helped her calm down a bit. She finished the salad prep in short order. She found her favorite dressing in the refrigerator. There was a low-fat poppyseed as well as some Italian. She pulled out the two chicken breasts and put them on a platter. Carmen asked, "Do you want to grill or should I? I haven't even seen the backyard yet."

Lyla said, "There is a gazebo with privacy curtains on the back deck. The grill is right outside of it. There are some comfortable chairs to sit in as well. The neighborhood is peaceful. I have not seen anyone yet. I can grill the chicken. Is there anything to season the breasts?"

Carmen said, "I found some garlic powder and something called 'Kickin' Chicken.' I sampled it, and it is a little spicy but should go well with the meat. Are you ready to cook?"

Lyla said, "Absolutely. It won't take long."

* * *

Dalton sat at the bar in his hotel room and heard a knock on the door. He figured it was the maid or his dinner being delivered.

Dalton was wrong on all counts. Standing at the door as he opened it were three police officers from the Sheriff's Department. He stepped back away from the door and said, "Can I help you, gentlemen?"

Sheriff de LaPaz spoke, "Mr. Dalton Craig, you are under arrest. Please turn around, and one of the deputies will pat you down and handcuff you."

Dalton yelled, "What the hell is going on here? I have done nothing wrong. I am directing a movie in town, and what are the charges?

Sheriff de Lapaz said, "I received a warrant from Los Angeles, California, indicating you are going to be charged with attempted murder and 1st degree murder for deaths that occurred in California. We have a helicopter ready to will fly you back to LA. Do you have any weapons in this room?"

8

DALTON SHOOK HIS HEAD as one of the deputies read Dalton his Miranda rights. The Sheriff continued, "You will be able to call your attorney when you get back to LA. Is there anything you want to take with you from here?"

Dalton said, "No, I just want to let the hotel know that this must be some mistake and the room should be locked and not entered until my return."

Sheriff de Lapaz said, "I will let the manager know. He is a friend, and I will explain the circumstances. I assure you that nothing will be disturbed. Let's go, Mr. Craig."

The three officers walked Dalton Craig out of his hotel and to an awaiting helicopter. The ride to Los Angeles took exactly an hour and twenty minutes. Mason was waiting on the roof of headquarters with Chief Dick Corsi and two uniformed officers. Dalton was assisted out of the helicopter, and Mason, walking to him, said, "Welcome back to Los Angeles, Mr. Craig. We will take you downstairs and get you situated, then you can call your attorney.

Dalton wanted to say something, but he remembered his lawyer, Sam Barfield, telling him that he should keep his mouth shut until he had a chance to speak with him, if ever he was brought in by the police. Regardless of the circumstances.

Dalton was fingerprinted, had his picture taken, and then he was brought upstairs to a large conference room. He entered the room, escorted by three deputies. Sitting in the room were Mason Delsson, Chief of Detectives Dick Corsi, State Attorney Camryn

Thomason, the Department Clerk Diane Smythe, Troy Phillips Los Angeles District Attorney, and Sam Barfield Dalton's Attorney.

Dalton was relieved to see Sam already there. Dalton was seated next to Sam.

After introducing those at the table, Mason began, "Good afternoon. We are here to question Mr. Dalton Craig about allegations made regarding the attempted murder of his late spouse, Carmen Craig."

Dalton stood up, yelling at the top of his lungs, "She is not dead. I talked with her two days ago." Sam grabbed Dalton and sat him down. He whispered into to ear to be quiet until he was asked to speak. Sam had to be forceful with Dalton because Sam knew Dalton was about to lose control. That would only show everyone Dalton could not control his anger. Dalton nodded, and Mason continued.

Mason said, "Mr. Phillips, as L.A. District Attorney, would you please explain to Mr. Craig the charges filed against him? It seems he does not understand these charges."

Troy Phillips stood and walked to the end of the table, where there sat on the table a small lectern. He said, "Mr. Craig, you are not being charged with the murder of your wife. The charge is attempted murder. We have evidence that you paid an individual to search for your wife while she was riding on your property. In light of new information, we are also able to match you up to several other murders. You will be charged in court in the morning for the murders of Belinda Cheeks, Karena Katrinka, Sarah Ostrov, Lynda Laffarty, and Jennifer Sandrew. We will disclose to you and your attorney all the evidence during discovery."

Sam Barfield rose and said, "Mr. Craig is innocent of these charges and will attest to that in court tomorrow. What time is he on the docket?

Troy Phillips responded, "He will be arraigned in State Court, Fourth Floor at 10 a.m. tomorrow. Any other questions?"

Sam replied, "Not at this time, Mr. Phillips. We will see you in the morning. Is my client free to return to his home today?"

Troy Phillips replied, "No. Mr. Craig will remain in custody here until the judge decides whether Mr. Craig is a flight risk based upon the severity and number of these charges."

Dalton was about to make another outburst, but Sam grabbed his arm and whispered something in his ear. Dalton sighed and resigned himself that there was nothing to be done at this point.

The officers in the conference room replaced the handcuffs on Dalton Craig and escorted him out of the room to the holding center downstairs.

Sam said to Mason, "I hope you have some strong evidence, Detective Delsson. My client is respected by everyone in Los Angeles. He has no criminal record. He had no reason to carry out any of the acts he is charged with. There may well be some repercussions if your evidence doesn't hold water. See you in the morning."

Mason did not answer him. He let Sam Barfield walk out the door. He knew these were the things a defense lawyer needed to say, but Mason knew the evidence they had against Dalton Craig.

Sam Barfield spent an hour with Dalton in his cell before he left the jail. He asked Dalton, "Did you kill, try to kill, or order the killing of those five women?"

Dalton shook his head no. Sam said, "Dalton, you need to tell me. In all honesty, did you do any of this?"

Dalton looked over Sam's shoulder. There, in the corner of the ceiling, was what looked like a small video camera that was more than likely recording their every word.

Sam stood, grabbed his briefcase, and said to Dalton, "I will talk to you first thing in the morning." He called for the deputy, who let him out of the cell. Sam left Headquarters with a nagging sadness. He had a bad feeling about this whole situation.

Bright and early, the next morning, Sam Barfield was able to talk with Dalton for thirty minutes. Dalton again assured him he was innocent. The Criminal Court of Los Angeles began promptly at 10 a.m.

The judge presiding in the case was the Honorable Bonita

O'Hara. She was tough, but open-minded, compassionate, and very authoritative. Judge O'Hara has sat on the bench for twenty-five years and was known to most everyone in the State justice system.

Court proceedings were called to order as Judge O'Hara entered and sat in her large black swivel chair. Judge O'Hara said, "Mr. Prosecutor, what are the charges in this proceeding?"

Troy Phillips began, "Your Honor, we are charging Mr. Dalton Craig with attempted murder in the first degree against his wife, Carmen Craig. He is also charged with first-degree murder for the deaths of Belinda Cheeks, Sarah Ostrov, Jennifer Sandrew, Karena Katrinka, and Lynda Laffarty."

Judge O'Hara stated, "Mr. Craig, would you please stand, and enter your plea at this time." Sam Barfield whispered something to Dalton, who then stood.

Dalton Craig stated, "Your Honor, I enter a plea of not guilty on all the charges. My attorney and I are anxious to go through discovery."

Sam stood as Dalton sat. Sam said, "We are awaiting evidence from the prosecution in discovery so we can prepare our defense. We would also like to request your decision on bail, your Honor."

Judge O'Hara replied, "If the prosecution has no objection, the court will recommend bail set at $500,000."

Sam Barfield replied, "We thank you for the decision, your Honor. We do, however, object to the high bail. My client has no history of being a flight risk. He also has no prior criminal record. Would you reconsider? I move to reduce or eliminate the bail and release Mr. Craig in my custody."

The District Attorney, Troy Phillips, asked, "Your Honor. Do you have a start date for the trial to begin?"

Judge O'Hara said, "Looking at the court's calendar. We will reconvene this case on Monday, the 14th, at 9 a.m. Two weeks from today." She tapped her gavel and said, "Court is in recess for fifteen minutes while I decide on Mr. Barfield's motion regarding bail."

Sam said to Dalton, "I will try to get this expedited. Don't worry.

Sit tight. and I will see what I can do." Dalton was released minutes later in Sam Barfield's custody with no bail.

* * *

The jury selection having been completed, the trial began on Monday, the 14th at 10 a.m. Troy Phillips was in the prosecution's chair, and Sam Barfield was in the defense chair.

Mason Delsson was in the first row on the prosecution side of the courtroom when the trial began.

Judge Bonnie O'Hara said, "Let us begin the case against Dalton Craig. Mr. Prosecutor, do you have an opening statement to the jury?"

Troy Phillips said, "Your Honor, the state of California will begin the case against Dalton Craig for the murders of Sarah Ostrov, Belinda Cheeks, Jennifer Sandrew, and Lynda Laffarty. He is also charged with attempted murder of Carmen Craig. The State will show that Mr. Dalton Craig had motive and opportunity for these crimes."

Judge O'Hara said, "Mr. Prosecutor, call your first witness."

Troy Phillipps stepped to the podium and said, "Your Honor, the State calls Chief of Detectives of the Los Angeles Police Department, Dick Corsi."

The court Clerk asked the Chief to raise his right hand and proceeded to swear him to "tell the truth and nothing but the truth, so help me God." Dick Corsi answers affirmatively and takes a seat in the chair to the left of the judge.

Troy Phillips began. "Chief Corsi, we know of your long service to the L.A. Police Department and your rise through the ranks to officer, then Detective, and for the past seven years, you are serving as the Chief of Detectives. Is that correct?"

Dick Corsi replies, "Yes, that is correct." Corsi looked into the crowd gathered for the trial and saw many friends of the Department as well as some City dignitaries.

Troy Phillips continued, "On the fifteenth of April of this year, you were called to respond to a call regarding a woman being found on her ranch, apparently thrown from her horse. What happened that day?"

Dick Corsi replied, "I sent one of my veteran Detectives, Mason Delsson, to the scene. He reported that the woman was Carmen Craig. There were no witnesses at that time. However, the coroner, Tracy Pine, indicated it was apparent at the scene, her horse had been spooked somehow, and the woman was thrown off and landed on a pile of jagged racks. Her face was disfigured but her clothes and identification indicated it was Carmen Craig."

Troy Phillips asked, "Who reported the incident to the police?"

Chief Corsi replied, "A man named Erickson Howard called 911. He is the Stable Master for the Craig estate. Dalton Craig asked where she was as it was not normal for her to be out so long. This concerned Mr. Howard. He jumped on a horse and went out to search for his boss to make sure she was okay. He indicated there was no one else around when he found Mrs. Craig's body on the cluster of rocks."

Troy Phillips asked, "How bad was her body disfigured?"

Defense attorney, Sam Barfield, stood and shouted, "Objection! Your honor, counsel is leading the witness."

Judge O'Hara said, "Sustained."

Troy Phillips said, "Sorry, your Honor. Chief Corsi, can you tell us anything else about Carmen Craig's condition and surroundings?"

Chief Corsi replied, "I received a call from Detective Mason Delsson when he reached the site of the body. Delsson reported that Carmen had landed face first on the rocks and she was bleeding from several punctures to her head. The injuries completely disfigured her face, so her casket was closed for the funeral. Her favorite horse named Sage was standing by her side when she was injured."

Troy Phillips said, "I have nothing further at this time."

Judge O'Hara said, "Cross examine, Mr. Barfield?"

Sam Barfield walked to the witness box and asked in a loud

voice, "So, Chief, you were not there to view the body. Is that correct?"

Chief Corsi replied, "Yes."

Sam asked, "Did you see Mrs. Craig when she was brought into the morgue?"

Chief replied, "No, I did not."

Sam said, "I have no further questions of this witness, your Honor, as Chief Corsi was unable to confirm what condition Mrs. Craig was in when she was found."

Judge O'Hara said, "Mr. Phillips, call your next witness."

Troy called out, "Prosecution calls Erickson Howard to the stand."

Erickson Howard was sworn in.

Troy Phillips asked him, "Did you find Mrs. Craig, the day she died?"

Erickson said, "Yes, that is correct."

Troy then asked, "Did you go look for Mrs. Craig of your own volition or were you requested to look for her?"

Erickson said, "Mr. Craig asked if I had seen her. I told him she was out riding. I then realized she had been gone for some time. Dalton then asked if I would go look for her because there were matters that he needed to discuss with her."

Troy then asked, "How long did it take you to find her, and what did you find?"

Erickson replied, "I guess I was out for a half hour when I came across her body on the rocks."

Troy asked, "What did you find? Was there anyone else around? Could you tell how she had fallen?"

Erickson said, "Mrs. Craig was lying face down on the rocks. There was a lot of blood. Her horse, Sage, was standing by her side. No one else appeared to be around. I really couldn't tell how she had fallen. I just assumed the horse was spooked and threw her off."

Troy asked, "What did you do next?"

Erickson said, "I checked to see if she was breathing. She was not. I called 911 and reported the incident. Then I called, Mr. Craig."

Troy asked, "Can you tell us what Dalton said when he heard the news?

Erickson said, "Mr. Craig yelled, 'Oh my God.' Then he asked where I was. I told him she was down by the pond next to the large rock formation. He said he would direct the police and emergency crews to that location. Then he said, 'The police are here now. I have to go.'"

Troy then asked, "Mr. Howard, how were you able to positively identify your employer?"

Erickson replied, "I have known Mrs. Craig for over fifteen years. She was dressed as she was when I saw her earlier that day, her horse was standing at her side, and she wore a watch that the stable crew and I gave her on her last birthday." Erickson was visibly shaken, and tears could be seen running down his cheeks.

Troy said, "So, Mr. Howard, if her face was so disfigured as the Detective reported, you could only assume it was Mrs. Craig. You did not actually positively identify her. Is that correct?"

Erickson replied as he composed himself, "Mr. Phillips, as I said, I knew her for over fifteen years, so I positively knew it was her."

Thank you, Mr. Howard," said Troy. "I have no further questions. Your witness, Mr. Barfield."

Sam rose and walked halfway to the witness box and asked, "Mr. Howard, did anyone else ever ride, Sage, Mrs. Craig's horse?"

Erickson replied, "No one ever rode that horse but Mrs. Craig."

Sam Barfield said, "Thank you, Mr. Howard. Your Honor, I have no further questions at this time."

Judge O'Hara said, "Mr. Phillips, call your next witness."

Troy Phillips stood and called out, "The prosecution calls Walker Craig to the stand."

Walker Craig appeared at the double doors that led to the hall outside the courtroom. He was dressed very casually in jeans and a Dri-Fit pullover T-shirt. He was sworn in by the bailiff.

Walker took a seat in the witness box, and Dalton looked at him disparagingly. Walker looked extremely nervous. He was biting his lip, and you could see the perspiration on his forehead.

Troy Phillips walked to the witness box and paused for effect. He asked, "Mr. Craig, do you think your father killed your mother?"

Before he could finish, Sam Barfield jumped up again and said, "Objection. Calls for a conclusion by the witness."

Judge O'Hara said, "Sustained."

Troy said, "I am sorry, Mr. Craig. Who do you think killed your mother?"

Walker was more visibly upset. He replied, "Mr. Prosecutor, after your investigation by the Los Angeles Police Department, it was determined my mother succumbed to injuries received after falling from her horse. Asking me who killed my mother is cruel and very unprofessional."

Troy was not phased in the least. He continued, "Mr. Craig, six women who were either dating, married to, or employed by your father were killed. Can you explain this?"

Walker smiled at the prosecutor and said, "Mr. Phillips, I am not a member of the Los Angeles Police Force. Nor am I a private investigator. You are alleging these six women were killed; yet I have seen no proof. Each of them may have met their demise due to accidental circumstances."

Troy took a different track. He asked, "Do you now or have you ever been in love with any of the women who have died around your father's ranch, home, or studios?"

Walker smiled and said, "Mr. Phillips, I respect what you are trying to do with this line of questioning. You are barking up the wrong tree. Though I was involved with several of these women, I have never wished them any harm or death, nor have I caused their deaths. For the record, I don't think my father had anything to do with any of the deaths. My father, Dalton Craig, is a powerful man in the film industry in Hollywood. There are many people my father has either not chosen for a role in his films, or he has beaten others to the punch in hiring an individual for a project. That being said, this does not in any way, shape, or form constitute a murder motive. However, Hollywood is a treacherous place full of people who need to make money and garner power."

Troy said, "Thank you, Mr. Craig, for that unsolicited diatribe. Now, if you answer my question. Have you ever been in love, or a relationship, with any of the women your father, Dalton Craig, has dated, married, or had a relationship with?"

Walker had a look of utter destain, knowing Troy Phillips would continue to be a bulldog during his testimony. "To answer your question, Mr. Phillips, I have not had a relationship or been in love with any of my father's women, except my mother."

Troy continued to drill at Walker, "What kind of relationship did you have with your mother?"

Walker replied, "I loved my mother. She took care of me and made my life wonderful when I was younger."

Troy then asked, "What about when you were older? Were you still close with your mother?"

"As I got into my late teens and twenties, my mother and I grew distant. I was trying to find myself, and she was into her horse breeding and her friends."

"What is the relationship with your father, Dalton Craig?"

Walker looked at his father seated at the defense table and frowned, "I have always tried to emulate my dad. He was successful in business, had a ton of money, and he had a line of women fawning all over him since I was in my early teens."

Troy Phillips said, "My final question is, 'How did the fact that your dad was unfaithful to your mother affect you, Walker?"

"What my mother and father did in their personal lives had no bearing on me whatsoever."

"Thank you, Mr. Craig. I have no further questions."

Judge Bonita O'Hara said, "Do you have any cross-examination, Mr. Barfield?"

Sam stood and walked to the witness box. He said to Walker, "Do you know anyone who would have a grudge against your father?"

Walker thought for a long moment, then replied, "I don't know of anyone here who knows my father as well as I do. He is aggressive in his determination to become the best at everything he does. In the business world, this might be considered to be a charlatan. A person described to be practicing quackery or a similar confidence trick in order to obtain money, power, fame, or other advantages through pretense or deception. A man driven, as is my father, will purposely or unintentionally step on or over many people along the way to reach his goal. There is no way of knowing how many people he has angered or ruined in the past twenty-five years. My guess is, there are countless numbers of individuals who would love nothing better than to see my father fall from grace or be in this kind of anxiety and drama."

Sam stood at his table and said, "The defense has no further questions at this time, Your Honor."

Judge O'Hara said, "Mr. Phillips, before you call your next witness, I think this might be an opportune time to take a twenty-minute recess."

After the break, Troy Phillips stood and said, "The prosecution calls Mason Delsson to the stand."

Mason walked in from the hallway and was sworn in. He sat in the witness box.

Troy Phillips asked, "Mr. Delsson, you have been investigating murders over the past several months. Correct?"

Mason replied, "Yes, I have."

"Can you tell me the names of the people you are investigating?"

"Yes, I can. It began with the accidental death of Carmen Craig. She is the wife of Dalton Craig, and they have a son together. She was out riding on the property she and Dalton own. She rode alone that day and was out longer than usual. They went to look for her. She was found lying on a bunch of rocks, having fallen or been thrown off her favorite horse. She was found face down, and her face had been injured beyond recognition. Her clothes and jewelry were used to identify her.

"Next was Karina Katrinka. She was a Polish-born actress. Karena was allegedly dating Dalton Craig just before her death. She was found by an actor who was lost on one of the lots of Gemini

Film Studios, which is owned by Dalton Craig. Miss Katrinka fell or was pushed off a second-story balcony and broke her neck in the fall.

"Then, there was Belinda Cheeks. She worked for Dalton Craig as his housekeeper for a few years. She was driving the family SUV to the grocery store when the brakes, having been tampered with failed, and she went off a cliff into a ravine. She was found dead by a passerby.

"Then Sarah Ostrov was reported dead. She was an actress who initially dated Walker Craig. Dalton Craig signed her to a movie contract, and she secretly began dating Dalton. She was also found dead on one of Gemini Studios' back lots.

"Next, we had Jennifer Sandrew's body washed up on the shore of Lake Tahoe. She had been on vacation with four of her girlfriends. The last time she was seen was an evening after the ladies had been out for dinner and drinking. She left the hotel room after that and was seen at the bar with Dalton Craig. He was vacationing with another lady who had returned to their room. Jennifer sat next to Dalton at the bar. They ordered a drink, then Jennifer left the bar and walked out of the hotel. Dalton left the bar less than five minutes later and was seen leaving the hotel. To our knowledge, Dalton was the last person to see Miss Sandrew before she was found dead.

"My private investigator was in Lake Tahoe at the time. When he called to tell me Jennifer Sandrew was found dead, I asked him on a hunch to check around Dalton's boat, anchored on Lake Tahoe. My investigator, Randy Keene, and the Lake Tahoe Sheriff, Antonio de La Paz, went to the boat anchored on the east end of Lake Tahoe. They found fingerprints on Dalton Craig's boat of Dalton Craig, Walker Craig, Fitore Fantazee, and Jennifer Sandrew.

"Finally, Lynda Laffarty was found dead just two weeks ago. She was Dalton Craig's first wife. They divorced, and Lynda never remarried, but had plenty of relationships after that divorce. Her last known relationship was with Richard Bruce, a waiter at a Lake Tahoe Restaurant, and more recently a freelance photographer.

They went out to dinner the previous night when she dropped him off at his home. According to Mr. Bruce, Ms. Laffarty returned home by Uber due to feeling sick from something she had eaten. Lynda was found the next morning by her housekeeper naked and dead on her pool deck.

"Six women are dead. All these women were either married to, worked for, or dated Dalton Craig."

Troy said, "Thank you, Detective. I have no further questions."

Judge Bonnie O'Hara said, "Counselors, due to the hour, we will adjourn for the evening and reconvene at 9:00 a.m. tomorrow. Court is adjourned."

Dalton said to his attorney, "Sam, I didn't kill any of those women, and we know Carmen is still alive. How are we going to proceed on cross-examination?"

Sam replied, "We are going to take one accusation at a time. We will end our cross with Carmen still being alive. The jury will realize you didn't kill your wife, and that may bring questions to their minds about the truth of the rest of the charges. We will have to refute the evidence they have for each case. That will be a challenge, but I think we will be ready. Good night, Dalton."

Mason Delsson walked into Chief Dick Corsi's office, "Chief, I am not looking forward to being cross-examined. There are way too many holes in our case. We have some circumstantial evidence, but I think we have covered everything. The question I have asked myself is: 'What if Dalton Craig did not kill anyone?'"

Chief Corsi said, "Well, who else do you think could have been the killer?"

Mason thought a minute and said, "You know, Chief, I have hypothesized several possibilities. I looked at Walker Craig. He is the son of a very rich family. He could have planned to kill his mother, with whom he never had a good relationship until way into his adult years. He hated the fact that his father was so successful in all his endeavors, but word on the street is, Walker couldn't get a hook-up in a women's prison. He dated several of the ladies, who were with his father, and that could have caused him to lash out at these women. Then I looked at the people who worked for Dalton. He pays them so well that I couldn't find a motive. I looked at the women he dated recently, like Keisha Kane. She would have no reason to exact revenge on Dalton, as their relationship is wonderfully sexual, and she has enough stability from her films and investments. I am also looking at Jodi Panicee. She is Dalton's secretary, who seems to have found her niche. I am racking my brain to come up with any other potential suspects. Do you have any insight on the situation?"

Chief Dick Corsi said, "There seems to be a bunch of people that are on the periphery of the action going on. I would look at those folks. They are the ones most disgruntled."

"Thank you, Chief. I will go through the list of candidates and let you know if I find anyone.

Mason left his office to prepare for his cross-examination.

* * *

Deyna Doll had been home for two weeks. She was well on her way to a full recovery and ready to go back to the racetrack. Her job at the racetrack was instrumental in her recovery, as she was able to work both from the hospital and when she returned home. Deyna could sit in her Florida room and work for a few hours at a time. She kept in almost constant contact with her partner, Susie Crull. Susie had been working long hours to compensate for the racetrack, not having her hardworking partner, Deyna Doll.

Deyna's phone rang. Seeing it was Sue Crull, she said, "Hello. How are you today?"

Sue replied, "I am ready for a short vacation. I spoke to Kevin about going to Europe, but he said he was too busy at the film studio. I wondered if you were coming back to work soon?"

Deyna said, "That's funny. I was just going to call you and let you know that I was cleared by my doctor to return. I can work four hours to start and see if my strength can take it. I would be able to manage things, do the paperwork, scheduling, and banking."

Sue said, "That is great news, but I wanted you to come to Europe with me. My friend has just purchased a home in Lisbon, Portugal. She still goes back and forth to the U.S., but I have rented it from her for a nominal fee. What do you think?"

Deyna said, "I wish I were up to it, but I had better wait until I can enjoy it better. Besides, I wanted to go to the trial of Walker's dad. I could go for a few hours, then come into work."

* * *

Mason Delsson was exhausted when he returned home after testifying in court. He spent an hour or so in the Chief's office with Troy Phillips. They had a plan to introduce Carmen Craig at the trial, but only if the defense mentioned that Dalton had seen her alive. They also discussed the strategy for Mason to deal with Sam Barfield's cross-examination in the morning. He walked into his house and grabbed a beer. He went out onto the back deck, and there sat Catie Gaynor, his next-door neighbor. She was sunbathing in a small polka-dot bikini. He let out a wolf whistle.

Catie said, "It's about time you got home. You work too much. Are you hungry? I have two steaks thawing, and the grill is hot. Interested?"

"That, young lady, is the best offer I have had a long while. Yes, please and thank you. The thought of cooking dinner made me want to drink more. I do appreciate it."

Catie said, "How was work? Didn't that trial start today?"

Mason said, "Yes. I testified for three hours. I have to testify again tomorrow. I am not looking forward to that. That is all I am going to say about that."

Catie said, "You haven't remarked about my new suit. Don't you like it? Do you think it is too much for the backyard?"

Mason said, "I was afraid I might say what I was thinking. So, I kept quiet. Now that you mention it, I love how you look in the new bikini. It took all the discipline I could muster to keep my lecherous eyes in their sockets. I would respectfully day it is way too sexy for the backyard, so I think you should take it off right here!"

Catie blushed and giggled. They had another drink while Catie scurried about making the sides, baked potato, and salad with homemade dressing. Everything was perfect. Catie said, "I am going to a Weight Watchers Workshop on Saturday at 9:30 a.m. I am supposed to bring a friend. It is not just for losing weight. The workshop also helps with recipe ideas and lots of motivation to be healthy. We could go for a light brunch afterward.

Catie invited him to join her as a friend for the WW meeting. He took her in his car on Saturday morning and drove to the workshop. Patricia O. was the leader. She was very sweet and well organized. Mary F, Linda D, Colleen and Katie, Chris, Richard & Karen, Bert, George, Suzi, Chris, Trish, Marne & Pedro. The group exchanged ideas for their weight loss strategies, how their week went, as well as what they cooked that week that was low-cal and delicious. The group was much of the draw. Not more than Patricia, the workshop leader. Mason vowed to join the group. He had some extra weight that he wanted to lose, and the support seemed great.

* * *

Friday morning, Mason was back in court. He was called to the witness box for cross-examination. After the bailiff called the court to order, Judge O'Hara said, "Mr. Barfield, you can begin your cross-examination."

Sam Barfield asked Mason, "Do you have any evidence that Dalton Craig killed any of these women?"

Mason readied himself and was a bit tense as he knew he wasn't fond of Mr. Barfield. Mason replied, "We have evidence that he hired a hitman to kill his wife, Carmen Craig. It was unsuccessful so he continued his spree."

People in court's gallery were buzzing, after this revelation. Mason continued, "We have eyewitness reports that Dalton Craig was seen leaving the home of Karena Katrinka and Sarah

Ostrov the night before each of them was found dead the morning after."

Sam asked, "Did anyone see Mr. Craig kill either of these women?"

Mason replied, "No. It seems the killer's modus operandi was to push them off a balcony in the late-night hours which lessened the chance to be seen committing the crimes."

Sam asked, "I suppose you have more charges against Mr. Craig, that you will have no evidence for?"

Troy Phillips shouted from his chair at the prosecution table, "Objection, your Honor. Counsel is leading the witness."

Judge O'Hara replied, "Sustained."

Sam then asked Mason, "Who else did Mr. Craig allegedly kill?

Mason replied, "As you have seen in discovery, the evidence we have shared with you points to Dalton Craig as the killer. He was seen working on the Craig Estate's car the morning that Belinda Cheeks drove to the store, then crashed down an embankment. In the case of Jennifer Sandrew, we found Dalton's fingerprints on his boat up at Lake Tahoe. Even more incriminating was the fact that we found blood on the railing of the boat that matched the blood of Jennifer Sandrew."

Sam said in a tone that dripped with sarcasm, "Did he allegedly kill anyone else?"

Mason said, "Are you telling me that you know of someone we missed?

Sam was livid, "You seem to know all about my client and his prurient interest in killing the women he once dated. Maybe I should ask you?"

Mason said, "We are looking into the death of Lynda Laffarty."

Sam Barfield was angry as he said, "Your Honor, I am finished with this witness. The prosecution has not provided anything but innuendo and has provided no direct evidence that Dalton Craig has committed any of these crimes. If they were, in fact, crimes."

Troy Phillips stood and said, "Your Honor, if it pleases the court, my next witness will be able to give some firsthand accounts of these crimes. The State calls Carmen Craig to the stand."

Judge O'Hara had to gavel the crowd noise down several times, yelling, "Order! Order! Order in the Court!"

The double doors to the courtroom opened, and in walked a stunning figure whose name was Carmen Craig. There was now silence in the court as she took the stand and was sworn in.

Troy asked, "Can you state your full name for the court, please?"

She said, "My name is Carmen Elizabeth Warner Craig."

Troy asked, "Have you changed your name?"

Carmen said, "No. I am just using my middle name and maiden name."

Troy said, "Would you like to tell the court the reason you use Elizabeth Warner now?"

Carmen said, "Almost a year ago, I went into my husband Dalton Craig's, home office. I was looking for my cell phone, which I thought I had left earlier that day while cleaning. I saw, on the top of a pile of papers, a note that read: C will be riding on Tuesday morning around 9 a.m. She usually wears a white cowboy hat. She will not be armed. Please make it painless. D. I knew that my husband was plotting to have me killed. He had faxed this note to someone. I made a copy of it and have it here."

Troy approached the witness stand and took the two sheets of paper from Carmen and went to Judge O'Hara and said, "If it please the court, the State would like to enter this as evidence Exhibit M. I have a copy for you and the defense."

Judge O'Hara said, "Mr. Barfield, do you have any objections?"

Sam Barfield stood and said, "Your Honor, we object to this witness as she was pronounced dead and was buried almost a year ago. We are shocked that she has risen from the dead."

Judge O'Hara said, "Mr. Phillips. Can you help me understand what is happening here?"

Troy said, "Yes, Your Honor. In the next few minutes, we will be able to clarify all of this."

The judge said, "Overruled. We will enter this as Exhibit M into evidence. Mr. Phillips, please continue.

Troy asked Carmen, "How did you react when you found the note on Dalton Craig's home office desk?"

Carmen said, "Well, my husband and I had drifted apart and were not as close as we were. I caught him cheating on me with several young starlets, but I kept quiet. When I saw the note, I began being extremely careful in everything I did. I assumed any stranger I met could be the potential 'Hit' person. One day, I was riding out on the ranch alone. My son Walker had canceled and said he could not ride. I was not out riding for more than ten minutes when I saw a person riding toward me with a gun pointed at me. They never got a shot off, as her horse was spooked by a rattlesnake. She was thrown off the horse, landing face-first on a pile of jagged rocks. It was a woman. She was about my size. Her name was Madonna Hakeem. I changed clothes with her, took her horse and gun. I wanted my husband to think I was dead, and his mission was successful."

Sam said, "Then what did you do? Did you return home?"

Carmen replied, "No. I rode her horse to the other side of the ranch, where I found this woman's car. I loosely tied the horse to the car's bumper. Inside the car, I found an envelope with Madonna's name on it. It contained twenty thousand dollars in cash inside. Her name was on the envelope in what looked like my husband's handwriting. I called for an Uber. I paid the woman in cash and told her to report to her company that I never showed. So, there would be no record.

I went straight to the airport and flew to Lake Tahoe. I called a friend who helped me change my name, and I called the credit card company to get new cards issued in the name of Elizabeth Warner. I changed my look enough that people didn't recognize me. I even attended my funeral, but from a distance."

Troy said, "That is a titillating story, but what else can you tell us?"

Carmen took a breath and said, "In Lake Tahoe, I watched my

husband bring a woman to the hotel across the street. I knew if he came to Tahoe, he would stay at the best hotel there. He is a creature of habit. I saw my girlfriends were staying at the same hotel as Dalton. I saw my friend, Jennifer Sandrew. She left the hotel after her night out with the girls. She left alone. She was followed by Dalton Craig a few minutes later. They walked a bit, then they stopped in the street, and had what looked like a blazing argument. Dalton left her and returned to the hotel. Not thirty minutes later, I saw Dalton leave the hotel once again. I saw our limousine pull up in front of the hotel. Dalton got into the limo without even a carry-on bag in his hand. I heard the next morning about the death of Jennifer Sandrews."

Troy asked, "Do you think your husband had anything to do with the death of Jennifer Sandrew?"

Carmen said, "No. I don't think so. I got curious hearing about all these deaths of women who were around my husband or dated him. I decided to investigate these deaths myself. The so-called accidental deaths made me wonder who was involved. I was anxious to solve these crimes so I could go back to living my life. I needed to hire my own investigator. I hired a lady I knew, whose name was Catie Gaynor. She had owned a houseboat for years in Tahoe, and I knew she worked in L.A. as a freelance investigator. She began her investigation of my family. I will let you hear from her what she found. Then you will know why I went into hiding, still fearing for my life."

Troy said, "I have no further questions. Your witness, Counselor."

Sam Barfield said, "Your Honor, we have no questions at this time but reserve the right to recall this witness."

Judge O'Hara said to Carmen, "You may step down." To Troy Phillips, she said, "Call your next witness."

Troy said, "The State calls Catie Gaynor to the stand."

Into the court walked Catie Gaynor. She was dressed in a simple black dress and black high heels. She looked radiant as everyone watched her walk in. She was sworn in and took the stand. Mason Delsson's jaw was opened until after she was sworn in.

Troy Phillips said, "Good Morning, Miss Gaynor. Could you state your full name and occupation?"

Catie said, "My name is Catherine Magdeline Gaynor. I previously owned the Boat House in Lake Tahoe, but I recently sold it to Del and Dolores Madison, who had worked for me there. I returned to L.A. and continued doing freelance work as a private investigator full time."

Troy asked, "Did Carmen Craig enlist your services?"

Catie said, "No. I worked for a lady named Elizabeth Warner. She asked me to investigate the deaths of the women surrounding Dalton Craig."

Troy asked, "Did you know Elizabeth was Carmen Craig?"

Catie said, "No, not until this morning."

Troy said, "Can you tell the court what you found in the investigation she requested?"

Catie began, "I began my investigation by looking at the possible suspects in the deaths. I looked at Kevin Syracuse, Diane Deal, Deyna Doll, Walker Craig, and Dalton Craig. I will take you through my investigation, beginning with Elizabeth hiring me. She gave me a copy of the note she found on her husband's desk. I searched Madonna Hakeem's apartment and found she had written notes from her conversations with the man who hired her."

Troy Phillips asked, "Were the notes from or to Mr. Craig?"

Catie nodded then replied, "Both, they were to and from Mr. Craig."

Troy then asked, "Miss Gaynor, how long have you practiced private investigation?

Catie replied, "I have worked as a private investigator both here in California and previously in Syracuse, New York, for the past twelve years."

Troy asked, "So after you spoke with Miss Warner, who we now know is Carmen Craig who did you investigate first?"

Catie said, "I looked at Kevin Syracuse. He has a strong dislike for Dalton Craig. It appears Mr. Syracuse and Mr. Craig have competed for actors, actresses, screenplays, as well as technicians in the film industry. Mr. Craig seemingly has beaten Mr. Syracuse to the punch on many occasions. Mr. Craig has also stolen some of the women Mr. Syracuse wanted to date. Mr. Syracuse is currently working to produce a movie telling the story of Dalton Craig. As you might imagine, the script calls for a reversal of all the situations between them. The script also calls for Mr. Craig to be framed for murder."

Troy Phillips interrupted Catie, asking, "Catie. Excuse me, but do you think Kevin Syracuse was behind the murders so he could pin them on Dalton Craig?"

Sam Barfield erupted with, "Objection! Your Honor, this line of questioning calls for a conclusion by the witness."

Judge O'Hara said, "Sustained."

Troy said, "Miss Gaynor, please continue. You were beginning to talk about Diane Deal."

Catie said, "I next looked at Diane Deal. She is a nurse but moonlights as an actress. She and Kevin Syracuse have a connection. I am not sure if it was a romantic involvement or a business relationship. She had a dislike for Dalton Craig as well. Dalton had rejected her five different times when she auditioned for roles in his films. This angered her to no end.

"She helped Mr. Syracuse write the screenplay for the film on Dalton Craig's life. Mr. Syracuse and Miss Deal played out scenarios in public from the screenplay, ensuring the filming would work and be realistic. I found no evidence of actual involvement in the murders.

"I then looked at Deyna Doll. It seems Miss Doll was accidentally shot when the Los Alamitos Racetrack was robbed. Deyna Doll was the mastermind behind the robbery. She and Kevin Syracuse were partners in a plot to ruin everyone in Dalton Craig's circle. This includes all the people he was married to, dated, or was in business with. She almost paid with her life when attempting to rob the racetrack owned by Cricky Amherst. Deyna and Kevin stole the money to help Kevin get out of debt. This would also finance Deyna's attempt to buy out Elegant Lace, a clothing boutique owned by her late partner, Jennifer Sandrew."

Kevin Syracuse was in the back row of the courtroom gallery. He got out of his seat and went behind the last row, bent over to avoid being seen. He was out of luck as the Sheriffs at the door put him up against the wall and put handcuffs on him. They read him his rights and walked him down to the Police processing unit.

Catie continued, "The gunman was aiming for Walker, and Deyna Doll walked into his line of fire. Kevin Syracuse had nothing to do with the actual killing of the six women connected to Dalton Craig. He only plotted the racetrack heist. He was not personally at the scene. He came up with the ruse of writing a book about Dalton's life to frame him for these accidental deaths, not knowing they would actually come to fruition.

"My investigation uncovered the truth about the deaths of Belinda Cheeks, Karena Katrinka, and Sarah Ostrov. The car Belinda drove off a cliff was doctored by the same person who pushed both Sarah Ostrov and Karena Katrinka off balconies; Ostrov off a sound stage balcony at Gemini film, and Katrinka off the balcony of her condo. Their neighbors both identified a second man going into their residences after Dalton had visited them. The man they saw was the same person who killed Jennifer Sandrew on a boat in Lake Tahoe, killed Lynda Laffarty, and hired a contract killer to kill Carmen Craig. It was Walker Craig."

The courtroom went into a loud buzz of conversation. People looked for Walker Craig. Some had seen him there, but he was nowhere to be seen.

Catie continued, "We also found a videotape from a security camera at the Craig Ranch that was not erased. It showed Walker Craig stabbing Greg Solomet on the pool patio at the Craig Ranch. Walker had been having an affair with Jodi Panicee and saw Mr. Solomet hitting Jodi at the pool. He went over to him after Jodi went upstairs to bed. He was passed out, but Walker slit his throat and threw him into the pool."

There was a commotion in the hall outside the courtroom. There was yelling and screaming. Suddenly, the door flew open, and

Walker Craig was in handcuffs, being dragged into the courtroom. He was yelling and screaming for his father, Dalton.

Dalton looked at Sam Barfield and said, "I can't believe this is happening. I thought for sure I would go to jail as someone was trying to ruin my life."

Mason Delsson walked up to Troy Phillips at the prosecution's table in the courtroom. He said to Troy, "That went better than we planned. I was glad to see Walker Craig come into the court today. I found it interesting that he sat idly by, watching his father, Dalton, be tried for the crimes that he, Walker Craig, had planned and carried out."

Troy Phillips said, "Thank you, Mason, for an outstanding job in sifting through all the reams of notes and interviews. It made it so easy for me."

Mason said, "Just doing my job, Mr. District Attorney. I must admit that seeing Carmen Craig in my dentist's office gave me the impetus to further investigate Carmen Craig. When she came to see me, all the lights and bells went off, and I was able to clearly understand who did what, when, and why.

"Then, my neighbor, Catie Gaynor's testimony, really told me how much I didn't know. She solved the case, putting all the missing pieces together."

Troy said, "You are good at what you do. We are lucky to have you in Los Angeles. Remember, everyone who works in criminal law has to get a break now and then, to be able to complete their jobs successfully."

Mason said, "Thanks, Troy. This case was so confusing in so many ways. There were a lot of potential suspects. We had to track folks in two different places in the state, as many went to Lake Tahoe frequently. The amount of time we spent doing interviews and the days we had private investigators following people caused much of the confusion we had."

Dick Corsi came up to Mason and Troy and said to Mason, "When you are done here, stop by my office. I have a bunch of questions I need answers to. I would rather not go to the Mayor's office to report on what happened with only transcripts of the trial to show him."

Mason looked out into the crowd, leaving the courtroom and noticed Keisha Kane. He also saw Cricky Amherst leave the courtroom in tears. The last person he noticed was Catie Gaynor. His neighbor, and soon to become his love interest. He wanted to talk with her. He wanted to pursue a relationship with this beauty, but more importantly, ask her why she kept so quiet. He jogged out of the courtroom and caught up with her in the parking lot across the street. He was out of breath but said, "Catie, how long did you know you were working on the same case that I was?"

Catie smiled, "I was on the case for a month and was just about ready to spill the beans and tell you what I knew. Troy Phillips convinced me that your pursuit of Dalton would help distract Walker Craig, motivating Walker to come to the courtroom every day. He thought he was going to get off Scott Free. Sorry."

Mason said, "I will only accept your apology if you have dinner with me at my house tonight."

Catie smiled and blushed, "Mason, are you going to woo me now?"

Mason said, "Catie, I have no stronger urge than to make you fall for me. The process will begin tonight. I have to get back to the office, but I will see you later."

Catie said, "I have been almost throwing myself at you for the past four months. I was wondering if you were ever going to make a move."

Mason jogged back to the courtroom. Dick Cordi was standing at the prosecution table with Troy Phillips. They all watched as Dalton Craig left the courtroom, walking with Fitore Fantazee, looking relieved and happy.

Dick Corsi said, "Mason, did you know about Walker's involvement all along?"

Mason said, "I began the investigation thinking it was Dalton Craig who had planned or carried out these murders. After speaking with the witnesses, and the people surrounding Dalton, it became very obvious that he did not have anything to do with the deaths of these women. I began to look at others as Catie Gaynor was doing. I targeted Walker Craig as the perpetrator, but I needed the evidence to nail him for these crimes.

Epilogue

MASON DELSSON AND HIS BOSS, Dick Corsi, were sitting in Corsi's office. Dick Corsi said, "So, Mason. I am a bit confused about who did what and why.

Mason said, "I knew some of the story, but Catie Gaynor had all the missing pieces of the puzzle. Well, let me give you the rundown. Belinda Cheek was unlucky to have been driving the car Dalton usually uses and lets Carmen do errands in. The brake lines were tampered with, and the car would not stop while going around a curve in the mountains, not far from the Craig Ranch. There were no witnesses to the accident. There was a random, untraceable call to the police. Our mechanic, who examined that car, said he was shocked that it made it as far as it did before it crashed. There was no fluid in the brakes. There is no question the brakes were tampered with.

"Jennifer Sandrew had dated Dalton Craig. She was still in love with him and saw him frequently. She also found Walker Craig was a good friend who helped arrange secret meetings with Dalton. He fell in love with Jennifer while listening to her tales of woe. She confided in Walker the mistreatment she received from Dalton, but she could not get away from his allure.

"It was Walker who had a message handed to Jennifer by a waitress in the Lake Tahoe hotel that said Dalton wanted to see her on the boat. The note said, 'If I am by myself, at the bar in the hotel, meet me at the boat.' Jennifer met Dalton and even had him buy her a drink at the bar. She asked him to meet her outside, where they argued. She went to his boat to see if Dalton would follow her. Dalton returned to his room to be with Fitore Fantazee. Walker was on the boat waiting for Jennifer. They took a boat ride, and only Walker returned. Walker then called his father and asked that the senior Craig return home to L.A. to help him deal with the police. We figure Jennifer and Walker also argued as she rejected his expression of love and his advances. Walker then pushed her. She fell and hit her head. He took the boat out for a short ride, dumped Jennifer's body in the Lake. Walker then returned it to the marina. Walker drove his rental car back to the Airport, and flew back to L.A. That is why he was late that morning for the meeting with Dalton in L.A.

"Dalton had a continuing relationship with Lynda and Sarah O. Walker hated Lynda, Dalton's ex-wife, for trying to get close to his mom for her money, while also continuing her relationship with Walker.

"Lynda Laffarty was married to Dalton. Early on in their relationship, Dalton discovered Lynda was with another woman. Lynda got out of the relationship but stayed friends with Dalton over the years. Kevin Syracuse wanted Lynda to appear in a film at his studio, but she turned him down. Kevin asked her out to dinner, and Lynda refused to go with him. Lynda was famous for recruiting young talent for Dalton's movies. Walker Craig later learned Lynda was getting a commission from Dalton each time a new starlet signed a long-term deal. Lynda stole potential lovers from Kevin Syracuse to satisfy her carnal lust for women, as well as put them in films with Gemini Studios.

"Carmen Craig overheard at a restaurant that Kevin Syracuse was planning to kill her to get back at her husband Dalton for their success in the film business, by framing him for the murder. Kevin had made a play for her years ago, but she shot him down. The day she was out riding, the lady who was hired to kill her wasn't such a good horsewoman. Her steed was startled by a snake and threw the woman off, and she went face-first into the rocks, just as she was pointing a gun at Carmen. Carmen then exchanged clothes with her as they were a similar size. Carmen took the woman's horse. She even gave up her favorite boots. The stranger was so disfigured that they would never guess it wasn't Carmen. Carmen found the stranger's identification in her car, so people never knew who the unlucky stranger was. Only one person knew it was not Carmen Craig. That person was Walker Craig. He had asked the stable master, Erikson Howard, to look for his mom. Walker recognized that it was not his mother but kept it from everyone. He was the one who hired Madonna Hakeem to kill his mother. Carmen figured this out when she found the note in Dalton's office. It was in Walker's handwriting.

"Sarah Ostrov was an actress Kevin Syracuse had dated, and he wanted to put Sarah into one of his movies. Just as he was going to sign her for the lead role, she signed with Dalton Craig. Then to make matters worse, Dalton began dating her. They were an item for a while until she started seeing Walker Craig. Sarah began traveling to New York, and was posing for *Playboy*, as well as other men's nude magazines. "The fact that she was gone so often and dated his father, Kevin Syracuse, and others in New York, led Walker to plan to end her life. He had a key to her house and hid there until she returned one night from New York. Walker snuck up on her when she went out onto the balcony and pushed her to her death.

"Christy (Cricky) Amherst owned the Los Alamitos Racetrack, which she inherited from her late husband, Patrick Amherst. She was friends with many elite women in Los Angeles. She dated Dalton once but saw him as a philanderer. She cut that off quickly. Dalton's son Walker asked her out. She knew it was to spite his father. She refused his advances. Cricky was a shoulder to cry on for all of her friends. Lynda Laffarty often went to her for love advice. Carmen confided in her early on in the marriage to Dalton. She introduced Kevin Syracuse to Sue Crull. Sue had drinks with her and Kathy Muller at Retreat Two restaurant. They talked about their relationships, as women will often do. Cricky was one of those spared from the wrath of Walker Craig.

"Kathy Muller, who lost several friends at the hands of Kevin Syracuse and his accomplices, inherited millions from Carmen but was elated to find Carmen had survived. Kathy and Carmen are still friends to this day. She still owns the Retreat Two Restaurant and stepped up to purchase Jennifer Sandrew's half of the Elegant Lace business to partner with Allie Campwick.

"Allie Campwick went on to marry a good-looking Rugby player from New York. They moved to Denver, Colorado, and have two beautiful children. She was thrilled to have Kathy Muller partner with her in the Elegant Lace store after her former partner, Jennifer Sandrew, was killed. She continues to quietly run her fashion business and raise her family.

"Greg Solomet worked in the insurance industry doing various jobs. He had worked in insurance for over fifteen years but didn't reach the level he had intended. He was very dissatisfied and wanted more pay. He subsidized his income by working many hours as a waiter at the restaurant called Retreat Two. He made a lot of money on tips. He worked half as many hours waiting on tables as he worked at his normal 40-hour week and made just as much money as his regular job. He saved his money for retirement and wanted to live in Paris. He lost his life pursuing a woman who he thought could improve his standing in the community.

"Erickson Howard was the Stable Master for the Craig Estate. He took care of Carmen Craig's breeding of her horses as well as the total management of the stables. He was a certified veterinarian but was able to work on the side as well. He had a severe gambling problem that led him to team up with Kevin Syracuse, who paid off lots of his gambling debt. This put him in debt to Kevin, who used Erickson's closeness to the Craigs to help carry out his plan to destroy Dalton Craig and everything dear to him. Erickson worked both sides of the fence. The perpetrators of all the killings paid him for his information. His loyalty to Mrs. Craig got him in her will when she was pronounced dead. He was in on the plot to thwart Carmen's killing. He followed Carmen the day she was targeted to be killed.

"Erickson had been in a bar and overheard the woman talking on the phone in the next booth about her task of riding a horse to get to some woman she was hired to eliminate. Her identity was revealed by Carmen, who found a note from Dalton to this woman in his den. She was identified afterward when her vehicle was retrieved from a riding stable very near the Craig Estate. Her name was Madonna Hakeem from Las Vegas, Nevada. She had rented the horse that she rode to track Carmen.

"Kevin Syracuse, a noted film mogul, tried to set up Dalton Craig by killing the people that Dalton loved. He wanted revenge for Dalton stealing all his women, his best staff, and all the best movie ideas. He would stop at nothing to finance his plan to destroy Dalton Craig. His studio, Aries International, was not as successful as Dalton's Gemini Pictures. Kevin began to produce a lot of XXX rated movies, at that time, generating three times the money he made on his regular production. He was not the man Deyna Doll heard talking during the racetrack robbery. Kevin was on set in Las Vegas at the time. He planned a movie script of Dalton Craig's life. He had too much to lose now, as his erotic films were making him barrels of money. He still wanted to get revenge on Dalton, so he wrote a screenplay exposing all the underhanded things Dalton Craig did with his studio and his family, as well as the women he stole from others, then discarded.

"Deyna Doll worked at the Los Alamitos Racetrack and was soon to be part-owner with her boss, Cricky Amherst. Deyna went to school with Kevin Syracuse and saw him regularly visit the racetrack. Kevin told her of his hatred for Dalton Craig. Deyna was also a designer and had studied design at the University of California at Berkeley. She worked with Jennifer Sandrew at the Elegant Lace Boutique on Rodeo Drive. Her goal was to own that or a shop like it one day. As if she were not busy enough, she sang in a small band at local clubs. The was called Two Way Street. Deyna wanted Kevin Syracuse to rob the Los Alamitos Racetrack. Deyna tipped him off about the holiday weekend receipts being held in their safe until the Tuesday after the three-day weekend. Kevin never took the bait. An unknown gang did the job.

"Deyna dated Walker Craig. He made her realize how poorly Dalton treated his family, his friends, and especially those women who worked for him. She helped Kevin plot the movie script. When produced as a movie, it would destroy Dalton Craig's image. Deyna was not charged with any crimes for the attempted robbery, as the police had no evidence that she was involved. She met Dennis Bellowso and fell in love with a great guy, so she married him.

"Diane Deal was a nurse working for a cadre of physicians. She was also having a torrid love affair with Kevin Syracuse. They had gone to college together and dated for a while before they graduated. She became overburdened with student loans from college and nursing school, so when she ran into Kevin, he made an offer to clear up her loans if she helped him with his revenge. She was on board immediately. Walker had hurt her badly after she had fallen head over heels in love with him. Little did Kevin know that Diane secretly had many a rendezvous with Dalton Craig. Dalton used her to get prescription medications for him, and they made a lot of money selling them to the actors and crew of his pictures. Diane discovered Dalton was keeping 90% of the money and threatened to tell her superiors if she went to the authorities. She was now used for sex by both son and father, and they both treated her like a common streetwalker. Diane wanted revenge. She helped Kevin Syracuse, her housemate, by doing as much as she could to get back at Dalton, but she wanted to set Dalton up by working with the police, claiming she was being blackmailed by Dalton. Diane Deal had become a triple agent, convincing Dalton, Walker, and the police that she was working for them. She gave Kevin the idea of making a movie about Dalton and telling of all Dalton's transgressions.

"Walker Craig was accidentally shot at the racetrack. Walker had become a nuisance to Dalton, his father, his mother before she died, and to Kevin Syracuse. Kevin had lost too many women and starlets to the Craigs. The people who robbed the racetrack must have had issues with all of the rich people in Los Angeles. Unfortunately, Deyna Doll got into the line of fire.

"Walker knew about how Dalton had treated Lynda Laffarty, as he saw them in the house together often when his mother was gone. These times, Lynda was at the house, she would spend a lot of time arguing with Dalton and asking for money. Walker also hated his father for trying to make him a mini-Dalton. He never wanted to be like him, as he saw through the empty veneer Dalton was showing to those outside the household. To punish his father, Walker would steal the women away from him, as Walker was much younger and much more attentive to these women. He gave them lavish gifts with the money he received from his mother. Walker had resorted to writing checks from his mother's bank account and signing her name. It took her a long time to figure that out, but by the time she did, Walker had stolen five hundred thousand dollars. She set up a repayment plan in return for not turning him in to the police. Dalton overheard them talking and scolded Walker profusely, embarrassing him in front of the servants. After that, Walker expressed his hatred for his father by letting Dalton catch him in a compromising position with two of the potential starlets in Dalton's home that Dalton had dated.

"Dalton Craig was a known control freak. Ever since he graduated from college, his sole focus seemed to be success in business and becoming the movie mogul he had dreamt about. His relationships with women were shallow as he used them as just toys in his game of life. He outwardly showed others his generosity and compassion for others, but deep inside, he was an evil, self-involved, egomaniac who was driven by greed. He put a contract out on Carmen because she had money he wanted to inherit, she was seeing other men, and she knew too much about his tactics with starlets and blackmailing them to work for less because of the tapes he made of them doing terrible things.

"When his wife, Lynda Laffarty, left him because he was

inattentive and mentally abusive, he feigned regret and tried to remain friends. He made sure she was taken care of and helped her purchase her restaurant, Retreat Two. Lynda always knew what Dalton was up to with his infidelity to Carmen, his second wife. Lynda had somehow endeared herself to Carmen, and they became fast friends. Dalton hated that and was cautious when dealing with Lynda. Lynda and Carmen could destroy him if he didn't keep them both happy. This was often on his mind.

"Walker Craig altered the brakes on the ranch vehicle that Carmen used. It was an accident that Belinda Cheeks took the car to go grocery shopping. She was not going fast, but lost control of the vehicle around a sharp turn, going down the mountain. It was accidental because Walker wanted someone else to use the car that day. Mainly his mother or father.

"Dalton had a violent relationship with Sarah Ostrov. She was with him when he found out she was sleeping with one of the photographers from *Playboy* magazine. Dalton asked her not to do a layout for *Playboy* because he was jealous and didn't want her to have real money. He told her it would ruin her movie career and violate the contract she had with Gemini Pictures. He wanted her to heed his advice. Again, she refused to be controlled. When the pictures came out in the magazine, Dalton vowed to end his relationship with Sarah Ostrov. It was then that Sarah began secretly dating Walker Craig. His lack of real power did not intrigue her enough, so she broke up with Walker. She did not fall from a second-floor porch on a movie set on the Gemini Studio's back lot. She was thrown off the porch by Walker Craig.

"Karena Katrinka was an actress from Poland. She dated Walker Craig. She lived at the Craig ranch while she became a movie star. She worked out at a local gym with Elijah Landon, whom she flirted with daily. Karena also had a fling during this time with Ryan Parker. That didn't last long, and she began to flirt with Dalton, who fell prey to her charms. She became pregnant. Walker was less than elated but wanted to do the right thing. Karena was found dead at her home. It looked as though she had been strangled. She may have been thrown off her second-floor balcony. She had been on hiatus from her television drama series.

"Jennifer Sandrew, who co-owned Elegant Lace, dated Dalton just after he left Lynda Laffarty. It was great for a while, then Dalton tired of her and moved on. This was hurtful to Jennifer. While on a trip to Lake Tahoe with her girlfriends, Jennifer spotted Dalton Craig getting off an elevator with a beautiful redhead. It was Fitore Fantazee who accompanied Dalton there. No one else had seen Dalton. The girls were all on their way back to the room. Jennifer was angry, so she got dressed up to go to the bar. The girls tried to stop her, but she was determined. Dalton was sitting by himself when Jennifer got down to the bar. She made some light conversation with him, had Dalton order her a drink. She left the bar before she finished her drink. One of the bartenders remembers seeing Dalton meet her at the front door of the hotel. Minutes later, the bartender saw them leave together. Dalton left after arguing outside the hotel. Jennifer went to his boat but found Walker there. Walker tried to console her to get her back in his arms. Jennifer rebuked him. He took her for a boat ride. Walker and Jennifer argued because Jennifer would not make love to Walker. Walker hit Jennifer in the back of the head. Then Walker dropped her overboard. He returned to his room, showered, and flew back to L.A. Thinking he got away with all these crimes. Lynda Lafferty told Walker that she knew what he was doing, so he killed her. He made them look like his father, Dalton, committed these crimes."

Dick Corsi said, "Whew, that is a lot to digest."

Mason said, "The six women killed met their demise by the person who should have been the closest to him. Walker turned out to be a spoiled rich kid. He went totally bad. He had little ability to hear the word NO. His mother and father both tried to get him into counseling to help him with his lack of motivation and his refusal to work for himself at an honest vocation. He was just a bad person."

Mason walked out of Corsi's office and went to his own office. Once he sat down, he picked up his phone and called Catie

Gaynor. She answered, "Hello, Mason. Before you speak, I wanted to apologize to you for keeping my investigation under wraps. I should have brought you into my understanding of things before we got into open court."

Mason said, "I thought we should sit down over dinner tonight and iron things out. I want to see you and tell you of my feelings."

Catie said, "Sounds great! Pick me up at 7 p.m. and we will find a restaurant we both enjoy."

Mason said, "Maybe we'll go to Retreat Two. We can get a quiet table and say hello to our friends like Sue and Kathy." They ended the call, both very happy.

After his office phone rang. He answered, "Hello, this is Mason Delsson."

Chief Corsi was on the line, "Mason, I just got a call from homicide. We just received a call about a double murder in the Hollywood Hills. I want you to investigate this one."

Mason said to Chief Corsi, "Here we go again!"

www.ingramcontent.com/pod-product-compliance
Lightning Source LLC
Chambersburg PA
CBHW021417110726
47901CB00008B/2197